BLOOD DEBTS

BLOOD & SHADOWS BOOK 3

BOOKS BY ALIANNE DONNELLY

BLOOD AND SHADOWS
Blood Moons
Blood Trails
Blood Debts
Blood Hunt
Shadow Hawk

THE REBEL COURT
Catch Me
Dearest Love
Sweetest Kiss
Rebel Heart

DAWN OF RAGNAROK
The Royal Wizard
Dragonblood
Prince of Deceit

THE BEAST
Bastien
The Beast

OTHER TITLES
Wolfen
Virtual
Function: L1VE

ALIANNE DONNELLY

BLOOD DEBTS

BLOOD & SHADOWS BOOK 3

This one is for my girls. Mia, the one-woman wonder, and always an inspiration. Heather, who never fails to cheer me on and restore my faith in myself. And Honour, my go-to person when I need someone to tell me, "This sucks. You can do better, so go do it." I don't think this series would have happened without you guys. I am blessed to have you as my friends.

Per me si va ne la città dolente,
per me si va ne l'etterno dolore,
per me si va tra la perduta gente.
Giustizia mosse il mio alto fattore:
fecemi la divina podestate,
la somma sapienza e 'l primo amore.
Dinanzi a me non fuor cose create
se non etterne, e io etterno duro.
Lasciate ogne speranza, voi ch'intrate.

~ As written on the entrance to the
slave barracks in the city-world of Rome

Through me the way into the suffering city,
Through me the way to the eternal pain,
Through me the way that runs among the lost.
Justice urged on my high artificer;
My maker was divine authority,
The highest wisdom and primal love.
Before me nothing but eternal things
were made, and I endure eternally.
Abandon every hope, who enter here.

~ Dante Alighieri (*Inferno*, Canto III)

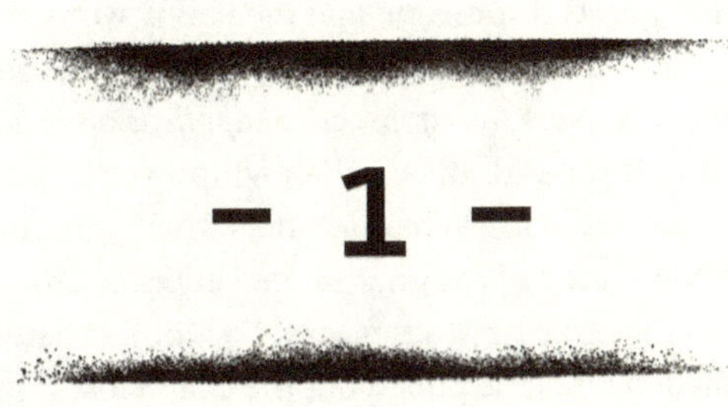

– 1 –

September 21, 3032 – Miramar Colony

The glass of whiskey slipped from her grasp and dropped in slow motion. Amelia felt the impact of it shattering at her feet before her ears picked up the sound, but she didn't dare look. All she saw was the gun pointing at her from five feet away.

"Welcome home, Dr. Chase," said the very large, smiling gunman seated at her kitchen table.

He knew her name. "Oh, my God." The whisper left her lips before she could stop it. Amelia dove for the com on the wall. It had a failsafe built into her security system in the event of something like this—the proverbial shit hitting the fan. Years of working for the government had taught her well.

"Don't bother," the man said. He pushed away from the table at the same time, the chair scraping so hard it would leave marks.

Amelia cringed and froze, her hands in the air. Her com link was voice-activated for normal emergencies, but a three-digit code would flood the apartment with a tranq gas she'd engineered to be harmless to her DNA. It was instantaneous, too. All she had to do was punch it in and run. If she could just get to it.

"I already disabled it. And the one in your lab."

A punched-in code. While her back was to him, Amelia cast a baleful look at the com and called herself a dozen kinds of idiot in her head.

It had made sense when she'd designed it. She hadn't wanted to accidentally gas her guests if someone said the wrong word. Everything else was voice-activated so there was no reason for anyone to even look at those coms. *Note to self: practical application is lacking…*

Heart racing, it took all of Amelia's willpower to ask without stuttering, "Who are you? What do you want?" She couldn't see him and was too scared of the gun pointed at her to chance a look.

"We'll get to that. For now, sit, please. You look exhausted."

Amelia flinched when he pulled out the chair closest to her with a nails-on-a-chalkboard screech. She took five seconds to compose herself and bid her genius escape plan farewell before she slowly turned around, expecting to be blasted at any second. But then, he wouldn't do that, would he? If that was his plan, he would have done it already. He wanted her alive, and there was only one reason why he would. The slight tremor from her hands became a full-body shiver.

"Careful around the glass," he warned.

The glass he referred to, or rather the pieces of it left, had held her favorite liquor, the one she only drank when the absurdities of life got to be too much. They were approaching critical zone now. Amelia sat in slow motion.

"You don't have to keep your hands up like that," the madman said. "Relax."

She put her hands on top of the table. "How did you get in here?"

The intruder pulled his chair back and sat facing her, still holding the gun pointed at her chest. He looked like he'd had plenty of practice with it. A laser gun, from the looks of it. Didn't use bullets, but concentrated bolts of theta particles in a stream powerful enough to cut a hole through concrete. It had a battery pack instead of a cartridge of rounds. It was also illegal, for obvious reasons.

"Same way I disabled your external com. I'm clever like that."

He smiled again. What did he think this was, a joke? She was so sick of psychopaths! Hadn't there been enough of them over the last few years? Hadn't a prison full of them been enough for anyone's lifetime?

Except, this one didn't look like her garden-variety New Alaska psychopath. She'd looked into hundreds of their eyes and seen the sickness inside. This guy was different. All she saw in him was calm, as if he wanted to will her to relax, and maybe a hint of amusement, as if at the same time he realized how ridiculous that was. He had dark hair cut in no particular style and shadow of a beard. When he smiled, he revealed strong, white teeth.

Amelia supposed he could be called handsome.

What? No! Remember the gun pointed at you?

Oh, yeah. The gun held in a big callused hand, attached to a big muscled arm, attached to a bulging shoulder. He might be as big as Hunt. Fascinating.

Jesus, Ams, she could hear Hailey's voice in her head. *Snap out of it!*

Amelia inwardly shook herself, horrified. What the hell was wrong with her? "What do you want?" she demanded, keeping her attention on the gun.

"I want to hire you," he said.

"You have a strange way of recruiting."

He looked at the gun. "What, this? This was to get your attention. Not even loaded." He set it down and twined his fingers together, leaning forward. "I have no intention of hurting you, but I'm not an idiot. I know finding a stranger in your home is a little frightening."

Har-freaking-har.

"I wanted to make sure you would hear me out before you went screaming to the police."

A pause, then he took the gun off the table and out of sight, making her blink up at him.

"You were looking at it really intensely."

Oh. She dragged her gaze away, to keep from staring at him.

He chuckled. "Looking for other weapons now? It won't help. I'd have you on the floor, disarmed and subdued in seconds. And I really don't want these negotiations to turn physical."

Something about the way he'd said the last part made her glance up at him again. He wasn't looking into her eyes anymore. He was staring at her chest.

Oh, shit! Amelia tensed, getting ready to run for it. Where was a good, sharp scalpel when she needed it?

The man frowned and shook himself. "Sorry, where were we?"

"On the floor, disarmed and subdued." Her voice shook.

He noticed and held his hands up in a show of peace. "Easy, Doc. I told you I mean you no harm."

"Uh-huh, sure. I believe you." Sarcasm, apparently, was panic-proof.

"Would it make you feel better if you had the gun?"

"Yes," she said eagerly.

He put it on the table in front of her.

Amelia stared at it, then up at him. She'd spent years surrounded by the most dangerous people the universe had to offer. There'd been those who'd frightened her simply by being in the same room, looking at her. And now one sat across her kitchen table, his gaze steady, and placed a gun in front of her. She had no idea what to make of it.

"As a show of good faith," he said.

Self-preservation kicked in. Amelia snatched it up and pointed it at him, squeezing the trigger. Nothing.

He didn't blink. "Told you it wasn't loaded."

She threw it at his head and shot to her feet, running for the door.

She almost made it to the hallway when he snatched her around the waist and lifted her off her feet. Amelia screamed and fought for her life, kicking and jabbing at him. The arm around her might as well have been granite, and the body it held her to couldn't possibly be human. He didn't sway, he didn't twitch a muscle. Amelia was tiring herself out fighting, and he didn't move. He acted like he held a scratching kitten.

Amelia dug her nails into his arm and pulled. Enough pressure to tear into skin, short of ripping out her nails.

The man groaned, but didn't let go.

He shifted, easily taking her weight with one arm, and with his free hand, caught both of hers in an unbreakable grip. "Settle down, Doc, you're only hurting yourself." His voice was strong and calm, while his arm bled all over her floor.

Holy crap! *Holy shit, I'm dead!*

Amelia fought harder.

The arm around her tightened, compressing her diaphragm. She gasped. It was a warning, she knew. If he wanted to, he could squeeze the life out of her, and he'd do it with the ease of an afterthought.

Amelia kicked back and her heel managed to connect with his knee, right under the patella. He hissed, shifted his weight to the other leg and tightened his arm around her more.

It was enough to cut off her air, and the strength leeched out of her fight. She still swung her legs back, but only managed light taps. Amelia sagged against her captor. Her head dropped against his shoulder, next to his jaw. Had he brushed it against her hair?

World going hazy… fainting…

The pressure relaxed and she gasped in a reflexive breath. It revived her enough to open her eyes, and tiny pinpricks of light flashed around her as she hyperventilated. A quick inventory of her body told her there was no major damage. She'd be bruised, but nothing felt broken. The madman had remarkable control.

As the world spun, her feet touched the ground and immediately buckled beneath her. But her captor didn't release her until she sat on the couch. A pillow appeared in her lap and she clutched it to her chest. Then his hand was on the back of her neck, pressing forward and down until her head was between her knees. "Breathe," he ordered.

Easier said than done.

She had no idea how long she sat there, wheezing, while his hand gently massaged the tense muscles in her neck.

Her perfectly ordered mind melted into chaos, random thoughts flying all over the place. *What kind of kidnapper takes care of his victims? Arterial blood is oxygenated and lighter in color than blood from veins. Runs quicker. DNA double helix can be altered into a triple. Quadruple is more stable. Stockholm Syndrome: developing sympathetic feelings for one's captor and identifying with their cause.*

Broken glass is good luck… but not mirrors. Mirrors are glass…

When she'd calmed herself, the madman let her sit up, and pressed a glass into her shaking hand. Whiskey. She downed it in one searing swallow. He replaced her empty glass with a full one. Amelia inhaled the aroma this time before she downed it, too.

Warmth burst in her belly; her head swam. She leaned back, still clutching the pillow. The glass was taken out of her hands and set aside. She was so very sleepy.

A big hand cupped the side of her face, tilted it up so she looked at him. He was a giant shadow, backlit by the fireplace. But she wasn't scared anymore. "Stay with me here, Doc."

Her eyes closed. *Just a short nap.*

Then she would wake up and all of this will have been a dream.

She passed out.

That went fucking well.

Gabriel blew out a frustrated sigh. Clearly, not one of his shining moments.

Or maybe that was a good thing. Lately, those moments of shine and glamour had centered on bloodshed. He assessed his arm with unconcerned detachment. Girl had some claws on her. Four angry scratches stretched long and deep from his elbow almost to his wrist. Might be the first time an injury made him smile.

He tore off the bottom of his shirt to wipe away the blood, and then left the wounds forgotten as he arranged the doctor's legs on the couch and covered her with a blanket he found draped over the armchair.

Damn! Fucked things up royally. Great going, Connors.

Not like I had a choice!

Dr. Amelia Marguerite Chase was almost impossible to get in touch with. He'd known there would be miles of red tape to prevent him from locating her, let alone getting to talk to her. Scientists of her caliber didn't associate with ordinary people.

So, yeah. Desperate times called for drastic measures.

Gabriel rubbed his knee as he dropped himself into the armchair, watching her sleep.

She had courage. Not many people he came across dared to tangle with him. They knew better than to provoke him. Even with the threat of punishment hanging over him, he'd never hesitated to break some heads. Most looked at him and turned the other way, fast.

He'd been nice with Dr. Chase, doing his best to keep her calm. But *nice* from him usually meant trouble. Tough to break old habits. Poor thing had to be scared out of her mind.

She frowned in sleep, drawing her knees up as far as she could, while still clutching the pillow. What would a woman like her dream about? he wondered. What would make her delicate features furrow with such concern?

Stupid question.

Blood welled on his arm again. He should bandage it before he left bloody streaks on her nice furniture. Gabriel got to his feet, wincing at the pain in his knee. She must have bruised a tendon. Shaking his head, a smile pulling on his lips, he left her to her slumber and went to the bathroom to utilize the wonders of a hot shower.

She'd probably sleep through the night, anyway. Maybe tomorrow, they could sit down like calm, rational people, and have a talk.

Hey, a guy could hope.

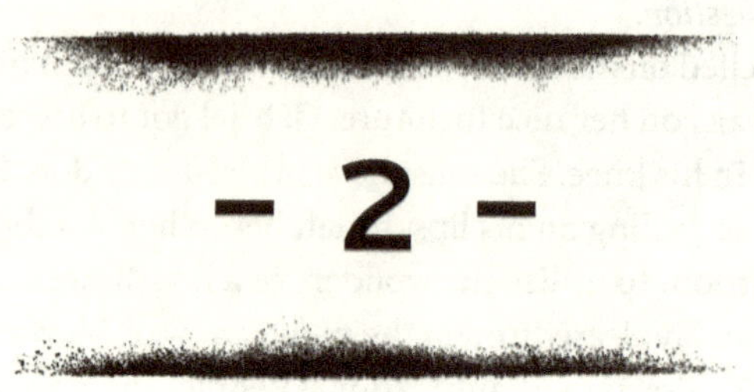

- 2 -

She woke up on the couch, holding a pillow. Amelia groaned. She hadn't made it to the bed? God, the last month was seriously getting to her.

Then again, what did she expect? It wasn't every day that one's sister decided to play mad scientist—on herself, no less!—and make everyone's life oh so very colorful for the sake of proving she could do it. Not that she hadn't. Proved herself, that is. It just would have been nice if Hailey had managed to do it without nearly dying and giving Amelia a heart attack in the process, that's all.

Spending months on the quaint, history reenactment planet of Torrey, where people thought it was fun to light candles instead of installing electric lights, hadn't helped Amelia's stress, either. After countless nights spent making sure Hailey pulled through, dealing with the fallout from her escapade, and keeping it all out of the public eye for both of their sakes, the best Torrey had had to offer in terms of luggage for her trip home had been a cloth suitcase, which had fallen apart the moment she got home.

Guess I should be grateful it held together that long, at least.

And after all that, she'd apparently passed out on the couch. Amelia spied an empty glass on the coffee table and sighed.

Well, that explains everything. Twenty-year-old whiskey went down as smooth as butter, but it had a kick. Must have knocked her on her ass after the trip she'd had. It explained the crazy dreams, too. Amelia chuckled. A huge stranger in her kitchen, with a laser gun that didn't fire. Ridiculous.

She sat up and stretched, feeling bruised all over. Her mouth was bone dry; she needed water.

But that would have to come later, she decided, making a face. She was still in her travel clothes. Forget the bed; she'd never made it to the bath. Raking her fingers through her mess of hair, Amelia got to her unsteady feet. What time was it? Night. Late, too. It was dark outside.

"Time," she said, surprised at how weird her voice sounded.

"Time," the computer replied. "Fifteen minutes, thirty-two seconds past eleven p.m."

Amelia yawned. "Bath. Hot, jasmine scent."

"Confirmed."

Shuffling her feet out into the hallway, she felt a sense of déjà vu. She frowned, looking at the kitchen, but there was nothing to see. On her other side, the stupid suitcase was still attached to the door where it had popped open and spilled her clothes. Amelia glared at it, too tired to even pretend she wanted to clean up the mess, and moved on to her bedroom.

Something was off. She couldn't quite put her finger on it. Was something missing?

She shook her head. It was probably the exhaustion messing with her.

The light was already on in the bathroom and she heard water. Ah, the luxuries of home. Amelia shrugged out of her travel shirt and rubbed her sore shoulders. Her socks came off next, which left her in a pair of jeans and a strappy tank top.

As she bent over, a shadow crossed the threshold on the other side of the bathroom door.

What the hell...

She straightened, watching the door and the light filtering out around it. Nothing happened.

Shaking her head again, Amelia reached for the door handle. Hesitated. Scowled at herself and reached again. Her fingers just brushed it when the door pulled open from the inside.

Bam!

Memories returned in a rush. Laser gun pointed at her chest, not loaded. Broken glass, whiskey all over the floor, running-caught-fighting-aching-wheezing… darkness.

Amelia looked up, *way* up into the face of the psychopath who had broken into her home.

And she screamed. No one around to hear her. She screamed louder.

He winced and covered his ears.

Amelia went for the first thing she could reach. A pillow. In her fright, she didn't care. She whaled it over his head again and again, until the thing tore apart and feathers rained everywhere.

When all that was left in her hand was an empty pillowcase, and she was breathing hard, she looked up at him again. The guy was covered in feathers, arms crossed over his chest, glaring at her. "Feel better now?"

Amelia screamed again.

"Knock it off!" he commanded, his voice booming.

Amelia shut up instantly.

He sighed, in what sounded like relief.

"W-who are you? What do you want?" she said, still clutching the pillowcase like a lifeline to sanity.

He looked down at himself. He was naked except for the white towel around his waist.

And now the feathers stuck to every wet inch of him.

What was going on here? Who the hell was this guy? Did she know him? Why else would he be in her home, *taking a shower*?

"Your bath is ready," he groused, wiping at the feathers. They just stuck to him more. He swore. "Go do whatever it is you women do to stop freaking out." And he brushed past her, padded on bare feet out of the bedroom, muttering to himself the entire way. He closed the door behind him.

Amelia was left gaping.

Amnesia? It was possible. Stress-induced selective memory loss maybe? But then why would she forget *him*?

No, she distinctly remembered the gun. Had there been someone else she hadn't noticed? Had this guy actually saved her from something? He appeared to be perfectly comfortable in her home…

Oh, God, what are you trying to talk yourself into now, Chase? Look at the facts!

Facts. Like the *fact* she was exhausted to the point of passing out on the couch. Or the *fact* she'd spent the last month either sitting at her sister's deathbed, or travelling coach on the cheapest possible interplanetary flights because everything else had been booked. Or the *fact* her life was turned upside down lately with telepaths, and beyond-unhinged killers, and genetically engineered shape-shifters, or that *she'd* had a hand in the latter.

The long and short of it: Amelia was losing her mind.

It was a liberating thought that made her smile. Right now, a hot bath and aroma therapy sounded like just the thing. She put the naked stranger anomaly on hold, nowhere near equipped to deal with that at the moment, closed and locked herself in the bathroom, stripped down, and crawled into her bath.

The warm goodness soaked into her immediately, and she felt her muscles relax. She sighed, wincing only slightly at the ache in her ribs. The scent of jasmine filled the hot air; she felt like she was in a sauna.

Amelia lathered and rinsed out her hair, then soaped up her entire body to wash off the last six months. Everything was back to normal now. Or as normal as her life could get, apparently. Her sister was now half snow leopard, but at least she wasn't dying anymore. And Amelia was back home, surrounded by familiar things. With the exception of an unexpected… house guest?

She glared at the sink where someone had set out a man's shaving kit. He'd come out wearing a towel, but there was her customary set of pastel green ones hanging untouched on the rack. He'd made himself at home here. A disturbing suspicion arose. Had he slept in her bed?

He wouldn't dare!

Then she remembered what had been out of place in her bedroom. The bed was turned down. She always tucked it perfectly neat before she left in the morning. Oh! The bastard was going down. She'd wait until he fell asleep and skewer his ass with the purely decorative fireplace poker in the living room.

Seething—was that blood underneath her fingernails?—she leaned back into the water up to her chin and breathed in deep to calm herself. "Music," she said. "Classical."

The computer beeped softly as it sorted through her extensive collection of music and arranged a playlist.

The heavy drumbeat and bass guitar that blared through the speakers made her slip completely into the water. She surfaced with her hair plastered over her eyes and bath water up her nose. "Stop!" Coughing, sputtering, she drained the tub and got out, wrapping a towel around herself.

That was it! No more. This was the last straw and something was about to break, big time.

Amelia stabbed her feet into her fluffy slippers and marched out of the bedroom. "Where the hell are you?" she demanded.

He was sitting at the kitchen table again, dressed in a pair of pants that had seen much better days, and feathers. He was picking them out of the angry scratches on his arm, but when he saw her, his hand froze above them, clutching feathers.

"How dare you!" she said, coming right up to the table. "You break in here, make yourself at home, attack me, and then you *reprogram my music*? I am going to kick your ass to Hell and back, you son of a bitch, you hear me?"

He didn't move. What the hell was he staring at? Amelia looked down, ire draining out of her in lieu of shock. Oh, right. Towel and fluffy slippers. Her rosy skin blushed deeper. She crossed her arms over her chest to keep the towel firmly in place. "I'm going to get dressed. You do not move a muscle until I get back."

His expression didn't change and neither did the direction of his gaze. Without blinking, he shook his head. "Not going anywhere," he said to her thighs.

Amelia swiveled and hurried back into her bedroom. Heart in her throat, she leaned back against the door after she slammed it shut. *Moron!* Where the hell was her superior intellect now? Quite possibly drained out of the tub along with the bathwater and the last of her sanity.

She locked the door and quickly dressed in a pair of sweatpants, clean tank top, and shirt. Her hair was still dripping, so she toweled it as dry as she could and finger brushed it back. Her extra pair of glasses was on the night stand. She snatched them up and put them on. Sharp eyesight couldn't hurt in a situation like this. Maybe it was time to do the vision correction procedure she'd been putting off for years now. Doctors couldn't be trusted. Amelia was her own physician, with the help of some very sophisticated equipment, but these were her eyes, and no matter how safe she knew the procedure to be, it still gave her the willies thinking about performing it on herself.

Taking a deep breath, she set that aside for the time being.

Okay, nothing to it. Just a stranger in my house. Be rational. Talk to him. Find out what he wants. Stall for time and get some kind of SOS signal out.

Nothing to it.

She'd dealt with worse dregs of society than this guy. Okay, so for all she knew, he was one of them, but he was *one* man. He hadn't tied or gagged her, which was his mistake and her very good fortune. She could get out of this on her own.

Had to. No one else was currently available to come to her rescue.

Amelia checked the clock. Midnight, exactly.

Squaring her shoulders, she unlocked the door and walked back to the kitchen.

What a way to start a new day...

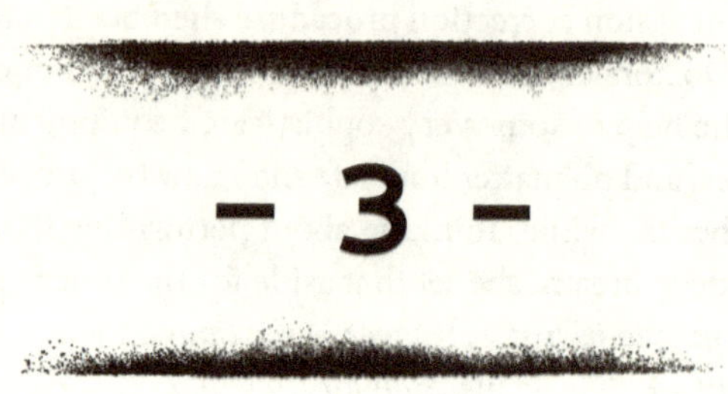

– 3 –

There were few things left in this universe that could rattle Gabriel. He'd seen it all, heard it all, and worse. But the sight of Dr. Amelia Chase, warm and wet from her bath, wearing nothing but a towel, yelling at him and calling him names just about rocked his world right out of orbit.

He'd seen her in pictures around this apartment, mostly in a suit or a lab coat, with someone or another shaking her hand and posing for the camera. He'd thought she was beautiful in them.

But this…

The woman had skin like silk. All peaches and cream, smelling like jasmine and heaven. Seeing her in her green towel and those ridiculous slippers, Gabriel had forgotten to breathe. Higher thought? Shit, putting a sentence together had almost been beyond him. All he could think was getting that towel off her and those smooth legs around him.

Gabriel leashed the thought in an instant. The woman was already terrified enough as it was. But how interesting that in her fear she fought instead of cowering. She was back in her room now, but his fingers still curled to tug that damn towel off her. His mouth was dry, wanting to lick every single drop from her skin.

Too long without a woman.

Yeah, way too fucking long. But it was better than the alternative.

He pushed to his feet and brushed the rest of the feathers off his torso and out of his hair. The woman had attacked him with a pillow. A freaking pillow. Though, he'd bet if she'd had the baseball bat he'd found earlier closer at hand, she'd have bashed him with it instead.

He pulled a clean shirt on over his head and sat back down, hoping she wouldn't come out of hiding until morning. Silently willing her to come back out without that towel.

And then she did, and he just prevented himself from shooting to his feet and startling her again.

She was dressed in loose slacks and a baggy shirt, something a woman would steal from her boyfriend. Did she have one? He hadn't seen any pictures of her with a man. It hadn't occurred to him to wonder until now. She lived here alone, he knew that much.

She came to the table more subdued than before, but her spine was stick-straight, and a pair of glasses sat on her pert nose. She looked like a kid playing dress up. So much innocence, Gabriel felt like he was tainting it by being in her presence.

The doctor cleared her throat. "In light of the unusual circumstances"—her tone said just how much of an understatement that was—"I am willing to put aside what happened earlier, for now. I believe it is… not impossible… for us to have a rational conversation. After which, of course, I will expect you to leave."

It would have sounded almost professional if he didn't keep picturing her naked. "Fair enough," he managed. "Please, sit."

She hesitated, but finally sat, leaving plenty of room for herself, in case she had to bolt. He really hoped she wouldn't. If he had to chase her down again, he might be tempted to do something stupid. "Who are you?" she asked, for the third time.

He answered only because she looked like she might actually hear him this time. "My name is Gabriel Connors."

"Do we know each other?"

"Not yet."

"Then what are you doing here?"

Where to begin? "Have you ever heard of the Romans, Dr. Chase?"

For a moment her gaze met his and he could see her wondering how crazy he really was. Then it was gone, and she answered as if it had been a perfectly legitimate question. "Of course. Who hasn't? But my work centers around the future, Mr. Connors, not the ancient past."

So innocent. "I'm not talking about the past, Doc. The Romans are… a society." And he used that term lightly. "A bunch of rich fucks with an archaic fetish." She hardly winced at his language, so he continued, keeping the information light, without the gory details. "They recruit *promising talents* out of college to cast them into their fantasy world. And I'm talking slaves, whores, and gladiators."

She frowned. "What?"

"It's like an elaborate game of make believe. They have an entire city built according to plans from ancient Rome, and they live and breathe that life. How many rich people do you know who like to pretend they're slaves?"

"Okay."

He raised an eyebrow. "That's it? *Okay*?"

She shrugged. "I spent the last few months on Torrey." As if that explained something. When he clearly didn't get what she was driving at, she waved it aside. "What do you mean by gladiators?"

Clever little scientist, getting straight to the heart of the issue. "Think of it as cock fights, but with humans. Sometimes animals. And humans who qualify for animals."

"Okay." This time she said it with a little less confidence.

"These people, the Patricians, they go all out on their sick games. When I say slaves, whores, and gladiators, it's not pretend. That's very real. Slaves get treated worse than dogs. Haven't seen a whore who hadn't gotten beaten or raped at least once a month."

"And the gladiators?"

"Fight to the death."

She nodded. A detached observer, taking in the facts. Gabriel was curious about what she might be thinking. Her face betrayed nothing.

"The system is merit-based. A whore who does her job well can be promoted to… I guess you'd call it companion status. Still doing what she was hired for, but exclusive to one man. Sometimes passed down to the son like a possession. But at least as a companion, she has some small income of her own, jewels and such to look pretty on someone's arm. Slaves can only get promoted to gladiator status."

"To fight to the death."

"Yes."

"Why?"

"Why, what?"

"Why would anyone do this?"

He shrugged easily, despite the arrow of old pain stabbing through his chest. "To prove something. Or maybe because they're desperate. With no other prospects, on some shithole planet, if the choice is street rat in the cold or street rat in ancient Rome… many don't even look at the fine print." It was never that simple. Rome had a way of burrowing itself under your skin. Yes, the desperate flocked there without a second thought. But there were those who walked into the great city despite being fully informed. *Because* of it.

But the doc didn't need to know that. It muddied waters already murky enough for her to wade through.

"What does this have to do with me?" she asked.

"We're getting to that, Doc," he said.

She waved him on. "At your leisure, then."

This might get tricky. "Gladiators," he said, "also have ranks. The best, the crowd pleasers, can ascend to champion status. They get paid well to fight in front of a crowd. Money, women, anything they want. All they have to do is spill some blood. They say a gladiator can fight his way to freedom, but I haven't heard of it ever happening. Probably a rumor they spread to keep the morale up. Keep them fighting."

"Fascinating. I still don't see what I have to do with any of this."

Gabriel sat back, stretched his legs and crossed his ankles. She was close enough that his legs almost touched her, and she shifted the slightest bit to the side to evade him. "There is another rumor among the gladiators, Doc. And this one I am tempted to believe."

She rolled her eyes, clearly humoring him now, and not with good grace. "Oh? Why is that?"

"Because the man spreading it was a half-crazy ex-con from New Alaska."

The good doctor blanched. The first true show of emotion since she sat down.

"After a few weeks, he racked up some kills, got drunk, and let his mouth run about some kind of experiments. Said the highest security prison known to man was some kind of cesspool of mad scientists messing with people's chemistry. Kept going on and on about people who never slept, and people who died in their sleep and were found disfigured beyond recognition. The most fucked up son of a bitch I ever met, kind of guy you'd cross the galaxy to avoid, and he was more afraid of the doctors than the mass murderer sleeping in the bunk above him."

Gabriel watched her reaction carefully, but aside from a nervous swallow, she said nothing. Her self-control was impressive. Just for that, he decided to prod her a little. "Care to comment on that, Doc?"

"What's there to comment on?"

Interesting. "This same guy," he continued, "told me one man survived. By the time they transferred him out, he was unrecognizable. With streaked hair and a creepy half-animal face, and his skin striped like a tiger. Feel free to jump in any time."

Dr. Chase shrugged.

"Your name came up in this particular story," he said. "The face of an angel, and the Devil's hand on her shoulder. His words."

She crossed her arms over her chest, which pushed her plump breasts together and up. Gabriel almost went slack-jawed at the simple gesture, so without artifice or subterfuge it caught him off guard. "How did you happen to hear all this?"

He had to search for his voice again. "I'm a gladiator. I thought that was obvious."

"I thought you said no one ever won their freedom."

Clever, clever scientist. "They don't. But they do get vacations. I got about three weeks of free time before I have to get back."

"Or what?"

"Or they track me, and drag me back. Already wasted a week here waiting for you."

"Yes, and why did you, again?"

"Because, Doc, you're going to help me."

"To do what, exactly?"

He pulled a folded picture out of his pocket. It was almost falling apart; he'd folded and refolded it so many times the color had faded to white in the creases. It had gotten wet a while back and one corner was torn off. But the subject was still recognizable. He slid it across the table to her.

Amelia held his gaze a moment longer, but he didn't blink. So relaxed, telling her all of this, feeding her some crap about slaves and gladiators, while her heart was racing and her composure was starting to crack.

Finally, she made herself reach for the piece of paper, dreading what she would find. Her heart sank when she carefully unfolded it. A picture torn from some ancient magazine. There were still remnants of writing in one corner, but it was no longer legible. No one wasted paper like this anymore. Everything in the universe was created and stored in computers. Paper was precious, and that made it all the more sacrilegious for him to have torn a piece of it like this. "A panther?" The shiny black big cat snarled at the camera, its mouth open wide, giant fangs gleaming.

"Did some digging while I was here," he said. That didn't bode well. "You covered your tracks pretty well, but there were some random notes here and there. I connected the dots, found out it was all true, and here we are."

"*Here*, meaning…"

"I want you to do to me whatever you did to the tiger guy."

Her heart sank more. How could he possibly know? There were no random notes; she'd scoured the place clean after what Hailey…

Hailey!

Would her sister never stop messing up her life? Amelia had wiped her own notes years ago, moved them to a different system, with only a secure uplink cleverly disguised as a bookkeeping file on her lab computer to connect to it. But she hadn't touched Hailey's initial work before she left for Torrey, wanting to preserve everything as her sister had left it, in case she needed it one day to, oh, save her own life.

What do I do? What do I do?

Play dumb. Not her strong point, but she could pretend with the best of them. "I'm afraid you'll have to explain."

"Naturally," he said. "Because you have no idea what I'm talking about, right?"

"God, what did you find in my notes?"

He hitched a shoulder in a shrug. "Just random words, really. Double DNA, successfully infected, despite low survival rate. Things like that."

Amelia folded the picture back up, buying herself time to think of something. "No," she finally said, and gave him the picture back.

"No," he repeated. "Just like that?"

"That about sums it up."

He drew his legs back and leaned his elbows on the table. "You'll reconsider."

"That confident, are you?"

"I got a few aces up my sleeve."

Oh, yes, how could she forget? "You think if you hold a gun to my head, I will do whatever half-baked insanity you come up with?"

He scowled. "You saw yourself the gun wasn't loaded."

"Well, I have nothing else to say to you. Good bye." She pushed to her feet and turned to get the door for him.

Something dropped on the table. "Ever heard of ferric diamonds? Fascinating stones. Diamonds that can conduct electricity and shimmer like fairy dust. *Before* they're polished."

Do not turn around. Do not *turn around.* Amelia turned. In the middle of the table lay a small, round stone that glittered like gold-sheened crystal. She could see the iron in it, but despite common sense, the carbon, the *diamond*, that encased it was completely unblemished by it. In all of her years of study, Amelia had never seen one.

"One carat of raw ferric diamond sells for about one hundred thousand credits to the highest-end retailers on Earth and any major colony," Connors continued in that deep, mesmerizing voice of his. "That little bit there is about eight carats. Keep it as a down payment. I'll give you two more, even bigger, to do this. One when you finish, and one more if I survive."

So pretty.

Amelia shook herself. "I have no need for more money."

He grinned. "Ah, Doc. A scientist like you, research is like an obsession. And after you cut all ties to the government… all the equipment downstairs can't be cheap."

Government employment wasn't exactly a matter of public records, but at least she had a fairly good idea about where he'd found out about it. In her lab. Her unsecured notes. As far as he knew, Amelia was currently unemployed and quickly burning through her reserves to power this place. He had no idea about her commercial contracts and patents.

"You're trying to pay me to kill you? An expensive way to commit suicide. And quite painful."

"No, I don't want to die. Just need an advantage before they chase me down."

"Why don't you sell the stones and use the money to disappear?"

Fury darkened his features. "I want to show you something." He came around the table, leaving the precious stone there, grabbed her hand and dragged her along to the front door. The suitcase was in his way. He sent it skidding with one solid kick. Amelia wished she could have done that herself. He took her down to the lab, making his way around her equipment in the dark, as if he'd done it so many times already he no longer needed the light.

At the main console, he released her and turned on the computer. He slipped a ring she hadn't noticed before off his finger, flattened it, and then he inserted the disc into a media slot. The holographic video played almost instantly. Like a scanned image, the disc created a scene in the middle of the room, and in the darkness, Amelia felt like she was there.

Everything was fuzzy; the recorder must have been covered by some kind of veil. An arena appeared in front of her, where three men in ancient armor battled with swords and shields. As she watched, one of them drew blood.

The wounded man dropped to the ground. It wasn't a fatal injury, but it was serious enough that blood stained the sand. As he struggled to his feet, a lion charged out of one of the darkened archways. It launched itself at the injured man while the others fell away. Blood sprayed as the man was torn apart. The other two fighters immediately teamed up to slay the beast, before they turned on each other.

The entire battle took less than five minutes, but it was enough to give Amelia nightmares for weeks to come. Finally, one man fell, and the other pressed the sword tip to his throat. But he stopped. Breathing hard, he looked over his shoulder, up into the crowds.

"Right there," Connors said. "That man in the middle of the balcony. That's the Caesar. All he needs to do is indicate his wish with a look, and it's done. If he sees a woman he favors, she's his. If someone wears a robe he likes, the person is stripped of it, willing or not. He only has to wave his finger, and a man dies."

Just then, the Caesar gave a signal and, without looking at his opponent, the gladiator stabbed through the loser's throat. The man on the ground struggled, but he couldn't budge the sword. It had stabbed into the ground and pinned him there.

"Caesar so loves to wave his finger," Connors said bitterly.

"Why are you showing me this?"

"Evidence," he said. "I need you to believe me when I tell you this is happening right now. I got a short reprieve, but there are countless others still trapped there. I plan to get them out."

Her tired mind picked up on something that didn't quite ring true. Amelia didn't know what it was but she didn't have to. He had to realize how idiotic he sounded. "By yourself?"

"It only takes one man to show the others what they're capable of. All the money in the world can't stop a raging warrior from slaying his jailer. But that warrior has to know he *can* do it."

Had he rehearsed that little speech in front of her mirror? "Like I said, suicide."

He shook his head. "Not if you help me. Not if I can take out the Caesar."

Ah, and there was the core of it.

"You're my one hope here, Amelia."

She flinched at the use of her name.

"If you don't help me, and I fail, I won't just die. The Caesar will have me *punished*. Along with everyone I associated with, just to prove a point."

"Oh, so it's not suicide you want to hire me for," she said. "It's aiding a murder. Well, that changes everything. Get out."

He blew out a breath in frustration. "The Caesar is the center of it all. Cut the head off a snake—"

"And two more grow back in its place." She knew this better than anyone. New Alaska had started out with one warden. There'd been five, one for each block, by the time she'd left.

And each had been worse than the guy before. There were nights when she still woke up from nightmares of prisoners breaking out in a riot, and wondered how someone like her had survived there.

It never took long to answer herself. She'd been too valuable, her research too precious to risk. She'd been guarded day and night, watched every second to make certain she was safe. Safe, and doing what they wanted her to do.

"I can do this, Doc," Connors said. "But not without your help."

She reached past him to turn off the projector. "I really don't see myself caring."

He caught her arm before she pulled away. "Of course you care," he said softly. He was staring into her eyes as if he could see her soul. His gaze was sharp, but somehow still hot. His fervor was evident. He *needed* her to do this. "I can see it, clear as day."

"Then you see what you want to see," she countered.

He half smiled, but it wasn't with amusement. "You hide your feelings; push them deep down so no one can touch you. But you do it to protect your heart, not deaden it. Because if you let yourself, you care too much. And it hurts."

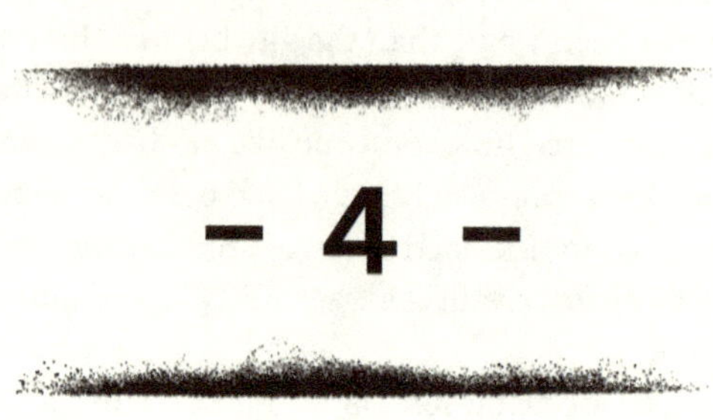

It was a shot in the dark, but Gabriel must have gotten a lot better at them over the years, because the truth of what he said was in her eyes. He wouldn't apologize. Thousands of lives had already been destroyed, and more got added to the count every goddamn day, because someone somewhere in the last twenty years had decided it would be fun to recreate antiquity. With all of its blood and gore. Amelia was the only one he knew of who might have the ability to trigger a change. Probably the only one alive who'd give a damn enough to try, if he played this right.

He'd thank her for it. On his knees, if he had to. For helping him bring down the Caesar, he'd willingly hand his life to her. But he would not apologize.

Amelia extricated her arm from his grasp, and somehow it was a pointed gesture with a clear message: Do Not Touch. She stepped back from him, seeming uncomfortable with being so close. Gabriel couldn't blame her. Taking her time, avoiding his gaze, she spoke. "If what you say is true—"

"It is."

"—and that video is authentic…" Amelia shook her head. "This is ridiculous. A single man can't change decades of money. You're talking about taking on the most influential people anywhere. You think they haven't already anticipated the possibility of petty riots?"

"The course of history has been changed hundreds of times by the actions of a single man or woman. Martin Luther, Joan of Arc."

"Attila the Hun, Adolph Hitler," she said, her tone arch. "What makes you think something you do will make things better?"

"*Anything* is better than this," he said, hardly able to grate the words between gritted teeth. She still didn't understand. She'd never been there. The recording was just the tip of the iceberg. One of several. "And to answer your other question, there is nothing *petty* about what I have planned."

No. For what they did, and continued to do, the Patricians would pay with currency they understood very well. Blood. Lots of it. They said that fear never touched the Caesar. It was unknown to a person who doled it out with a twitch of an eyebrow. Gabriel could prove a very effective tutor. He would teach the Caesar to fear shadows.

One single being. The smallest signal. And all of Rome shuddered. The Patricians played their games, pretended they were better than everyone else. The enlightened society. They couldn't see they were as much slaves to the Caesar as the people who cleaned out the latrines were to them. The only difference was they dressed better doing it.

Cut the head off a snake... and two more grow back in its place.

Perhaps. Everything in life was a gamble. It was just a matter of how high the stakes were. He might not bring the Republic to its knees, but he might be able to free a small portion of it, including himself. Wasn't that a worthy enough undertaking?

"You might come to regret those words," Amelia said. "There are things far worse than this. You're asking me to do them to you. At best, you survive and go on a killing spree. At worst, you die." She shuddered, as if she was remembering. "Horrifically. In pain like you have never felt before. I've seen men beg for death. The lucky ones didn't survive long enough to speak."

It was as much a confession as it was a warning. "I've got nothing left to lose here."

She scoffed softly and looked at him with pity in her gaze. "You don't know how wrong you are about that."

"Does that mean you've made up your mind?" If she said no, could he force her to do his bidding?

Yes.

Amelia drew a deep breath and exhaled on a defeated sigh. "I need to think about this."

"Tick-tock, Doctor."

She nodded. "I'll have an answer for you by morning."

Gabriel was tempted to push, but by the looks of her, that was the surest way to push her in the wrong direction. "Fair enough," he said instead. "It's late. I'm sure you're tired from your trip. Sleep on it." He typed a sequence into the computer to get access to the building's systems. Voice only worked for her as the owner. He would be changing that soon.

"What are you doing?"

"Just a precaution," he told her. "In case you happen to get cold feet at night, I don't want you bolting for the door."

She swatted at him to get to the controls. "You're locking me in?"

Gabriel held her aside with ease. A simple command here, a push of a button there, and it was done. The front door wouldn't open until he decided to let it. "Temporarily."

"*Argh!* This is unbe-*freaking*-lievable." She was still grumbling to herself when she headed back up to her apartment.

Gabriel finished with the computer and hurried after her.

"I try to be rational," she said to herself, loud enough for him to hear, "and what do I get? No, no, no, there is no *rational* with this guy. Freaking baseball bat to the head probably wouldn't work."

"Probably," he allowed.

She turned around with a gasp, a hand pressed to her heart.

Gabriel grinned. "I've been told I have a very hard head."

A wet lock of hair fell over her eye, and he had to amend that very soon, his head wouldn't be the only part of him suffering from that particular condition. "*What* will it take to get rid of you?"

"You know the answer to that."

She swiveled and continued to the kitchen without a word.

"Come on, Amelia. One life among many. You've never heard of me before I showed up, and you'll never see me again once I'm gone. What's the problem?"

"*Do no harm,*" she said. "That's the problem." She took a bottle of juice from the cooler and slammed the door shut. There would be a fresh bottle in its place the next time she opened it. Such a simple thing, a self-replenishing cooler. Standard in every home of every civilized colony, on every inhabited planet. A man who's had to kill for a drink of water might easily resent those simple little luxuries.

He frowned. "That hasn't stopped you before. What, you suddenly grew a conscience since the government cut all ties?"

She took a big swig from the bottle. "Right. Because everyone is free and unfettered outside of the Republic. No one could possibly understand the life of a slave. Poor you and your friends. Such a tough life you have." She pointed at him. "That's the biggest fallacy in your argument, Connors. You think you'll be free once you fight your way out of Rome."

He raised an eyebrow. "You're saying someone forced you to do those experiments?"

Amelia rubbed her forehead. "I'm going to bed."

"Yeah, good idea." Long day. He could use a few solid hours of sleep.

They reached the bedroom at the same time. The door was open, and they clashed, trying to go through it at the same time. Amelia jumped back. She crossed her arms over her chest.

"What?" he said.

She cleared her throat and raised an eyebrow, waiting for something.

Gabriel almost groaned. "Right," he said. "Your bedroom. I'll go crash on the couch."

"Oh, please," she replied. "Don't let me stop you from going to a hotel. Really."

He scowled. "Can I at least get a pillow?"

Amelia scoffed.

Gabriel didn't budge.

There was no way she could beat him in a battle of wills, and she was beginning to realize it. She rolled her eyes. "Fine," she said on a cute little growl and marched into the room, shoving past him. A second later, she tossed an empty pillowcase at his head and slammed the door in his face.

Gabriel glared at the feathers still hanging off the tear. "That's fine," he called. "I'm used to sleeping on the hard, bloodstained ground. Being a gladiator and all."

No answer.

"Amelia?"

Nothing. *Damn.*

Amelia clutched the baseball bat, poised next to the door in case he decided to come in. He didn't. After a while, she heard him move away. She propped a chair under the door handle just in case.

Bloodstained ground… right.

She stayed by the door for a good long while, but then her hands started to cramp and ache. Finally, she surrendered her vigil and went to bed.

Amelia wished she had her garden here. Nothing worked better to soothe troubled thoughts than lush greenery. She'd had a greenhouse on Torrey, but she hadn't had time to finish one here. The few potted plants she had in the sunroom above the lab weren't near enough to soothe her now.

At what point had her life taken this turn for the bizarre? There were so many little things, so many insignificant choices over the years, all leading to this inevitable conclusion. Things like choosing to go to a different coffee house, rather than wait in line in the one she usually went to. She'd met her mentor there.

Taking an interest in biochemistry. The only schools specializing in it were government-run.

Accepting the first job offer that had come her way. Who cared if it was for the government? If the pay was good and the work was interesting, what else could she ask?

It turned out, she could have asked for a lot more. But by the time she'd figured it out, it had been too late.

One door closed, another opened. And if it didn't, she crawled through a window.

And now a suicidal squatter was in her apartment, insisting the shortest instance of freedom was worth more than a lifetime in slavery. Amelia understood. She'd fought with everything at her disposal to get her freedom.

That was precisely the problem.

There'd been nothing to do about Tristan, her first successful experiment in DNA alteration, except cover her tracks. Hailey had almost died, and in the process nearly exposed herself as a shape-shifter. Both now had the rest of their lives to look forward to, but it came with a high price. Anonymity. If they exposed their abilities, the authorities would stop at nothing to put them under a magnifying glass. And she'd be the one forced to look through it.

And now here came Connors, wanting to become a shifter for the express purpose of outing himself. One life among many, he'd said. Another fallacy in his argument. It was never about one person. In this case, it wasn't even about his friends.

If he exposed himself, he'd be putting everyone at risk. That included Amelia, and every patient and subject she'd ever come into contact with. Tristan would be first on the list. Hailey not far behind.

Amelia was an expert at calculating probabilities; she played causality like a pro. A always led to B, regardless of C or D. It was a matter of predicting all possible outcomes and compensating to avoid the bad ones.

There was no avoiding anything now. If what Connors said was true, and they came looking for him, Amelia was in trouble one way or another. The bastard had dropped her into the middle of a maelstrom without a life vest. He had no idea what he was getting into—what he was getting *her* into. It pissed her off that he was such a damn hypocrite.

A hero and savior, sure. About to martyr himself for the good of the Romans. Right. He would only have to ruin a few other lives to do it. But who cared about them? They were no one. People he'd never met and would never come into contact with. Faceless strangers who didn't register and didn't matter.

Was this what he considered triage?

Were a few lives acceptable as collateral damage when it came to saving thousands?

Amelia shook her head at herself.

Connors didn't think like that. He had tunnel vision so bad, he didn't realize there *were* people about to be trampled beneath his charge.

A always leads to B.

It wasn't unreasonable to assume Connors had come straight here.

Like it or not, there was already a target painted on Amelia's back. No matter what she did from now on, it would always be there. But maybe she could somehow minimize the risk to the others.

Maybe if she played her cards right—assuming she had any—she could keep them safe.

Amelia got up and went to the window. She pressed her hand to the windowsill. The entire bottom portion acted as a scanner. It matched her handprint to a very small database of allowable combinations, and a compartment opened in the floor below the window.

She took out the paper files and sat down with her back to the wall, using the light filtering in from the street to examine their contents. There were three files, and each one was there for a different reason. All of them were paper, one of only two surviving copies. Nearly impossible to trace, so easy to destroy.

Some of the contents made her want to close the files and never look at them again. Amelia made herself look. In the end, they only mirrored what was already permanently stored in her memories. There was no escaping any of her past sins. She would take them to her grave.

Amelia closed the top file and set it aside. The rest of them she placed back into their hiding place in the floor. The compartment was set on a timer and closed automatically after sixty seconds, unless something disturbed the location, in which case, it slammed shut and locked.

The moon was full tonight. Amelia could make out its bright glow from behind a cover of thick clouds. There was rain on the night air. Probably another storm on the rise. This region was known for them.

Rain makes the flowers grow.

Not here. Everything within a mile radius was pavement and warehouse. People here didn't care much for plants of any kind.

A shame. At the darkest times of her life, flowers have always had a way of brightening her outlook on the future. Her first apartment had turned into a hothouse, one plant at a time. She missed that place. And with its vast natural beauty, she even missed Torrey.

She put the file on her nightstand and crawled back into bed. There was only one pillow left. Amelia curled up with it and closed her eyes, patiently waiting for sleep to pull her under.

Bracing for the nightmares to come.

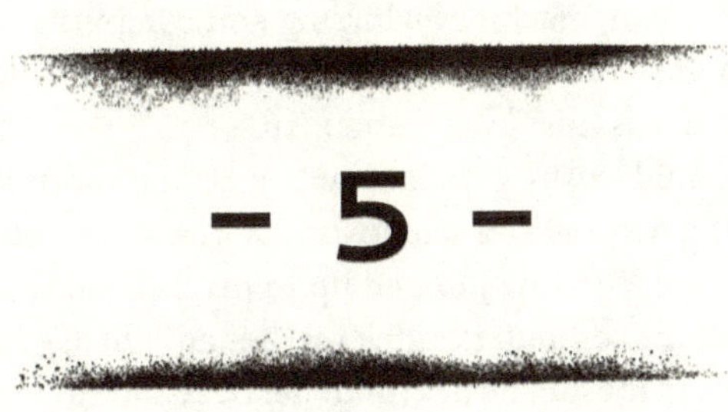

– 5 –

"It wasn't a dream."

Even if she wanted to convince herself otherwise, the evidence stared her right in the face. A chair propped against her door and a paper file on her nightstand. One of the ones she'd hoped never to have to pull out again. Amelia took her time washing up and dressing. It was almost noon, but it wasn't as if she had anywhere important to be.

Her stomach growled for sustenance. After a cautious peek out the door and judging it safe to emerge, Amelia went to the kitchen. She poured thick mango-peach juice over a readied bowl of cereal in the meal nook and sat down to the table.

The ferric diamond was still there, in the same place it had landed last night. Amelia stared at it while her cereal got soggy with the juice. She didn't reach out for it… didn't move. Why would he leave it there?

"Connors?" she called.

There was no answer.

Dare she hope he'd changed his mind and just left?

Doubtful. A gladiator used to fighting and conquering—a good one, as evidenced by the fact he was still alive—wouldn't leave well enough alone. So where the hell was he now?

Suspicion. *He wouldn't…* "Connors!"

Nothing.

He would! The bastard!

Amelia abandoned her cereal and left the apartment, heading for her lab.

The light was on, machines whirring and computing. And in the middle of them, Connors was on the floor, doing push-ups.

"What the hell is this?" she demanded.

He paused mid-push-up to look at her. "Good morning," he said. "I'm gathering data, as you scientists like to say. It's a stress test." A computer beeped, and he jumped up to his feet. He wasn't winded or sweaty and the computers didn't register any change in heart rate.

Amelia tossed the file she held onto her desk and stopped the functions he'd initiated. "Push-ups aren't stress," she told him. "Don't pretend to know what you're doing." He had round, pale gray patches stuck to his temples, the side of his neck, and on the inside of his wrists. One of her inventions, just recently patented and rolled out to every major healthcare facility. She cringed at the blatant misuse and took his hand to peel the wrist patch off. "These are not toys," she told him.

"Then you might want to take back the rest of them, too."

His tone… was he teasing her? Amelia took off the patches on his temples and on his neck. "As I was saying," she said, tossing the used patches into the trash can behind her.

"What about these?" he said while her back was turned.

Amelia froze. How much worse could it be? She braced herself and turned around. "I'm going to kill you," she growled. He'd stripped off his shirt, revealing his handiwork. The idiot had wallpapered himself in the damn things. It looked like he put a patch over each major organ.

He must have wasted a full pack of them! "I'm going to beat you to within an inch of your life and toss you out behind one of the warehouses. And you know what?"

"Tell me."

"I'm going to enjoy it."

Connors tossed his head back and laughed.

Amelia blinked. Okay, so she wasn't as big and tough as he was, and she wasn't up on the popular threat-of-violence lingo these days, but surely she wasn't *that* laughable.

"You're funny when you don't try to be," he said, still heartily amused. Bastard. He took off the patches one at a time and, following her example, tossed each into the trash. Amelia wanted to weep for each one. "I was waiting here for you," he explained, "and got bored. You got a nice lab, Doc."

As the patches came off—*Oh, God, there were more on his back!*—her tunnel vision slowly cleared past them to the scars that crisscrossed his torso. There were two long, parallel lines across his back, like whip lashes. His chest had a number of cuts, most of them fully healed and old, but one or two looked freshly healed.

"I like computers," he said in praise. "Or I used to, before all this shit—"

"Battle scars?" she asked, cutting him off.

His good humor faded a little when he peeled off the last patch over his right kidney. He was looking at the same thing she was—a long, straight scar that ran from his left clavicle, across his chest to his right side, to just where the ribs ended over the liver. "Badges of honor," he replied, but he didn't sound very proud. "Hammer strikes that honed the blade."

When he met her gaze again, it was almost measuring. Was he self-conscious about them? "Come on, Doc," he said. "You must have seen worse than this."

What she'd seen didn't compare to this on any level. She'd treated self-inflicted wounds, and ones caused by treatment. She'd seen men bleed to death in front of her eyes before she could identify the source of damage. All of them had been dirty wounds. That's how she'd thought of them. She'd felt tainted treating them.

Connors was the first man she'd seen whose scars were a fact of life. On him, they were a testament to his strength and will to survive. At least two of his scars would have been life threatening. He'd received them fighting for his life. As a scientist, Amelia should have been impassive, looking at them. As a woman, she wanted to know how he'd gotten each one. She wanted to ask if it had hurt.

There was another scar on his forearm. It looked like it had come too close to severing part of his limb. Amelia's hand reached for the arm, as if she weren't in control of it.

Connors caught it in a flash, squeezing her wrist enough to let her know he could crush it if he chose to. It startled her into looking up into his eyes again. *Don't,* they warned. Holding his gaze, Amelia reached with her other hand and pried the last patch out of his grip. He released her when he realized what she was after.

Amelia held the crumpled patch up to him. "This is not a pulse patch." Those had been discontinued years ago. Similar in appearance, but limited to monitoring blood flow to specific areas of the body. They were second generation medical tools, compared to her version, generation ten. And if that's what Connors thought these were, if that's how long he'd been out of the loop, she shuddered to think what else he might have messed up if she hadn't come down when she had.

"It is a multisystem monitoring patch. It has about a million micro-scopic connections that plug into a person's body and transmit vitals and system information to the computer over there. It costs about three thousand credits to make, six to buy. One can monitor every last detail about a person's anatomy and bodily functions for a month." Diagnostic applications alone were limitless. One small patch, and a physician could monitor what ailed his patient for a full month. It was a breakthrough that had made her a fortune.

Connors had the good grace to look thoroughly chastised. His face flushed, and he ducked his head. "Sorry," he muttered.

"Don't touch my stuff again."

She tossed the last precious patch into the trash. Once they adhered to the skin, the microcomputer inside tuned into the wearer's body. It would be useless for anything else now.

"Have you made a decision yet?"

"The decision's not mine," she said.

"I don't follow."

Obviously. "Whether I agree or not, I am already knee-deep into this, thanks to your sudden and inexplicable arrival in my home. You already screwed up my life. Now the question is whether you are willing to screw up your own." She handed him the file and took her seat at her desk.

"What is this?" he said, opening the paper folder. "What am I look-ing at?"

"A few possible outcomes to this scenario," she said.

The first few pages of the file were her handwritten notes. Much like journal entries, except about others, not herself. She waited for him to skim through them and turn the page. After the notes came pictures. She expected some kind of reaction from him. Shock, disgust, and fear were all possibilities.

Those pictures depicted the worst of what could possibly happen to him. Fates Tristan and Hailey had avoided by a sheer stroke of luck and a whole lot of painkillers. They were death portraits at their worst. People with their skulls split open and brain matter splattered everywhere; with broken, contorted limbs that no longer looked human. With fur to hide the bruising underneath, and massive fangs in dislocated jaws. People whose final act had been to reach out hopelessly for some kind of help that never came.

People she'd killed in the name of science and progress.

Amelia expected him to toss the file back in her face and walk out without a backwards glance.

Instead, his only outward reaction was that he turned the next page slower. He didn't gasp, or make a sound, just frowned at what he was seeing and, without looking up, made his way to her desk and perched on the edge of it, still leafing through the file.

When he got to the end, he closed it and placed it neatly in front of her. "When do we begin?"

Amelia was inherently a good person. It showed in every word she spoke and every action she took. Gabriel had never seen anything so gruesome as those pictures. The notes he'd come across in his search here hadn't come close to scratching the surface of her studies. Amelia was meticulous about keeping her secrets.

She'd shown him the file to educate him. Or possibly scare him. Odds were good that the Caesar already knew where Gabriel was and would come looking for him. Amelia was right: she was already involved, no matter what happened. And despite all of that, she was still trying to convince him doing this was not a good idea.

All of those people had died, as she'd warned, in terrible pain.

But she left out the most pertinent fact in this situation.

One man had survived.

And if one had, another could. Gabriel hadn't come this far to turn back now.

She closed her eyes and shook her head a little, probably calling him all kinds of idiot in her head. "I'll need to do some tests." She glared at him. "The *proper* way."

He winced.

"After that, I'll need to procure several DNA samples and find the right match for your chemistry. Once I get the serum ready, it's a matter of a few injections."

"How soon will the serum take effect?"

"That depends," she said. "I have some choices to make. The man you're staking all your hopes on—the survivor—only began showing signs of metamorphosis after a year."

A fucking *year*?

"However," she continued, "some recent developments lead me to believe it is possible to expedite the process."

"By how much?"

She glared. "It is dangerous, and the chances of failure go up exponentially the faster you try to achieve something."

"In for a nickel, in for a dime," he said with a shrug. "What are these recent developments you mentioned?"

"You should know that to stand a chance, there must be certain chemical markers present in your makeup. It seems to be a prerequisite for any kind of success that the subject be chem-resistant."

"What does that mean?"

"It means your body cannot have incorporated the mandatory chem-treatment administered to children in infancy."

"Why?"

"The two work at cross purposes," she explained. "The chem-treatments balance out protein production and seal DNA strands to make them stable. What I need to do is open the DNA strand to introduce a new one. You can have one or the other, but not both."

"I see. So what do you need first?"

"I'll need a sample of your blood to test for this resistance."

Gabriel pulled a small blade out of his boot.

"Jesus!" Amelia jumped to her feet so quickly she sent her chair rolling back all the way out the door. "What is the matter with you?" she demanded.

"You said you needed blood."

"Yeah, drawn with a syringe into a sterile test tube. God, how long have you been living in antiquity?"

Too damn long. He sheathed the blade and rolled up his sleeve, proffering his arm without a word.

She still looked spooked, like she'd run if he turned his back. "It's just for carving," he said to put her at ease. "I carve wood when I get bored on bed rest."

Amelia didn't look convinced. She nodded toward the back of the lab. "Over there, please. In the seat."

Gabriel sat in the chair, noting the metal restraints built in. "Manacles, Dr. Chase?" he said. "Careful, or I'll start getting all kinds of naughty thoughts in my head."

When she came to him with a tray of instruments, she was wearing a white lab coat, gloves, and a glare. She sterilized his arm over a vein and poked a long needle into it, letting blood drip into a vial. At least she hadn't tied him down. "This is for typing," she said when the vial was full. She closed it, shook it, then set it aside and attached a tube to the needle in his arm. "This will be for more extensive tests."

"Bleeding me dry?"

"Not yet," she said. "Though later, you might do that all on your own."

Gabriel smiled. "I'm not worried."

"Oh?"

"I know you wouldn't let me die like that."

She put a soft rubber ball into his hand. "Squeeze this every five seconds."

"Yes, ma'am."

Amelia checked everything, then went to a station far to his right and put the small vial of his blood into a machine. From beneath the table, she pulled out a couple of bottles and a small bag. She returned to him and gave him one of the bottles. "Fluids and sugars, so you don't faint."

Not likely, but he was getting a little thirsty.

She clinked her bottle against his. "Here's to insanity."

"Cheers," he said.

The bag turned out to be cookies, which she nibbled on while waiting for the blood bag to fill. She sat hunched on a tall chair, swinging her legs like a kid. How easily she put him from her mind. This wasn't the Amelia who'd yelled at him last night and clawed his arm bloody. She was a stranger now, an apathetic machine performing a task. And he felt like an insignificant slab of meat on her exam table.

It shouldn't have bothered him.

It still did. So he decided to do something about it. "Don't I get a cookie?" he teased.

"No."

Gabriel frowned. "How come?"

"This is my breakfast," she replied.

"Not a very healthy one."

"Unfortunately, it's all I get, seeing as there was a lunatic squatter loose in my lab when I was preparing a proper one and I didn't get the chance to finish."

"Oh, sure," he said. "Blame it on the house guest. It's all their fault. I'm beginning to think you don't want me here."

Amelia raised an eyebrow at him. "Thank you for stating the obvious."

Now he scowled. "Did it ever occur to you that I might be of use?"

She chuckled. "Oh, this I gotta hear."

"I can fight."

"I don't have any enemies."

"I am strong."

"You're the heaviest thing in this complex. The rest I can lift by myself."

How quickly she'd demoted the qualities that made him a famous champion in Rome, loved by the bloodthirsty crowds, and adored by the lusty women, to nothing more than a quirk of his genetic makeup, and just as appealing.

"I'm good with computers," he said. True. And with all the computers she had here, he could keep himself amused for weeks, making it easier for her to do her job. The little patches transmitted something? He could make her a receiver that could pick up on those soft signals from other planets.

Amelia shrugged. "Good enough to lock me in here until you decide to release me. Not impressed."

Well, then there was only one thing left. His favorite. "I can make your toes curl with a kiss." He could do a hell of a lot more than that. He could make her wild with want; tease her until she begged him to fuck her. He grew hard just thinking about it—stripping her of that cool indifference and inhibitions, until she clawed him and bit him; anything to get some relief.

"Got a boyfriend for that," she said, the faintest blush stealing across her cheeks.

"Liar." Gabriel was satisfied to see cracks forming in her professional mask. The good doctor wasn't as aloof as she liked to pretend. He could use that.

"Am I?" She hadn't met his gaze and it occurred to him he could make this whole process a hell of a lot more enjoyable. For both of them.

"Either that, or your *boy*friend lets you travel on your own and live here all by yourself. Guy like that doesn't deserve a woman like you. Wouldn't know the first thing to do with you." Her blush intensified, making his heart beat double time. Yes, this was the true Amelia, not the automaton she pretended to be.

"I'm here and he's not. His loss." And Gabriel's gain. He reached out to touch her rosy cheek, not in the least deterred when she moved out of the way. "Must be lonely here all by yourself. Are you sure you can't find some use for me? I have so many." He could make her arch like a cat to his touch. "In the bedroom…" He could become an addiction she'd never rid herself of. "In the kitchen…" He could make her so craven for him that one heated look would make her wet and needing. "Here…" The posh Roman ladies had taught their favorite whore well. "Any way you can think of."

Amelia sighed. She hopped off her chair, put the bag of cookies on his stomach, and dusted off her hands before she reached for gauze to wipe away the blood that had trickled out around the syringe in his arm.

Gabriel wouldn't let her hold anything back. And when he finally fucked her, he'd do it so hard and so long she would forget all her past *boy*friends. She would scream his name when she came. Over and over again. "And some you'd blush to imagine."

She removed the needle and put pressure on the puncture mark with one hand, while she manipulated the plastic bag of his blood onto a cart with the other.

"Nothing to say? No witty remarks, Dr. Chase?" Gabriel's knuckles were turning white. He opened his hand and let the rubber ball drop to the floor. "I guess your silence will have to be enough, then. I know you won't admit it, but I'll bet your heart's beating a little faster." His was drumming a primal beat that demanded he snatch her down and taste those pouting lips.

She put an adhesive bandage on his arm and brought his wrist up to bend the elbow.

"Bet that lab coat is starting to feel hot, isn't it, Amelia?" He wanted to tear it off her. See her in nothing but those sexy glasses on her nose. "Your hands look unsteady," he noted. He wanted to feel them on him, his imagination already running rampant with the feel of that cool touch on his overheated skin. He'd take his time melting her until she burned. Until she seared him—and he knew she would. This woman would brand him forever. "Tell me, do you ever crave, Amelia?"

Her gaze finally snapped up to meet his, her eyes burning bright blue.

Gabriel's eyes followed the smart line of her nose to her parted lips and stuck there. "I do," he said.

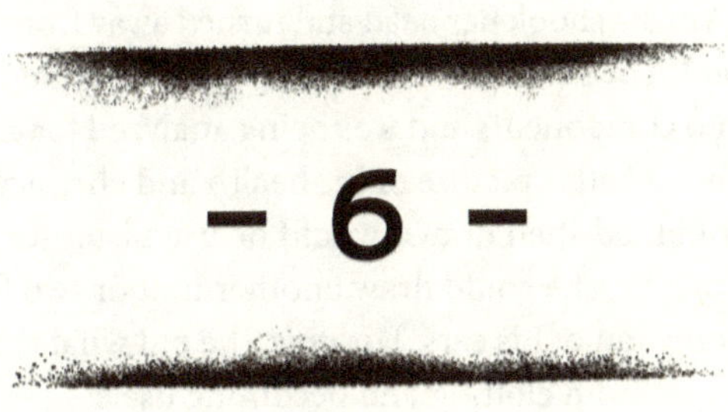

– 6 –

"I crave all the time," he said, staring at her mouth, and Amelia almost melted.

Heart beating faster? *Yep, quite a bit.* Lab coat feeling hot? Heat crawled up her spine, making her cheeks burn. It was all she could do to keep from panting.

How the hell did he do that? Was she really that desperate and deprived? Amelia hadn't been born yesterday. Hell, she'd spent most of her life in a male-dominated field, and then New Alaska, where over ninety percent of the population was male. She knew exactly what to expect from men and how to guard against it.

But Connors just had to go all deep-voiced and intense, and years of training flew directly out the window.

"And what does a man like you crave?" Her voice was breathy, her mouth was dry, and she was talking stupid. Why was she encouraging him?

He frowned, and then raised those chocolate eyes to look into hers again. Amelia felt invaded by his steady stare. As if he could see through her, right into her soul. She'd never felt so exposed before, not even around Hunt, who'd willingly admitted he could read minds.

What was worse, Connors knew it, too. His mouth quirked in a brief, wry smile. "It would only scare you."

"I don't scare easily." *Liar!*

"Neither do I," he replied.

Now, why did that sound like a promise?

Losing it. Amelia shook her head and turned away from him to deal with his blood. The small amount in the vial she'd gotten earlier had separated into components and was being analyzed for anomalies. It would give her a better picture of his health and chemical makeup.

The unit of blood she'd drawn would be used later for more tests. Tomorrow, maybe, she could draw another unit or two for when he started bleeding out of his ears. For now, she put what she had into a cooler to keep it from clotting and becoming useless.

When she went back to her computer, Connors followed. "You really do have a nice lab," he said. "Bit cold, though."

"The thermostat is voice-activated," she said. "Feel free to turn the heat up."

"Oh, I will," he said.

Moments later, the lab was sweltering and Amelia was deep in research mode. It tended to happen when she got really focused on her work; everything else ceased to exist. She'd missed meals before, had gone entire days without food because she'd been so preoccupied with her latest project that she hadn't noticed the passage of time.

As she browsed the restricted databases for the necessary compounds on one computer, and typed in a code to piece together a formula on another, Amelia easily fell into the natural rhythm of her work. This was what she loved, what she excelled at: being presented with a problem and coming up with a solution, even if it meant creating and overcoming several other sub-problems in the process.

Her research into the biology and traits of the black panther was fascinating. The name was an umbrella term for three separate species of animals: the jaguar, the leopard, and the cougar, all of which could produce offspring with black pigmentation. Amelia read reports on all three and, based on its size, *Panthera onca*, the jaguar, would be the best fit for Connors.

Matter could neither be created nor destroyed. While several scientific theories have challenged this law in the past, and some had managed to succeed, it was one of several unquestionable rules in the game of shape-shifting. Nature would only allow the bending of so many of her rules before she struck back.

In theory, Amelia had the basic formula to give a human being the ability to change his shape into another living being. In practice, however, certain species were incompatible with each other.

Early DNA tests have shown anything other than another mammal was not a viable option. Beyond that, size was another factor. The closer an animal specimen was to the subject's size and weight, the better the chances of success. Survival, however, was another matter altogether. Not even Amelia could predict that.

There were three zoologist researchers currently in possession of numerous strains of *Panthera onca* DNA. Two of them used these samples in conjunction with a breeding program to keep up a healthy population of jaguars in their habitats. Each individual was tagged and its DNA recorded, along with specific data about them, including age at the time of tagging, sex, weight, and special characteristics.

Of those two databases, one was run by the man who had supplied Amelia with all of her DNA samples in earlier trials. Dr. Matthias was meticulous about his record-keeping, often following individual animals throughout their lives and recording detailed histories. As far as sources went, his was the most trustworthy.

There was only one problem. Amelia couldn't be sure Dr. Matthias could keep a secret when it came to the government. Hunt's success was a secret from *everyone*. Her superiors had demanded her research notes in exchange for Hunt when she'd decided to leave New Alaska. They might spend years, decades, trying to decipher her notes, only to discover they all led to a dead end and no solution.

The knowledge Amelia had, in the wrong hands, could prove catastrophic. She'd learned long ago how little value human life held these days. She could not risk anyone in any way involved in these studies to be recruited by people in power. Whether of their own will or against it. No. She couldn't risk contacting Dr. Matthias again.

Instead, she set to searching the other database for a viable specimen. It was a painstaking process of reading copious inconsequential notes and observations, wading through a mess of records cataloged by location, rather than species, and unsearchable.

By the time she got through the last of it, her notes listed five different DNA samples by name and serial number, and she sent an informal request for them and six others from her alias account. Many scientists had the equivalent of a stage name, which they used to market their consumer products, while their true names and credentials were only used for government contracts. The government allowed this and looked the other way so their employees could make a decent living on the side and feel less like lowly slaves to dictatorial tyrants.

No sooner had she sent off the request, than her computer turned off.

Amelia gasped. "What the—"

"You've been at this for hours."

Connors! "Are you crazy? You can't shut off a machine like that!"

He shrugged, completely unrepentant. "Sure you can. You just flip a switch."

The other computer, the one decrypting her formula was still running. Her shoulders slumped in relief. Thank God, at least he hadn't touched that one.

"You should take a break," he said.

"I thought you were in a hurry."

"I thought you didn't care."

He pushed her e-pad aside and set a steaming plate of pasta in front of her.

"Where did this come from?" It smelled so good her mouth watered for a bite. Creamy Alfredo sauce, pieces of chicken perfectly baked and still juicy. Amelia always overcooked it and made it as dry as dust.

"I told you, I have my uses." He was grinning.

Amelia had been gone for months. There was nothing in her kitchen that hadn't come prepackaged and preserved in some way. "Where'd you get the ingredients?"

Connors rolled his eyes. "I called for delivery."

"I didn't hear the doorbell."

"Yeah, exactly. You were too busy being mesmerized by the shiny numbers on the screen. I *told* you I was making dinner. Did you hear me?"

Amelia leaned back in her seat and crossed her arms over her chest. "If you don't like the way I work, you're more than welcome to take your jewels elsewhere."

He ducked his head, but Amelia saw his smirk. She shrugged. Not like she meant to be subtle about the double entendre. "Eat. You must be starving."

"I'm perfectly fine."

As if on cue, her stomach growled loudly.

Amelia rolled her eyes. "That doesn't mean anything."

Connors shook his head and perched on the corner of her desk. She was surprised it didn't crumple beneath his massive weight. "Angel, your stomach's been growling for the last two hours."

"Don't insult my intelligence with your nicknames. My name is Amelia. Dr. Chase should do fine for you." God, was that real cream and cheese on that pasta? *Don't stare. Don't stare!*

Too late. His big, callused hand came into her field of vision. He picked up the fork and twirled some pasta onto it before he speared a piece of chicken. "Open wide," he cajoled, raising the morsel to her lips.

Amelia shook her head.

"Come on, just a bite?"

"I—"

He pushed the fork past her lips and she had to take it, or make a pig of herself.

"—will not be fed like a child," she finished around a mouthful. *Heaven.* The sauce was delicious. The flavors melted in her mouth, became more complex with the scent. She could almost taste truffles in there. She glared at Connors. "I hate you." She loved this.

"Duly noted," he said, already offering another bite.

It was so good, Amelia almost forgot herself and let him feed it to her, too. At the last second, she stopped his hand and took possession of the fork. "Fine, I'll eat."

For five hours Gabriel watched her work. She'd been so focused on it she hadn't glanced up from the computers once. He *had* told her he'd be cooking dinner. He'd also asked her what she was in the mood for. *Something hot, maybe?* Nothing.

He could have called in an army of chefs and set up a stove right in front of her nose and she wouldn't have noticed.

But now she put the same kind of concentration into eating. Amelia was in rapture over a simple pasta dish, something he'd cooked a thousand times before because it was quick and hearty. She smelled every forkful before she put it in her mouth, as if she savored the scent, and she hummed with each bite.

Watching her lips close around her fork was by far the most erotic thing he'd ever seen.

"Where'd you learn how to cook like this?"

"Huh?" Gabriel shook himself. "Uh, college. My roommate was a culinary arts student."

"Really? What did you study? No wait." Amelia took another bite. "Computers, right?"

"Nope," he said. "Want to guess again?"

Another bite. She sighed this time, as if it was too much goodness to bear. Ten seconds passed before she came to herself again and remembered they were in the middle of a conversation. "First tell me how you know so much about computers."

"Now this will be a one-two-three approach."

"Like the combos I taught you. Left, left, right. Right?"

"Har-har. Pay attention, or next time we spar I'm going for blood."

Gabriel blinked away the phantom voices, shut out the easy laugher. Pushed the sudden stabbing pain in his soul to a dark corner of his mind until it was back to a steady ache in his psyche. He shrugged. "Just do, is all. Computers have rules that make sense. I can figure out how things work, look into the belly of the beast, and rearrange its innards. I can alter it into something completely different, without killing it." Shining laugher in those bright eyes. Cut short. Brutally silenced. "Machines I get. Other things tend to be more complicated."

"So what *did* you study?"

"Why so curious all of a sudden?"

She smiled; the first genuine smile he'd seen on her face. "Part of the job description," she said. "Need to match a cat to you so it'll work."

"You're looking for a cat that fights with swords and likes computers? Good luck."

Amelia laughed. "Aim high and settle."

"Never," he said, a little thunderstruck by this quicksilver change in her. She was done with her dinner now, and she'd propped one foot on the edge of her chair and the other on her desk. Her chair was leaned back as far as it would go and every time she bobbed back and forth, Gabriel expected the front wheels to come up off the ground. "Why would you want to set yourself up for disappointment?"

She shrugged, her eyes still bright with contentment. Or was it happiness? "I think it's less depressing to dream and hope, even if you end up disappointed. Otherwise, you're just a grouch settling from the start because you think you'll never find that perfect thing anyway."

"Well, if you put it that way."

Amelia bobbed again, and the front wheel came up for a second before she leaned forward and made it drop back down. "Speaking of matches," she said, "I need to put you in the scanner."

"More fancy tests?"

"Oh, there will be a *lot* more of those. Back in the chair, please."

The chair with the manacles.

Gabriel sat while she turned on another machine and took her e-pad. She adjusted her glasses higher up on her nose. "Why do you wear those?" Surely a scientist of her caliber could fix something as simple as nearsightedness.

"They serve a dual purpose of making me seem threatening and vulnerable at the same time," she said distractedly.

Her immediate answer surprised him, but as he considered it, yeah, it made sense. The first image most people probably had of Amelia was a stern-faced woman in a lab coat with glasses perched on her nose. "Mad scientist" came to mind, which wasn't far off the mark. But without those glasses, no matter how smart, she would be at a huge disadvantage in a physical altercation. No doubt that dichotomy confused people enough to give her an edge.

Gabriel grinned. Clever, clever woman.

A moment later, a holographic image of him appeared between them. It was a perfect replica, except it had no clothes. Then his skin disappeared, displaying the muscles. Creepy. The muscle layer was the next to disappear, revealing his organs.

"My what nice innards you have," Amelia said.

"All the better to impress you with."

She chuckled, but was already distracted, looking more at her e-pad than the projection. "You had some damage to your organs. Looks like your kidney took a beating."

More than once.

"Lungs look good, heart is strong."

"Thank you," he said.

The image changed, now showing only his skeleton. "Very few damaged bones," Amelia said. "That's interesting, given your occupation."

"Guess I'm just lucky," he said bitterly. Gladiators fought to kill, not wound. They used blades and spears, not fists unless there was no other option.

The projection zoomed in on his skull and it became the size of Amelia's desk. Then it was his brain slowly spinning in mid-air. "No structural anomalies," Amelia said. "But then, insanity often doesn't show up on brain scans."

Gabriel frowned. She was back in efficient-researcher mode, distracted and talking purely for the benefit of her subject sitting in the chair. He didn't like it. What happened to the smiling, happy Amelia from a minute ago? "Can you zoom in on other body parts with that thing?"

"Of course," she said. "Why? Is there a particular area of concern?"

"You could say that. I am concerned about some muscles I haven't been using much lately. You know what they say. Use it or lose it. And I *really* don't want to lose these."

She lowered the e-pad to glare at him. "You just want to see your penis blown up to three feet."

Gabriel did his best not to laugh, but his voice came out choked when he said, "It wouldn't be too much of a stretch."

"Please," she muttered, going back to her notes. The image changed again to display his nervous system. "You think I haven't heard that one before? Besides, it's not muscles that make you go hard."

"You're right," he agreed. "It's more strategically placed fatty tissue. Soft skin, plump lips…"

She tapped her stylus against the e-pad. "It's blood flow."

"No, I'm pretty sure I never got hard during a fight. That's something a guy would notice."

Amelia blinked at him. "What? That's not what I meant."

"Well, unless you plan on putting your theories into practice, maybe we should focus on something else. My balls are blue enough as it is, without you teasing me with all your scientific pillow talk."

She sputtered. "I wasn't, I… *you* started this!"

"And since you won't let me finish, I'm changing the subject."

"Oh, by all means," Amelia said, "please finish. But do me the courtesy of waiting until I'm out of the room." She turned her back on him and headed for the door, her lab coat billowing righteously behind her.

And Gabriel couldn't let it go. He shot to his feet, caught her in the hallway, and had her pressed against the wall before he knew what he was doing. God, she smelled so damn good. He felt her tremble when he nuzzled in her hair to get more of that scent. His dick turned as hard as steel and his shoulders shuddered. "You think that it's easy?" he said, not recognizing his own voice. "A good rubdown, get off, and get on with my day? What if I want more than that?"

"Yesterday you had a gun pointed at me," she said. She was very still, barely breathing, but Gabriel felt tension in her. *Fight or flight, Doc?* "Today you pulled a knife out of your shoe. Now, what, you're going to try to seduce me?"

"Would you blame me if I did?"

"I don't know what you could get away with in Rome, but out here, rape is a crime."

He was scaring her. Gabriel pushed away enough to look her in the eye, but couldn't make himself release her completely. "I never took an unwilling woman to my bed. They always sought *me* out."

"My, it must have been wonderful for you there. It's a wonder you ever wanted to leave."

His hands fell away from the wall, and he stepped back, effectively shut down and impressed as hell by her strategy. Amelia didn't waste words; she struck where she could do the most damage. Fight or flight? She was free now, but she wasn't fleeing. The woman, so much smaller than him, so much weaker, stood her ground before him like an equal. No, a superior. She'd judged him to be her lesser.

Gabriel couldn't blame her; he'd proved himself to be little better than the animal he was paying her to make him into. It shouldn't have mattered. But it did. *Her* opinion of him mattered. Gabriel wanted her respect, at least. He'd spent too much time being regarded as a piece of meat. Here, with Amelia, he *craved* having her treat him as a man.

"I apologize," he said. "I was out of line."

"*Way* out."

He nodded. "Way out."

Amelia regarded him in silence for a moment.

"Am I forgiven?"

"I want you to unlock the door," she said. "There are supplies I need. Things I have to pick up myself."

"Can't do that. You'd run as soon as that door opened."

"Just where do you think I'd go? This is my home."

"My guess? As far from here as you could get."

In the past, Amelia had only ever understood Stockholm Syndrome in the context of a psychology textbook. As part of her studies, and her training in New Alaska, she'd been required to gain a deep understanding of the human psyche. Now she was about to get a giant heaping of personal experience on the subject.

But the lines were blurred here. Was Connors her captor, or an eccentric employer who liked to micromanage and keep close tabs on his employee? For the price he was paying, did she have grounds to complain? After all, she'd agreed to this.

Was he a good guy, or a bad guy? He had the wherewithal to kill her many different ways, with instruments or with his bare hands, and yet he hadn't hurt her. Subdued her? Yes. Disconcerted her? Constantly. Made her hot and bothered? Far more than she was comfortable admitting, even to herself. But whenever push came to shove, she'd drawn blood, and Connors had backed off.

And he *cooked* for her. Of course, this could all be a ruse to lull her into willing submission, but why go to all that trouble now, when she was already doing what he wanted her to?

Did she want to get away from him? Absolutely.

But she also wanted him to tower over her again as he'd done a second ago, and coax him to kiss her. Tristan had his Dara. Hailey had found her Jeremy. What was so wrong with Amelia? Why did she have to be alone? It wasn't fair.

And now here was Connors who… well, okay, so he might be batshit crazy, but he also seemed to have trouble keeping his distance from her. What was more, he was letting her set the pace.

If Amelia wasn't careful, if she let her guard down too much, she might end up doing something very ill-advised. And it would be all her doing. Her fault for not being vigilant. She'd done that before, and her sister had nearly died. Amelia knew what was at stake, and yet the prospect of letting her guard down, letting the chips fall where they may, had never been as appealing as it was right now.

She was so damn tired of being strong all the time. Putting up a front to hide any weakness. Was she crazy to consider letting loose for a while?

"Listen," she said, hoping she sounded less frantic than she felt. "I need to get some air. I can't stay locked in here twenty-four seven."

Those perceptive eyes of his searched her face. "Then I'll go with you," he said.

"Won't you get into trouble if you show your face?"

"Not unless you cause a scene," he said, unconcerned.

"That's a lot of trust you're putting in me."

Connors shrugged. "You already hold the scissors, Morta."

Amelia frowned. "What?"

He looked at her as if she'd slapped him. "You're kidding, right? You don't know who the Fates are?"

She crossed her arms over her chest and raised an eyebrow. "Do you know what deoxyribonucleic acid is?"

Connors nodded. "Point taken. The Fates personify destiny," he explained. "Three women who control all living things, even the gods. Greeks, Romans, even Normans, had some version of them. In Roman myth, Nona spun the thread of life, Decima measured its length, and Morta cut it."

"So, in essence, you called me Death. *Mors, mortis, post mortem…*"

"Well… yeah," he said, looking like a little boy who'd been caught in a lie. "But think of it as a compliment."

Amelia gaped. "In what way can *Death* possibly be regarded as a compliment?"

He sobered and met her gaze dead on. "If I had to choose between a death at the hands of the Romans or yours, I'd choose you in a heartbeat."

It was dark, already late, but when Gabriel looked up at the sky, he couldn't see a single star. In Rome, all the houses lit up at night and the scent of burning oils and firewood filled the air. But outside, the streets were always dark and, looking up, Gabriel could see a vast eternity of glittering gems. Nothing better than the stars to remind a man of his insignificance.

Amelia walked fast. She wasn't trying to get away from him, or get in front of him; it just seemed like her natural pace. She walked with purpose and direction, as if this outing had a time limit.

"So where are we going?"

She was leading them out of the industrial district with its block-like warehouse monstrosities, into a bright, perpetually busy corner of the city made up almost entirely of squat little houses somehow attached to skyscrapers behind them. It wasn't like the shopping malls he'd briefly entered and very quickly left again when he'd first arrived here. The shops in this area were all small and crammed with things he had no names for. Stalls were set up outside, with merchants hawking food and who knew what else. Everything that could be cooked or burned was for sale, be it animal or plant, and a rich steam-slash-smoke combination clogged the air until Gabriel found it hard to breathe.

Artisans? Not quite. More like family owned businesses, selling imports from their place of origin. So this was the international district. The guy who'd delivered the groceries earlier had mentioned it. It amazed Gabriel that so many merchants could thrive here this way. Everything was so cramped there was no room for signs or advertisements of any kind. Every merchant sold only what he could make appealing to the people passing by. If not for the skyscrapers and sophisticated roadwork beneath his shoes, Gabriel would have thought he was back in Rome.

"There are some things you don't buy through computers," Amelia said. She wove through the throngs of people so nimbly, he was having trouble keeping up with her. It didn't help that he was a head taller than everyone around him. While the crowds could meet Amelia's gaze and move out of her way, they showed no such consideration to the faceless pillar of flesh following in her wake.

When she stopped at an intersection, waiting to cross the street, he caught her hand in his. "So I don't get lost," he explained when she looked up at him in surprise.

The crowds moved again, and the two of them were swept along to cross the street. Amelia headed for the edge and Gabriel stayed close, hoping his size would intimidate people into making room for them. It didn't. There really wasn't any room *to* make.

Then they were in front of a doorway, and he had to duck his head low to enter. Inside, the shop was dim and hazy with incense smoke that made his eyes water. Carpets overlaid each other all over the floor, and there were giant wooden chests set up haphazardly, filled with odds and ends. On the shelves against the walls were jars of things he couldn't identify. It was probably safer not to try.

Amelia cleared her throat. "You can let go of my hand now."

The biggest jar held something that looked like a white root in the shape of a human. It reminded him of mandrake, but this was much bigger and so detailed, he could make out fingers and toes. Was it artificial? "I'd rather not," he said, unable to look away.

"Here," she said, "hold on to this instead."

Gabriel stared at the wooden statue she'd given him. It was some kind of monkey thing, sitting with its hands on its up-drawn knees, and in between them was a massive dick, pointed right at Gabriel's forehead. "What the..." He dropped the thing and wiped his hand on his shirt.

When he tore his horrified gaze away from the statue to ask if she was trying to give him a heart attack, Amelia was gone. "Amelia!"

"Over here." Her voice sounded smothered.

"Where is here?" He weaved between an armored statue and a dried-up mummy.

"Right here," she said, appearing from behind a bookcase. She was holding a mesh bag and a carved wooden box.

"What have you got there?"

She shrugged, taking her loot to the shop owner. "Stuff," she said.

Two minutes later, they were out in the melee again, and Amelia was pulling him across the street into an alley away from the crowds. Gabriel breathed a sigh of relief.

Until they emerged out the other end into an even bigger one. By then, he had no idea where they were anymore, or how to get back. If she left him there, it might take him a week to find his way back to her lab again. He had a feeling these crowds never lessened.

The next store they entered was more of a greenhouse. Three long tables stretched end to end across the space, all covered in dirt and plants. There were planters on the ground, too.

"Molly?" Amelia called. "Oh, Mooollyyy!"

"Millie?" a female voice called back. A second later a scarf-covered head popped up among the flowers. "Millie!" the woman cried and got to her feet to come greet them. She looked like a mole. Thick glasses sat on her tiny, sharp nose, making her eyes look enormous. Her thin lips were pulled into a surprisingly brilliant smile, which might have made her pretty, if she wasn't covered in dirt.

"Millie?" Gabriel frowned. He was ignored.

Molly the mole rushed forward and embraced Amelia. Both of them laughed and cooed; clearly this was a reunion of some sort. "Where have you been?" Molly said. "One massive order to Torrey and then nothing for *months*!"

Amelia ducked her head. "I'm sorry. I had sort of a family emergency."

"Oh," Molly said, and that tiny non-word carried a world of understanding. "Everything okay now?"

"Oh, yeah!" Amelia nodded eagerly. "Brilliant, actually. I'm working on another project now."

Molly held up her hands. "Wait, let me guess. You got swept off your feet by mister Hunkypants over here and decided to bring him home, and then you realized your house sucks, so you finally decided to take my advice and do that expansion for the garden." She grinned. "How'd I do?"

"Uh, well…"

"That's exactly right," Gabriel chimed in, starting to like this Molly. He put his arm around Amelia, ignoring her sputters to turn his charm on Molly. "We met on a techies forum. Can you imagine? Her picture didn't nearly do her justice." He shook his head at Amelia in admonishment. "Bowled me over the first time I saw her. I knew she was brilliant. But brilliant *and* beautiful?"

Amelia pinched him so hard he was certain blood was welling under his skin.

Gabriel grinned. "Anyway, we've been together ever since. Inseparable, you might say."

Molly squealed and clapped her hands in delight. "I knew it! I *knew* you were hiding something from me—and shame on you!" She openly ogled Gabriel. "Should have brought this one around a lot sooner."

Amelia fought to extricate herself from his grasp and, because he was feeling generous, he set her free, but snagged her hand and twined their fingers together. "Well, like he said, I've been—*ahem*—held prisoner by—"

"—her lust," Gabriel finished.

Which made Amelia's jaw drop almost to the floor.

Molly's eyes went wide. "Really?" She sounded disbelieving.

For some reason, Gabriel took offense to that, so he decided to lay it on even thicker. "You have no idea," he said dramatically. "It's a constant marathon with her. Bedroom, kitchen, lab. She's always ordering me around." He grinned. "Good thing I can keep up."

"What? That's not—"

"Hell, she even locked us in for a while. *Man*, that was fun. We tore that place up good. Feathers flying everywhere. I think I still have some of them stuck up my—"

"*Anyway*," Amelia cut in, glaring daggers, while Molly watched them, looking more and more confused. "I'm here to purchase plants. Lots and lots of plants. Bulbs and seedlings are good, but I want something thick and fully grown, too."

Gabriel leaned into her. "Just wait until we get back," he said and cupped her ass.

She stomped on his foot with all her might. It barely registered past the feel of those luscious curves. He couldn't make himself let go until she knocked his hand away with the wooden box. Amelia gave Molly a pained smile. "Sorry, we can't stay and chat longer. Got lots to do."

"Uh, yeah, sure," Molly said. "I got tons of new stuff today. Come on, it's in the back. You can have your pick. You want the trees too, or just the ferns and flowers?"

Amelia shrugged. "You know me."

Molly looked contemplative, almost disappointed when she met Amelia's gaze. "No," she said, "I really don't think I do." Then she flashed a quick look at Gabriel and turned to lead them back, not noticing how Amelia's face fell at that pronouncement.

Amelia refused to look at Connors again while they were in the shop. She kept her attention on Molly and all of the treasures the gardener was showcasing for her. She hadn't been teasing about the ferns—she had giant bushes of lush green leaves; a single plant that came up to her waist would hide her legs from sight completely if she stepped into the planter.

There were also exotic palm trees that bore some kind of fruit; heady-scented flowers; and fast-growing vines, too. Amelia bought them all, planning to lose herself in gardening for the next couple of days so she wouldn't have to deal with her insufferable jailer.

What the hell had gotten into him? Weren't they supposed to be *not* causing a scene?

She shook her head, listening to Molly explain how to care for all of those plants. She would not be examining his motives for provoking her. Besides the fact he was a dead man walking, she didn't *care*. Nope. Not one bit. Didn't want to know why he'd tried to act like her lover in front of her one and only friend in this colony. Didn't care that he'd grabbed her backside like it belonged to him—and she had *not* liked it!

Amelia was only flushing because it was hot in the greenhouse. That was all.

Wait until we get back. She inwardly snorted. The only thing that would be happening when they got back was her closing herself into the half dome above the lab and locking the door while she played in the dirt.

She'd spent weeks haggling with contractors to carve out a little place for her Eden. No one had wanted to do it without a permit, though she owned the entire damn building and fully accepted the risks. And when they'd finally gotten it done, Hailey had had to go and…

Well, anyway, it was all ready for her to start planting now, and she wasn't letting anything else stop her. She even had an irrigation system set up; she just had to program it to the right amount and frequency.

One day, Amelia would have herself a real greenhouse. Big enough to fit a rain forest in. Maybe a waterfall or two. There would be rocks that were really cooled cabinets for beverages, and curtains of vines would hide all artificial doors. It would be just her and nature. Lots and lots of nature. She might even get tropical birds to sing in there.

Amelia wrinkled her nose. Maybe not. Animals made messes. She'd then have to clean up after them. Better to let the plants take over. She could always play birdsongs and nature sounds through the audio system.

Molly gave them a cart to transport the plants back to Amelia's home. It was already programmed to go there, and would come back again on its own when the weight sensor registered no more load. Before Amelia knew what was what, they were saying good bye, and Connors was ushering her out of the shop with a hand at the small of her back.

She would have kicked him, except this visit had left her feeling more than a little down.

"All right," Connors said as soon as they were outside. "Spill. What are the plants for? Are you making human-tree shape-shifters? Engineering sentient plants to sniff out intruders?"

Amelia blinked up at him. "There's science," she said, "and then there's science-*fiction.*"

"Right," he retorted. "I'll keep that in mind." Two seconds later: "So what are they for?"

Amelia rolled her eyes. "I like greenery."

"And…"

"And, nothing. That's it. I like plants. I'm making myself a hothouse."

Connors frowned.

"What?"

"Is everything okay?"

Hysterical laughter bubbled up inside of her, but by the sheer force of self-control, she managed to tamper it down to a chuckle. "Are you seriously asking me that?"

"You just seem…"

"Tired? Frustrated? Irritated. No, I have it—"

"Sad."

Amelia shut her mouth. "Just walk," she said.

They went to two more shops before turning back toward home. Thunder was rumbling ominously, and by the time they made it out of the international district, a few random drops of rain were already falling. Amelia steered them toward the edge of the sidewalk where overhangs provided some cover at regular intervals.

They were under one of those overhangs, still four blocks away from her building, when the heavens opened and a deluge poured down. Amelia was ready to dash through it, but Connors held her back. "Just wait until it eases."

As if to mock him, a bolt of lightning jagged across the sky right above them. He pulled her farther away from the edge to the wall, hunching over her like he wanted to shield her. Rain here wasn't the romantic kind where people went out to dance in it. It was frigid cold and, though the air temperature was very comfortable, Amelia's breath still misted before her, and she was glad for Connors' closeness. After the greenhouse and the stifling crowds, she was starting to feel chilled out in the open.

When she shivered, he leaned in closer to say, "Put your arms around me."

Amelia shook her head.

He grasped her arms and did it himself, pulling her into the warmth of his chest. "Body warmth only," he assured her.

She couldn't make herself walk away. The longer the rain continued, the colder it got. Hail was coming down now, chunks of ice drumming all over the overhang and ricocheting off the pavement. She winced every time a big one dropped, expecting it to punch through the overhang and onto her.

"Easy," Connors soothed. The storm hit a crescendo, and his arms closed around her, loosely at first, and then tighter. At one point it sounded like the overhang would buckle beneath the falling ice.

Finally, hail eased to rain again, but it was only a short reprieve. Amelia's fingers were freezing at his back, but she unclenched them, releasing his shirt to take his hand. "Come on," she said, teeth chattering, and pulled him into the rain.

They ran the final stretch. Amelia was soaked and frozen through by the time they got into the building, and her lungs were burning from the run. She leaned back against the door, soaking in the warmth of the hallway.

Connors went straight to the lab, but came back out a minute later as the climate control kicked into gear and the air started to warm up. "You're cold," he said, looking at her breasts. She didn't have to check to know her nipples were beading against her top. He came to her as if he couldn't stop himself. "You should go change."

Asssstute asssessssmment. She was shivering again, and her teeth were starting to chatter. Common sense said: *Go change.* But Amelia was lacking in the self-control department at the moment, depending on the door behind her to stay upright. Her building was a study of evolution. The previous owner had repurposed a warehouse and renovated to incorporate the newest advances in climate control, which included self-heating walls and floors, but he must have skimped on something because there were hot and cold spots all over the place. There was a hot spot five feet away in the ceiling, practically radiating heavenly warmth. Amelia lurched away from the door to stand underneath it for a moment. Just long enough for her legs to regain their ability to hold her up.

Because he was as soaked as she, Amelia waved Connors over.

He turned his face up to the ceiling, and his chest heaved in a sigh. Amelia had to stop herself from reaching out to touch it. "Better than a fire," he said.

Amelia followed suit, closing her eyes and soaking up the warmth on her face. She was already starting to regain feeling in her cheeks. A good sign.

When she opened her eyes again, Connors was watching her.

Her next breath hitched in a soft gasp at the sheer hunger in his eyes. He raised that big hand of his and brushed the back of it gently against her cheek, then down to her neck. Amelia was so cold, his touch burned, but she wanted more of his heat. It was the only thing in the world right now that could warm her.

His gaze drifted down to her lips and stuck there for long moments. Then he leaned down closer, slowly, giving her ample time to stop him. She didn't. His kiss was as soft as his touch, a gentle brush of lips at first, a maddening hint of what he could give her. He made her want it; made her quiver for more than this.

Amelia rose a little on unsteady toes to increase the friction. Connors sucked in a breath. His hand cradled her nape, and he crowded her against the wall, one arm snaking around her waist to lift her up a little. Just enough so they were on a more equal level.

And then he *really* kissed her. Amelia moaned at the delicious, bruising pressure. His tongue delved in deep, coaxed hers to play, and she kissed him back, clutching at his shoulders while he mastered her mouth. She lost herself in the moment, gave herself free reign to feel. To touch and be touched and—*Oh, my!*—he hadn't been kidding! Her toes curled as he made love to her mouth.

It was an expert kiss, almost practiced, but quickly evolved into something wild and out of control. The more out of control he got, the more Amelia loved it, straining for it, nails digging into his shoulders, adoring the way it made him shudder.

Her feet touched the floor again, and Connors released her, ending the kiss with a last lingering caress. Before she could pull him back, he put an arm's length of distance between them, leaving her breathless and unsteady, leaning against the wall. "Not sorry I did that," he said, backing up to the opposite wall.

Amelia couldn't come up with an answer. With the hotspot heat wave still flowing over her, her lips throbbing and her legs unsteady, she felt almost dream-like. This couldn't be real, could it? And if it wasn't, why shouldn't she enjoy it for a little while?

"Ah, God, look at you," he breathed. His hand reached out again, but he pulled it back and looked away. She could see a muscle jump in his jaw. "You need to change out of those wet clothes before you get sick."

"Is that really what you want me to do?" She didn't recognize her own voice.

"No," he said, surprising her with the raw honesty. "I want you to come here so I can rip them off you and fill my hands with that sweet ass of yours. I want your hands on me again. I want my cock in you and have you scream my name when I make you come."

Her sex clenched at his words. She could imagine that happening so easily. Wanted to see if it worked practically as well as in theory.

"So you need to go to your room now and lock the door," he said, hands clenching into white-knuckled fists at his sides. Those hands had been so gentle before, but now looked absolutely brutal, as a gladiator's hands should be. The sight slowly pulled her out of her reverie.

"Why?"

Connors turned his dark gaze on her again, looking her straight in the eye. "Because once I start, angel, I won't ever stop. I won't ever let you go."

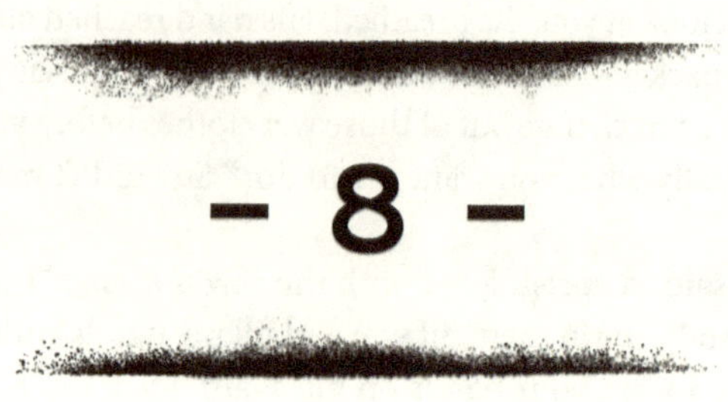

– 8 –

September 23, 3032

"There's a messenger downstairs."

Amelia. On all fours. Digging in the dirt. Her back was to him, as it had been ever since she'd run to her room yesterday. Damn, the woman had an ass to die for. And any other time, Gabriel would have found some excuse to get up close with her like that.

But not today.

She wouldn't face him; refused to look at him. Today she'd come to the lab for all of two minutes. She'd checked the computer readouts, informed him he was a "suitable candidate," and promptly retreated up here. Not once had she looked him in the eye. She didn't say one word more than she had to.

"It's something you need to sign for."

Gabriel had told the truth last night. He *wasn't* sorry he'd kissed her. He only wished Amelia would let him do it again. *Should have kept my mouth shut.* He'd scared her, and now she was in full flight mode. Avoidance was the best form of defense. There was nothing he could do if she refused to confront him about this, and nothing he said or did made her rise to the bait. Dr. Chase had completely shut down.

"I'll be right down," she said absently while she carefully removed a bulb from the wooden box she'd bought last night at the shop of horrors, and positioned it in the dirt. It was hot in here. Gabriel had found this room locked down tight while he'd been waiting for her to arrive. Hadn't understood why she would lock an empty room. Now he could see the different levels for what they were—strategically placed platforms for planters. The room was its own micro-system, completely cut off from the rest of the building, air- and watertight. As dry and cool as the lab was downstairs, so the room above it would be hot and humid.

"You need any help in here?"

"I got it," she replied. She dusted off her hands, but they were still covered with dirt by the time she came to the door. Which he was blocking.

She cleared her throat, silently demanding passage.

Gabriel didn't budge.

"Move, please," she said, looking somewhere in the vicinity of his chest, but she might as well have been staring off into space for all she saw. It bothered him enough that he wanted to snap her out of it.

"Look at me," he said.

"What for?" Amelia shrugged a shoulder. "I already know what you look like."

"That's not very friendly of you."

Her mouth tensed into a thin line; the first show of emotion he'd seen from her all day. "You're here to get treatment. Not to be my friend."

"But I could be, if you let me."

She laughed, and it was a bitter sound, completely lacking humor. "Oh, boy. You need to decide what the hell you want from me, and do it right quick. You threaten me, you flirt with me, you embarrass me in front of my friend, then you *kiss* me—"

"As I recall, you kissed me right back."

Finally she looked up at him, her blue eyes flashing lightning, and Gabriel conceded he probably shouldn't have reminded her of that. "Then you chase me away," she continued, clenching her teeth as her ire rose. "And now you want to be *friends*? Try to see where I might have an issue with your attitude. And *move!*"

He turned enough to let her squeeze through. Amelia shoved at him hard when she passed, and marched down to the front door.

Gabriel followed close behind.

The messenger was a teenage girl with purple hair, dark eye shadow, and a pierced lip. "Delivery for Dr. Chase?" she said, looking utterly bored.

"Yes, that's me," Amelia said. She pressed her thumb to the e-pad the girl gave her, signed her name, and took the sealed carrier, already ushering the girl out. "Looks like it's time to get to work," she said, taking the carrier to the lab.

"What is it?"

"The DNA samples I ordered." She set it down on her desk and went to wash her hands and put on her lab coat.

Gabriel stared at the carrier. His future self was inside that thing. Either his salvation or his death. As Amelia was so fond of telling him, either would bring pain. He could handle pain. It meant he was still alive. Still had a life worth living.

Amelia came back all business again with a tray of dishes and instruments.

Decide what you want from her.

Gabriel watched her set up a work area near her fancy machines. She put on a pair of gloves and carefully opened the sealed carrier, pulling out frozen vials in bands of three. She checked each trio against her notes, and then set it down on an iced surface of her table.

Amelia became completely absorbed in whatever she did. Nothing jarred her concentration. Not even conversation. To be the subject of that focus. that kind of intensity…

The doc didn't do anything by halves. Gabriel was now beginning to realize this was what bothered her. Since he'd met Amelia, he hadn't finished anything when it came to her. It had to be frustrating that she couldn't place him squarely in any one category because he kept changing the parameters.

Decide…

"Why so many samples?"

"There actually aren't many," she said. "Each sample is divided into three portions for testing purposes. Here." She tapped on one of the screens to pull up a DNA strand.

Gabriel came closer to follow along with her explanation.

"This is your DNA. All living things have DNA similar to this. The

Devil is in the details. There's only about a three percent difference between the DNA of humans and chimpanzees. Beyond that, in humans, there are tiny differences which account for physical characteristics, intelligence, temperament, et cetera."

"What I need to do is match a panther's DNA anomalies as closely as possible to yours. That's one third of it. I need to make sure the two will actually fit together chemically, and I can't do that with numbers and formulas. Then I need to match a trigger to both strands. That will allow you to change your shape from one to the other. Once I have that, and I am sure the sample is viable, I'll use the last third, the untouched one, to actually create the serum."

"Sounds complicated."

"It is."

"Can I help?"

He didn't realize how close he was standing until she shifted away. "This is a delicate process. I'll need space and some peace and quiet. If you want to make yourself useful, you can program an irrigation system up in the solar."

"You sure you're not only trying to get rid of me?"

All night long, Amelia had tossed and turned, remembering his kiss. And when she'd finally fallen asleep, she'd dreamed about it. Only it had ended differently in her dream—with Gabriel carrying her into the lab and sweeping some glassware off the table. He'd laid her on it and ripped her shirt down the middle, the way he'd said he would. He'd suckled her nipples so hard she could feel them throbbing even now and when he'd mounted her...

In the complete privacy of her mind, she couldn't call him by his last name anymore. Hell yes, she wanted to get rid of him for a while! Every time she looked at him from the corner of her eye, she remembered that kiss and her dream, and that was a dangerous mental place to be when she literally held his life in her hands.

"I need to concentrate right now," she told him. "Believe me, you don't want me to mess this up."

"Fair enough," he said. Amelia almost sagged with relief. Until he said, "How long do you think you'll need?"

A decade. Maybe two, to get that dream out of my system. "I don't know. Why?" If he said something suggestive and inappropriate, she might deck him. Or jump him. Possibly both. As off balance as she was, it wasn't an unreasonable assumption.

"Lunch break," he said.

Oh. "Maybe two hours," she said. "Two and a half."

"Sounds good. I'll see you then."

She waved absently, counting the seconds until he walked out the door.

But, of course, he wouldn't leave it at that. "By the way," he said from the doorway, "you were mistaken before. I know exactly what I want. I just haven't figured out the proper way to get it."

The next trio almost slipped out of her hands. God, his tone! And she could *feel* his gaze on her. She set the trio down carefully and braced herself against the table. *Do not look at him. Don't—*

She looked.

But Gabriel had already turned away. A second later, he was gone.

And for some reason, Amelia felt disappointed.

~

Two hours later, Amelia hadn't heard a peep from upstairs.

She'd already eliminated seven of the eleven samples as incompatible. Her pool of resources was starting to grow shallow. If she couldn't find a suitable fit, she'd have to order another batch, which would mean another delay. More time with Gabriel.

Hoping for the best, Amelia took one of the next trio of samples and carefully removed the miniscule plastic rectangles with a grouping of cells between them. She inserted it into the extractor and started the sequence.

"Incoming call," the computer said. She had the volume set on low in the lab so it wouldn't jar her concentration.

Amelia frowned. Hadn't Gabriel blocked all of the coms?

Or had he only blocked outgoing calls?

She sucked in a breath. "Answer," she said at once.

A small picture-in-picture appeared on her screen. She tapped on it to make it bigger. Hailey was there, wearing sunglasses. Her hair looked gray now, obviously wet. Hailey's reckless transformation had not killed her, but the shock to her system had leeched out the color from her hair completely. She would forever wear it as a reminder of how close she'd come to dying.

There was hissing in the background. Was she on a beach? "Ams! Where the hell are you? I've been calling for two days!"

"I was…" *attacked in my own home and taken prisoner by a madman who is paying me a fortune to try to make him into a shifter. And now I'm dreaming about him screwing my brains out on the sterile table in the lab.* "…busy." She had to clear her throat to find her voice again. "What's up?"

"Are you okay?" Hailey said with a frown. "You look different. Kind of glowy."

Glowy? She had no idea what to say to that.

Thankfully, Hailey didn't seem to care. "Anyway, guess what?"

"You're pregnant."

"Uh, no. Guess again."

"You got a job?"

Hailey raised an eyebrow. "Actually, yes. It seems *someone* roped me into this scientist gig, and now I got a title, the deed to a humongous lab on Torrey in my name, near unlimited research sources and some place called *Royal Technologies, Inc.* depositing hefty sums in my account every week. But that's not it."

You're welcome, Amelia thought. The company paid Hailey royalties from sales of some thermo-regulator patches the two of them had developed recently. It pretty much guaranteed Hailey would never have to work again for the rest of her life.

"I got married!"

It shouldn't have been unexpected, but that it had happened so quickly was a surprise. "Good!" Amelia said. "That means you have someone else to drive crazy now. Happy days!" Actually, they were happy. Jeremy Calen, the telepath Amelia had originally hired to track Hailey down, was a good man. One of the very few true gentlemen left in the universe. But he would never be cowed by Hailey, no matter how wild or out of control she got. Maybe he'd be a steadying influence on her. A sister could only hope.

Hailey laughed. "I'm not *that* bad, am I?"

Amelia raised an eyebrow. "Sweetie, look in the mirror. That's all I have to say."

"Oh, speaking of, look what I can do." Hailey took off her sunglasses and leaned closer. Her skin changed color, faint rosettes blooming on her face. Her eyes became outlined in dramatic black, and then some of the rosettes faded while others became darker. "I never have to wear make up again!"

Brilliant. The woman who'd single-handedly made herself into a shape-shifter, then saved herself from a horribly slow and painful death, someone who had at least three times the strength and speed of a normal person, with senses so sharp she could pinpoint a rabbit deep underground, was most excited by the fact that she looked pretty.

"Glad to see you finally got your priorities straightened out," Amelia said.

"Har, har," Hailey said dryly. "So listen, Jer and I are going to be indisposed for a while, but I want you to come visit us on Torrey."

"You're settling down?" This was a shock. Hailey was such a free spirit, Amelia couldn't imagine her with a steady home and hearth.

Hailey shrugged. "Maybe. So when are you coming over?"

"Oh, I don't know, Hailey. I'm sort of in the middle of something right now."

"You mean something is actually more important than seeing your baby sister shackled to the normal life and teasing the ever-living hell out of her for it?" She frowned. "Wow. Must be serious. You're not in trouble, are you?"

Well…

"'Cause I got the Special Unit on speed dial now, and some super awesome new tricks I'm dying to show off."

Somewhere to the side, out of the picture, Amelia heard Jeremy mumble something about saving that for later, which made Hailey laugh.

"I'm good," Amelia said. *For now.* "Got everything under control." *Not even close.* "Just got a few things I need to take care of. A contract, sort of." *For the price of three ferric diamonds and my soul.* "But once it's done, I will definitely come see you." *Unless something goes very, very wrong.* "Got any news on Tristan and Dara?"

Hailey gasped. "You mean you're not keeping tabs on them?"

Amelia glared.

"Okay, okay. They're good. Last I heard, the asshole—sorry, *Tristan*—was picking names for his litter. He and Dara were arguing about the wisdom of naming the firstborn Hunter Hunt. But to be frank, we've kind of been avoiding each other whenever possible so…"

Amelia's mouth twitched. She dearly hoped they wouldn't do that to the child.

Jeremy said something else, and Hailey nodded to him. "I have to go now. The tide is coming up, and there's these bioluminescent little squid things that light up the beach at moon rise." She blew an exaggerated kiss. "*Mwah,* darling. I'll try to check in at some point." She winked and the screen went dark.

"Bye," Amelia said belatedly. She almost missed her sister. Almost. In the absence of a friend, there was no one for her to talk to about the complication that was Gabriel Connors.

"Who was that?"

Speak of the devil… "Professional consult."

"About bioluminescent little squid things?"

The screen blinked green and a whole lot of text streamed over it. The DNA was a match. Because the machines and computers were all linked through internal logic, the program was already extracting all of the necessary variables to plug into a formula for the trigger. It would try all possible options and then choose three that fit the best. Afterwards, it would be up to Amelia and her steady hand to test whether any of them were viable.

But that wouldn't be for some time. While the computers worked, she had some time to spare on a lunch break.

"Good news?" Gabriel asked.

"Possibly," Amelia replied. She checked everything over, and then stripped off her gloves and coat. "I might have found a suitable match. But I won't know for certain until the trigger analysis is finished. Which means I have time for lunch."

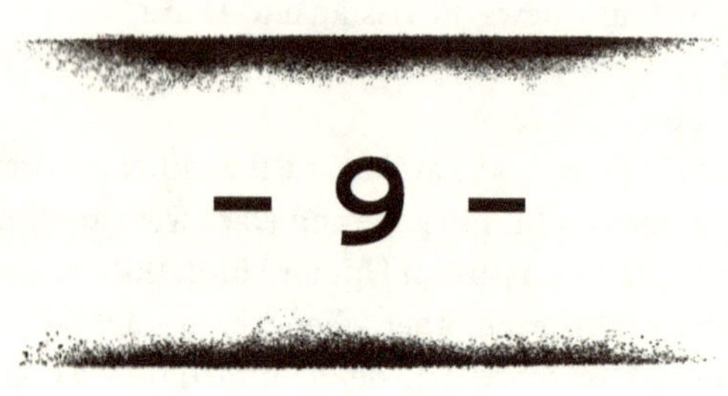

- 9 -

September 24, 3032, 1:35AM

She was in her solarium, but it felt more like a jungle. The plants were overgrown, hiding the pathway completely. The entire floor was covered with soft moss. It was hot and humid, the glass walls and ceiling trapping heat inside.

Amelia followed a path from memory to the artificial waterfall. The surface of the pond glistened and glittered in the moonlight. She could see something moving beneath the surface and frowned. Fish? But she hadn't ordered any.

Then something drew her gaze to the waterfall itself and she watched as a looming shadow emerged. Clouds moved overhead, allowing moonlight to spear down and bathe the man in its glow.

Gabriel.

He stood waist deep in the pond, water trickling down his upper body. "Come to me," he said, his gaze holding her captive; mesmerizing. "Come," he said again, holding out his hand.

Amelia's breathing became shallow. She knew what would happen if she succumbed to that hypnotic voice. Her body heated in anticipation while her mind screamed to stay away. She stepped over the edge into the pond. Her dress soaked instantly and slowed her down, tangling around her legs.

"Come," Gabriel repeated, closer now. He disappeared beneath the

surface, but she still heard his voice, commanding her.

The water was warm. His hands on her legs felt hotter. Amelia gasped when he caressed his way up her leg from the outside, his mouth following the same path on the inside.

"Come," he said again, and this time his meaning was completely different...

~

Amelia woke with a start, out of breath. Her sheets were tangled around her legs and she was an inch away from falling off the bed. She moaned. This could not keep happening! How was she supposed to stay professional and detached when she kept dreaming things like *that*?

Now she wouldn't be able to sleep at all.

But maybe...

She raised her head to check the door. Locked. Chair firmly in place beneath the doorknob. Amelia bit her lip. Should she? *Could* she? It was nothing but a physiological impulse, after all. Perfectly natural and acceptable. No one ever had to know. Not that it was anything shameful...

Amelia closed her eyes. She could still see him half-naked in the water, dark eyes burning for her. She couldn't hear his wicked whisper anymore, but she remembered, and it made her shiver. A braver woman would have gone out there and made use of him, as he'd so insistently offered. A smarter woman would have stocked up on other alternatives.

Amelia groaned. Neither was an option. With only a small, regretful sigh, she turned her head into her pillow and slipped her hand into her pajama bottoms.

A noise outside her door stilled her before she could get a good stroke. She stopped breathing. A voice. Gabriel? Was someone else in her home? *Oh, God, what now!*

Amelia kicked her way out of the tangle of sheets and reached for her baseball bat. She tiptoed to the door and strained to hear more. It was definitely Gabriel. Who was he talking to?

She carefully set the chair aside, eased the door open, and slipped outside, as quiet as a mouse. His voice was coming from the living room, where he'd made himself at home, but it was dark in there.

Amelia approached cautiously, clutching the bat, ready to bash someone a good one. Now he sounded agitated, mumbling something she couldn't decipher.

He was—she approached the couch and frowned—sleeping?

Gabriel's arms twitched, and his brow furrowed. Definitely asleep. Dreaming. On the heels of her own, very disturbing dream, Amelia blushed. Dreams weren't transferable, were they? As far as she knew, Gabriel wasn't a telepath. Thank God for that.

Just to make sure, she checked all of the shadows and hidey-holes for more intruders. There was no one, and the system was undisturbed. No one had gotten in, or made a call. Relieved there wasn't another foul plot afoot, Amelia set down her bat.

Wow, he looked really troubled. She wondered what he dreamed about. "Gabriel?" Should she wake him?

He stilled at the sound of her voice, head turning toward her.

"It's okay," she said. "Just a dream."

"Caesar," he said, almost as a sigh. He had to be dreaming about Rome. By the looks of him, it wasn't anything good, but the way he'd said that… almost reverently. Yet he wanted to kill the Caesar.

"Easy," she said, reaching out a tentative hand to brush his hair back.

"Fucking bitch!" he suddenly snarled. His eyes snapped open, unseeing, and before she could pull back, his hand shot out and grabbed her around the neck.

Amelia choked on a scream that never made it past her throat. She pried at his hand, desperate for air, but the more she fought, the tighter he squeezed. Growing lightheaded, she knew any longer and it would all be over. In a last ditch effort to save herself, she slapped him. Hard.

Gabriel felt the sting of a slap. Incensed, he shook his head hard and found himself in the dark living room, his hand wrapped around Amelia's throat, not the Caesar's. With a harsh yell, he released her, horrified.

Amelia fell to the floor, coughing, wheezing. She was holding her neck while trying desperately to get away from him any way she could.

"Jesus." He couldn't believe what was happening. "Christ, I'm so sorry," he said, reaching for her, needing to touch her to make sure she was alive and unharmed.

She crawled faster.

"Amelia, please. I didn't..."

She reached for something, then got up to her knees and swung with all her might.

Gabriel saw the bat too late. It connected with his side before he could brace himself and sent him sprawling.

The sharp, burning pain shocked him. He couldn't breathe. Every time he tried, he felt the tip of something burying deeper. "What the hell was that?" he yelled. Or tried to. He could barely get enough breath to manage a groan.

"You... almost killed me!" she wheezed, obviously trying to yell, too. In the absence of her voice, she reached for the lamp beside the couch and turned it on manually.

Gabriel glared at her. "Unintentionally," he growled.

Her face was screwed up in a pained grimace, and she was holding her neck. He couldn't see how much damage he'd done. "Yeah, well"—a harsh cough racked her frame—"me too."

Holding his ribs, Gabriel scowled at her.

"Okay, not really," she amended. "I may have meant to hit you with a baseball bat."

"You feel better now?"

The sarcasm must not have come across very well. "Yeah, I do," she replied, seeming surprised.

"Good," he retorted. "Because I think you broke something." Gabriel had broken limbs before. Usually because of some sort of heavy animal. He'd thought he was used to the pain, but those times had been bee stings compared to this. Every movement he made, even to take a careful breath, sent agony shooting through his torso, and he didn't need a medical degree to guess he was seconds away from puncturing a lung. Clearly, heavy animals had nothing on little Dr. Chase and her bat. Gabriel struggled to sit up, made it to the couch, and decided that was far enough.

Amelia cleared her throat and winced in pain. When she pulled her hand away, he could finally see how raw and red her neck looked. "Are you okay?" he asked gruffly. Logic said if she could whale on him with that bat hard enough to break a rib, she'd be fine.

"I'll live," she rasped. Then, grudgingly, "You?"

Gabriel made a face. "Think so. Could probably use a doctor, though."

The sigh she breathed was a clear sound of resignation. "Come on," she said, taking hold of his arm on the uninjured side. "Let's get you to the lab."

Another stab of pain made his vision cloud over as he pushed to his feet, and he pitched forward, nearly going down again and taking Amelia with him. By some miracle, he managed to stay upright. By another, he made it to the lab without tumbling down the staircase. He eschewed the manacle chair in the back in favor of perching gingerly on the edge of Amelia's desk. It was closer.

She left him there while she gathered instruments and wrapped some kind of bandage around her neck. "What is that?" he asked.

Amelia set everything down onto her desk behind him, then took his hand and placed it over the bandage. It was cool to the touch. As far as wordless explanation went, that one was straight to the point and made him feel like shit. "I'm sorry," he said, brushing the pad of his thumb over her jaw.

She shrugged, saving her voice now, and set to work. The doc had brought out an interesting array of tools. Gabriel couldn't see all of them, unable to twist around and look, but the ones she used were truly fascinating. A square blue patch placed over the rapidly darkening bruise numbed his side within seconds. He'd have breathed a sigh of relief if he wasn't worried about puncturing a lung.

Amelia checked the injury on a scan, pointing it out to him, confirming she'd broken not one, but two of his ribs and bruised the muscle. Counting off from his armpit down, she located the injured ribs and kept her hand on the spot while she reached for a nasty looking syringe.

"Uh, what is that?" It looked long enough to reach his hip bone through his nose. And it wasn't exactly on the thin side.

Amelia ignored him and jabbed the thing straight into the break, injecting it with something that seared like a hell bitch. "Ow, *fuck!*" The muscle spasm made him double over. He gripped the edge of the desk, trying his best to breathe through it, but his lung felt branded.

When she pulled the needle out, Gabriel was relieved that it was done. Then she jabbed it right back again, into the other break. This time he gritted his teeth against the pain, but couldn't bite back the sound that ripped out of him. All of a sudden, he didn't feel bad about her neck anymore.

She pulled the needle out and tossed it aside, keeping a hand on the injection site as if to soothe it. With her free hand, she cupped his cheek to make him look at her and raised an eyebrow; a wordless question. He couldn't begin to answer. Amelia sucked in a breath and blew it out in demonstration.

When he didn't copy her, she did it again. It wasn't as if he was trying to suffocate himself! *Holyfuckingshitthathurt.*

Amelia let go of him to scribble something down on her e-pad and held it up to him to read. *Breathe!* the note said. She'd underlined it three times.

"Trying," he growled.

She pointed to the note again.

Glaring, Gabriel let go of the precious little air left in his lungs and sucked in a fresh batch.

Amelia nodded in encouragement.

He did it again, only because she was looking. The woman had eyes like sapphires, with a faint webbing of green lines over the irises. It was like looking into a gem held up to the light. Almost made him feel like he could do anything for those blues. Gabriel silently willed her not to look away.

When he was breathing as normally as possible, she patted his cheek, already dismissing a would-be crisis and turned to her implements again. Gabriel caught her hand to stay her. Amelia looked surprised at the gesture, then blushed. She held up a roll of bandages, showing him she still had work to do.

He was forced to release her.

She was careful bandaging his torso, and Gabriel was grateful for the little consideration. His insides still burned enough that a muscle in his back twitched every so often. But by the time she was finished, the pain had eased enough that he could breathe easily. Amelia scanned him again and showed him the damaged ribs. Whatever it was she'd injected him with, it now surrounded the broken ribs like a splint on the inside. Gabriel poked at the spot, and the image changed. The bandage wasn't solid. It adjusted to his body, holding the break together, but still flexible enough to allow for movement. Just like the bone itself would, if it weren't broken. Fascinating.

Astonishingly painful to administer, but fascinating.

Seeing he was sufficiently impressed, she turned the scanner off.

The trip back up the stairs was easier. He could temper the impact of his weight better going up. Gabriel would have gotten up there without any help, but he didn't tell Amelia that. Not when she was so obliging in ducking under his arm and holding on to him as a support.

It felt… nice.

In the hallway, she stopped him, looking from the living room to the bedroom.

Bedroom, please.

Amelia regarded him to decide, and he put on his most innocent expression, tossed in a wince to make it believable. She narrowed her eyes in suspicion, but turned for the bedroom.

There *was* a God!

She straightened the sheets for him, fluffed the pillow a little, but let him lie down on his own. Nodding in satisfaction, she spun on the balls of her bare feet toward the door.

Gabriel caught her hand again.

"Stay." Wait, that wasn't right. He'd meant to say, *Thank you.*

She gave him a don't-be-ridiculous look and tugged on her hand to free herself.

"Oh, come on," he said. Still no, *thank you.* "You owe me for this."

She pointed at her neck.

"Well, yeah, okay," he allowed. "But I didn't stab you with a drinking straw and pour lava into your neck, did I?"

Amelia scuffed her foot guiltily, and he frowned. "Did you know it would hurt that much?"

Studying the floor most intently, she shook her head in the negative.

Oh, son of a… "Was that some kind of experimental trial thing you injected me with?"

A hedging nod.

"Oh-ho-ho, you are so busted." For all she knew, the stuff could have been toxic. It felt toxic. And she hadn't hesitated to use it! Just gathered it up like another harmless bandage. "And you *are* staying with me tonight."

Her gaze snapped up to his, and she opened her mouth to argue.

"Ah-ah, save your voice. You're staying to make sure I don't croak before sunrise."

Her mouth compressed into a thin line, and she stomped her foot, probably calling him all sorts of ugly names in her head.

Gabriel almost smiled. "C'mon," he said, "you know you want to."

Amelia turned away, but not before another blush stained her pretty cheeks.

He waited for her to gather the courage to face him again. When she did, it was with a bracing breath and a resolute nod. She pulled her hand free and made a series of strange gestures—a comical dead face among them—from which he surmised she was only staying to make sure he didn't die.

Oh, and he was supposed to stay on his side of the bed or she would do something cutting to some part of his anatomy.

"Right," he said when it looked like she was finished.

In answer, she narrowed her eyes into slits and pointed a finger at him as if to say, *You watch yourself, buddy.*

"You know," he said, choking back a chuckle, "you're really funny when you don't try to be."

In answer, she drew her lips back in a snarl.

But she did march her luscious ass around the bed and got in it with him. All the way at the edge, outside of the covers, lying flat on her back like a corpse, but she was there.

Gabriel sighed and closed his eyes, wondering what it would take to coax her closer.

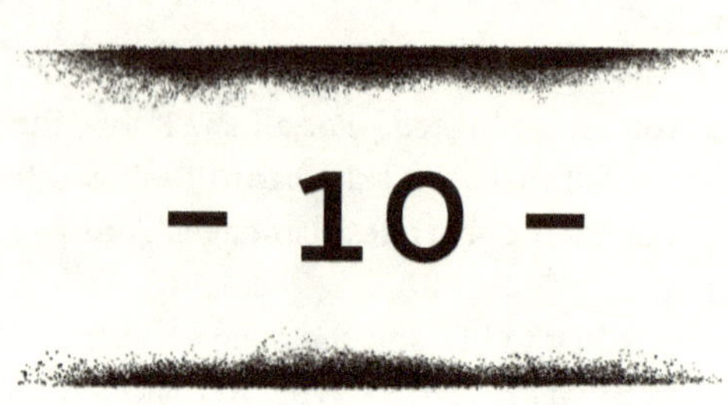

– 10 –

Silken sheets slipped over her heated skin, making her arch for more. Contact. Heat. Friction.

She could feel Gabriel's hands on her, confident and sure, touching her as if he had every right to. Amelia gasped when he palmed her bare breasts possessively. His palms were callused and rasped over her nipples, making them bead to his touch. She wanted his mouth on them.

And then, as if she'd summoned him with her thoughts, he was there, suckling and kissing her flesh. Electric sparks of pleasure zinged from her nipples down to her sex. Her cry for more was muted in this place. She was glad for it, even while she knew Gabriel was fully aware of how desperate she was for him.

She grasped his shoulders to ground herself, but he took her hands and brought them down to her sides, holding them prisoner while he feasted on her breast, kissing and licking his way up to her throat until she shivered, then down to her belly until she arched her hips up to him. But he never settled in either place.

Instead, he slid back over her until his face was above hers, noses almost touching. She couldn't focus her eyes, but she felt the heat of his gaze on her. Amelia wanted to clamp her thighs around his hips, feel the hardness of him against her core, but he denied her, trapping her legs with his. Gabriel raised his head a little, and she gasped, scorched to her soul with the hungry flames in his dark gaze.

He kissed her, ravaging her mouth, allowing for nothing but full *participation. He tasted her, possessed her. Amelia writhed. Though he was no longer holding her wrists, she could not move her hands. "Still," he whispered against her bruised lips, but she couldn't keep still.*

Amelia strained for more, caught his lower lip with her teeth and sucked until he groaned and kissed her so deep she forgot to breathe.

Her arms were still immobile, but he'd freed one of her legs, inserting his powerful thigh between hers. He moved.

Oh, God, yes!

His chest rubbed over her nipples, and his thigh pressed against her core.

Yes!

Amelia wriggled as much as his weight on her would allow, rocked against that thigh while he held still and watched her, his devil's gaze missing nothing. He wanted this; wanted to see her take what she needed. It was there in his eyes, the tight set of his mouth, and the taut muscles of his shoulder.

It embarrassed her and thrilled her, made her wet for him, the friction against her clit a poor substitute for his hard cock slamming into her, filling her.

Please, she begged silently. She couldn't bring herself to say it out loud. She craved the feel of him inside her, the hard pumping rhythm of his thrusts. She needed him demanding over her, behind her, under her... any way she could get him.

Moaning, she bucked her hips against him more. So close! He could sense it, too. His gaze burned hotter, his body pressed closer, his hand palmed the curve of her hip, guiding her movements.

The full-body orgasm slammed into her so hard, she nearly screamed. Her vision darkened while it rocked through her, and all the while she felt Gabriel's gaze on her.

Still humming with pleasure, she returned to herself, half-opening her eyes to find herself in darkness, their positions reversed. "Christ," he breathed, staring at her with something like awe.

Exhausted, sleep weighing down her eyelids, Amelia couldn't do more than settle in and drift off.

~

A tickle against her hand stirred her from sleep. She almost groaned. It couldn't be time to wake up already; she'd just gotten to bed. Her body felt spent. Bruised, even. And her mind was so fuzzy, she didn't want to open her eyes. *Just a few more minutes…*

Amelia shifted her head on her pillow—

Not a pillow.

She went as still as a statue, muscles tensing and strange butterflies fluttering in her belly. She racked her brain for memories. Patched up, went to bed, told Gabriel to keep his hands to himself. Fell asleep. Had the most amazing wet dream ever…

Wait… It *had* been a dream, right?

Right?!

Dread killing off the butterflies into a cold weight in her stomach, Amelia cracked one eye open.

Oh, God!

So not a pillow!

The side of her face was pressed into Gabriel's shoulder, her hand was over his on his chest and—*Oh, God!*—was she straddling his leg? That sure as hell didn't feel like her bat against her hip.

She made herself cautiously tilt her head back to look at him. Maybe he was still asleep. If she shifted carefully, she could extricate herself, and he never had to know what she'd done. She'd broken two of his ribs last night. He'd probably sleep the whole day away.

His smug, shit-eating grin told her better than words ever could about how royally screwed she was. "Good morning," he said, looking like he was biting back a laugh.

"Oh, God!" Amelia scrambled away fast as she could. "Holy shit— what the hell!" Her throat still felt raw, but she barely felt it past her mortification.

"Easy," he said, not bothering to cover up his chuckle. He reached for her, but she slapped his hand away and moved farther. Her palm slipped off the edge of the bed and her upper body followed. Amelia yelped, reached out blindly to catch herself. Gabriel snatched her by the elbow and pulled her back, freely laughing at her now. "Will you calm down?"

Amelia slapped at him, frantic to get away and repress any memory of this ever having happened, but he wasn't having any of that. The more she fought, the less freedom she had, until she was pinned beneath Gabriel, exactly the way she'd been in her dream.

This couldn't be happening!

Her arms were pinned to her sides, her legs held immobile by his, and his body weighed her down, effectively putting an end to her struggles. She couldn't even head-butt him because he was so close, her neck strained backwards to get away. And, damn it, what the hell was he smiling about!

"I made it clear you were to keep your hands to yourself," she said in her best, you-piss-me-off-by-breathing voice, but her face felt on fire and the rebuke carried no weight whatsoever. Especially since her voice, still raw from last night, sounded morning-after sexed up, rather than stern.

"Yeah," he replied, grinning at her, "but I figured our arrangement went out the window when you rolled onto me and dry humped my leg in your sleep."

"Oh, God," she moaned, wishing the ground would swallow her and spare her more embarrassment.

"Good dream?" Gabriel teased.

Amelia twisted and fought to get away, but she gained no ground.

Gabriel nuzzled against her hot cheek and murmured at her ear, "You're beautiful when you come."

A hot shiver almost made her turn into a puddle. Oh, man, she was in so much trouble! Schooling her body's responses—as if *that* was ever going to happen, with his morning erection poking at her belly—she took a breath to calm herself. "Get off me," she said, doing her best to sound professional. If the way he smiled against her jaw was anything to go by, she'd failed miserably.

"Why?" he challenged, his mouth roaming where it shouldn't.

Panting now? *Really, Amelia? Amelia Marguerite Chase… a total out-of-control wanton.* Hailey would say it's always the quiet ones.

His tongue flicked over her earlobe, and she gasped, her body responding to him eagerly. Far too eagerly. Quiet ones, indeed. In thought, and in dream, too, apparently. Amelia was never one for half measures.

What had he asked?

Oh!

"Because I can't fraternize with my subjects." There. That should do it. Except as far as excuses went, that one came out sounding lame. Damn, she should have made it more convincing.

He caught her earlobe between his teeth, and she had to bite her lip to keep from doing something stupid, like moaning.

When he pressed an open-mouthed kiss to the sensitive spot below her ear, Amelia's head moved of its own accord to give him better access. "That's not what you were saying last night."

God, what had she been saying? Amelia vaguely remembered begging.

"That's not what your body's telling me now." Another kiss, followed by a languorous lap over her pulse.

Amelia gasped and shivered. This was too much. She'd never been good at dealing with embarrassment, but with this absolute lack of control over her own body thrown in the mix, she was completely lost. Torn between straining closer, giving him more, and fighting like a hellcat to get away and run. Somewhere far, where she would never have to look at him and remember what she'd done.

She made an effort to form a coherent sentence. "I don't even know you."

That brought his head up, and he looked into her eyes, so like her dream version of him that she felt moisture gather between her legs. The man was sex incarnate first thing in the morning. And those eyes…

"You know more than most people have bothered to find out," he said in his husky morning voice that vibrated in his chest, straight into her, stimulating nerve endings that had no business being stimulated. "You know me inside out, angel. Literally."

She wanted him to kiss her. "I met you days ago," she said to remind him, and herself. "We're practically strangers."

Gabriel frowned. He shifted, releasing her hands. It was her opportunity to free herself, but then he braced himself on his elbows and, with feather-light touches, brushed her hair out of her face. Amelia was too stunned to move. "Why are you so against this?" he asked, sounding genuinely perplexed.

"It's irrational."

"Maybe it's fate."

He kept touching her face even after her hair was subdued. Light brushes of his fingers over her brow, her cheekbone, down to her jaw. Amelia closed her eyes so he wouldn't see how much she enjoyed it. She *shouldn't* enjoy it. "After three days? Be serious."

His thumb caressed her lower lip, and she swallowed against the impulse to suck it into her mouth. "Well," he said, "let's do the math here. Been a while for me, but as I remember, a normal date is, what, about four hours long? With several days between that and another?"

Amelia curled her fingers into the bedsheets. This was an impossibly weird conversation to have in such an intimate setting. She couldn't concentrate, couldn't think when he kept touching her as if… almost like… he liked it. He wasn't trying to seduce—though he was succeeding with frightening ease—just wanted to touch her. "S-something like that," she said, struggling back to the discussion.

"Well, we've spent about three days together now, nonstop. Multiplied by twenty four hours, divided by standard date time, we passed date eighteen about two hours ago. You already know me in ways only a doctor or a lover can. So the only issue left is me getting to know you."

Amelia stilled, opening her eyes.

"That's really what you're fighting, isn't it?"

She met his gaze before her own darted away. She made herself look at him again.

"Why is that?" he asked, almost gently, as his hands settled on either side of her face. Close, but not touching. "What is it you're afraid I'll discover?"

Too much. Her body tensed, arousal quickly draining out of her until all she wanted was to get away. She couldn't answer him.

Gabriel knew when he'd pushed too far. Her gaze became bleak, almost afraid, and he could feel the fight return to her body. Whatever progress he'd made, he was losing it, and fast. Clearly, that had been the wrong thing to say. Amelia wasn't a woman who let others in easily. And he knew that, so why the hell had he pushed?

"Let's put a pin in that for the moment," he said, trying to somehow salvage the situation. Gabriel had had his fair share of women. Probably more than his fair share. Sex was nothing new to him. It was an enjoyable pastime, a release from all the fucking blood of the arena. He liked it. Sought it out whenever he could. Rarely turned a woman away when she came to him, or summoned him to her. There wasn't much he hadn't done or tried at least once. He'd learned the games Romans played, even learned to enjoy some of them.

As far as experience went, Gabriel's was wide and varied. He had a knack for learning what a woman told herself she liked, and what she really *needed*, and he could deliver both. It was almost a game where his partners set the rules, and he got to enjoy getting around them.

But last night, being awakened like that, watching Amelia masturbate on him and feeling her body quiver when she came, so completely guileless and innocent in her sleep, had been the most erotic experience of his life. *That* hadn't been a game. And he didn't want it to be one with her, ever. For once, he wanted something for its own sake. Not because it was fun, or an escape, but because…

Christ. Gabriel just wanted her so badly he'd do anything to have her. "Forget about all the scientific variables. Pretend the past never happened." *If only.* "Pretend nothing else exists. Focus on the constants. Just you and me. Here and now." *The way it should be.* "Can you do that?"

Her tongue darted out briefly to wet her lips, and he gritted his teeth to keep from diving after it. "By definition, the variables will always alter—"

"Goddamn it, Amelia." If he let her, she'd slip right back into scientist mode. "Stop thinking like a machine. Life is not an equation. I'm not asking you to change the rules of the universe here." He took her hand and placed it against his cheek. "I'm asking you to feel."

Her hand was cool against his face, hesitant, but she didn't pull away.

"What do you feel?"

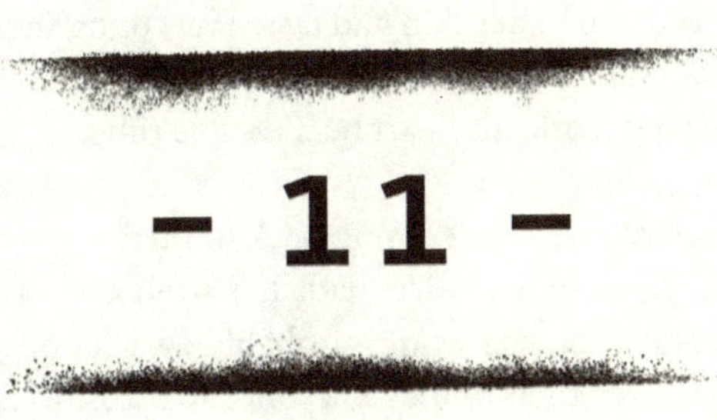

Amelia's throat worked, and her eyes darted as if she couldn't decide what to say. Finally, she met his gaze again, and there was a fragile acceptance on her face. "I can't get emotionally attached to my subjects," she said.

Battle lost.

"*But.*"

Gabriel held his breath while she searched for words. "But…?" he prompted.

Her hand left him to cover her eyes. "God, I can't believe I'm going to say this."

Hope. "Say what?"

She made a frustrated sound that reminded him of when she'd stomped her foot last night. Gabriel wanted to smile. He pulled her hand away and coaxed her to look at him. "Come on, angel, talk to me."

Amelia took a deep breath for courage and, without looking at him, said, "As two consenting adults, we could make some sort of temporary arrangement."

He groaned. "We need to work on your communication skills." Right. Because her formally delivered, cool and controlled proposition *hadn't* just made him hard enough to hammer nails.

"I-is that a yes?"

Sex without emotional attachment. With Amelia. For however long he had here. Without emotional attachment. He could kiss her whenever he wanted to, take her wherever and however he could. He could strip her down to her skin and taste everything she hid beneath that lab coat. And with no emotional attachment. The thought of getting her naked made his heart beat double time.

No emotional attachment.

Why the hell did he keep coming back to that?

Because the hitch in her voice made her seem a whole hell of a lot more vulnerable than she would probably ever let on. There were women who treated their bodies as a tool and took lovers as casually as they chose a new dress to wear in the morning. Gabriel had met plenty of them. But Amelia wasn't one of them. She liked to pretend she was, and maybe she'd convinced herself she could be, but he could see the little chink of fear in her eyes that told him it was all an act.

"Just sex," he clarified. "Nothing else."

She nodded. "That's the deal."

He'd love to be inside her head right now and see what she was thinking. "You really want that?"

Amelia reached up and twined her fingers together at his nape, pulling him down. "It's a mutually beneficial solution to our situation," she said a breath away from his lips, and pulled him closer for a kiss before he could argue.

Christ, he'd missed kissing her. Gabriel shifted his weight, freeing her legs, and she immediately raised her knees to cradle him. He groaned into her mouth and tugged her top up to fill his hands with her breasts. The little sound she made was muffled, but all the encouragement he needed. He massaged the soft mounds that fit so perfectly into his hands, brushed his palms over her nipples.

Amelia broke their kiss with a gasp as she arched into his touch. "God, it's just like my dream."

Pure masculine satisfaction made him grin like an idiot. "*This* is what you dreamed?"

She moaned and moved beneath him. "Kiss them," she said.

Don't have to ask me twice. Gabriel shifted lower and flicked his tongue over her tight nipple. Amelia cried out and hugged his head to her chest. He sucked the tempting little nub into his mouth, loving the way she writhed against him from just this. So damn responsive.

Could he make her come like this?

Using his tongue and teeth, he teased her while he pinched her other nipple. She went wild, nails scraping his scalp and neck. When he raised his head to look at her, she demanded, "More!"

Gabriel groaned and speared his hand into her pants. "God, so wet." Her knees clamped down on his hips, and she bucked up into his hand. He turned his attention to her other breast, matching the rhythm of his suckling to his stroking fingers.

"Yes," she cried when he dipped a finger inside her. He shuddered at the feel of her, so hot, squeezing him. She was close, and damn, he wanted to see her come again.

"Look at me," he said.

She didn't. So he stopped stroking.

Amelia moaned, nails digging into his shoulders to spur him on. He *really* wanted to. "Look at me," he said instead. "I want to see your eyes. I want you to know this isn't a dream."

He felt her shudder, her sex squeezed his finger tight, but she didn't come yet. And she did look at him. Those beautiful blue eyes looked at him and *saw* him. "Now," he said and pulled out of her almost completely before he thrust two fingers into her and ordered, "Come for me."

Her orgasm overtook her, and her mouth opened on a soundless cry. Oh, but she wasn't getting off that easily. Gabriel kept thrusting, kept up the steady rhythm, holding her at that peak, rubbing inside her while he massaged her clit with his thumb. She hid her face in his shoulder.

"Look at me," he told her.

Amelia shuddered in his arms. "I c-can't."

"Yes, you can." He picked up the rhythm, making her head fall back onto the pillows. She looked at him with dazed, heavy-lidded eyes as her second orgasm overtook her so hard, she arched up into him and screamed. "Beautiful." Christ, he couldn't wait to feel that with his cock inside her.

She was panting, her entire body quivering, as he slowly eased his fingers out of her and freed himself from his pants. Amelia could feel his hand shake as he guided the tip of his erection over her wet flesh. She nearly came again, just from that. Whatever he'd done to her had made her hypersensitive to his touch.

Her pants between them kept getting in the way, and she somehow maneuvered herself to take them off. Gabriel cursed when her hand brushed his cock in the process. When she was free of the pants, she reached for him, curling her fingers around the base of his erection. She squeezed, and Gabriel fell over her with a pained groan, catching himself on his hands above her. "Put it inside you," he rasped.

Amelia stroked him, up to the head, slick with her moisture, then back down. On her second pass, she swirled her thumb over the top. His chin dropped to his chest and he cursed again. "Amelia," he said in warning.

She stroked him again, reaching with her free hand to cup his balls. His back arched, and he bucked into her fist, but stopped himself. "Think you can play with me?"

"Turnabout's fair play," she returned saucily and twisted her hand on his cock.

He growled. "Oh, but I'm not finished with you yet." He reached between them again and stroked her clit, making her gasp, but she held back. Held out for all she was worth. He spread her with his fingers, trying to maneuver so he could do what she refused.

"Look at me," she said, giving him back his own words. She couldn't believe she was doing this.

Gabriel's gaze snapped up to hers again, with a touch of surprise and a swirling inferno of hunger.

Amelia held his gaze as she brought the head of him to her entrance, but moved slightly when he thrust so that he slipped up over her. Both of them cried out as he slid over her clit, and her sex clenched hungrily for him. He never broke their stare. He spread her more, and she couldn't drag this out anymore.

She brought the tip of him back to where they both wanted it, and with a slow push, he impaled her, going as deep as he could possibly go. He pulled almost completely out of her and thrust again, starting another chain reaction that made her shatter into a million pieces. Gabriel swore and let himself drop on top of her, snaking his arms around her to pull her to his chest.

They rolled until she ended up on top, but Gabriel held her immobile as her spasms went on, as he pumped his hips up, thrusting into her to keep it going. Amelia had no control over what her body did, and Gabriel reveled in the way she bucked and shuddered. With a curse, he rolled them again and drove into her harder, faster, deeper. She felt him come inside her. Felt him tense over her and pull her so close she couldn't breathe for a moment. His groan of pleasure rumbled through her. She could love that sound.

As her senses slowly returned to her, she found Gabriel watching her with an almost-tender expression. "Beautiful," he said, and when he kissed her, that, too, felt like praise.

His words brought her down from cloud nine, and Amelia started feeling awkward again. She pushed at his shoulder, silently asking for release.

Gabriel slid out of her as he rolled to his side, and Amelia blushed again. He was smiling, watching her like he wanted to get right back to it again. By the looks of him, they could spend all day doing this, and she wouldn't object if that was what he wanted. He'd just given her the best sex of her entire life. *She* wanted to lick her lips and say, "More."

The audio system beeped softly. "Virus database updated," the computer said, and Amelia crashed back to reality.

Gabriel frowned. "What does that mean?"

"It means it's time to get back to work."

The lazy contentment drained out of his face. His eyes became hard, determined. Amelia was glad for the change. She needed to get them back on track. For a moment there she'd let herself forget the true nature of their circumstances. This man might die very soon. Most likely by her hands.

Amelia went to snag a quick shower to compose herself, leaving him to his own devices. She needed a moment to focus. *Can't afford this distraction.* The smallest mistake could mean his life.

When she came out, Gabriel was leaning against the wall next to the bathroom door, arms crossed over his chest. "You locked the door," he said.

The four words were spoken in a sullen, grumbling voice still rough enough to make her body clench in memory of what they'd done. And there went her composure again. She'd never had anyone question her personal routines before, but she felt unaccountably as if she owed him an explanation. Or an apology?

Before she could formulate an answer, he slipped past her into the bathroom. He didn't close the door all the way.

Puzzled, she left him to it and took her breakfast to the lab. Immersing herself in work would clear her head. And she needed a clear head to do what he'd hired her to do. She couldn't think about what they'd just done, or about what might happen once they were finished here. Amelia had a job to do.

A report was already prepared for her to review. The panther DNA was a safe match, and Amelia had three triggers ready to test and a prep agent ready to administer.

Gabriel would be pleased.

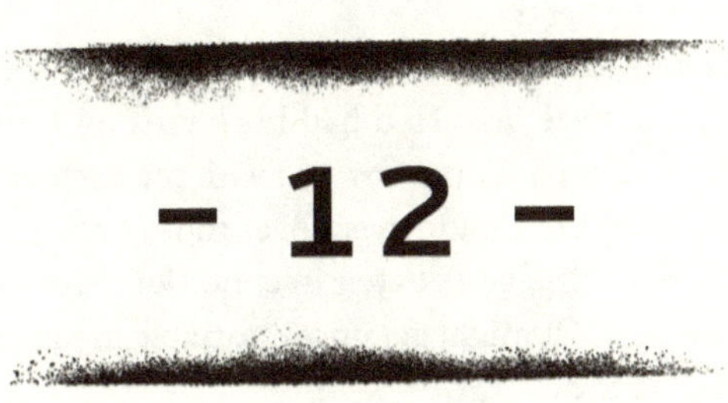

Gabriel was pissed.

Though he really shouldn't have been. It wasn't as if Amelia had deceived him. No, she'd spelled out the terms of their liaison quite clearly. Neat little arrangement. Mutually beneficial solution.

He snorted. Yeah, he should have expected this. All the benefits of sex without the messy complications of emotional attachment.

Which apparently meant as soon as she'd gotten hers, Amelia rolled out of bed and into her lab coat to diligently assist him in his soon-to-be very painful suicide. She was nothing, if not efficient.

He felt used.

Not that he'd expected hours of cuddling, but a quick fuck and then back to the business at hand hadn't been in his plans, either.

It should have put his head back in the game that things were moving forward quickly. With any luck, he'd get the treatment and be on his way before the deadline. It was great news. He ought to be happy.

Instead, he was disappointed as hell he didn't get to taste her.

Gabriel stabbed his legs into his last clean pair of pants, aware yet unimpressed that his ribs held. Snatching an apple from the kitchen, he went in search of Amelia.

Of course, she was in the lab.

She'd put on classical music and turned the heat up. Her feet were bare, and beneath that damn lab coat she wore shorts and a strappy tank top. The woman looked like a sexpot archaeologist rather than a scientist.

"What's with the heat?"

She hardly looked up from the microscope she was bending over. Damn, she had a sweet ass. He'd had his hands on it minutes ago. The sight of it clad in pants and covered with the back of her lab coat offended him. Nothing should ever cover those curves, except him. "The DNA seems to integrate better in conditions similar to the human body," she said. "It might get uncomfortable in here for a while."

Oh, she had no idea.

Gabriel came up behind her and caught her around the waist, pulling her against him. Predictably, Amelia straightened, but instead of gaining ground, all she did was lean into him more. He took full advantage, palmed her breast, knowing it would make her melt against him. She could pretend to be the detached scientist all she liked, but it changed nothing about the way she responded to him, so eager for this. Gabriel could play her like a fiddle with his touch, make her sing him a symphony. But right now, all he wanted was to rattle her composure and prove she wasn't as untouchable as she liked to think she was. The rest would come later.

"You treated me bad, angel," he said, nuzzling in the side of her neck. "Cut me deep." Her head fell back against his shoulder. "I thought we had something."

"We had sex," she said. "Nothing more."

Gabriel scowled. He pinched her nipple lightly through her top, gratified to feel her breath hitch. "Would you care to change your answer?"

Amelia cleared her throat to disguise her moan, but he wasn't fooled. "Great sex?" she said.

In reward, he kissed her neck and trailed his hand over her taut waist beneath her shirt. "I could have helped you shower."

Her hands were fisted at her sides. Gabriel felt the tension in her body, her struggle not to respond. It only made him more determined to make her. He nipped her shoulder and angled his hand down, barely brushing inside the waistband of her shorts.

Amelia caught his hand before he could get any farther. "Yes, you're very helpful," she said. "But we never would have made it out again."

Most likely true. Something he'd like to put to the test. He sighed and released her. "One of these days," he said when she turned to face him. He could see her pulse throbbing in her neck, which was miraculously unbruised. Gabriel wanted her again. For hours and days. He'd had a taste of her passion, and he wanted more. If he wasn't careful, Amelia would make him an addict.

"One of these days, what?" she challenged, back straight, chin high. But her cheeks were flushed and her eyes were bright with want. God, he could slake her so easily, if only she would *let* him.

"One of these days, angel, I'll get you all to myself. Without this lab, without any distractions." Craving the heat of her, he leaned in close. "And then I'll keep you out of your head with pleasure for so long, you won't remember how you've lived without it before. And you won't ever want to go back."

"Assuming you survive, of course."

Gabriel tensed, desire cooling in a hurry. *Damn her.* He stepped back a respectable distance and speared his hands into his pockets to keep them to himself. "Yes. Assuming I survive."

Disappointment flashed through her eyes. Or maybe he'd imagined that. As the music transitioned from a symphony to a violin solo, Amelia broke their miserable little staring contest and brought up a mess of data on the computer screen. "The serum is being synthesized. I found a match and a trigger that seems to be working. Once everything is ready, it shouldn't take more than a day to administer. But, of course, I can't give any guarantee it'll work."

"Uh, right. Great." Something was wrong here. This thing between them shouldn't be so complicated. Amelia wanted him; he was sure of it. And he sure as hell wanted her. So why wasn't he stripping her down on one of the tables, or the manacle chair?

Amelia faced him askance. "You're not changing your mind, are you?"

"What? No. Absolutely not. I'm just… thinking."

She raised an eyebrow at him before she turned back to her work, snapping a vial into an injection gun. "About what?"

"You," he said. "What else is there worth thinking about?"

The gun wavered in her hands. "How about that you might die

this week?"

"So you keep telling me. Is that how you keep your mind off what we did?"

"In the chair, please," she said.

"Does it work?" he asked. "I'd really like to know this, you see." She walked away from him, toward the manacle chair, giving him no choice but to follow. "Because no matter how often you keep reminding me that I'm a dead man walking, all I keep seeing is your face when you came for me." He could still feel the way her body had tensed against him, how she'd clutched him and dug her little nails into his back. He could feel her heat squeezing his cock, and her scent was all around him still. He couldn't seem to get rid of the memory. It kept coming back to him, and he had to remind himself he wasn't in bed with her anymore.

Amelia wouldn't meet his gaze. It was probably a good thing. If she showed, or even hinted, she was thinking the same thing, he'd be on her in a split second. "Sit," she said.

"I won't let you forget it, Amelia." Somehow, after sating themselves on each other, they'd left things frustratingly unfinished. Gabriel cupped her cheek, coaxed her to look at him. "You can't blow this off. We have something here." Damned if he knew what it was, though.

"This is the first part of your treatment," Amelia said, but her voice was unsteady. "It's to prepare your body for the shift. If it's successfully integrated, it should help you heal a lot faster."

Gabriel dropped his hand and took a seat. "And if it isn't?"

"Then you're shit out of luck and the first change will kill you."

He snorted. "Good to know."

"Luckily, your current injury gives us a chance to test it and recalculate if something goes wrong." She turned his hand palm-up on the armrest and put the injection gun to his vein.

Gabriel caught her hand to stop her. "A kiss for good luck?" *Come on, angel. Give me something here.*

He thought she would refuse, but then she licked her lips and brought them to his. Gabriel let her set the pace, didn't push for more, just gently coaxed her to open to him. Her kiss was sweet and slow, almost like she was trying to soothe him. Or to apologize.

He reached for her, intending to pull her into his lap and kiss her proper, when the needle stung his arm and the gun injected the serum.

Amelia pulled back, looking into his face. Probably checking his pupils or something. "Are you okay?" she asked.

"No," he answered. "Kiss me again."

She wanted to. He could see it. Instead she stepped back. "I need to monitor your vitals in case something goes wrong."

Gabriel growled and pulled her down into his lap. He clamped his arms around her to keep her there.

"What are you doing! I told you—"

"Just stay still a minute and let me enjoy this. I won't try anything."

"Then what's the point?" Always thinking. But she stopped struggling. Even if she was still tense.

"Consider it an experiment."

"Experiment."

"Uh-huh. I postulate that holding you like this will relieve my anxiety and slow my heart rate."

Amelia looked at him for a moment, then tensed, straining away. He instinctively tightened his hold on her. "I want my notepad," she said. Gabriel allowed her enough room to reach for it.

When she settled back, she relaxed against him. "Every experiment needs data." Tapping in commands, she brought up a miniature scan of his body, along with all of his vitals. His heart rate had slowed and evened out, and his had BP lowered.

Amelia looked at him, seeming astonished.

Gabriel shrugged. "I told you."

"Amazing," she mumbled, checking and double-checking everything on her small screen. "And the serum is working. Your ribs are knitting back together. Can you feel it?"

He winced. "It itches like crazy."

She smiled at him, and it was like watching a brilliant sunrise. Wriggling out of his arms, she ran to one of the many cupboards and pulled out another gigantic syringe.

"Oh, now wait a minute," he said. "We're *not* doing that again."

"Have to," she said. "The bandage is permanent unless I dissolve it. If I don't, after a while your body will form a fluid-filled cyst around it, and I'll have to go in to remove it surgically."

Gabriel glared.

"Come on, don't be such a baby."

He choked. "A baby?"

"Look at it this way. If you can't handle this, then you sure as hell can't handle every bone in your body stretching, distending, and breaking to accommodate a new shape. We might as well give up now and save you a lot of pain."

"Fine," he growled. "But next time I'm getting knee-walking drunk before I let you do anything to me."

Her mouth quirked. "Noted." She adjusted the chair so it stretched out into a gurney. "Lift up your shirt, please."

Gabriel grinned. "You do it."

She hesitated.

"Come on, after this morning, you're still shy? About something so simple? Not like I'm asking you to pull down my pants and suck my di—"

"Fine," she said quickly. With the syringe at the ready, she pulled up his shirt and touched the needle to his side.

"No anesthetic this time?"

"I'm not going deep. You shouldn't feel more than a prick." The needle stabbed through his skin and muscle. He felt it enter the chemical bandage, but there was no pain. Amelia pressed along the rib as she injected the fluid. "It's dissolving into saline." Still no pain. At least not from the injection. As she dissolved the one on the other rib, he flexed his abs, ready to sit up, and winced. Without the bandage support, the freshly healed breaks strained. They were whole, but still fragile, and felt like a deep bruise he couldn't ice.

"Damn."

"What's wrong?" Amelia tossed the syringe onto a tray and grabbed her e-pad again. "Vitals are stable, BP slightly elevated. No adverse reaction to the bandage or solvent. Are you in pain?"

The monitors suddenly blinked and shut down.

"What the—"

"Gladius!"

Gabriel sat up so fast, he felt one of the ribs crack again. *Aw fuck!*

Now he was in pain.

And in trouble. A whole lot of trouble.

Amelia spun on her bare heels to face the intruders she hadn't heard enter as the computers booted back up again.

"Unauthorized system shutdown," her computer system said. "Initiating diagnostic scan."

Three large, muscled men accompanied the tall, curvy woman with a ridiculously red wig. "I am getting so sick of people coming in uninvited," she muttered.

The fake redhead smiled beatifically and opened her arms to Gabriel. They were weighed down by at least two pounds of golden cuffs and bracelets. "My Champion. Gladius, how I've missed you!"

Amelia transferred her gaze to Gabriel. He was sitting up, staring at the quartet with murder in his eyes, a muscle jumping in his jaw. "Friends of yours?" Amelia asked.

He said nothing. Her e-pad beeped insistently. His heart rate was through the roof. Who the hell were these people?

"Will you not greet me properly, Gladius?" the woman inquired, and though the request was sweet and almost hurt, there was an underlying edge to her voice. It wasn't a request; it was a command.

Out of the corner of her eye, Amelia saw Gabriel's hands curl around the edge of the gurney, knuckles white. "Shit," he breathed.

His vitals were going haywire. She had to calm him somehow. "'Gladius'?" she repeated, keeping her voice carefully neutral.

"Latin for sword," the woman said, seeming delighted to have someone to speak to. Her arms had lowered, and she now had her hands clasped demurely in front of her.

"Also for penis," Gabriel added. Amelia could see the effort it took for him to release his death grip on the gurney. She couldn't be sure, but she thought he'd called the woman a bitch under his breath.

Amelia set the e-pad aside. "Give me your left hand," she said.

He looked at her in surprise, but complied.

Holding his forearm in one hand, she placed the other over his recently broken ribs. "Push your shoulder down and your chest out to the right," she said. He was reaching across his torso to her. If his ribs still bothered him, he would feel it now. "So she just called you a dick?" she said to take his mind off things.

Some of the tension left him, but Gabriel still wouldn't look at her for more than a second. "She thinks the Latin makes it sound classier." He showed no reaction to her touch, but she could feel the fracture. It had to be causing him pain. It didn't show past the seething rage in his eyes.

Amelia released his wrist, and he subtly brushed his fingers over the length of her arm as she let go of his ribs, too.

The redhead woman huffed. "Well, aren't you going to introduce me?"

"No," Gabriel said simply.

"So rude, my Champion."

"Go fuck yourself," he snapped. "How's that?"

Amelia expected the bodyguards to step up, but they didn't twitch.

The redhead shivered. "Will you watch?"

Now was as good a time as any to ask. "Why is she wearing bed sheets?" The woman had white sheets draped over her from shoulder to ankle. They were held in place by golden ropes tied around her waist and shoulders. It looked like she'd be naked if she took one wrong step.

Amelia's question was ignored.

"Gladius, I missed you so," the redhead said, mewling. "Come give us a kiss."

Amelia wanted to snarl at her. "He needs to rest. He's been injured recently."

The redhead gasped—so obviously an act. "Goodness me, what happened?"

"A brawl," Amelia said. "I was there when it happened. Offered my services as a medical professional. Mr. Connors has been a patient here for a while now."

"Why would you care if Mr. Connors got hurt?" the woman asked, sounding perplexed.

"Because he did it in defense of me," Amelia lied without hesitation. She didn't like the woman's theatrics.

"Ah, sentiment." Her tone said how precious she found it.

One of the bodyguards snickered. "You ran away to play doctor?"

Oh, good. So it wasn't only Gabriel in Rome with an infantile sense of inappropriate humor. Now she knew where he'd gotten it.

"I still have a week," Gabriel said. "Why are you here?"

Curious, he hadn't asked how they found him.

"Silas," the redhead intoned, "explain."

"The fair Honoria, Caesar of Rome, has given you leave to venture out of the city," Muscle Number Two said. "She has *not* cleared you to leave the planet."

All pretense of civility left the redhead. "I don't know how you managed to get off-world, but rest assured, those who aided you *will* pay." Then she smiled. "Now, my Champion. You had to know we'd find you eventually. So why have you come here? Who is she to you?"

"Wait," Amelia said, inserting herself into a conversation which did not in any way pretend to include her, and turned fully to Gabriel. "*She's* the Caesar?" Honoria, and not the man in the recording he'd shown her that first night. "The Caesar is a woman?"

Gabriel nodded tensely, not taking his gaze off the intruders.

"How'd you manage that?" she asked Honoria.

The redhead shrugged a shoulder and set down the instrument she'd absently picked up. Something told Amelia nothing this woman did was an accident, or without purpose. "Killed the last Caesar in his sleep," Honoria answered easily.

Cut the head off a snake… another grows in its place. If the former Caesar had been the merciless ruler in the recording, Amelia couldn't imagine how much worse this woman could be, that Gabriel felt he had to take her out no matter what the cost to himself.

Honoria was meandering around her lab, looking bored, but those deceptively uninterested eyes missed nothing.

"Diagnostic scan complete. Reinitiating last session. Please enter password."

Amelia tapped on her e-pad to shut down all screens, and Honoria swung her cold, viper gaze to Amelia. "Something to hide?"

"My work is proprietary. Yes, I try to keep it from others."

"Enough with this," Honoria said. "You're coming back with us. Now."

"I'm afraid I can't allow that," Amelia said. Gabriel wasn't going anywhere until he was good and ready.

Honoria raised a perfectly groomed eyebrow. "You think you have a say in this, Doctor?"

Gabriel tensed behind her, his vitals spiking again.

Amelia made sure to keep her voice steady and professional. "As his physician, his welfare is my concern. I cannot in good conscience clear him for duty until I am assured he will be able to hold his own. What would be the point of healing him if he ends up getting himself killed the moment he steps foot back in the arena?"

"Doc," Gabriel said in warning, but Honoria was considering the quandary. Or rather, considering an opponent. Amelia knew when she was being measured, hated it with every cell in her body, because she'd been subjected to that sort of look countless times in the past. She'd accepted it as a fact of life before. Now, it made her want to give this Caesar something to look at. Who the hell was she to judge Amelia?

"You needn't have bothered coming after me," Gabriel said, distracting her. He'd shifted closer, holding his ribs, and the small motion was enough to tell her it would be unwise to antagonize the redhead right now. "I would have come back on my own."

Honoria shot him an I-wasn't-born-yesterday look. "I'm certain you would have." She considered Amelia again, and said, "Very well. I will allow you the rest of your free time here. I expect you back in the arena at the end of it—"

"Or you'll kill me, good and bloody," Gabriel finished for her. "Yeah, I know."

Honoria smiled. "No, sweet Gladius. I will kill your doctor here. Good and bloody, as you say. And I'll make you watch." The sheer venom in her tone, the way she looked as if she would enjoy doing those things, made Amelia take an involuntary half-step back.

"I said I'd be back," Gabriel snapped, savage hatred pouring off him.

"And now I know you'll keep your word," Honoria said, her tone once again civil. "Patch him up well for me, Doctor Amelia Marguerite Chase, and I'll make sure you never want for anything for the rest of your life."

"Save your threats and bribes," Amelia said. "I don't work for you. You don't frighten me." She would not show how unsettled it made her that Honoria knew her name.

Honoria blinked. "Oh, but my dear, no one touches my champions, unless I say so."

Out of spite, because she was sick of people ordering her around, sick of them forcing her hand, and the decisions she had to make, she ruffled Gabriel's hair. "There. Touched him," she said. "What are you going to do about it?"

The smile that stretched across Honoria's face gave Amelia chills. "Silas," she said pleasantly, "break her arms."

Three things happened then, all at once. The one called Silas grunted and started forward. Amelia dove for the biggest syringe on her tray, filled with a chemical solution that, without the reactant, would dissolve tissue on contact. And Gabriel shoved to his feet, taking a stand between Amelia and the others.

Silas and Gabriel stopped, nose to nose. Neither man moved to attack, nor did they make way for the other. "Back off, minion," Gabriel said low. A warning.

Amelia palmed the syringe and edged closer to Gabriel.

"You dare defy me," Honoria hissed.

"Call off your dogs," Gabriel ordered. "You know they can't match me."

"I should have them flay you out of your skin!"

Amelia heard the chill smile in Gabriel's voice. "Try it. I'll break their necks, and gut you before you can scream for help."

Fury swirled across Honoria's features. She was as tense as a rock, hardly breathing, her face turning so red it clashed with her wig. Four against one, and it appeared that Gabriel still had the upper hand. How was it possible? Just how good of a killer was he?

Finally, Honoria breathed out in defeat, though she was still livid. "Silas, heel," she said and, like a good dog, Silas obeyed. "This isn't over, Gabriel," she told him. "At the end of the day, don't forget *you* chose this. You owe me blood."

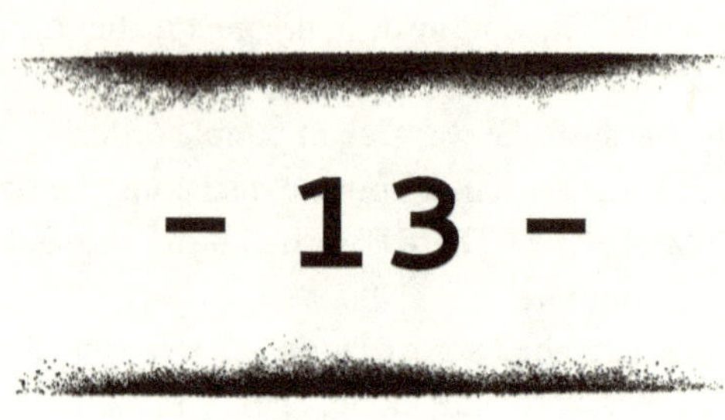

– 13 –

The moment the queen bitch and her evil minions were gone, Gabriel wheeled on Amelia. "Did you go stupid on me? What the hell is wrong with you?" His side was throbbing, his jaw ached, every muscle screamed for him to go after Honoria and finish her off.

But none of that held a candle to the mind-numbing terror he'd felt when Silas came after Amelia. To break her arms. Except he wouldn't have stopped there. And Honoria wouldn't have called him off.

"Seems like you missed a prime opportunity there. Why didn't you just end it?"

"You don't think I wanted to?" He stalked her as she retreated. "You don't think I've stood before that sadistic cunt a hundred times before, *inches* away from ripping her head off? It's an illusion, Amelia. A great big fucking game of make-believe. I can't take out one of her dogs without two more crawling out of the woodwork. And it's not me they would have come after first."

Amelia's eyes were huge. "Gabriel, you need to calm down."

"Fuck calm!" All of the house systems were centralized to one control unit. A security flaw he was going to remedy as soon as he found out how in the holy hell Honoria managed to get in here to begin with. He swore when he brought the diagnostics up on screen. "We may need to relocate. It's not safe here."

"All right, fine. Whatever you say. But right now, I need you to sit down, okay?"

"*Sonofabitch!*" They'd gone around his protocols. Completely by-passed all of his security measures and used the science number cruncher to confuse the system into a reboot. Which meant whatever Amelia hadn't password protected was now Honoria's.

"I will sedate you if you make me," Amelia threatened.

Gabriel slammed his hand down on the keyboard so hard he crushed it.

"All right, mister. You need a time out."

"Amelia, please tell me your work is secure on this system." He couldn't bring himself to check.

"My work is not *on* this system," she said, and relief made him sag. "All data comes from and returns back to a different location, with biometric and password security. The connection shut down when my computers went offline."

So they wouldn't have gotten anything.

Amelia went to the central console and placed her hand on the screen. After she input her password, all of the monitors turned back on, streaming with data that hadn't been there after the reboot. "There," she said. "See? Now will you please sit down?"

Gabriel hung his head. "I'm sorry. For all of this." *If anything had happened to her...*

"I knew what I was getting into."

He glanced at her sideways. She couldn't have possibly known. But the quiet confidence, the self-assurance in her, made him believe her. There was a strength in Amelia that could only have been forged in fire. "I never wanted this to touch you."

"If that were completely true, you wouldn't have come here in the first place," she said with a shrug. There was no censure. "Now come on. You managed to re-break your ribs. I need to see how much damage you did."

Gabriel returned to his chair and let her examine him. Her hands shook a little when she probed his ribs. "Does this hurt?"

"No." He covered her hands with his, seeking her gaze. She wouldn't look at him.

"Good. That means the serum is working. Once we start with the change agent, I'll have to monitor you to make sure this one doesn't disintegrate."

"Is that possible?"

"Very," she said, consulting her e-pad, "if the compounds react to each other. I'm testing for all contingencies before starting the treatment, though." He knew she was only talking to calm him. It only worked because, though it was obvious she was trying, she didn't sound like the emotionless scientist. There was tension in her; her movements weren't as fluid as he was used to seeing, and she was so pale, Gabriel wanted to take her into his arms and erase the last ten minutes from both of their memories. Go back to this morning when all that mattered was her being there with him, completely.

"Is that why the tiger guy didn't change for a year?" he asked, keeping the conversation going because he needed to hear her voice to steady himself. "Because of a cross-reaction?"

"No," she said in a tone he was beginning to recognize. The woman was a trove of information, but when she talked like that, she only gave the bare minimum. Only enough to shut him up. She was hiding something. "In his case, the trigger was non-reactive. He went through a different process."

Gabriel decided to probe for more. "Then this is a theoretical possibility?"

"It's all trial and error. We learn by doing. Every body is different, reacts differently. There's no such thing as standard or normal. No basis for comparison."

Realization dawned. "In other words, it didn't happen to the tiger guy, but it happened to someone else. There were others who went through this."

Amelia blinked at him. "Yes," she said. "You've seen them."

In the file. The images of people who'd been killed by the changes.

"No," he said, starting to understand the undercurrents to this whole thing. "You said the tiger guy was the first success. But the cross-reaction didn't happen in him. Means it couldn't have happened before, otherwise you would have altered the compounds. Which means it must have happened *after* him."

For less than a second, Amelia went so completely still, he could practically hear her heart stop. Then it was over, and she turned her back on him and returned to her desk.

Gabriel went after her. "What are you keeping from me?"

"Nothing that concerns you," she said, all cool authority, not looking at him.

"If it has relevance on what you're doing to me, then it damn well does concern me. You're a good doctor, Amelia. Don't you think a patient should have all the available facts to give an informed consent?"

"You demanded *my* consent without knowing *any* of the facts. And when I gave them to you, you didn't care! What makes you think you get to ask for more now?"

Gabriel drew back. "So it's personal." Amelia wouldn't be this up in arms if it was some faceless stranger. She'd shown him plenty of those. But with the tiger guy, she kept everything vague and never gave more than she absolutely had to. She was protecting her patient. How much closer to her had this mysterious other person been, that she refused to acknowledge his very existence? "You did this to someone close to you."

"No, she did it to herself," Amelia snapped. "Without my knowledge, or consent. She put her life on the line for the stupidest of reasons, much like yourself, and she died three times because of it!"

"*She?*"

Amelia slammed her e-pad down and shoved to her feet. "I'm not discussing this with you." Then she marched out of the lab, dropping her coat on the floor along the way.

"Honoria will be back," he called after her. "We still need to leave!"

She shouted back something extremely unflattering before she disappeared upstairs and out of sight.

Gabriel blew out a frustrated breath and dropped into her abandoned chair. He let the momentum spin him around a couple of times. Great. Just great.

When the computer screen came into his view, he dropped his feet to the floor and stared. In her haste to escape him, she'd forgotten to log out. Scruples made him hesitate for all of five seconds before he brought up the search window. He'd never been able to access these files before; hadn't even found them. Because he hadn't been able to find the connecting uplink. Now that the connection was open, all of Amelia's work was right there for his inspection.

Within moments, he was scanning her files, organized chronologically. He skimmed through the early trial, not interested in the failures. The first success was labeled THNA. Gabriel didn't know what that stood for, but the description was almost identical to what that nut from New Alaska had told him. NA… New Alaska? Then what was the TH?

He let that go for now, focusing on the results. The guy had almost died moments after the virus had been administered. Amelia had suspended the experiment, and the following treatments had been aimed to stabilize his condition. A year of treatments.

Cause of transformation: Unknown.

Trigger: Unidentified.

He'd changed spontaneously?

The information cut out, seemingly mid-sentence. Except there weren't sentences, only random notes.

The next entry was labeled HSCT. The acronym was a link to another file.

Gabriel checked behind him to make sure Amelia hadn't come back, then selected the link.

The screen went black, and then a low resolution video popped up, the picture adjusting automatically to fit the screen. It was a little out of focus, but Gabriel could easily make out a woman. Her face looked deathly tired. Her skin was sallow, and she slumped in her seat, though her voice was strong as she spoke into the microphone. *"Statistically, a sister virus strain, a mutated version of the virus originally used, would have the best chance of being successful. Similar enough to perform the same function, and just different enough to avoid an attack by the subject's immune system. Apparently, the subject has developed a defense against the original virus, so I had to improvise. And hey, it only took me fifteen hours to come up with a workable serum."* There was a wry, amused sort of way-to-go-me pride in her voice, but the strain on her face revealed more emotion than she probably wanted it to.

She was dying, and she knew it.

Gabriel fast-forwarded to a part where the woman was looking directly into the recorder. *"This is a risky procedure. At best, the subject*

*will become infected with the regenerative agent, and some of the virus'
indicators. At worst... at worst, the solution contains a cell or two of
the full, live virus, in which case, introduction into the blood stream
will mean immediate infection."*

She went on to describe the progression of the disease, and the
increasing risk, given the number of injections she was going to be
administering to the subject. The longer she spoke, the more unsettled and weary she became. Even her off-hand comment about a date
didn't seem to brighten her spirits.

Then she took a syringe and injected herself. *She* was the subject.
HSMT. T, for Torrey, the place where this was recorded. And the rest
of it: Hailey S. Chase.

Gabriel turned off the video and logged out of Amelia's uplink.
He felt as if someone had knocked the wind out of his freaking soul.

Her sister. Amelia was protecting her sister.

~

Amelia shook so much she tripped going up the stairs. By the time
she made it to her green room, she was hyperventilating. The thermostat was turned up almost as high here as it was in the lab, but the
humidity was much higher. She couldn't breathe.

She couldn't go outside to breathe.

Amelia dropped to her knees and hung her head, burying her hands
in soft, dark soil, seeking familiarity and comfort. Plants, the earth,
had always been a soothing presence in her life. Today, both failed to
calm her. She fisted her hands in the soil, feeling miniscule granules
bury so far beneath her fingernails it hurt.

Hailey is safe, she told herself. Her younger sister was off somewhere
on an exotic honeymoon with a man who could read minds. She was
nowhere near danger, and if it found her, Hailey and Jeremy could
damn well take care of themselves.

Amelia *knew* this.

So why was she still having a panic attack?

She wanted to cry. She wanted to scream until she passed out. She
wanted to break things. Most of all, she wanted to get the hell out of

her life. To escape the mess she'd made and go somewhere far from it, where no one knew who or what she was. Where she could start over with a clean slate.

It wouldn't clear my conscience.

And that was the crux of it. Amelia could run; she had the means. But she could never run far enough to escape her memories. She wished she could accept her past as easily as Gabriel had accepted his. But he had only killed people. Amelia, for all intents and purposes, had tortured them to death. She'd made their own bodies turn against them. She'd made them suffer, sometimes knowing they would, and recorded the results, like none of it mattered.

Amelia was far more of a monster than he could ever be.

She and Honoria should get along quite well.

That was one thing monsters and scientists had in common: they did not feel while working. Emotion clouded judgment. Made a scientist clumsy. Made her make lethal mistakes. Sympathy, compassion, remorse, and fear had no place in a lab.

Amelia closed her eyes and made herself not feel. She analyzed her body's responses, focusing on the facts, not the emotional triggers. Elevated heart rate. Constricted airways. Lack of oxygen in the blood, and thus in the brain and major organs, causing lightheadedness and weakness in the body.

The next breath came easier. The one after, even more so.

Amelia released her death grip on the soil and braced herself to stand. She had to hold on to the wall while her legs steadied and the room stopped spinning. One of these days there would be a chaise set up there, by the palm trees. And over there, by the window, would be an artificial pond, maybe a little waterfall with lotus flowers floating on top.

One of these days, this place would be a miniature Eden she could escape to and pretend she deserved to be there. For now, the plants still needed to grow and mature. And Amelia still had a lot to make up for.

Light, cool mist caressed her overheated skin. The irrigation system turning on. Amelia picked up the control unit to check the settings.

Gabriel had actually done an amazing job. Not only practically, but aesthetically. He'd programmed the system to water each type of plant as needed, in a sequence that had a rhythm to it. Stunned, Amelia looked around, watching and listening to the sprays of water sound out the *Blue Danube* waltz.

She could almost hear the melody.

Wait, she did hear it! The control unit in her hand had a volume option. She'd thought that meant water volume. Amelia turned it up and smiled. Johann Strauss at his best. And the water did follow the beat! Not only that, as she watched the sprays around her, it was like seeing an orchestrated performance.

Gabriel had done this. She'd given him a task to get rid of him for a while, something that ought to have been menial and boring to someone of his talent, and he'd done this. It was so beautiful, it shamed her.

Amelia set down the controls, rinsed off her hands, and left the Eden she didn't deserve. There was dinner to order and a stack of movies waiting to be watched. She had a year of new releases to catch up on. Perhaps some mindless entertainment was what she needed.

The kitchen had an uplink to a hundred neighborhood restaurants. Thankfully, Gabriel hadn't disabled it. Amelia ordered food from three different places, gathered light snacks for the wait, and set up the movies to play in sequence, skipping the end credits.

Gabriel returned from the lab as she was about to settle in to watch. She could hardly bring herself to look at him, but when she did, the strange look on his face made her frown. "Something wrong?"

He shook himself. "No," he said.

The way he was looking at her, as if she was a mystery he was resolving, made her uncomfortable. "Look, about before…"

"I was being an idiot," he said. "Just wanted to get a rise out of you."

Her mouth quirked wryly. "It worked," she said. Then she sobered. "About the other person—"

"You don't have to tell me. I get it."

"Oh?"

He winced and shrugged. "You, uh, left the link to your files open."

"I see." Amelia put the snacks down before she threw them at him. *Stay calm, stay rational.* "So you snooped."

"Yes," he said and, to his credit, he looked duly guilty. "I'm sorry."

"Did you shut it down afterward?"

"Of course I did."

She nodded. The backs of her legs were to the couch, but she wasn't sitting down. Neither was he, still standing in the living room doorway. "So what did you find out?"

Gabriel dropped his gaze to the floor and rocked back and forth on his feet, hands in his pockets. "I found a recording of your sister."

Stay calm. Hailey can take care of herself. Far better than Amelia could now. Hailey had the advantage of her snow leopard.

"You realize I have to kill you now," she said, needing the humor to calm herself and dispel the awkward situation.

His gaze came up, and he smiled crookedly. "If you must," he said, as though extremely put out. "I suppose I have no choice but to let you try." And from the change in his tone, it was clear where that attempt would lead.

Amelia's relief was weak, but it was there. She made herself release the tense breath she held, and settled on the couch. "Maybe later."

Gabriel ventured a step or two into the room and raised an eyebrow at the TV. "Dr. Amelia Chase watching a movie? How… ordinary."

"I sometimes find it useful to engage in activities average people enjoy. For research purposes, of course."

"Of course," he agreed.

Amelia smiled. "Would you care to join me?"

"Well, if you're sure it won't bias the results of your study."

She shrugged. "Repetition tends to remove bias."

"Then I accept your most gracious invitation."

"Good," she said. "Park your butt right here and shut up. The movie's starting."

Gabriel chuckled. "Yes, ma'am." He sat close enough that they touched from knee to shoulder and stole a piece of candy out of the snack pile.

She glared, put his arm around her, and drew her knees up so she leaned against him. Then she stole the candy back. "There, that's better."

"As usual, Dr. Chase," he said, snagging a snack of his own, "I cannot find fault with your logic."

– 14 –

September 28, 3032

For two days, Gabriel played House with Amelia. Something had changed the day Honoria made her presence known—and Gabriel was under no illusion she'd actually left. Gabriel was more determined than ever to finish the treatment and put an end to that farce.

But at the same time, he was reluctant to see this thing with Amelia end. However messed up their circumstances were, the days he'd spent here with her were among his most pleasant memories. Three mornings now, he'd gotten to wake up to the sight of her in his arms. She snuggled close to him in her sleep each night, almost compulsively.

He got the pleasure of watching her eyes open, all liquid warmth like he'd never known existed. He got her sleepy smile, and the kitten-like purr. He got to kiss her, and take her, or have her take him. He'd even coaxed her to share her shower, which was quickly becoming his favorite pastime. Watching water sluice over that soft, creamy skin, getting to caress every inch of it, making her come in his arms while she clutched the handle bar when her knees did that buckling thing that made him feel like a god—oh yes, sex in the shower, definitely among his favorites.

But no matter how happy and carefree those days were, each night after the lights had gone out and Amelia was asleep, Gabriel remembered why he was here. With nothing to do but to think or dream,

Gabriel plotted his revenge.

And each night, guilt and remorse ate him alive. Because these happy, carefree days were anything but. All of it, every moment he spent with Amelia, was tainted with what he'd dragged her into. With the knowledge that this was an all too brief escape. Because, no matter what happened to him once he left, he was never coming back here.

The serum was as ready as the machines could make it. Now it was up to Amelia to tweak the smallest details of the composition to make it viable. It was a tedious task that involved her sitting at her desk and staring into a microscope for hours on end. It hardly looked like she moved at all, but on the screen she'd set up to record the process on a sub-molecular level, he could see how much she was actually doing.

Today, she'd told him, was the final step to stabilizing the virus. It was almost time.

As he fiddled with the wiring in the manacle chair, Gabriel felt each second pass him by; time he was losing. Time he would never have again.

Gabriel looked over his shoulder at Amelia. She was so focused on her task, she probably didn't know he was still in the lab. The speakers crooned some depressing classical song. There were a lot of those playing lately. He'd dubbed the genre "Death of Santa Claus."

The lab was as hot as a desert. Gabriel didn't bother wearing a shirt in here anymore. He had no idea how Amelia could stand it in her white lab coat. Her hair was up today in a haphazard ponytail, and her flushed cheeks were the only indication she noticed the heat. Was she even breathing?

Just then, she carefully let go of her instruments and sat back with a tired sigh, rubbing her eyes.

Enough was enough.

"Change music," he said, and the song stopped mid-melody. "Randomize all."

A second later, easy drums rumbled through the lab. Amelia made a face, but said nothing. The drums eased off, replaced by soft, sweet violins, and she returned to her microscope. She settled into her zone again, and he wondered whether he should warn her.

Too late.

The violins trailed off and a beat later, heavy bass and drums exploded through the speakers.

Amelia jerked and straightened away from the microscope, hand to her heart.

"Probably should have warned you, right?"

Amelia stared at him. "You do realize the smallest mistake here could kill you?"

Gabriel grinned. He wasn't worried. "I'm dead one way or another."

She glared.

He shrugged. "Everyone dies sometime."

"Yes, well, I'd rather not have any more black marks on my record."

"You're working too hard."

"Just doing what you asked."

"Well, as your boss, I say it's time for a break." He closed the side panel on the manacle chair and pushed to his feet. "Change song," he said, and the song got replaced by a slow one. Perfect. "Come here," he said.

She shook her head. "I need to finish this."

Gabriel rolled his eyes. He went to her instead and pulled her to her feet. "Later."

"But I—"

"It's just a dance," he said and pulled her into his arms. They fit together. And holding her made his restlessness mellow out. "See? This isn't so bad."

Amelia's foot came down on his in a misstep. "This isn't working," she said, pulling away.

Gabriel spun them around, deliberately fast to put her off balance. She wouldn't fall; he held her tight. "Hmm, you're right," he said. "Maybe you should let me lead."

"I thought I was."

That made him smile. "Just relax. I might actually know what I'm doing here."

She opened her mouth to say something.

He kissed her to shut her up. Amelia melted into him, as he knew she would, her body tuning into his every motion on instinct. The most accomplished temptress in Rome couldn't affect him as much as this woman, clinging to him so trustingly. Practiced sensuality was nothing compared to Amelia's artless grace. She was brilliant, beautiful, funny, caring, and so damn strong, it humbled him.

He was falling for her.

Gabriel ended the kiss on a lingering caress, drawing back a little to look into her sleepy-sexy blue eyes. "There, see? Easy."

The song ended with, *The pieces I've become are yours to make whole again, make me whole again,* and Amelia blinked up at him. "I have to get back to work," she said.

Gabriel nodded. *No emotional attachment,* he reminded himself and made his arms release her.

Amelia caught one before he withdrew completely. "Kiss me again?"

He kissed her hard, pulled her in so tight her feet came up off the floor, and left her as dazed and breathless as she made him. It was payback, punishment for making up idiotic rules and invading his thoughts, even when he didn't want her to. For all the times she made him want to say, *Fuck it,* and forget his plans. For being so damn cool and collected when all he wanted to do was crawl into her skin and stay there forever.

"Back to work, then, Dr. Chase."

Gabriel turned his back on her and returned to whatever he'd been doing to the exam chair. It was a good thing. At least he didn't see her gaping at him like a fish out of water. God, but that man could kiss! He was her own personal stash of some pretty potent aphrodisiac, and two days of indulging hadn't nearly been enough. Now she wanted more.

He thought she worked too hard. The only reason it was taking so long was that she couldn't concentrate on her work. He only had to walk into the room and her focus went up in smoke. He looked at her, and she melted. He smiled, and she forgot why she was in the lab to begin with.

The man was dangerous. She'd never been this frazzled before.

Amelia went back to her microscope. She was almost finished. The first and second rounds were clean and ready. That left the third to do and the antivirus, in case something went wrong. Amelia could have started the treatment already, if she was certain she could finish the last round in time, but that was not about to happen with her mind all over the place like this.

The injections had to be administered within a certain time frame. A few minutes early or late wouldn't make a difference, but any more than that, and she couldn't guarantee a positive outcome. Then again, all of this would most likely end in disaster, anyway. The best she could do was lower the risk as much as possible.

So Amelia cleared her mind of Gabriel and the effects he had on her, and focused on her work. He left the lab at some point, and she switched the music back to classical. The last round of the serum was the most complicated and took the longest to clean up and stabilize.

By the time she finished, her head ached, she was sore all over, and her stomach screamed for sustenance. She turned off the heaters with a sigh of relief and dragged herself upstairs to get food.

"All done for the day?"

"All done, period," she said.

Gabriel straightened in his chair as if someone had goosed him. "So when do we start?"

Amelia glared at him. "Food first."

"Right," he said. "Yeah, of course."

In the time it took her to get to the table and sit, Gabriel had pulled out plates of leftovers and heated them up for her. He made himself sit while she ate, but she could hear his foot tapping under the table faster than a mouse's heart beat. And he was watching her like a hawk.

Just because she could, and because he deserved it, Amelia dragged it out, ate slowly and sipped her juice after every bite. Gabriel said nothing, looking like he'd explode any second. She half expected him to jump up and pace, or force her to eat faster. It amused her.

When she leaned back, Gabriel stilled, eyes huge.

After a few seconds' rest, Amelia sighed and set back to eating.

He glared at her, but she ducked her head to hide a smile. With sustenance and fluids, her headache was easing, but the residual soreness in her body remained. She needed to work out the kinks, maybe go for a walk or do some yoga. She glanced at Gabriel.

Nope. Won't be doing any of that any time soon.

Finally, she finished. Gabriel shot to his feet again to put the plate and glass in the dishwasher. "All done," he said and grabbed her hand, pulling her along. "Lunch break over."

Augh! Amelia wanted to kick him. She stumbled on the stairs. Gabriel caught her and righted her, but didn't spare a moment on pleasantries, just kept dragging her along. She glared daggers at the back of his head the whole way to the lab.

It was already much cooler than before. The computers were on standby, the serum injections were neatly aligned on a tray, ready to administer. Gabriel let go of Amelia's hand to look them over, then he put the tray on a hover table and sent it to the exam chair as carelessly as if he was tossing junk into the trash.

He turned right back to the lab table and rooted through the drawers until he found a pack of patches. Casting her a look, he reconsidered and handed them to her instead, then stripped off his shirt and tossed it aside before going over to her cabinets and making a mess of everything inside, looking for something else. He returned with a loaded tranq gun and extra rounds.

"What are you doing?" she said, taking the items from him.

Gabriel sat in the exam chair and pointed to the shackles. There was a symbol laser-etched into them. As close to a name as scientists have gotten for the alloy they were made of. "These things are unbreakable," he said. When he put his wrists into the manacles, they snapped closed. He jerked his arms, apparently to test them. "They should be able to hold me if I get out of control. They won't open unless you say the command."

He'd voice-locked them? What. The. Hell.

"But I have no idea about the rest of the chair. Amelia," he said, looking at her like he was about to jump into a shark tank to save the world, "if I break free, you need to take me out."

Amelia looked at the stuff in her hands, then at the injections, and nodded solemnly. She put a monitoring patch on the inside of his elbow and set everything else aside.

Gabriel tested the manacles again, moved around in the seat for all the worlds like he was getting ready to endure who-knew-what. When he was done, he sat tensely, fingers curling and uncurling.

"Comfy?" she asked.

He sucked in a deep breath. "Let's do it!"

Amelia picked up the first injection gun and stuck it into his arm, releasing the serum into his bloodstream. Gabriel was holding his breath, his eyes squeezed shut. Amelia checked her watch, counted to five seconds, then patted him on the arm. "Congratulations. Phase one was completed successfully."

Gabriel released a breath on a "*What?*" His eyes snapped open wide. "That's it?"

Amelia's mouth quirked. "What did you expect, black fur and a fractured skull?" Of course that would be what he'd expect, after everything she'd scared him with by now.

Gabriel looked down at himself. "Well how do you know it was successful?"

"Because if it wasn't, your heart would be arresting right now."

"Oh," he said lamely. "So, uh… you going to let me out of here?"

Amelia rolled her eyes and set to cleaning up. She marked the time and put the rest of the injections back in their place. The tranq gun she put on her desk, just in case.

"Amelia?"

She took off her lab coat and hung it from her chair, checked all systems and shut everything down. The lights were the last to turn off as she came to the door.

"Amelia!"

Giggling inwardly, she walked out, shouting over her shoulder, "Unlock."

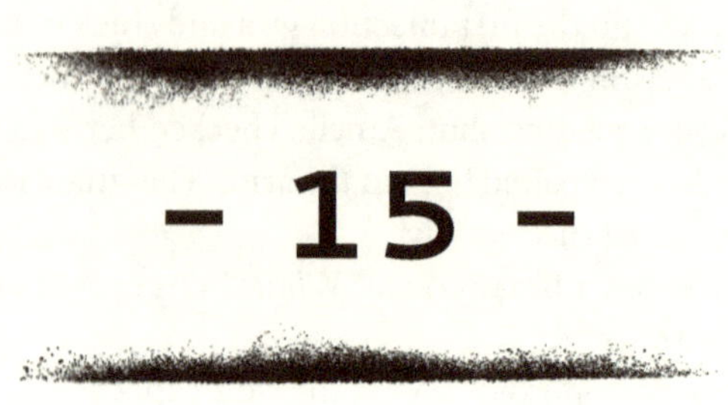

– 15 –

Though Gabriel didn't seem to realize it, the serum *had* taken effect rapidly. To anyone else he would have appeared restless, impatient. Probably no more than he had before, but Amelia picked up on the subtle changes.

Like the way he paced now, head canted down like a predator. Or the way he tilted his head sometimes as if he heard something she didn't. He licked his teeth a lot as if checking for fangs, probably not realizing the action itself was more animal than human. He didn't talk much but he did look at her every so often. And whenever he did, his gaze was so piercing and intense, Amelia expected him to pounce on her. It was getting to the point where she didn't know if he wanted to kiss her neck or bite into it.

As a scientist, she knew his expectations and impatience were amplifying everything, making it seem more than it was in reality. It was probably speeding up the transformation, too. But as a woman locked in a building with a man who would soon be turning into a feral beast, she was getting a little nervous.

This place wasn't equipped the way her lab on Torrey was. She didn't have a cage here to lock him, or herself, into. She could close herself in her room, but if he wanted to get in bad enough, he would.

Amelia monitored the changes in him on her e-pad, checking vitals and the progression of the virus. By seven o'clock, the virus had spread through his entire body and the real changes began. He'd only received a small dose so the changes were subtle. With the next injection they would become more pronounced, and the last would seal the deal.

She'd put on another movie to dispel the tension, but it wasn't working. Gabriel couldn't sit still for five minutes before he got up to pace and explore. He touched things like he'd never seen them before. He searched through every nook and cranny, looking for something that clearly wasn't there if the frustrated half-snarl was anything to go by.

At one point, he went into her bedroom and closed the door. Amelia didn't know what he did in there when it got so quiet, but she figured she probably didn't want to. Taking her e-pad with her, she left the apartment and ducked into her green room.

The fertilizer she'd gotten from Millie was working like a charm. Everything was bursting with life, growing so fast, the place was well on its way to becoming the jungle Amelia wanted it to be. She still didn't have her chaise. Instead, she'd dragged a small mattress to the palm trees for the time being.

She took a short walk around to check on every plant, then went to the windows and turned her face up to the sun. There was no music playing today. She wanted to be able to hear Gabriel in case something went wrong. The e-pad screen showed everything in order with his biology, so she relaxed a little. If anything had been wrong with the first injection, she'd have known by now.

A small rustle of movement had her spinning around to look for the intruder. Behind the giant fern, crouching in shadow, Gabriel was watching her. He stood when she spotted him and stalked toward her, holding her gaze. His eyes were different. The rich chocolate brown was fading. The way he moved was different, too; his feet made no sound on the floor, and though he brushed against the plants, his gait was so fluid they didn't rustle.

Amelia stood still as he approached her, coming toe to toe with her. Gabriel searched her gaze, then slowly lowered his head to her neck and breathed in deep. She shivered. "I can smell you," he said, his breath hot on her skin. "You're everywhere here. Sweet." His nose nudged into her hair. "Enticing." His tongue touched her ear, just barely. "You're like a lure I want to follow, even though I know it's a trap."

The rumble of his deep voice made heat coil low in her belly and her hands curl at her sides. She licked her lips to bring some moisture to them, and his light brown eyes snared on the action, waiting for her to do it again.

She did. Gabriel pounced so fast she jerked back, but the window pane was right there to stop her. He crowded her against it, held her still as he delved into her mouth, chasing her tongue's retreat. The way he kissed her—*Sweet God*—it wasn't a kiss at all. He licked into her mouth, tasting her, feasting, gorging himself like she was his favorite dessert and he couldn't get enough of her. His fingers dug into her arms painfully, and Amelia gave a cry.

Gabriel shoved himself away with a snarl, shaking his head sharply as if to dislodge a bad memory. His hands curled in his hair so hard the skin was pulled taut over his forehead, his eyebrows high. Amelia rubbed her sore arms, off balance and grateful for the window at her back. "It's the changes starting," she explained, watching his chest expand with massive breaths.

"I feel it," he said, eyes squeezed shut, jaw clenched. His entire body quaked with the strain of standing still. He was still hard, and even without animal senses, Amelia could tell how much effort it took to keep his distance from her, how much he wanted *not* to. "It's like I'm losing control. Can't think. Burning up." His hands dropped to his sides, leaving his hair a mess. But he brought them up again in front of him, watching as he curled his fingers into tight fists and straightened them out again repeatedly. "My hands aren't my own," he said.

"It'll probably get worse before it gets any better."

"Tell me."

Gabriel's pale eyes were almost desperate when he turned them briefly on her. He looked away again with a sharp inhale as if the mere sight of her was pushing his limits. He needed a distraction. "Think of it as the panther being born inside you. It's still young, unsure, testing its limits. It'll be part of you. You can't fight it. The more you try, the more it'll fight back. I think what you need to do is… teach it." That sounded so awkwardly lame. "Maybe not 'teach it' in the usual sense, but accept it, and give it room of its own." *Not much better.*

Bah! She felt all of eighteen years old again, standing in front of a class, trying to explain something she herself didn't understand.

Frustrated with her inability to do a better job of it, she let out a tense breath. "Okay, let me think this through a little before I say something stupid."

Gabriel's mouth quirked at that. A good sign.

"You're adding something to yourself that shouldn't belong. It's not going to be easy, or comfortable, but there's no going back now that the process has begun. All I can tell you is that you need to strike a balance between accepting the animal inside you, without losing yourself to it. Does that make sense?"

"Perfectly."

That didn't make her feel any better.

"I have to learn to be myself and something else at the same time. No big deal."

"A bit late for sarcasm now, don't you think?" she retorted.

"It's never a bad time for sarcasm." In spite of his crappy mood, he looked better already. There was still tension in his posture, but his breathing had evened out and his features were more relaxed. He glanced at her again, testing himself. "When is the next injection scheduled?"

Amelia checked her watch. "In a few hours. You should try to get some sleep."

Gabriel snorted. "Right. Have you ever slept while being invaded by a foreign consciousness?"

She bit back a smile. "Can't say I have."

With a bracing breath, he shook his head. "Can't shut down now. Need to keep my mind working."

"What do you want to do, then?" It was a safe guess he wouldn't resume his out of the blue sexual attack. Intercourse wasn't exactly an intellectual exercise. Well, she'd have to live with that.

"What I *want* to do?" he repeated with strained amusement. "Is throw you down on that mat and rip your clothes off with my teeth. What I *want* is to taste every inch of your skin, put my head between your legs and lick you for hours. Put you on your hands and knees and fuck you so hard, you won't be able to walk straight for days."

Amelia didn't have time to shiver before he was in her face again. His voice dropped lower, like a rumbling purr that made the muscles in her belly tighten and her hands curl at her sides. "And I want to make you come around me so many times, you won't be able to look at me again without thinking about it."

He nuzzled in her hair, bracing his hands on the glass on either side of her. Inhaling deeply, he tensed again. "Ah," he said on an exhale, and his eyes glowed. "You like that idea."

Amelia nodded with an awkward jerk of her chin. Her tongue darted out once more to nervously moisten her lips. Her heart was racing in anticipation, and it was all she could do to keep her breathing even. She had no idea what might set him off. He said it himself, he wasn't in control. It was a dangerous situation to be in. And still she grew wet for him, her hands itching to bury in his hair and tug him down for another one of those wild kisses.

Gabriel groaned. "You don't know what that does to me."

She had a pretty good idea!

"So you need to distract me."

There were a lot of things Gabriel might have expected from this change. Internal injuries galore, new shape to change into whenever he needed it, heightened strength and speed, possibly aggression, too. But he hadn't expected this insane sensory overload. He could hear Amelia's heart beating like a drum. Her breath was like ocean waves. He could smell the faint underlying nuances of her unique scent, separated into thousands of components swirling in his nostrils. When he touched her—hell, when he touched *anything*—it was like feeling it for the first time. Gabriel could *taste* the plants here, and the moist earth. And his sight… there were no words to describe it.

His thoughts were different, too. It felt like his brain was being partitioned like a computer hard drive. The border between the two parts was tentative, fragile at best. Just enough to let him know there was something new and foreign present, but not enough to actually keep it separate. Its influence was complete. He'd said his hands weren't his own. His mind didn't feel like his own, either.

There were no voices to intrude on his thoughts, no separate consciousness he could discern. There was only a heightened awareness of everything around him, as if he'd never encountered any of it before.

Curiosity about every little thing made him itchy and restless. It pulled him in a hundred different directions at the same time.

Yes, he needed a distraction.

"Tell me how you came to work for the government."

Amelia tensed instantly. "I was recruited."

"And was it everything they promised it would be?"

She shifted her weight, eyeing the door past his shoulder. "Do we have to talk about this now?" Gabriel knew she'd give anything to not discuss her past. He sensed her need to flee from it, and him. She'd been running from it long enough.

"Was it?" he persisted.

"What does it matter now? I'm out. End of story."

"Ah, angel, when it comes to you, I'm curious as a cat." It was true. All of the other wonders in this new, bright, and shiny world he was discovering paled in comparison to the mystery standing before him, wrapped in silken skin and golden hair, skittish as a foal to get out of his reach.

"Curiosity killed the cat," she said archly.

"Good thing felines have nine lives. I'm willing to give one for you."

She reached up, probably to adjust her glasses, but her arm got stuck with her elbow at the window and her hand at his chest. Before she could pull it away, Gabriel captured it with his own. She fought him, plainly uncomfortable. Not with his nearness—he'd all but cured her of that with repeated exposure—but with the topic of conversation. "I don't see how any of that is relevant now."

"Indulge me."

Amelia glared. "Haven't I been indulging you enough lately?"

Gabriel grinned. "Not nearly." He leaned in closer, brushing his nose against hers. "So?"

She closed her eyes and sighed in exasperation. "It wasn't exactly the career highlight I hoped for."

"Go on."

"I was…" She looked around, anywhere but at him. "I was hired to do research. On the effects of chem-treatments and the reason why people are becoming resistant to them. At first it was only statistical analyses, drawing conclusions from data other researchers have gathered. Every once in a while I'd have access to a lab to do some studies of my own, but nothing major."

"They wanted you to prove yourself."

"No," she said dryly. "They wanted me to prove I could do what I was told and keep my mouth shut about it. See, that's the thing about the way the government operates. They don't order, they give *suggestions*. One day a man with a friendly smile comes in carrying a briefcase of money, tells you your efforts have been noted and the higher ups want to reward progress and developing talent. Spins a pretty story about how you're free to use the funds for anything you might require. And he'll be sure to tell you it's perfectly acceptable to branch out into other areas of interest. Like, say, human physiology and what effects certain things have on it."

"Suggestions," Gabriel said. "And what happens if you choose not to take them?"

Amelia smiled bitterly. "Every once in a while they request progress reports on your work. If they don't see what they want, you get a subtle hint that maybe the reason your research is hitting a dead end is because you haven't considered the effects of sleep deprivation or certain toxic cocktails on human physiology. And if you still don't fall in line, they stop playing nice."

Her gaze dropped, and she slumped a little against the glass. The sheer misery emanating from her made Gabriel want to growl. "I've seen good scientists, geniuses, the kind of people willing and able to take on the task of saving the world, get blamed for… horrible things. Planted evidence, quick private trials with a jury on government payroll. Some of those people I've never heard from again." She frowned. "They were my friends."

Gabriel gritted his teeth. There was hurt in her, running deep, and far back. She'd lost people close to her the same way he had. Only less bloody. Gabriel had seen those he cared about get tortured and executed. But Amelia never knew what had happened to her friends. She'd had to go on, burdened by the suspicion they might still be alive somewhere, held prisoner, suffering. It looked like that suspicion never left her, though on some level she had to know those people were long dead.

"You are a strong woman, Amelia." To have lived with the threat of death hanging over her head and come out the better for it.

She met his gaze. "You don't get it. *They* were the strong ones. They stood their ground and fought against what was wrong. All I ever did was what I was told." Her eyes squeezed shut again. "And the things I've done…" In a whisper almost too soft for him to hear, she finished, "Even made the Shadows take notice." Gabriel's eyebrows twitched down into a frown at that.

Shadow? She couldn't mean the soldiers… Gabriel had had a run-in with them once before. When a guy in a midnight blue uniform had shown up to shake his hand after a fight, Gabriel had had the shock of his life, discovering the secret army everyone whispered about as urban legends were actually real. For a couple of days after, he'd almost expected the soldier to come knocking on his door to recruit him.

To his surprise, the knock had come. But it had been a representative of Rome at the door. And he hadn't come for Gabriel.

When Amelia opened her eyes again, they were haunted.

"How did you get out?" he asked to bring her back to their conversation. Dwelling on past horrors helped no one. He didn't want her thinking about the time she'd been at her weakest; he wanted her to remember how strong it had made her become.

Amelia straightened her shoulders and raised her chin, and suddenly she was herself again, as if that little action, standing straight was all it took to shake off the bad memories, push them back for the time being. When she answered, her voice was once again cool and controlled, as if nothing had happened. As if he was a stranger asking what time it was.

"Ironically, with the very research they were paying me to conduct. One of my subjects survived the introduction of animal DNA into his system. I put in for a transfer under the pretext of requiring a different environment to further develop the study. It was enough physical and professional distance that I was allowed to abandon all my other projects. When Tristan later died, the study died with him, and they had no more use for me. I ran like hell and never looked back."

Her tone said she was done talking about this. Gabriel wouldn't get any more out of her now. He pushed himself away, enough to give her some breathing room. Enough that she could slip past him if she wanted.

Instead, she blinked up at him. "Hey, you want to see something amazing?"

Gabriel raised an eyebrow. "Are you going to get naked?" He *definitely* wanted to see that. Especially if she did it slow. Possibly to music.

She gave him a look that clearly questioned how he'd managed to crawl out of the primordial goop. "Come on." Taking his hand, she slipped around him and pulled him out toward the front door.

"Uh, where are you going?"

Amelia grinned at him over her shoulder. "Trust me," she said.

The door was locked. Her password and biometrics wouldn't work; Gabriel had reprogrammed the security after Honoria's little visit. Nothing and no one was passing through the door in either direction until he deemed it was safe. Of course, Amelia, being who she was, tried anyway, and her shoulders slumped in defeat when the door still wouldn't budge.

"I don't know whether to kick the door or you."

Gabriel took pity on her. He nudged her aside and hacked the system from the small console. It wasn't as easy as he made it look to open the door. He gave them one way out and back in again. The only way he could be sure they wouldn't walk in on a nasty surprise. If they came back and the door didn't open, they'd know someone had gotten inside. And that someone would not be getting back out again.

The door opened, and he ushered Amelia through it. Just like the first day, she led the way out of the neighborhood and into the chaos of the international district. Like then, he caught her hand to keep her close.

Fuck. The hypersenses were bad in Amelia's apartment, but a thousand times worse out here. It was like getting punched by giant fists from all sides. The noise deafened him; the scents confused the ever-living hell out of him. He couldn't scent Amelia anymore, and she was right in front of him!

So many people yelling, and shoving, and waving foreign things right in his face… He nearly punched some guy who shoved a reeking bowl of goop right under his nose. Amelia pulled him away before they caused a scene.

They made their way through the crowds at a snail's pace while Gabriel ground his teeth and focused on Amelia's back to keep from lashing out at strangers. It was the most agonizing half hour of his life, at the end of which they emerged on a street with deadlocked traffic. Transports hovered in place, having nowhere to move. Gabriel had no clue how long they'd already been waiting there, or how long before they could go on. It looked to him like they were all just parked and the people had forgotten to get out.

"And this is why we walked," Amelia told him. She led the way again, weaving between the transports to get to the other side of the street. The traffic eased the farther they got until they were in a neighborhood as seemingly abandoned as Amelia's. The houses were different here. Not older, exactly, but old-fashioned. Amelia slowed their pace to a stroll, linked her arm with his, smiling up at him mysteriously.

"What have you got up your sleeve?"

She grinned. "You'll see."

The neighborhood ended abruptly, as did the path. It was a dead end, like a border drawn on the ground. Gabriel could imagine a single road circling the colony and everyone inside going about their business, but no one ever touching that boundary. Beyond the pavement was nothing. Dried grass, a boulder here and there. For a couple hundred yards it looked like a wasteland, and then the ground gave way sharply.

Amelia led him to the edge of the cliff and pointed. "Look."

Gabriel's eyes widened. He was gazing out at a completely different world. It was at least a thousand-foot drop from the edge of the cliff down to the valley, but what he wouldn't give to be able to jump off and glide across the land.

It was wilderness. Untouched, untamed, a forest at his feet, spreading hundreds of miles in every direction. He could see the glint of a waterfall in the distance. There were birds of prey circling high above, hiding among the clouds. With his enhanced senses, Gabriel could hear creatures far below him, so many he'd never be able to count them.

He could see the trees… glitter. Gabriel squinted. That wasn't right. But it was. The leaves, plants, flowers—all of it glittered as if it was artificial, and yet he could scent that it was all real.

"The entire valley is a massive crater," Amelia said. "Minerals in the soil affect everything that grows here; they soak into plants and alter them somehow. Things grow bigger, more beautiful, but as soon as they're disturbed, they wilt and die. It's like a giant, living jewel box. You won't find another place like it anywhere in the universe. It's the biggest national park on this planet, completely cut off from civilization, and no one is allowed down there without permission. No camping, no fires, no hunting, fishing, or foraging."

An eagle's cry echoed as the bird swooped down as if in free fall, disappearing into the tree canopy. Gabriel heard it catch something, and a moment later it emerged with its prey secured, flying off.

"Miramar doesn't have much in the way of attractions. There are cities, jobs, people, and whatever they decide to build to entertain themselves. But it has this." She said it with pride.

"Is that why you live here?"

"That, and other reasons."

"Which are…"

"Many and varied and not up for discussion," she said and smiled. "Why are you so nosy?"

"Never met a woman so disinclined to talk about herself before." Gabriel tugged her down to sit close to the edge of the cliff. Safer than standing where a strong breeze could knock her off balance. He settled her into the circle of his arms so both of them still had a perfect view of the park.

"Hmm, let's see… something about me. I was born not far from here. I have a younger sister. You've seen her."

Gabriel winced at the subtle reprimand.

"Our parents divorced when I was young, and our mom died a couple of years after that."

"That must have been difficult."

She shrugged. "We got through it. Now tell me about you."

"Me? What's there to tell?"

"Gee, I don't know," she said dryly. "How about where you grew up or what you studied in school? Or, hey, here's a good one: How did you get into Rome?"

"I was recruited," he said, repeating her earlier words.

"And was it everything they'd promised it would be?"

"Touché." He should have known better than to rehash that conversation.

"Well?"

"It was worse."

Amelia tugged his arm tighter around her, and he pulled her closer on reflex. It felt good to hold her. And not having to look into her eyes made the words easier to say. Still, he kept the details to himself. "The most insidious thing about Rome is that it's completely voluntary. They make damn sure all their legal ducks are in a row. The recruiters paint a pretty picture of the city; show you Rome at its best. They don't lie; that would be against the law. They tell you the parts you want to hear until you get the impression it's all an elaborate game of pretend. By the time they get around to asking for a signature, you don't even want to read the fine print."

"What's the city like?"

Gabriel didn't have the right words to describe it. "Hot and cold at the same time. It's almost like a desert, except for some oases scattered around. If you stand on the sand with your bare feet, they'll burn. But you look into the people's eyes and you feel like your blood is freezing in your veins. The Patricians… most of them are dead inside. No souls, just greed and malice. You can see it in them. Hear it in their voices."

"What about the actors?"

Gabriel squeezed his eyes shut and nuzzled in her hair. He didn't want to think about the actors. He'd had his fill of terrified expressions, people flinching whenever someone came too close, people beaten and left for dead like so much garbage in the streets. Men with thousand-yard stares, broken by what they'd seen and done. By what had been done to them. Women weeping behind their veils where no one would see; branded, disfigured so they were forever tied to their masters.

"Let it go, angel," he replied. "Some things are better left unsaid."

He could sense her growing agitation. "You don't have to protect me, you know."

Gabriel smiled and stood, pulling her up with him. "How do you know that's not exactly what I'm supposed to do?"

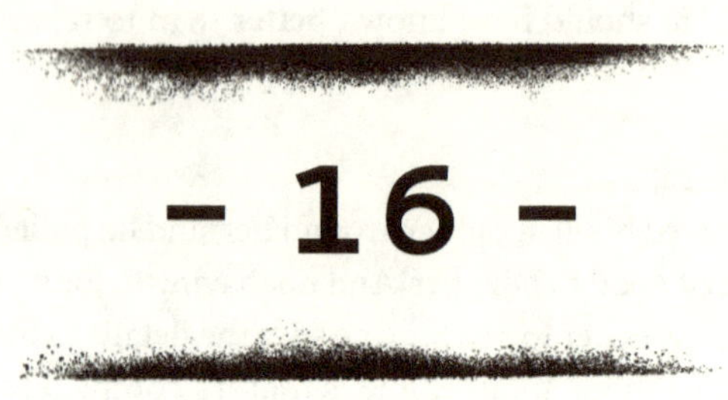

– 16 –

September 29, 3032

"It's time." It was almost a relief to say the words. Amelia was so on edge, loud noises made her jumpy. And the day had started out so well. She'd woken up snuggled so close to Gabriel they'd almost been one being, and she'd never been so comfortable in her life.

But it had gone downhill from there. The closer they got to second injection time, the more tense they were. Even watching a movie didn't help. For the last hour or so they couldn't even look at each other. Paradoxically, now that the wait was finally over, they weren't exactly jumping for joy, either.

Gabriel dragged his feet to the exam chair and sat down like he was sulking. He didn't lock himself in this time, just sat there staring balefully at the tray of syringes. His eyes were back to normal, at least. Thank God for that. He wouldn't be permanently affected like Hailey.

Amelia smiled. "How are we doing?"

"You tell me."

"Well, the regenerative serum is working after the first introduction of the virus. You're about halfway there. And you're still alive." She tilted her head. "I thought you'd be more excited."

"Excited? Sure. You're destroying my human nature so I can go on a killing spree. What's not to be excited about?"

Amelia frowned. "You—"

"Will you stop saying I chose this?" Gabriel speared his hands into his hair. "I remember, okay? I was there."

"Have you changed your mind?" she asked softly. Nothing would make her happier than to stop this right here and now. Except it was one injection too late to go back to the way he used to be. She'd never arrested treatment midway before. Finishing it might kill him, but stopping now and leaving a DNA strand destabilized definitely would.

Gabriel dropped his hands onto the armrests and met her gaze. She waited for him to make up his mind, careful not to betray her thoughts. She made herself breathe under his scrutiny, not wanting to influence his decision either way. *If he asks me what to do...* She would have no idea what to tell him, was afraid she'd say something wrong and make everything worse.

"No," he finally said, and her heart broke a little. "No, I haven't. Too late now to go back anyway, right?"

Amelia dropped her gaze to the syringe tray. "Right."

"Right. Have to see this through."

She gave an infinitesimal nod and picked up the second virus injection. Only one left after this. And then he'd be gone forever. No more obnoxiously loud music, no more ruined supplies and equipment. No more life-changing sex and being held all through the night.

Game face on. Can't afford mistakes.

Amelia squared her shoulders and brought the syringe to Gabriel's side.

"Hey," he said, catching her hand. "Look at me."

Somehow, she did.

"Whatever happens, I want you to know none of it was your fault. You didn't do anything I didn't ask for."

"And you think that makes a difference?"

Gabriel released her. "It should. I wouldn't have traded this time for anything. Whatever price I have to pay because of it, I'll pay it gladly."

You'll pay with your life!

Couldn't he see it? Didn't it matter to him one bit that he would die? It made her so mad how little regard he had for his own life. Like he had absolutely nothing to lose. Like there was no one he'd be leaving behind.

Amelia shook herself. "Kiss for good luck?"

"No," he said. "Just a kiss."

She leaned in and Gabriel met her halfway for a kiss that somehow felt like goodbye. He was gentle, coaxing, and so perfectly under control, he was a completely different man from the one who'd had her trapped in the greenhouse yesterday, demanding answers.

Amelia bit.

"Ow!"

"If you're going to kiss me," she said, "do it right." And before he could say anything, she kissed him with everything she had, clutching his hair. Finally, he went along with the program, cupping her nape to hold her close as he took over.

The computer started beeping, dragging her out of the pleasure haze. Amelia broke away, leaned her forehead against Gabriel's.

"What is that?" he asked, sifting his fingers through her hair.

"It's a timer," she said, taking hold of his arm to find a vein. "The safest time to administer the injection is until the beeping stops. You ready?"

"As I'll ever be."

It took less than a second to inject him, and the moment Amelia pulled out the needle, the beeping stopped.

"So what happens now?"

A sonic boom shook the building and the lab plunged into complete darkness. Lights, computers, coms, anything electronic was down, including the emergency systems. Amelia blindly reached out to Gabriel. She could hear him moving; he wasn't in the chair anymore. "Gabriel?"

His arm slid around her from behind, pulling her into his chest. "Stay still and quiet," he said, maneuvering her around. She had no sense of direction in the absolute darkness and any sort of movement threw her off balance. Gabriel steadied her and pushed her to crouch in a corner somewhere. "Don't budge until I tell you. Got it?"

Amelia nodded. "Yes," she said. "What's going on?"

"I'm going to find out." More movement. "By the way, this night vision thing? Pretty fucking awesome."

Amelia chuckled, but her heart wasn't in it. She wasn't exactly scared of the dark, just the things that went bump in it. And this was looking to be one big, giant bump.

As if on cue, something big went *thud*. There was a distinct grunt and sounds of fighting, then silence. "Gabriel?"

Nothing.

More fighting, and this time there was a loud crash. Amelia winced and covered her ears, hoping it wasn't her new DNA code breaker that just got smashed. Someone gave a shout, and then there were more sounds, more people, and what she imagined to be fists flying left and right. "Don't let him get away!" someone yelled.

"Get the lights back on!"

"Hold him—*umph*."

"Gabriel!" she called again, as loud as she could to make herself heard.

"Get the woman!"

Amelia slapped a hand over her mouth. *So stupid!*

Gabriel gave a savage roar, and the fighting intensified. It was closer, too. Something huge got shoved out of the way, and then it sounded like they were right on top of her. Amelia covered her head, making herself as small as possible.

"Get the fucking lights!"

"Got him!"

Oh, God, what happened?

When the lights came on, she had to squint through the brightness. There were five huge men in her lab. One was on the floor bleeding, two held Gabriel between them like they were holding on to a tree. There wasn't a single face unmarred or unbloodied. Gabriel's head was down; was he unconscious?

One of the men still standing stomped across the broken implements all over the floor to get to her, glass crunching in his wake. Amelia screamed when he grabbed her and hauled her up so high, her feet dangled a good couple of inches off the floor.

The sound roused Gabriel, and he raised his head. Amelia swallowed a giant lump. His left eye was swollen shut, and his right eyebrow was cut and bleeding freely. He had to squint and blink to keep the blood from his eye. His cheek was bruised and his lip busted. *Jesus,* did they hit him with a sledge hammer?

"All this trouble for one little whore," the one who held her muttered.

Amelia dragged her gaze away from Gabriel to look at her captor.

"Still," he said, leering, "she's got potential."

Gabriel struggled against the two holding him. By their oaths, she could tell he almost got away from them. Smartly, he kept his mouth shut.

Amelia took strength from him. She drew back her head as far as she could and snapped it forward, butting her forehead against the guy's bulbous nose. The loud crunch of bone wasn't nearly satisfying enough to make up for the splitting headache she gave herself.

But he did let her go. With a savage oath, he reared back and dropped her. Amelia found her feet too late. Her knees buckled, and she dropped unceremoniously on her ass. And *ow!* Now she hurt at both ends.

Gabriel smiled as much as his busted lip would allow. "That's my girl."

That earned him a vicious punch in the stomach, and he doubled over again.

Brokenose came after her. Amelia scooted back, slipping more than actually moving. He was reaching for her again when heretofore silent Intruder Number 5 barked, "Enough! The Caesar wants them alive."

Brokenose did not take that well. He bared his bloody teeth at Amelia, his eyes promising retribution somewhere down the line.

She did the stupidest thing she could: opened her mouth. "I could set that for you," she said. "I think I've got a hammer or a shovel around here somewhere."

Brokenose leaned over her, blood and spittle dripping from his chin onto her. "You think you're so clever? You just wait. The Caesar will tire of you soon enough. And then you're all mine."

"Marek!" the apparent boss snapped.

Like a temperamental dog, Brokenose snarled and straightened, turning to face his master.

"Pick up Lars and clear out." He had the airs of a general. The guy was built like a tank, hardly a neck to his name, but he stood at ease with his giant arms loosely behind his back. He was missing an eye, but the one he had left was as cold as ice. This one wouldn't blink at ripping a child's head off.

Amelia had seen his type before. Her stint in New Alaska had been nothing if not an eye-opening education about the human character. The Marek person was a loose cannon. Easily provoked and easily defeated with his own temper. But this guy was smart, and he was calculating. He was the type who'd wait until his enemies were asleep, and then sneak into their bedrooms and disembowel them before they could call out for help. And he'd probably enjoy doing it.

"You two," he said to the ones holding Gabriel, "hold him up."

One of the henchmen adjusted his hold to free an arm, and then raised Gabriel's chin for the general guy to slap him. Amelia pushed to her feet, frantically looking for a weapon of some kind. Everything was a mess. Her implements were all over the floor and out of reach. The only thing close by was Gabriel's last injection and the now empty syringe. She swiped both off the tray and pocketed them, then picked up the tray itself. It wasn't much, and it wouldn't do enough damage to stop these guys, but it might slow one down a little. Maybe.

As if he'd read her thoughts, the general turned on her and narrowed his eye at the tray. "Feeble, Doctor. Hardly worth my attention."

"And yet you take the time to tell me that? I think I'll keep this at hand."

He chuckled. "Be my guest." Then he dismissed her and turned back to Gabriel. Marek was already gone with his fallen comrade, so there were only three now, blocking her way out. And they still had Gabriel hostage. Beaten, but she could already see signs of recovery. If the general noticed, too, they were screwed.

The man slapped Gabriel again, rousing him. "Ah, welcome back," he said.

"Hey… Soren," Gabriel mumbled. "Long time. You still alive?"

"And doing quite well, thank you for asking."

"Ah, that's a shame."

"Why are you here?" Amelia demanded. "The Caesar said he still has time to come back."

"The Caesar changed her mind," Soren said without looking away from Gabriel. "Her *Gladius*"—from his tone, he knew exactly what the word meant and enjoyed throwing it in Gabriel's face—"is to report to the arena day after tomorrow, rain or shine. He's going to be the main attraction." He turned to her to add with a smile, "She was nonspecific as to his condition."

"Are you willing to bet your neck… uh, your life on that?" Amelia challenged.

Soren raised his eyebrows. Or tried to. The scar bisecting his eye must have damaged a muscle on one side, so that eyebrow came up only part of the way, and crookedly. "Your girl's got guts," he said to Gabriel. "You should talk to her about that. It's gonna get her killed one day soon."

"She's smart, too," Gabriel said. "Smart enough that she could have gotten out of here by now if she wanted to." He glared at her in reproach.

Amelia shrugged.

Soren looked at her, then back at Gabriel. "We'll take them both," he announced. "I don't know what the hell is going on here, but I have no doubt the Caesar will want to know about it." He jerked his head toward the door, and his henchmen dragged Gabriel kicking and fighting outside. Then, like some perverted version of a gentleman, he inclined his head to Amelia and motioned her forward. "After you, Doctor."

"I'm guessing that's the easy way."

"I prefer to think so."

She wasn't about to risk the hard way. Not with this guy. "Are you on good terms with the Caesar?" she asked, edging forward.

"Quite good."

"And Gabriel is her Champion." Another small step.

"Indeed."

She nodded. "I suppose she values the both of you quite highly." She was next to him now and he wasn't jumping her. A good sign.

"What are you getting at?"

Amelia shrugged. "I'm only thinking out loud. Because if she does value her assets, it would make sense she'd arrange first class transport for them." And she preceded him out the door.

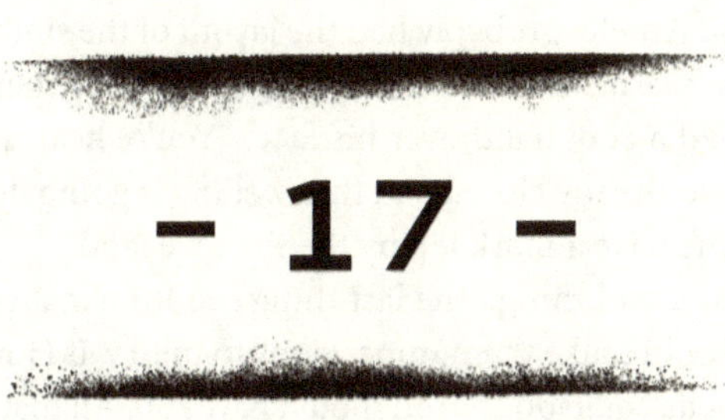

– 17 –

They trussed him up with thick ropes, hands tied to his feet behind his back. For all that the queen bitch had contracted a private shuttle to transport them all back, Gabriel was on the floor, having fallen off the seat during takeoff. He fucking hated Romans. They were so damn cocksure there was no way Gabriel could escape, they left him and Amelia alone in their cabin. Then again, it wasn't like they had anywhere to run. Plus, he was pretty sure they were being monitored constantly. A suspicion Amelia confirmed by subtly inclining her head toward the starboard corner.

"You could have gotten out," he said.

"Yeah? And how exactly did you see that going in your mind? I run past the four massive behemoths blocking the only way in or out, make it to the street where no one ever stops for a red light, and what? Yell for help before they catch up to me?"

She had a point. Damn it! He should have thought this through. They'd used an electromagnetic pulse strong enough to rattle the building. Which meant if Amelia had somehow managed to get away, she'd probably have had to run a mile to find a working transport.

Amelia sighed and slid off her seat to sit on the floor with him. "Guess we're in trouble, huh?"

Gabriel snorted. "They haven't invented a word strong enough for what we're in."

"Oh, I don't know. I could think of a few choice ones."

He grinned despite himself. At least she wasn't freaking out. Ever the cool scientist. Amelia probably had the layout of the shuttle, number of people on board, and how many weapons each of them carried.

She brushed a cool hand over his face. "You're healing," she said. "The cuts have already closed and the swelling is going down. At this rate, you won't have a mark left by the time we land."

Which was a bad thing. The last thing the Romans needed was a serum that could make them impervious to injury. If Honoria found out what Amelia could do… "You should have run. All that technology, don't tell me you don't have some kind of panic room in that place."

"I do, actually," she said. "It was disabled the moment they shut the building down. Although, truth be told, I didn't even think about it until now."

Brilliant.

"Every last failsafe and security measure I engineered failed miserably, and all it took was one man and an EMP," she grumbled. "I'm beginning to think I'm not as smart as I thought."

"You? Never." Amelia was a scientist, not a strategist. Her defenses might have failed, but he had complete faith in her ability to think their way out of this. "Your superior intellect must have decided the challenge wasn't worthy of it, so you subconsciously sabotaged the game to show off what you're really capable of."

The look Amelia gave him could have frozen the sun. But all she said was, "Here, let me try the ties again." She leaned over him, prying at the thick ropes. She'd worked her fingers raw once already and couldn't budge them. "Nope, not coming loose." She sat back on her heels with a frustrated sigh.

"I'll live." At least until they dumped him into the arena. Then he couldn't make any more promises.

Amelia glanced at the recorder and met his gaze. She dragged him up to sit on his heels. Not an ideal position, but better than lying on his side. His shoulder ached and his entire arm had already gone numb. When he was steady, she slipped a hand into her pocket and pulled out a syringe. *The* syringe. The last injection.

He couldn't believe she had it. In all the chaos, Gabriel had completely forgotten about that. "How long before you need to use that?"

he asked, keeping his voice down.

She looked at it, then met his gaze. The brilliant blues were filled with regret. "I'm sorry," she whispered.

Right before she jabbed the needle into his arm.

Gabriel groaned and leaned back against the seat. Fire spread through his veins, burning him from the arm up to his skull. His vision darkened as if he was about to pass out, and he doubled over as far as his bound arms would let him.

"I'm sorry," she whispered again, catching him so his forehead leaned on her shoulder. It brought her mouth to his ear. "It's a huge risk, and I have no idea what this will do to you. But I know what will happen if they find the shot and take it."

Christ, he was on fire! Muscles contracted in spasms he couldn't control, breath locked up somewhere between his throat and his lungs, not going up or down. He felt his heart drumming up a storm, so hard his insides quivered with each beat. His arms down to the tips of his fingers cramped, threatening to break his bones, and his abs tightened so much he could feel them tearing.

And that was just the beginning.

Amelia was talking to him softly. He had no idea what she was saying, but past the ringing in his ears, her voice comforted him. Not enough to stop the process. The ropes bit into his wrists and ankles, blood welled in the wounds, and still the fucking things didn't budge a fraction of an inch. His head pounded like his brain was trying to push his skull out. Any minute, his eyes would pop out of their sockets.

Then his face felt like it exploded. The pain was indescribable. Sharp pops surrounded by dull aches so intense, he wanted to cut his own head off to stop it. He felt his face change shape. His nose flattened, upper and lower jaws expanded; he felt himself snarl, and his upper lip split.

Some miniscule remnant of self-preservation made him fight back. Somehow, Gabriel willed his face to change back, though it felt like ramming his head against the wall again and again. He bowed his back, forcing his airways to open so he could breathe. Once he could get air into his lungs, some of the pain eased. Like working out a Charlie horse, his body let go of the tension slowly, by sharp degrees, and left him boneless, weak, and gasping for breath.

He was still leaning on Amelia. Even that contact hurt his bruised flesh, but he didn't have the strength to stay upright on his own. In his mind, the panther stretched and yawned, arrogant and self-assured. Gabriel could already tell it'd be a pain in the ass. "It worked." Holy shit, *it worked!* And he was still alive!

Sort of…

Someone burst in the door, pulled him and Amelia apart. Without her support, Gabriel dropped to the floor again, groaning at the impact. He couldn't see a damn thing. His eyes were swollen shut, and his nose whistled when he breathed.

"What the fuck is going on?" Marek demanded. Soren must have sent him.

"Get your hands off me," Amelia yelled. Gabriel could hear her struggling.

He pried an eye open to see what was going on. Just in time to see Marek's paddle-sized hand slap Amelia across the cheek. Her glasses went flying, and Marek closed his hand on her throat and lifted her up almost off the floor.

"Let her go!" Gabriel shouted, pain splitting in his upper jaw and nose. The panther raised its head, showing a modicum of interest in what it saw as sport. It was freaky. Especially because it kicked the healing into gear. He could open his eyes again.

Amelia was struggling in Marek's grip, clawing at the massive hand at her throat. Her face was going red. "Marek! You son of a whore, I'll kill you for this!"

Something glittered in Amelia's hand a split second before she jabbed it into Marek's throat. The bulldog of a man dropped her and stumbled backwards, yanking the syringe out of his jugular. It dropped out of his hand as his knees gave out, and he crumbled to the floor like an overstuffed puppet.

Amelia coughed and wheezed, feeling along the floor for her glasses. Relief washed over Gabriel when she found them and put them on, leaning back to catch her breath. "I'm discovering I hate being choked," she wheezed.

Soren appeared in the doorway. Impassive as ever, he looked over

Gabriel and Amelia, glanced at Marek's still form, and walked away. The bastard left Marek's body there like he couldn't be bothered to care.

"Will he be back?" Amelia asked, wincing. She didn't have her supplies now. Her neck was already bruising and swollen, and her throat was probably as sore as hell and would be for a while.

"No," Gabriel said, hating to hell this being completely helpless shit. He couldn't gather enough energy to try to loosen the ropes binding him. "Check Marek for weapons."

Putting near death experience at the top of the Sucks Major Stinking Ass list. Amelia knee-walked to the dead-weight bastard with the IQ of a rabid carrot. He'd fallen face-first, and she had to turn him over to get to his pockets. He weighed at least a ton, and after holding up Gabriel and getting the fear choked out of her, it took her a while to get it done.

Marek was as ugly dead as he'd been alive. Her face still throbbed where he'd hit her, and it pissed her off. Amelia drew back and slapped the dead weight across his disgusting face as hard as she could. Son of a bitch almost broke her glasses.

"He's dead, angel," Gabriel said. He had a tender smile on his face, like he was proud of her and amused at the same time.

"Yeah, well, I'm still pissed. So sue me." She rooted through his pockets but found nothing of use. Just a pack of matches and some strange-looking coins. "How are you doing?" she asked Gabriel. For a moment there, while he'd been changing, she feared he'd be dead for sure. It was a miracle he lived through it.

"Not bad, considering I feel like I want to die."

Amelia turned to stare at him. "Don't ever say that, not even as a joke."

He nodded solemnly. "Fair enough. You got anything?"

"No." She blew out a frustrated sigh and went back to Gabriel. "So this Soren guy. Sends a man to check on the prisoners, lets him die, and then leaves him where he fell."

"Yep."

"Hmm."

"Just the type of guy he is."

And she'd bet Rome was full of people just like him. She couldn't wait to meet them all.

So much for her quiet, normal life. Amelia had been so sure, once the mess with Hailey was taken care of, she'd get to enjoy her life, worry-free. Well, not completely worry-free. Her sister was a shape-shifter, after all, and her new brother-in-law could read minds. She shuddered to think what their children would be like.

Just went to show all good plans eventually hit a great big brick wall.

Amelia eyed the dead Marek. He'd be getting really gross soon. *Almost like old times.* Another dead body in front of her. Cause of death: Amelia Marguerite Chase. And here she was without her menthol rub. She couldn't bring herself to regret her actions this time. She only wished she'd gotten a few good hits in *before* he'd hit the ground without a pulse.

"All right. Seeing as how I'm about to take a grand tour of Rome, you might want to tell me a little more about it."

Gabriel swore. "I'm so sorry, Amelia."

She waved that aside. Sorry wouldn't help her. If she was going to survive in a place so far out of her area of expertise, she'd need all the help she could get. *Just another assignment.* She'd get through it. She'd learn and adapt, and at some point, she'd find a way out like she always did, and maybe then the universe would finally get off her back and let her live out the rest of her life in relative peace.

Gabriel looked so pathetic lying there all tied up, she took pity on him and righted him again. With his help, she maneuvered him so he could lean against the seats since he was still weak from his partial shift. "We don't have time to play 'shelter Amelia' anymore. I need to know what you know. Call me paranoid, but I don't think they'll be keeping us together once we land. I'd rather not go in completely ignorant."

He hung his head in defeat, but nodded. "You're right. Okay."

For the next five hours, Gabriel told her everything he knew about the grand city of Rome. He described the layout of the city with the Coliseum at its heart. The arena was the center of everything. It was a livelihood for some, entertainment for others, and hell on earth for the rest. He told her about the grand gardens, flashes of bright green in an otherwise sandy landscape. Some were so big, people could get lost in them. Others were little more than a gazebo of trees, with marble benches and a fountain.

Gabriel was a well of knowledge about Rome. He knew where the most beautiful statues were, where the best musicians played, and the best wine was poured. And he knew which parts of the city she should avoid at all cost. Places where disease was so thick in the air, it could be smelled from half a mile away. Places where people entered and never returned, where criminals and cutthroats reigned supreme.

The most distressing part of the lesson came when Gabriel told her that while the Patricians weren't big enough classicist to use public restrooms, they did have public baths. Which she might have to use.

"You mean… Bathe. Naked. In front of other people?"

Gabriel nodded. "The baths are segregated for men and women, but attendants are of both genders." A quick smile flashed across his face. "I haven't spent enough time in the women's baths to know all the current trends, but as I recall, the male attendants there were eunuchs. The poor bastards."

"Should have read the fine print."

"Thoroughly, and with a magnifying glass," he agreed.

"Tell me about the arena."

The look on his face made her wish she hadn't asked. The deadened tone in which he described it made her as sick as the things he talked about. Some gladiators were more like employees; they had their own living quarters and showed up daily to train and fight. Others were not so lucky. Those with cheaper masters were kept in underground cells like prisoners—they had a bunk, a bathroom corner, and a jug of water. The door was locked all the time, except when they were training or entertaining the crowds.

The only time a gladiator had company was when he was allowed to the public baths or when he was rewarded for good service. In the baths, or anywhere in the city, they were treated like superstars. Women loved them, attendants fawned over them, gave them whatever they wanted. All for the price of spilling some blood as magnificently as possible.

As reward, they sometimes got women. Amelia retched a little when Gabriel explained what that meant: slaves and whores brought to their cells to repay a service with another.

"D-did you ever…" She couldn't finish the sentence. Wasn't sure she really wanted to know the answer.

"Did I ever have women brought to me? I'd be lying if I said no." Gabriel sounded even less inclined to talk about it than she was to hear about it. But he was talking. And he was honest, though it was difficult. Amelia was grateful for that. "But I told you the truth before. I never took an unwilling woman to my bed."

Amelia nodded. *Got the picture. Loud and clear.* A gladiator as popular as he must have been, women probably signed up on a waitlist for the privilege of having him sleep with them.

"Besides, that didn't last long. When Honoria got my contract, she came up with a new way to *reward* me."

"I'm sure." *About ready to stop talking about this now.* Amelia flexed her fingers and hands. They were starting to cramp, tightly curled as they were. She shouldn't have asked. Hadn't she learned by now not to ask questions she didn't want answers to?

Gabriel's gaze warmed, and he smiled a little sadly. "You don't need to look like that," he said. "I got out of it."

"Out of what, exactly? And how?"

His smile turned savage, and Amelia's stomach did a nasty dive. Whatever he was about to say, she knew she'd regret hearing it for the rest of her life. "Honoria likes to fuck her gladiators after battle," he said, "but she hates to be sullied by blood."

– 18 –

September 30, 3032 – Rome

They landed as the larger of the two suns reached its highest point. When the shuttle opened, the hot desert air felt like stepping into an oven. Gabriel was instantly parched. He was used to this heat, but one look at Amelia told him she wasn't doing so well with it.

"Home sweet home, huh?"

Gabriel didn't have to do more than look at Lars to wipe that shit-eating grin off his face. The guy's nose was still crooked, his face looked like a punching bag at the end of a week-long practice, and he was favoring his left side. In contrast, Gabriel didn't have a mark on him. After the beating he'd taken and the "partial shift" as Amelia called it, his only issue was being a little unsteady on his feet.

And that royally pissed off Lars. It was humiliating to come out of a fight looking worse than your opponent. Lars had been knocked out cold in the first three minutes and slept through everything. Bastard should be happy he was still alive. Gabriel had had his neck in his hands, one decision away from snapping it like a twig. At the very last second he'd chosen not to kill Lars in Amelia's lab.

Ah well, live and learn.

When he didn't get the rise he'd been aiming for, Lars screwed up his face and left in a huff. Soren had assigned him to clear out Marek's body. Funny how their roles had switched. Gabriel put both of them out of his mind and turned his attention to the sight before them.

Home sweet home. Hats were too trite for this place; this was where you laid your life. From the shuttleport at the top of Mt. Olympus, they could see all of Rome spread out before them. The Coliseum all but glittered in the noonday suns, the streets were filled with people and colorful streamers, and banners were hung everywhere.

That arrogant bitch must have announced Gabriel's return to the arena. A brilliant move on her part. If all of Rome knew he was back, *all* of Rome would be watching him and inadvertently making sure his ass stayed put. It was better than assigning an armed escort to shadow his every move.

Next to him, Amelia was watching the city like a warrior about to go into battle. She stood straight and steady, but he could scent her anxiety. Amelia was scared, and with good reason. "Just remember everything I told you," he said.

"I have an excellent memory."

Their transportation arrived in the form of a group of horses decked out in the highest finery known to Rome. Golden beads were braided through their manes, irritating the horses into tossing their heads to get them out. The saddles were polished to a shine and adorned with bright red trimmings and streamers. The reins had fucking bells on them, and Gabriel wouldn't be surprised if their shoes were golden. Why anyone would do this to such a naturally elegant, majestic animal was beyond him.

"Horseback riding, on the other hand," Amelia said, "could be a little problematic." Her dignified gulp was only audible to Gabriel's overly sensitive ears.

"Don't worry, I won't let you fall."

"You ride with me," Soren told Amelia. The son of a bitch had called for his own horse, Demon. A subtle name for a subtle mount. The steed was already stomping up a dust storm, snorting and chewing his bit. He'd been known to take digits. "You're in the chariot, Champion."

The guy who dragged him to the chariot had to be new. Gabriel had never seen him before. Perfect. His hands were freed of the ropes, but New Guy tied one of them right back up to the chariot. It was for show, nothing more. That rope wouldn't hold him if he decided he was done playing nice. But it wasn't meant to. It was a visual reminder of the leash around his neck. Amelia was their insurance policy, and all of them knew it.

New Guy tied off the rope and yanked on it to test the knot. He noticed Gabriel examining his free hand and explained, "So you can wave. Try it."

Gabriel punched him in the nose. "Yeah, that'll do." His mouth quirked up at one corner. He'd take his satisfactions where he could get them.

"Mount up!" Soren ordered.

Gabriel's jaw muscles jumped when Soren mounted his horse and dragged Amelia up to sit across his lap. She clutched the saddle's edge so tight, her knuckles stood out pale white. Demon was already picking up on her tension, and he wasn't exactly docile with an empty saddle on his back, let alone a rider. Two riders? Gabriel hoped for Soren's sake he wouldn't let Amelia get hurt.

At least they took it slow going down the hill. At the foot of the mountain, the welcome party was already in full swing. It was like they were greeting a damn hero. Flower petals carpeted the city streets, with more raining down as they passed. There were so many people, soldiers had to hold them back so the entourage could pass. Women shouted his name, tossed him handkerchiefs and other things. Men threw coins at his feet and chanted his "nickname."

Nothing said *We love you* better than chanting *penis* over and over again. God, he hated Honoria so much. Gabriel kept his gaze forward and his hands still until New Guy shoved into him from the side.

"Wave," he growled.

Gabriel's temper flared. His free hand tightened on the reins, translating the tension to the two horses pulling his chariot. They whinnied and tossed their heads, jerking suddenly to the left and spooking New Guy's mount. Caught off guard, the soldier didn't have time to catch himself before he was thrown off, landing with a heavy thud on his back. Riderless, the horse ran for it. It took three of Soren's men to catch and calm the beast.

Amelia shot Gabriel a worried glance, quick as lightning. All he could do was hope his pair stayed put, otherwise he'd be dragged across Roman dirt on his stomach.

"Have you ever seen a more beautiful sight?" Soren said at her ear. His nearness made Amelia want to shudder. The only thing keeping her from doing it was that she was too tense, holding on to the saddle with everything she had. There wasn't a loose muscle in her left to shudder.

She made herself look around. The path they were on wasn't the stomped sand it appeared to be. Nothing natural was that smooth. It had to be synthetically bonded somehow, making it as tough as concrete while still golden like sand. The buildings around her looked ancient in design, but there wasn't a crack in the walls anywhere. The roofs were all slanted the same way, which meant they utilized solar energy. And the people were dressed simply enough, but adorned with glittering, faceted stones no antiquated tool could have cut.

It was a lie. All of it. A pretty veneer hiding a simple fact of life: people were too used to their modern creature comforts to give them up for the sake of pretense. "As a matter of fact, I have." Torrey, for all that it drove her crazy with its lack of amenities, was what Rome only pretended to be. Genuine. Amelia would choose that over this farce any day.

Soren chuckled. "Your defiance intrigues me."

She leaned more forward to get as far from him as possible. "Don't get too excited. I'm about as far out of your league as a woman can get." She was still human. This guy? She had her doubts.

His gloved hand brushed her hair, and she almost jumped off the damn horse to get away from him. The horse must have sensed it, because he stopped and tossed his head back, almost hitting her.

Soren pulled on the reins mercilessly and dug his knees into the mount's sides. "Settle down, Demon."

"Demon? How fitting."

"This beast is a lifesaver. When he's not trying to kill me."

That was it. "Let me down, I want to walk."

"Look!"

Amelia looked up from the saddle, daring a glance forward past Demon's monstrous head. The crowds opened up, the buildings became background, and all she saw was a sea of people alongside a wide path leading up to a magnificent marble palace. It was raised high, with bright white stairs leading up to a gigantic platform. Like some sort of temple, it had columns supporting the roof and carved scenes of battles everywhere.

At the foot of the staircase was some sort of stage with billowing canopies. There were people there, waiting for them to approach.

"We go on foot from here."

"Oh, thank God." She slipped off the horse immediately and would have fallen on her face if one of the soldiers hadn't caught her.

Once their conveyances were taken away, their little company moved forward. Amelia felt like some kind of sacrificial offering being dragged to the altar. It didn't help that they were walking over a long red carpet made solely of silk sheets. She expected them to catch on her shoes, but they didn't. Probably because every five feet or so there were people crouching on either side, holding the fabric in place and adjusting it when it was ruffled.

Amelia swallowed back a wave of nausea. These had to be slaves.

Soren noticed her looking. "They're getting well paid for the service they provide," he said.

Gaunt faces, sunken eyes, clothes immaculately clean for the celebration, but the colorful strips of cloth tied around their arms for decoration weren't quite wide enough to hide the bruises. The crowd's cheering wasn't quite loud enough to disguise the shouted commands and insults when someone failed to adjust the silk fast enough.

"Tell me," she said, "how much do they pay you? What is the current price of a human soul?"

"You think coming here has changed me."

"Oh no, I am pretty sure the way you are is precisely *why* you came here in the first place."

"Then you're afraid coming here will change you."

Amelia gritted her teeth. "I don't plan on staying long enough to find out."

Soren didn't twitch, as if what she thought or planned was completely irrelevant because she had no hope of succeeding. "In any case," he said, "this place doesn't make people the way they are; it merely enhances traits already present. You'd be surprised how meticulous we are in our recruitment. For example, our mutual friend over there." He inclined his head toward the front of the entourage, where Gabriel walked tall and proud ahead of them. "He is special, you know."

You have no idea.

"Any street thug can be dressed in a costume and pitted against an opponent in the arena. More often than not, they will fight to the death, probably for the sheer pleasure of it. Amateurs clubbing at each other with sharp bits of metal. They draw blood, the blood draws a crowd. Doesn't take much more than that."

His voice grated on Amelia's nerves. She wanted him to shut up so much, she was willing to try making him and risk the consequences. But apparently he was in a chattering mood, like a gossipy hen over a pot of tea and cookies.

"But Gabriel, he has courage. Strength. Some would say showmanship. These are traits not easily found among the general population. He was chosen for the arena quite deliberately because of them. And he has flourished here. Rome didn't make Gabriel, Dr. Chase. It made him better."

"That should be your new catchphrase. Come to Rome! Reach your highest potential. And then die."

"You just described life," he said. "Isn't that what we all strive for? To reach our highest potential? And then, of course, everything comes to an end some time."

"Right. You just expedite the process. An entire lifetime, fast tracked to what, ten years, if that?"

He merely inclined his head.

"And that so-called potential you mentioned. What exactly is that? Being the best slave you can be? Moaning the loudest you can while dying of some disease that wouldn't be an issue in proper society?"

"Show me a city without disease, Dr. Chase. Show me one where people don't rob, or steal, or fight for money. What you speak for so passionately is an idea, nothing more. It can never become reality because of one simple, painful fact of life."

"And what is that?"

"Human beings are essentially animals. With base instincts, needs, and wants. Greed, hunger, lust, even misery. All of these things are ever present in our makeup. Some manage to suppress them with intellect, but most take pleasure in drowning themselves in one or the other. I believe they call it instant gratification. People get what they want, when they want, by any means necessary. You'd be surprised how many times that translates to violence in some form or another."

The most frightening thing about his little speech was that he was absolutely right. Amelia was a scientist who'd spent the better part of her adult life studying human nature. She knew what he was talking about, had seen it firsthand many times in the past. Had often lost faith in humanity because of it. She could easily find evidence here to support everything he'd said if she wanted to.

Amelia inwardly shook herself. *Can't think like that!* This man was a monster. This place was an abomination of what society should be. She ought to know better than to let emotions cloud her judgment.

Just breathe. Get ahold of yourself. You have a brain, so use it!

Yes, Amelia could see evidence all around her to support his claims. If what Gabriel had told her was true, all of these people had signed up for this. They'd chosen, even if they hadn't known all the facts beforehand.

But that was only part of the story. Amelia made herself see the other side. There was one more human trait Soren had neglected to bring up: self-preservation. Yes, people might sign contracts without fully understanding of what they entailed. But once they discovered the truth, no one in their right mind would choose to stay here of their own free will.

It was a matter of degrees. A man thrust into boiling water wouldn't stay in it unless something stopped him from escaping. But a man in a bath gradually warmed to boiling might not realize the danger until it was too late. Either way, the outcome was bad.

Amelia looked around, taking in the faces around her. There were many Patricians, as Gabriel had called them; the rich pretending to be noble to live out some sick fantasy. But among them, the faces of their indentured employees stood out like beacons. She could see a dozen. Then two, then three. Very soon she lost count. But the more she saw, the better she could distinguish between their plights.

She could tell the ones in boiling water apart from the ones in the heating bath. The former were broken. They rarely raised their gazes, never touched anyone, flinched when someone came too close. They were the quiet mice that went through life hoping and praying they were invisible. Because when they weren't, bad things happened.

Like the man who got ruthlessly whipped across the back for not getting out of the way fast enough. Or the woman crouched by a column with long matted hair falling over her face; she probably hadn't seen a bath in months. Her arms were spotted with infected cuts and wounds.

But those who hadn't yet realized they would die here, they had a far greater impact. Their eyes were hungry, desperate. They *wanted* to be seen. They *wanted* whatever they could get. They spoke, begged, cried, and reached out to the Patricians for mercy, taking beatings in stride because they were still worth the scraps they got for their pain.

They still had hope that one day they could beg enough, save enough to get out.

"You're wrong," she told Soren as they reached the canopied stage. She recognized Honoria at the forefront. Those behind her had to be her council. "People can choose. They can choose to be better than this. The Patricians simply choose not to be."

All of this pain was nothing more than sick entertainment. There was no reason why a single person had to do what these slaves were doing, when simple, cheap technologies and devices could easily take over the tasks. They were here because the Patricians enjoyed watching them suffer.

This was what came of money and sadism joining together on a massive scale. She'd seen it before in shady underground labs, sanctioned and funded by a heartless government. But Rome was worse. Rome flaunted it all like a badge of honor. This was their world, as they imagined the world should be, and in it, they were gods.

"You mean people like Gabriel?" Soren said. "You think because he left he is somehow better than everyone else here?"

Honoria rose from her seat and everyone around them either bowed low, or fell to their knees. She came forward, opening her arms to Gabriel. "My Champion," she said. "Welcome back."

He will not kneel, Amelia thought, worrying her lower lip. Seconds ticked by and still he stood, silent and strong before the Caesar. *He will not kneel.*

"I suppose he didn't tell you."

"Tell me what?"

He was going to do it. He would kill the Caesar right now, here in front of everyone, with a hundred guards at the ready to slice him to pieces. Amelia hardly dared to breathe, waiting to see what he would do. Her hands clenched into fists at her sides. If push came to shove, she would have to get a weapon somehow. There would be chaos. A mob of this size, people would fall left and right and get trampled to death in seconds.

"We didn't seek out Gabriel," Soren said. "He came to us."

Amelia tore her gaze away from Gabriel's back to stare at Soren. *Impossible.*

But the sheer satisfaction in his one remaining eye was proof enough that he spoke the truth. He had no reason to lie.

And still, she sought Gabriel again. He was the hero here. The one man willing to stand up to a corrupt regime and bring it crumbling down, even if it meant his life. Gabriel had strength and courage, but he also had honor, and compassion, and conviction. Soren was trying to drive a wedge between them. Maybe he suspected they were close and was trying to divide and conquer. Either way, it wouldn't work. Gabriel would prove him wrong. He was still standing!

As if her thoughts called to him, he turned and found her in the crowd. His gaze met hers, and a sigh of relief escaped Amelia. This was the man who'd fought to keep Soren and his men away from her. He'd told her everything about this city so she could be prepared. He'd shown her more care and compassion in the last few days than anyone else had in her entire life. Gabriel was worth believing in. She'd trust him over anyone else in this damn city.

Amelia smiled a little, wanting to reassure him she was all right.

A muscle jumped in his jaw. He didn't smile back. Instead, Gabriel turned back to Honoria and lowered to one knee, bowing his head. "Hail our radiant leader, Caesar Honoria."

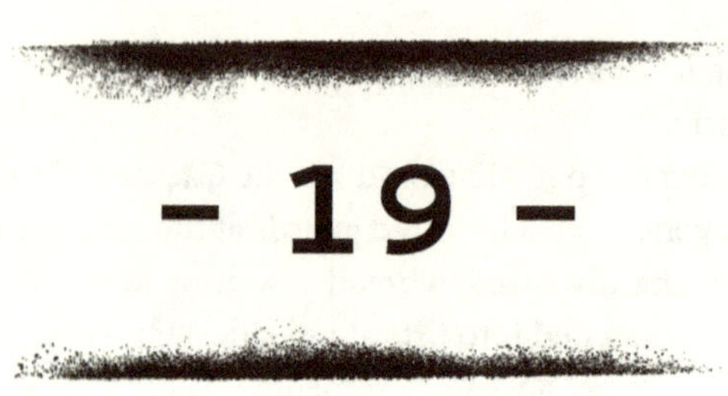

– 19 –

"Our Champion has returned!" Honoria announced, and the crowd went wild. Naturally, the queen bitch would milk this for all it was worth. "And tomorrow, he takes his rightful place of honor in the arena."

Gabriel's hands ached to wrap around her neck and throttle the life out of her. The panther bristled and paced back and forth across his mind. It was restless, agitated. Too many people, too much noise. It wanted to lash out. Gabriel itched all over; he wanted to roll around in the dirt to stop it.

"But tonight, we celebrate!"

That was his cue. Gabriel pushed to his feet again, wondering if it was possible to kill a person simply by hating them enough. Honoria had made a circus spectacle out of him. She'd summoned what looked like everyone in the city, her entire army lined the promenade, her bodyguards surrounded her, and her best men-at-arms were at his back. And still he would have lunged for her the second he'd reached her chaise.

Except Amelia was standing three inches from Soren. She'd die before Gabriel could get his hands on Honoria.

Damn it! This wasn't how it was supposed to happen! Amelia should never have been here. If not for her, Gabriel could have killed Honoria ten times over. Probably died ten times over, too. But that wasn't the point. He had to get Amelia out of here.

As the crowd erupted into song and dance, the council dispersed, and Honoria's men-at-arms drew closer. Soren had Amelia by the arm, pulling her in front of the Caesar. "Your Radiance, a gift for you." He shoved Amelia forward until she was next to Gabriel but she wouldn't look at him. For once, he was glad.

Honoria smiled. "Dr. Chase, wasn't it? I hear you are quite deadly with a needle."

"You were misinformed," Amelia said, her professional mask firmly in place.

"Is that so?"

"The needle wasn't what killed him. It was the air pushed through it into his blood stream."

Honoria laughed in delight. "Oh, you clever creature. Killing a man with air! You must tell me all about it."

"There's nothing to tell," Gabriel told her. The last thing he wanted was for the fucking Caesar to latch on to Amelia.

"Gladius, where are your manners? You don't interrupt women in conversation."

"My apologies," he retorted. "I wasn't aware you considered yourself to be a woman, otherwise I would have interrupted long ago."

Honoria's nostrils flared. "You disappoint me, Gabriel." It was the first time she'd used his real name since she'd come into power. He was getting to her. "Take him to the baths. Guard him every second. He's not to pick his teeth without someone there to see it."

"What about me?" Amelia asked.

Honoria smiled at her. "You are too adorable for words. I think I'll keep you."

Gabriel stilled to his core. *No…*

"And I have something for you. Call it a welcome gift." Honoria snapped her fingers, and a slave girl brought a silver chest on a red velvet pillow. Honoria opened it and withdrew a necklace. The chain was platinum and the pendant on it was perfectly round and polished into a mirror shine. It was a locket with God knew what inside.

"Don't," he grated.

Honoria ignored him. "You see this engraving?" she told Amelia. "That is the likeness of Asclepius, god of medicine and healing. I thought it fitting, given your profession."

Gabriel made a grab for it, but the men-at-arms pulled him back. Before he could do anything about it, Honoria hung the chain around Amelia's neck. "There," she said. "It will bring you good fortune."

Gabriel struggled against the men holding him. "Amelia, listen to me," he said. "Don't let anyone take that from y—"

Soren elbowed him in the stomach so hard, Gabriel saw stars. He doubled over, hoping he wouldn't throw up his own spleen. Coughing weakly, gasping for breath, he raised his head to see Amelia. Two tenets were unshakable in Rome: decorum and the bulla. As long as someone wore "outside" clothing, they were outside the Roman order of things, and neither soldier nor the Caesar could touch them. The first thing a newcomer did after signing their life over was to don Roman garb, which was exactly what Honoria would force on the two of them now.

And that thing was a bulla. It was traditionally given to girls as a protection from evil and taken away and burned on the eve of their marriage. These people took it one step further. If a woman gave away her pendant or lost it somehow, it was taken as an open invitation to sleep with her. A woman without the pendant good as lost the rights to her own body.

Honoria might as well have collared Amelia and tied her to a post. She'd given the bulla and she could take it away if her new pet displeased her.

Gabriel flexed his muscles to get free, but even with the animal's added strength, he couldn't budge. The panther riled at this; it was offended. Prideful bastard didn't like that it couldn't do what it wanted and that something mildly interesting was being taken from it. It looked at Amelia and saw the only tolerable being around. The panther might not understand why Gabriel was frantic to get her out of here, but it took its cue from him.

Gabriel's head pounded like a drum, and his hands were unbelievably itchy. He curled his fingers into his palms and felt the sharp prick of claws. He didn't dare look down to check. His mouth pulled into a snarl, splitting on the inside, but he somehow kept it from parting all the way, keeping the outward mask human.

Honoria's perfume was so cloying, he wanted to sneeze, and her bright red wig hurt his sensitive eyes. *So bright… begging to be prey.* Gabriel couldn't tell whether that was his own idea or the panther's.

Amelia frowned at the pendant, then looked Honoria in the eye. "Thank you," she said.

"You guard that thing like your life depends on it," Gabriel told her, struggling to keep his voice level. It was rumbling a little, like a suppressed growl. What would be next? Fangs? Black fur and a fractured skull? If he betrayed anything, Amelia wouldn't just die. They'd make her suffer.

"I told you to take him to the baths," Honoria snapped. "And for goodness sake, give him some proper clothes."

Her loyal dogs obeyed, dragging him away.

The panther reared its head and growled, and Gabriel felt his teeth sharpen. "Don't lose it!"

"Well, wasn't that interesting?" Honoria said.

Amelia palmed the pendant again. "This is your insurance policy, isn't it? What's inside? Some sort of tracking chip?"

Honoria laughed. "My, aren't you a paranoid one. Look around, sweetheart. Do you really think I need something like that to know where you are? No. This is for fun. Now come, there's a great celebration tonight, and you still have to get ready."

Amelia had a bad feeling about this *getting ready* the moment Honoria took her hand to lead her up to her grand palace. The platform she'd seen from below was even bigger from up close. It could hold a battalion. There was an army of slaves and servants bustling about, readying tables and seating areas. Setting out thin, flexible sheets that would cool or warm dishes placed on top of them. The torches on the walls were lit with a spark controlled by remote. Naturally, everyone in ancient Rome had had those.

More translucent canopies in every color of the rainbow were being hung from each column. They were also automated to close and retract by remote. Everything was being checked to make sure it would work. Amelia half thought there was a timer set for every action, but no. The Caesar probably had slaves to keep time. And guards to brutally whip them if they missed a beat.

Past that madness, the palace actually had walls. It wasn't a full cube building, either. It was a broken, hollow square. Past the hallway running left and right into a U, the space was open in the middle. It was a garden with water spilling over the walls, and three fountains in the middle spraying up glittering droplets. There were trees here, and flowers. Not quite as tropical as Amelia's green room, but so much more beautiful because it was outside.

The air was cooler here—she could actually take a deep breath without burning her lungs in the process—and the billowing, transparent sheets draped above from end to end provided a little shade from the two suns. Amelia felt her tension drain out of her in a rush that made her sway. The tranquility of the place was breathtaking.

"Do you like it?"

"Yes," Amelia said on a dreamy sigh. Then she woke the hell up. "And by that I mean, no. I don't like it, I don't want to live here, will never sign anything binding, and I don't like you. It. Here. This place. I don't… like it?"

Honoria smiled and pinched Amelia's cheek. "So adorable!"

Amelia had nothing to say for herself. She hung her head, keeping her gaze on the ground so she wouldn't gawk anymore. The building in the far back was completely separate from the one they'd entered through, creating a clear pathway into the garden on each side.

"These are my private chambers," Honoria said. "Servants sleep back there, but this is where I bring only my most honored guests." She led Amelia through the place on a grand tour, showing her where her rooms would be, and then pointed out what she called the garderobe, a small room with a modern toilet inside. Thank God for that.

"And here is the bath."

Amelia cringed at the word, girding her loins for what she was about to see. But the chamber they entered was fantastically beautiful. There were two large pools in the middle, one cold, one hot. The walls were marble, carved and laser-printed with colors… an ancient version of porn. There were tables set up along the walls for towels, soaps, and oils, and a couple of chaises in the corner with a tray of fruits and a metal jug of something.

"I'm sure you're worn out after your journey," Honoria said. "My servants will attend your bath and bring you fresh clothing. When you're ready, you may go to your rooms to rest, or perhaps the garden."

Fresh clothing? She looked over Honoria's outfit, and those of the serving women around her. "You're going to make me wear bed sheets, aren't you?"

Honoria smiled mysteriously and made her exit.

"Fantastic," she said on a resigned sigh.

For the next two hours, Amelia endured the indignity of having strangers bathe her. She didn't want to, but the alternative was to bathe on her own and have the serving women get beaten or whipped for having neglected their duties. They told her as much, eyes wide with fright, as they begged Amelia to let them take care of her.

So she gritted her teeth and endured. The hot bath came first. They tossed flowers into the water and poured in some kind of scented oil and let her soak like a chicken in marinade for a while. *This isn't so bad.* She managed to relax for all of a second.

But then the women came back and insisted on scrubbing her with washcloths. Every. Last. Inch of her. They washed her hair, too. Then they helped her out of the hot bath and over the slippery floor to the cold one that knocked the breath right out of her. More scrubbing continued until she was red from head to toe. And not from blushing, either. Those washcloths, as soft as they were, in combination with the cold water, rubbed her completely raw.

Amelia shot out of the pool the moment they released her.

But it still wasn't over!

While she'd been in the cold pool, someone raised the temperature in the room until it felt like a sauna. The women, Lillian and Rosalie were their names, brought out oils and proceeded to massage them into Amelia's skin. She could tell they were as uncomfortable as she was, probably because she wasn't making it easy on them. When a third woman came in carrying a tray of razors, Amelia snapped.

"What are you doing?"

The new woman blinked at her as if no one had ever spoken to her before. "I… I'm here to shave you," she said, showing her the tray with its assortment of blades. All shapes and sizes like a neat little collection of torture tools. Amelia had been around enough scalpels to know when a knife was sharp enough to cut flesh like butter.

"No."

"But my lady—"

"No. I've been a good sport about this, I've let you women do things to me some of my past boyfriends hadn't been allowed to do. You've bathed me, oiled me up, and thank you for your effort. I actually feel slightly better. But no way in Lucifer's red hot, sulfur spewing, ever-burning hell am I letting you anywhere near me with those blades. Are we clear?"

The woman nodded and scurried away.

Amelia let out a sharp breath of relief. "God, I hope she doesn't get in trouble for this."

Lillian and Rosalie ducked their heads, snickering.

Amelia raised an eyebrow. "Something funny?"

"It's just…" Rosalie started.

"It's been so long since we met someone normal here," Lillian finished.

Little did Amelia know that that sentence would be the highlight of her day.

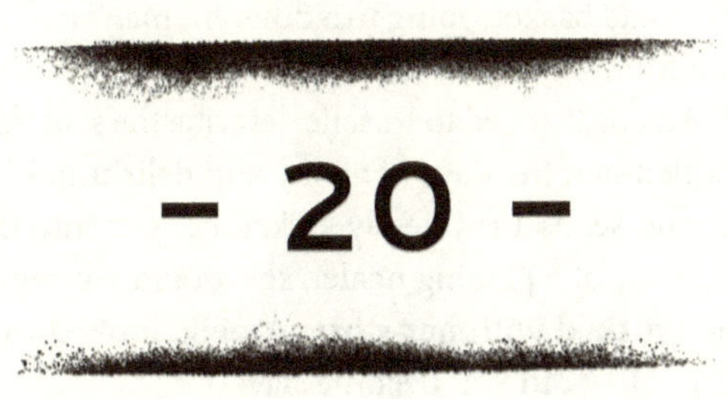

– 20 –

By the time the larger sun went down, Amelia was as ready as she was ever going to be. Rosalie helped her put on the stupid bed sheets that passed for the height of fashion here. At least they were a flattering shade of blue that brought out her eyes. Lillian tried to arrange her hair up, but it wasn't working out, since Amelia's hair barely reached her collar bone. They tried to talk her into a wig but, like the razors, that just wasn't going to happen. So instead, they pinned it out of her face with silver adornments to match the pendant she wore.

Noticing neither Lillian nor Rosalie wore one, Amelia asked Lillian what it was, and without meeting Amelia's gaze, the girl explained the basics of its function. Well, tried to. It was hard to catch her meaning with all the "you knows" and awkward hand gestures.

"I don't understand," she said. "You mean I can't have sex while I'm wearing this?"

Lillian and Rosalie exchanged an uneasy glance. "No, mum," Rosalie said. "That's no' it at all." She busied herself cleaning up while Lillian moved closer to the doorway as a lookout. What was going on here?

"Hurry up," Lillian said.

Rosalie nodded and, without looking at Amelia at all, she began. Her words were halting and her cheeks blushing as she spoke about how her mistress had taken her bulla as punishment for having flirted with her son. How the men of the household had looked at her the moment it was torn from her neck. Amelia couldn't understand how the girl could talk about it all. At the age of eighteen, she'd been passed around like a bread basket, going to a different man's bed every night. If she refused him, she'd been beaten.

Horrified, Amelia listened to Rosalie describe the staff infection that had nearly killed her, the days of agony and delirium. Her mistress, sick of all the noise, had ruthlessly kicked her out into the street. If not for the charity of a passing healer, she would have died.

When she finished with her story, Amelia looked to Lillian for confirmation. "How did you become slaves?"

Rosalie hesitated, but after a moment, redoubled her efforts to fold a satin sheet. She shrugged. "Renegotiated my contract."

"You can do that?"

Lillian snorted. "Sure you can," she said bitterly. "That's what I did, too. I used to be a weaver's apprentice. When she croaked, I couldn't find work elsewhere. Only had a year left to my contract, but in Rome, without someone's patronage, I wouldn't have lasted a week." She breathed a big, almost happy sigh. "So here I am, a member of the Caesar's household. Better lodgings, more food, clean clothes, baths every day if I want them, and no one beats me with a cane unless the Caesar is upset. All I have to do is bear it for another twenty years."

Amelia couldn't even process that.

"Word of advice," Lillian said. "Don't touch anything that might look like a contract. They have ways of getting you to make your mark, whether you know it or not."

Amelia stored that away for later. "But wait. I've seen other women without these things. Both rich and poor. Are you telling me all of them are treated this way?"

Lillian shook her head. "Many choose not to wear them. But we're most definitely not all treated the same. A rich lady can have her variety. But a slave is still a slave."

So that was why Gabriel had been so adamant about her keeping it on. Just what was she supposed to be here in Rome? She didn't have a master, or an employer, and she definitely didn't have status. She was nobody. Her very existence here depended on Honoria's mood. Any time the Caesar chose, she could cut her loose and let her fend for herself.

Amelia barely registered the slave girls leaving. She was pissed. And she was scared. Honoria had good as chained her. But it wasn't for her. The bulla had been a test. And Gabriel had failed it, revealing a weakness Honoria would exploit at the first opportunity. The Caesar would dangle her in front of Gabriel and make him do anything she wanted. Or else.

First chance she got, she was going to wring Honoria's neck. Or maybe pour acid in her bath.

Lifting one foot at a time to flex her ankles and get used to the straps of her sandals, Amelia mentally centered herself. The Caesar might know what made Gabriel tick, but she didn't know Amelia. If they were to have any chance of getting the hell out of here, she'd have to play it cool and controlled. She was a scientist. And this was a prime opportunity to observe her subject in his native habitat.

Gabriel was probably already feeling the panther inside him and it would wreak havoc with his mind for a while. For his sake, she had to stay objective and in control. Amelia was no good to either of them if she let her emotions get the best of her. *I have a job to do.*

It was time to clock in.

The back house was quiet behind the oasis. The smaller of the two suns was little more than a bright star. It produced no additional heat, and very little light. It was like a prolonged sunset when the sun is millimeters away from slipping behind the horizon. Beautiful, but useless as suns went.

Torches had already been lit, burning fragrant like incense, and their scent and soft light created a heady atmosphere. Amelia emerged into the dark garden, enjoying the cool breeze. Those fountains and waterfalls acted as some sort of natural air conditioning. The ground had retained the heat of the day—she could feel it through her sandals—but the air was comfortable out here. Amelia gave one last longing sigh. One day she would have a garden like this, she vowed. And she would damn well live to see that day.

From the garden's front edge, she could already see shadows moving, hear music playing. It was like nothing she'd ever listened to. String and air instruments blending in a heady, pagan rhythm so different from the classical melodies she was used to, that her heart beat in symphony to it. It was music to dance to, to make love to. To *live* to. *Hailey would love it.* Amelia stepped foot into the front portion of the house, into a reverberating amplifier. Somehow the hallway captured the music, made it bounce around the walls, and threw it back outside much louder than before. She'd love to know how they'd done that.

Out in front, the party was already in full swing. It all looked like a dream. Amelia was sure she'd walked over white marble coming into the house. Now the terrace was covered with silks and pillows, furs and all sorts of other things to hide what lay beneath. Lamps behind the soft canopies cast shadows of dancers from all sides, their forms swaying sensuously to the music's steady beat. It was a passionate dance, as primitive as the music itself. Amelia wondered how many of those dancers were trained acrobats, to stretch and bend the way they were. Or was that a trick of the light?

She tilted her head at one pair. Even without the benefit of seeing their expressions, the way they always kept close, kept touching, their faces a breath away, indicated a depth of connection she almost envied.

Do you ever crave, Amelia? Gabriel had asked her once.

I might be beginning to, she thought in answer.

There were three other shadow couples, clearly hired performers rather than guests. As the music intensified, so did their dance. Amelia hastily looked away from one pair getting a little too caught up in the moment. She dropped her gaze and hurried away, making her way through the gathering crowd.

She almost ran into a group of women. Only the flutter of skirts in her field of vision made her stop before she mowed them over.

"Gladius is back, did you hear?" one of the women whispered excitedly.

"My slave girl saw him enter town," another replied. This was clearly a private conversation, but Amelia couldn't move her feet from the spot. There she stood, making herself an innocuous part of the crowd, listening in on what they had to say. She felt like a voyeur eavesdropping on them. It was embarrassing and immature, but for the life of her she could not make herself move an inch. "I made her tell me all about it while I made use of that little toy I told you about."

The others tittered at this. "You might as well admit it wasn't so little, Juliet."

This Juliet chuckled. "With pleasure. It wasn't." Then, with a wicked smile in her tone, she added, "I'd had it fashioned after Gladius. Gods how I missed him."

Amelia's face burned, her stomach tightened, and her brows drew together in indignation. *Should not be listening.* She was torn between walking away and going up to Juliet and slapping that look of longing from her cosmetically altered face.

Another woman in the group chimed in with a sympathetic hum. "As do I. Now there's a man who knows how to pound a woman into ecstasy." A disgustingly dreamy sigh followed, which made Amelia want to retch. Still she stayed right where she was. "Even my husband couldn't find complaint when he found out. He said he'd rather see a blissful smile on my face than hear my shrill voice when I come."

What the hell!

Gabriel had slept with these women? And not just slept. From the sounds of it, he'd gone far above and beyond the call of duty. Amelia felt her nostrils flare. She pressed the back of her cold hand against her cheek to cool it. *A bunch of gossiping hens. Don't believe a word they say.* Did they have no shame at all? They were talking about him like a piece of meat! And out here where everyone could hear!

"I was his first, you know," one woman boasted, and Amelia dropped her hand in shock. "Back when he first came here. I was the first, and for a heavenly while, the only one who got to have him." For a moment she was relieved. The woman had almost made it sound like he'd been a virgin until that time, which was ridiculous. Then the dark-haired aristocrat patted her already perfect hair and added with fake humility, "You all have me to thank for teaching him all his impressive tricks."

I can't hear this! Amelia covered her ears to block out the argument that ensued about who'd taught Gabriel what. She was almost hyper-ventilating, tense from head to toe, wanting to scratch those women's faces off—for what? Amelia backed away, putting some distance between her and the group before she did something violent. She realized with a baffled sort of wonder she might be… no, not might be. She *was. Jealous.*

People brushed past her as she walked backwards, seeking some sort of shelter from her crazy emotional outburst. *Get ahold of yourself!* She had no business feeling anything about any of this. Amelia rooted her feet, dropped her hands to her sides, and made herself stand still while she calmly and rationally collected her thoughts and explained to herself that—

"Heavens, the things he said to me while he fucked me out of my wits made me come so hard I nearly swooned. Gladius is a god."

—that someone was about to get their face ground into the dirt and flattened with a three ton statue.

God, what was happening to her? *This isn't me. I don't do this. I don't* feel *like this.* Never before had she had so much trouble with her emotions running rampant. And it wasn't just the jealousy, although that was a big part of it.

She was in a strange place where the rules worked against her. Her safety was in serious jeopardy, she was being manipulated left and right, she had no allies here and no way to contact those few she had outside of Rome. On top of all that, Gabriel was out there somewhere, probably freaking out as his mind and body changed, and if it didn't kill him, he had a whole lot of self-inflicted torture to look forward to. Nothing was going according to plan. There was no way to salvage the situation, and everything kept going from bad to worse! She hardly knew up from down in this place, and the only thing she was certain of was that she had to get out. Now.

It took every ounce of her already frayed control for Amelia to walk to the grand staircase off this madhouse. Dread settled in the pit of her stomach when she looked down from its edge at the daunting sight below.

While she'd been ruminating, the smaller sun had set, casting Rome into darkness. But it wasn't complete. Standing there, she could look out over a large area of smaller buildings. Every street branching out from the main corridor was lit up with torches. It was a more daunting sight than full darkness would have been. The shadows cast by torchlight were worse than ghosts, dancing over walls and the ground. Amelia was in no way superstitious, but even she got nervous at the sight. Light enough to remind her how dark it was.

A smidgen of false hope in a wholly hopeless situation. And that was before she looked down.

The staircase was lined on each side with soldiers standing at attention, facing forward like statues. A row of them stood at the very bottom like an army of bouncers keeping unwanted guests outside. They were all armed with spears, metal helmets gleaming on their heads, and bright capes billowing in the breeze to reveal swords strapped to their hips. When she edged toward the first one on her right, his head swung around to her, a pair of sharp eyes staring at her from an unsmiling face. She edged right back away from him.

Two pairs of firedancers were putting on a show in the middle of the staircase. They were sensuous and masterful, bending every which way and running the burning ends of their wands over their bodies in time to the music. They were so sure, so focused, and so damn close to tripping and falling down those stairs, Amelia was afraid to watch.

Honoria stood in the center of the topmost step, looking down. At first Amelia thought she was watching the show, but every once in a while, the Caesar would give an infinitesimal nod and another person or two would make their way up to join the party. She was passing judgment over who could enter. And she didn't even have the decency to go down there and tell the people to their faces.

Sensing her presence, Honoria spoke to her without ever looking away from that line of guards. "This is how you create the elite, my dear. Create something the people want, and then deny it to all but a chosen few."

Keep it together. Amelia left her to it. She wound her way through the growing crowd to get to the food tables, giving the groups of women a wide berth. A man painted white to resemble a statue stood to the side. When she reached for a glass, he filled it for her, moving his arm and nothing more. "Thank you," she said, cautiously sniffing the contents. Wine. There were about a million ways it could have been drugged or poisoned without altering the taste or color. And about a hundred different ways she could be incapacitated or killed by drinking this. Right that second, Amelia was so damn thirsty, she didn't care. She downed the contents in two large gulps, making a face at the taste.

Of all the ways to make alcohol, Amelia didn't understand why people would make or drink one that tasted like spoiled fruit juice.

Without a word, the man statue refilled her glass.

She glared at him and set the glass down, turning to leave, and almost ran into Soren. "Rome suits you," he said. "You are the talk of the party."

Whose talk? she wanted to ask. Because the women sure as hell weren't talking about a female nobody. Since she couldn't answer him without snarling, Amelia forced an uneasy shrug and looked him over to buy some time to find her normal voice again. The general wore a set of bed sheets like her, only his didn't reach past the knee and were tied around his waist with a wide leather belt. He didn't have the golden laurel that sat on many a man's head here, or the golden cuffs. His only adornments were a pair of leather bracers with cleverly disguised blood stains. His hair was wet, combed back in a way that would have been handsome, if not for the ugly scar on his face.

"Did you just get out of the shower?" she asked. *Hurrah! An intelligible sentence has at last emerged.*

Soren laughed. "You could say that." The light made his remaining eye gleam dangerously. She'd bet he'd had a whole harem of women to bathe him. "I see the Caesar has restrained herself tonight."

Amelia looked over the opulence of the terrace, the mountain of food being consumed and wasted, the fountains of wine that poured out onto the floor, and sometimes into someone's mouth. "I can see how you would think that."

"What I mean is most of her parties tend to be clothing optional." He drawled the words while he leered at her. The guy couldn't have any depth perception whatsoever, and still Amelia knew there wasn't a single detail about her that went unnoticed. *Gross.* "But I'm sure it won't be long before this is, too."

"I really didn't want to know that."

Soren chuckled and leaned into her personal space, fingering the pendant resting at the swell of her breasts. "Liar," he said at her ear.

Amelia shuddered. He smelled like scented oils and sex, and he sized her up like the next course of dinner. Except when his gaze snared on her pendant, his mouth twisted as if it disgusted him, and she saw his hands curl at his sides.

She had to get away from him somehow, but the table was at her back and he was caging her in. Her hand reached behind her along the table for something to use against him.

"My friends and fellow citizens of Rome," Honoria said, and the music hushed. Everyone faced her, including Soren, who turned toward his Caesar like the good little soldier he was. Amelia took the opening to edge around him and put some distance between them. "It is time to welcome our guest of honor this night. Our Champion, Gladius!"

She'd timed it perfectly. As soon as she said his name, Gabriel topped the staircase and came to a stop next to her. He looked magnificent, dressed in nothing but a leather kilt of some sort and a pair of sandals, a silver cuff nestled between the muscles of his upper arm. The sheer power emanating from him was overwhelming. He radiated strength, wearing his scars proudly. Probably because the sight of them excited the partygoers, rather than repelled them. The crowd cheered while he stood next to Honoria like a statue of Hercules, stoic and untouchable. Expressionless.

Only Amelia noticed the rigidity of his stance, the tight fists curled at his sides, the tense set of his jaw and—*sweet God!*—the pale sheen of his eyes.

When he'd had enough adoration, Gabriel moved to walk away, but Honoria stopped him with a single touch of her pale, feminine hand on his arm. His eyes didn't just glitter when he looked at her; they shone, catching the light of the oil lamps. Amelia gasped, praying he could control himself. A shift triggered by strong emotion like fear or rage was dangerous. It could kill him, even with the regenerative serum working properly.

"Not so fast, my love," Honoria said.

My love? Another wave of irrational jealousy rocked her on her feet. *It's a test. Stay neutral.* Hard enough to do here without provocation. But the way Honoria ran the backs of her fingers up and down Gabriel's arm made Amelia as twitchy as hell. Especially when she noticed the Caesar's touch was very deliberate, tracing a long scar on his arm. Even from so far away, Amelia felt Gabriel all but vibrating in agitation. He couldn't get away, but he wanted to. Badly. Either that, or turn on Honoria and rip her apart.

"I have a gift for you."

From the way Gabriel tensed again, he too must have caught the malice in Honoria's voice. "I don't want anything from you," he growled.

"This, you will accept," Honoria said with the full authority of the Caesar. She turned to address the crowd. "Ladies, friends, members of the highest circle of my regard. Tell me, has our Champion not proven himself beyond compare?"

"Yes!" they chorused, drawing closer.

"And have the gods not smiled upon his form, and strength, and skill?"

"*Yes!*"

"Has he not entertained us to our hearts' delight?" Her gaze lighted on Amelia. "Pleased us well with his tireless determination?"

"*YES!*"

"Oh my, yes," someone close to her sighed.

Honoria smiled like a cat holding a mouse by its tail. "And is there anyone among us who would bar him from her bed?"

"No!" By now, all of the women had gathered at the front, leaving the men to watch all this like some show being put on for their amusement.

Amelia backed into the shadows to get out of sight. All those women were ogling Gabriel like they were starving and he was a feast.

"So much for tonight's entertainment," a man to her left muttered.

"Bastard's going to get the pick of the flock again," another replied. "Just watch, he won't leave any for the rest of us."

The first one hummed in agreement.

He wouldn't!

Would he?

Already the women were all but drooling for him, touching themselves and panting like dogs. It made her uneasy, the intensity with which they coveted him; he had to feel it. Didn't it unsettle him? She glanced at Gabriel. He looked mildly annoyed. That was it.

When the women started moaning and whining, Amelia's earlier jealousy evaporated in an instant, and she felt sick. This was sick. All of it. Gabriel had slept with these women, a rabid pack of bitches in heat, already breathing pleas his way. His Adam's apple slid up and down. He couldn't be unaffected. This had to be wigging him out as much as it was her.

Amelia swayed, suddenly lightheaded. She rubbed her eyes, but the soft sheen of dreaming wouldn't go away. She glanced at the glass of wine she'd drunk, feeling like an idiot when her body started to heat up. It was too warm. Her heart was beating faster. Amelia licked her lips, thirsty for more of that wine. Her muscles loosened, and she felt sleepy and needy at the same time.

Honoria had drugged her. All of them. It was in the goddamn wine.

She squeezed her eyes shut in a feeble attempt to clear her mind, but without her vision, she had no balance whatsoever. And her ears picked up on things that couldn't be real. Amelia braved a look to her left, saw shadows moving, shifting. She squinted to focus her eyes, and gasped. A soldier leaned against one of the columns while another took him from behind. He grunted, and his arm muscles jumped, and Amelia thought he was in pain, but then her gaze dropped lower to the hand he had wrapped around a woman's hair, holding her mouth to his cock.

Amelia dragged her gaze away, but not before she noticed two more men watching the trio and masturbating. One snatched a passing servant girl and shoved her to her hands and knees. A woman squealed on her other side, and Amelia moved out of the way a second before a pair dropped to the table. The woman on her back, a man between her legs, driving himself into her. Another woman rounded the table and climbed on top of it lifting her skirts so she could straddle the first one's face. The girl eagerly hooked her arms around those thighs.

It horrified Amelia that she was growing even more aroused by this. Her breasts felt heavy and wetness gathered between her legs. She was shivering from need and terrified someone would take advantage, that she might welcome it. But the men spared her only minimal attention. Only looked long enough to notice the pendant at her neck. Amelia clutched it like a lifeline and prayed this was one self-imposed rule no Roman would break.

She sought out Gabriel again, needing the distraction of her one solid anchor. But the moment she looked at him, memories of his mouth on her, his hands stroking her, the feel of his cock hard and thick in her hands, filling her body, overwhelmed her, made her clench and…

Amelia shook her head to make herself focus, but it only made her dizzy. She ached for him, knowing it wasn't real but a reaction forced on her by whatever Honoria had spiked the wine with. She'd only had a glass. How much had the others drunk? No wonder they were acting this way.

Honoria let the crowd work itself up to a fever pitch, until Amelia was certain they would mob Gabriel and damn the consequences.

She couldn't be here, hated that it was affecting her like this. Amelia was almost panting in desperation. She breathed deep to ground herself, almost moaned when the simple act of inhaling made her nipples brush against the fabric of her gown, sending little shocks through her spine.

Honoria smiled in satisfaction. "You see, my Gladius, what a generous mistress I am to you? Look at this. Look at all this bounty I have laid at your feet."

As if they were ordered, the women promptly fell to their hands and knees, arching, looking up at him, and it was all Amelia could do not to follow suit. Gabriel stood there, staring into space. Amelia bit her lip until it hurt. The pain helped to clear her mind a little, but not enough to shake this off completely. The silver adornments in her hair made her scalp ache. She pulled them off, tossing them carelessly to the pillow-covered ground.

"All this beauty, offered to you on a platter. That is my gift, my Champion. Tonight, you may have your pick of these women, and rest assured, not one will deny you. Have two, have ten. Have them all, if that's what you wish. I would keep nothing from you." To the women she said, "Ladies, I leave it up to you to prove your worth to him."

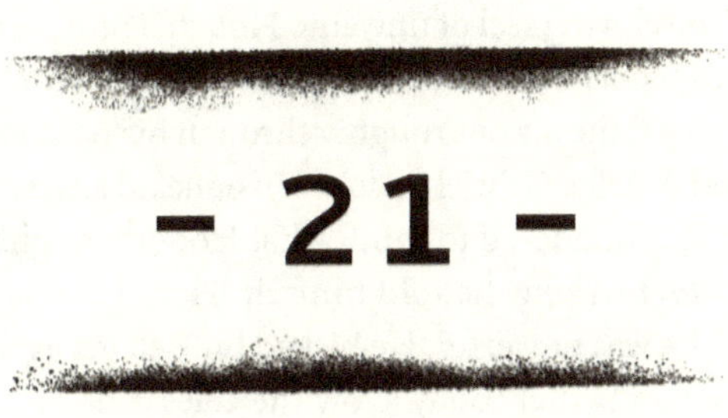

- 21 -

The whore Honoria had had her eunuchs bathe him. The ones happiest to be rid of their balls. He'd roared them out of the bath and bristled the whole time he'd washed and dressed, doing his damnedest to hide his face underwater when his upper lip split clean to his nose, which flattened down like someone had punched him. True to her word, she'd had at least one soldier watching him the whole damn time. He'd nearly drowned, waiting for his face to return to normal.

And now this. He'd already been walking a razor's edge before, but now...

"...prove your worth to him."

The moment she said it, all hell broke loose. In seconds, Gabriel was surrounded by women, many of them naked, touching, grabbing, hanging onto his arms and holding onto his legs. He felt tongues on his skin, while a couple of women dry humped him like dogs in heat. He felt sick.

Gabriel clenched his teeth, felt his canines lengthen until they poked his flesh. He welcomed the pain, focused on it, breathed back the panther panicking at such chaos. It wanted to lash out and fight its way to freedom. Every time a woman moaned his name, the panther roared inside his head, demanding to be let out. So it could run. Even an animal knew it should be getting the fuck out of there.

When his muscles started to cramp, shifting under his skin, he shoved his way out of the crush of female flesh, not caring who got bruised or bloodied in the process. He shook himself off like an animal to get rid of the cloying feel of unwanted touch. His nose was filled to the brim with scents he couldn't shake, but he made himself breathe in deep and expel the air out roughly through his nose to clear it. He needed to find Amelia. Gabriel hadn't seen or heard anything about her all day long. He shuddered to think what Honoria might have done.

She won't do anything, he told himself. Honoria was as cunning and cruel as she was powerful. He kicked himself yet again for losing it the way he had earlier today. Now the Caesar had a pretty damn effective weapon against him, and Gabriel had no idea how she'd use it. He could only hope Amelia was smart enough to stay on her toes and not let herself be manipulated.

And then he saw her, standing in shadow, clutching the edge of a table and staring pensively at a point on the cushion-covered floor, while people around her fucked like there was no tomorrow.

Gabriel growled so low, it was more a physical vibration than an actual sound. Whether anyone heard him, he'd never know, but they must have sensed *something* because no one got in his way as he went for Amelia, and those coupling hastily moved away.

They might as well have not existed to Gabriel. He had eyes only for Amelia. She was dressed in typical Roman garb, flowing blue fabric draped over her and tied with silver ropes. The bulla glittered around her neck, and her hair was free and loose. She looked beautiful. Her scent cut through the cesspool of Roman garbage, granting him the first moment of clarity he'd had all damn day. But it was off.

Her mouth was set, her shoulders rose and fell in tight breaths, she was flushed and her brows were drawn. He recognized the signs as disgust. Even the panther recognized it. This had to be the first time it had ever felt the bitter sting of humiliation. Fangs receded, muscles loosened, but his spine remained rigid.

Gabriel made himself step forward, wanting nothing more than for the rest of the world to disappear. Someone groaned loudly, and Amelia shuddered. *Welcome to Rome,* he thought bitterly. Hatred for everything in this place filled him until it oozed from his pores.

She sensed his approach, tensed up, but wouldn't look at him. Christ, she couldn't even look at him. His stomach tightened; he felt sick knowing she'd seen this shaming display and would probably see far worse before they managed to get out of here. Gabriel wanted to put his arms around her, wanted to be for her what she was for him—the only good, clean thing in this place.

But right now, she probably saw him as another part of this. Her revulsion hit him like a full-body blow to the senses. *Look at me,* he silently willed. His hand rose of its own accord, forefinger gently touching her chin to coax her gaze up. *God, angel, save me.*

She lifted her chin, but her gaze remained fixed on the floor. Then she raised her gaze to his, and he saw how dilated her pupils were, finally recognized the scent battering at his brain, overlaid with something sickly sweet and wrong. That wasn't disgust making her so tense; it was arousal. Unnatural.

Gabriel's hackles rose, making his scalp itch. The sociopathic cunt had drugged her. "Are you with me, angel?" he said softly, not wanting anyone else to hear. He couldn't be sure she caught his words.

Amelia swallowed hard and latched on to his wrist, nails digging crescents into his skin. She didn't say a word; didn't have to. He got the message loud and clear.

When he scented Honoria behind him, he damn near snapped. "This is the one you want?" she asked, as if she hadn't known all along what his choice would be.

"You said you'd deny me nothing," Gabriel growled.

Amelia squeezed her eyes shut, but then somehow squared her shoulders and met his gaze again. She was fighting it, doing her damnedest to get herself under control, though it couldn't be easy. Gabriel knew the brand of aphrodisiac Honoria favored. It mucked with the brain as much as the body, and took a damn long time to wear off. And the more a person ingested, the worse it got. Amelia couldn't have had too much, otherwise she would already be writhing on the floor like the others.

He wanted to sag with relief. They'd get through this. Somehow.

"True," Honoria said. "But you both are my guests of honor. I was going to give her the same consideration I gave you."

"No need," Amelia said quickly. "I choose him."

"Are you quite certain? There are some fine male speci—"

"She's sure," Gabriel snapped and took Amelia's hand. Damage done. Now all he could do was control it as best he could. They were getting out of here. *Now.* "Thanks for the party. Gotta run." *As far away from here as we possibly can.*

"My apartments are at your disposal," Honoria said.

"And those recorders you have hidden in every corner of them will be at yours, right? No thanks."

He pulled Amelia along through the mass of bodies, keeping her close and grabby hands away. The firedancers were still on the staircase. He had to make his way around them to get to the bottom where the guards still stood at attention. "Move," he growled.

The guards looked up toward Honoria.

Gabriel didn't trust himself to turn. She must have given a nod, though, because the guards stood aside and let them through. He'd never been so relieved to step foot onto sand before. "Are you okay?" he asked, never slowing, leading the way through the darkened streets of Rome.

"No," she said, breathing heavier than should be necessary. "Maybe. I don't know."

He kept a steadying arm around her, glad for the cool night breeze. It would help clear her head.

"Where are we going?"

"Somewhere far less glamorous than the palace."

Her head bumped against his chest as if she couldn't hold it up anymore, but somehow she managed to raise it again. "Oh, thank God."

He almost smiled at that. Almost.

The streets weren't empty tonight. There were hundreds, if not thousands, trying to get to Honoria's little get together. Most of them would be turned away, but that had never stopped a Roman before. There would be many more parties tonight, scattered around the arena, held by scorned, prideful Patricians doing their very best to show everyone they hadn't really been trying to get in. They'd had their own plans from the beginning.

Gabriel stalked the streets, taking them farther from the epicenter of chaos into the quiet, dark alleys of the outskirts. The house he sought was empty. A nice little hideaway Honoria might or might not know about. Whether she did or didn't, she never came here and neither did her men.

"Step where I step," he told Amelia, releasing her hand so he wouldn't pull her off balance.

"What do you mean? I can't see anything."

He stopped in the doorway. "Close your eyes and let them adjust to the dark." He could walk this path with his eyes closed, but then he'd done it thousands of times before. Amelia needed to see where she was placing her feet.

After a moment she nodded. "Okay, I think this is as good as it's going to get."

"Can you see the floor?"

"Barely."

"Good enough. Step where I step. Nowhere else. And don't touch anything."

He led the way, checking behind him to make sure Amelia was following his directions. She had her arms spread out for balance and stepped lightly with her toes first, testing the floor before she put her weight on it. *Good girl.*

They circled around the main room, a random path of zigzags, until they were facing the front door again. Gabriel stooped to feel for the edge of the trap door. When he opened it, the window shutters closed one by one and the door locked. Electric lights turned on inside the tunnel, illuminating the ladder rungs.

"Are we getting out of here?" Amelia asked. He could hear the hope in her voice.

"No," he said, bracing for the wave of disappointment that washed over him a second later. "Just going where Honoria won't find us." He helped her down the ladder, following behind her so he could close and lock the hatch.

The tunnel was more of a maze. There were paths leading to dead ends—literally—and paths that kept going in circles big enough to confuse the hell out of the unwary traveler. There were so many booby traps, even Gabriel didn't know them all anymore. But he didn't have to; he knew the only safe way through these catacombs. That was enough.

"What is this place?"

"You'll see," he said. They were almost at the end. He didn't want to ruin the surprise.

The tunnel opened to a spacious cavern. Parts of the walls were still rough stone, as if someone had started carving them smooth but was interrupted before he could finish. There was an underground stream running through here. It was channeled around the chamber's walls, but a small side stream had managed to branch off to run through the center.

This was as close to home as it could be. There was furniture that almost looked modern, electricity, a computer system, and an emergency com system. It was capable of connecting to the world outside of Rome, but Honoria had ways of monitoring when signals went in or out. If he used it, she'd find this place in an instant.

Amelia brushed past him into the cavern. "Did you do this?" She turned full circle, looking around with a sort of wonder he'd never seen in her eyes before. She wasn't a scientist observing her surroundings now, wasn't taking mental notes. For once, she was looking and just *seeing*.

"No," he said and left it at that.

Amelia came back to him, holding his gaze. She touched his cheek with feather-soft fingertips. The scent of the drug was fading. She was getting back to herself. "Your eyes are pale."

Gabriel wasn't surprised. "After the day I had, yours would be, too." His voice came out softer than he'd intended. Weighted down with years of shit no human being should ever be forced to carry. Being back here always brought it up to the surface. His brief escape into Amelia's home, into her life, made coming here all the worse. He'd let himself forget with her. Now it all came back with a vengeance.

Amelia dropped her hand and pulled away.

Gabriel frowned. "What's wrong?"

"Soren told me something today."

He groaned. "Of course he did. Amelia, you can't believe—"

"Is it true they didn't recruit you?"

That son of a bitch!

"You haven't lied to me about anything else so far," Amelia said. "So tell me the truth. Did you ask them to bring you here?"

A muscle in his neck twitched. "He shouldn't have told you that."

"Is it true?" she insisted.

Gabriel's shoulders slumped a little. "Yes," he said.

"Why?"

I'm going to win her, Gabe.

She's not a contest, man, think about this!

I am. I have nothing to offer her now. But once I do this, my name will mean something.

Suddenly weary, Gabriel dropped onto the couch and leaned his head back. The angle was awkward, but at least he didn't have to look at Amelia. "It's a long story. Anyway, it doesn't matter now."

"Funny, I seem to recall telling you almost the same thing about my past, and you still demanded to know. You told me I knew everything about you."

"Everything worth knowing."

"Well if it's so inconsequential, then what's the harm in telling me? And goddammit, what the hell was in that wine?"

"I never said it was—"

"It's simple, Gabriel." She blew out a frustrated breath. The drug would linger in her for a while. Once the sharp arousal subsided, it tended to leave a person hypersensitive and unsatisfied. "You owe me. Those ferric diamonds aren't going to do me a damn bit of good if I never get out of here. I'm kind of depending on you to *survive.* And it's not exactly a comfort to know you might not have a plan to get out yourself. I know this was a suicide mission for you from the start, but are you willing to get me killed, too?"

Gabriel shot to his feet. "Is that what you think?"

"And what should I think?" she said, getting in his face. "You had Honoria right in front of you twice now, and you did nothing."

"You were standing right next to Soren!" And the general's hand had been on his sword the entire time.

"You're a gladiator. From the looks of it, a pretty damn popular killer."

"That would not have saved you today if Soren decided to pull his blade." God, if only.

She ignored that and continued on her tirade. "You apparently chose this. For reasons I can't begin to guess, because it scares the hell out of me to think about it. And you want to kill Honoria at any price, even if it means your life. Tell me, which part should I be comforted by?"

"Don't do that. Not you. You know better."

"I *don't* know!" she cried desperately. "Don't you see? I don't know anything, except what you choose to tell me. So tell me!" Her fear hit him like a punch in the nose. She was breathing hard, and her eyes glittered like she was about to cry. "Please," she said. "Just tell me."

Gabriel turned away from her, unable to stand the sight of her fighting to keep her tears at bay. Amelia wouldn't cry; she was too strong for that. What killed him was that she shouldn't have to be. He sat back on the couch and dropped his head into his hands. Christ, what a fucking mess. "I told you my college roommate was a cook." The words halted there. Everything in him rebelled against burdening her with this.

Tell her. She deserves to know.

He sought the panther for some sort of support. The beast lounged back, seeming relaxed, now that the mass of horny females was gone, but its gaze was too predatory, too fixed on Amelia. For now, it was watching, biding its time. But the interest was there and Gabriel had no way of knowing if it was lust or bloodlust in those pale feline eyes.

"Well there were three of us in the room," he said, pushing back the panther and any awareness that it was there inside him. "Jack was the cook, Alex was the engineer, and I was the fighter. Had a personal trainer on call every day, courtesy of my scholarship. Fought tournaments every chance I got. Won, too. More often than not.

"There was a girl living in the room across the hall. Paige. Pretty little thing. Genius with computers. She'd come over, take cooking lessons from Jack, self-defense lessons from me, and in return, she'd teach us about computers. Alex always did his own thing, but he was always there for that lesson. He loved that girl..." *Enough to do something stupid.* "And she had no idea."

Amelia came to him, sat on the ground at his feet. She didn't say anything, didn't touch him, but her nearness was enough.

"Then one day this guy came in, told Alex he'd have to prove himself to get a girl like that. Said he had the perfect way to do it. Three-year contract, fame, glory and all that other crap, and then he could come back for Paige with a fat bank account and a name worth taking. So Alex signed up. We tried to talk him out of it, but he wouldn't listen."

"He came here," Amelia guessed.

"He came here."

"So what happened to him?"

"He did well. So well that by the end of three years, the Caesar wanted to renew his contract indefinitely. But Alex had Paige waiting for him at home. He respectfully declined, and they backed off with a smile. A week before he was scheduled to come home, he called us all to brag. We teased him like crazy for being dressed like a statue. He proposed to Paige that day, with me and Jack as witnesses. Happy times.

"Four days later, they found Paige's body three blocks from campus. Poor thing was beaten so bad, we couldn't even make the identification. Her hands were broken, and she had skin under her fingernails. You know what that means?"

"She fought back, like you taught her to do."

Gabriel nodded, the old bitterness coming back to the fore. "I taught her to be brave, so she fought when she should have run," he said. "Against men like Soren and his goon squad, she wouldn't have stood a chance, but she fought anyway. They could have made it quick, but they let her struggle and fight because it amused them. That's what happens when the Caesar is about to lose something precious." The rest of the story spilled out uncomfortably past the lump in his throat.

"Alex must have found out somehow. Last message I got from him was some cryptic code and a map to this place. He never made it to the shuttle home. We were best friends, the four of us. I wasn't about to let it go, and neither was Jack. But of the two of us, I had the best chance of getting in. Jack stayed behind in case something happened to me. He died in a transport collision exactly one year after Paige. Around the time I got to be a *damn popular killer*."

Everyone he'd ever cared about. Dead. Gone forever, leaving nothing behind but old recorded messages and the sound of their voices. Those would never leave him. Not as long as he lived. Gabriel blinked away the memories of broken bodies, bloodied faces that had once used to smile and laugh, enjoying life to the fullest. He dragged himself out of that dark place where his nightmares came from, where he retreated when he missed his friends the most, becoming almost catatonic for hours on end, remembering.

He found himself looking at Amelia's hand, tucked trustingly into his. He squeezed it, grasping on to that fragile thread of compassion he would not find anywhere else.

"Your friend Alex built this place," she said softly.

"Among other things," he replied, having to clear his throat to find his voice. "He built the tunnels as a game. Must have realized something wasn't up to snuff and added the traps later on. Caesars put their faces on every building in Rome. This is the only place they couldn't touch. After all that promise of fame and glory, this cave is the only thing he had that they hadn't corrupted."

"Did you ever find whoever killed him?"

"The old Caesar gave the orders," Gabriel said, anger clearing the last cobwebs of pained misery. "Honoria was the one who carried it out."

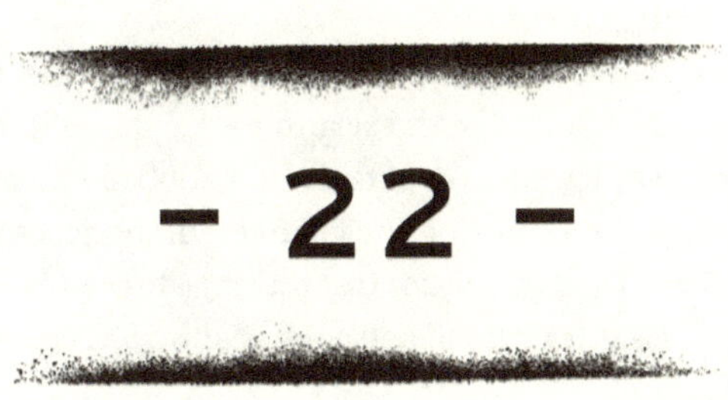

– 22 –

His face changed when he said it. Cheekbones widened, nose flattened down a little, teeth sharpened, and eyes glowed pale brown, almost white. He didn't seem to notice any of it. "All this time, everything you've done, was for revenge?"

Gabriel's eyes flickered when he met her gaze. "If you had a chance to go back to all those sons of bitches who took your friends and make them pay, wouldn't you?"

Amelia swallowed with difficulty. "Yes," she admitted. She wouldn't have hesitated. She'd have found a way; developed a virus, or a poison, something to make sure nothing could save them. She'd make them suffer for days, even weeks, for the lives they'd destroyed. Not just the scientists. Their friends and families; everyone who'd ever cared about them. How many calls had she had to make, informing someone's wife or brother that the man they knew, looked up to, loved, was never coming back? How many times had she had to sit there impassively while a child cried, begging her to bring his mother back?

The only difference between her and Gabriel was that he had what Amelia could never get: the face of the person responsible. He knew exactly who to go after, and now that she knew why he was so determined to do it, she couldn't imagine another course of action but the one he was taking.

His face softened and he smiled, compassion making his eyes darken. "I know that look," he said. He reached out to cup her cheek, but his gaze snared on the dark claws that tipped his fingers. Brows drawn, he stared at them.

Amelia took his hand in hers. She checked his nail beds for damage, but found none. "Looks like the serum took," she said. It made her edgy that this was happening outside of a controlled environment. She had no way of monitoring the changes taking place inside him, no tools or meds for damage control if things turned bad.

But Gabriel was still alive and appeared healthy. She could be grateful for that, at least.

"So what happens now?"

"Now," she replied, "I think it's time you tried a shift. It's better if you initiate it intentionally than have it happen on its own. This way, you should be able to control it better." Amelia pushed up from the ground, but the hem of her skirt was stuck beneath her sandal. She was pulled up short, jarred off balance, and tipped forward.

Gabriel caught her, laughing as she ended up on top of him on the couch. "I can't believe you're actually wearing that," he said.

"I didn't exactly have a choice in the matter," she grumbled. Stupid dress. Everything these Romans wore was like a nymphomaniac's dream design. It was made for the express purpose of being taken off.

"Those bastards," Gabriel said, eyes glittering with mirth.

"Right?" *He* understood. "They tried to shave me!"

Gabriel laughed.

Or not. Amelia glared.

He took one look at her face and laughed harder. "Oh man, I would have loved to have seen that. Please tell me you threw the razors."

"No," she offered grudgingly. "The girl ran away too fast."

Gabriel snorted with laughter, his eyes starting to water. Every time he almost had himself under control, he burst out laughing again.

Amelia felt her lips twitch in answer. She would not give him that satisfaction. She waited him out until his amusement at her expense finally subsided. "I can't believe people actually choose to wear this."

His gaze turned hot and moved down over her, making her feel overheated again. She could have sworn the drug was wearing off, but clearly it was more insidious than that. "It has its uses," he said. "But I can see you hate it. So allow me." He tugged on one of the silver ropes the girls had tied her up in. One little tug, and the whole intricate design, which had taken half an hour to achieve, loosened. *Nymphomaniac's dream...*

Gabriel tugged the rope off her, leaving her draped in blue fabric like the bed sheets they were. The material gaped at the sides, allowing him to slip his hands beneath it. She gasped softly at the feel of his rough hands on her sensitive skin. He caressed her waist, her hips, the curve of her ass, then skimmed his hands up her back to her shoulders. "Gabriel," she breathed and licked her lips.

"Missed you, angel," he murmured, applying a little pressure to bring her closer. "Thought about you all day long."

She was kneeling on the stupid skirt, couldn't get close enough when it kept getting in the way like that. Amelia shifted her weight to free her knees one at a time so she could straddle him properly, with the front of the dress stretched over her between them. "And what have you been thinking?"

He licked the seam between her lips. "Let me show you." His mouth sealed over hers, stealing her breath. Amelia held on, submitting to the measured thrust of his tongue against hers. He led the way, showing her exactly how he wanted her to respond. When she tried to match him, his hands on her tightened in silent reprimand. When her hands skimmed over his bare shoulders to his chest, nails lightly raking against his skin, a low growl rumbled inside him, making her hands still.

He took his time, displaying his dominance with incongruously gentle licks and touches. Amelia became dizzy, her sex squeezing emptiness while he palmed her hips coaxing her to ride him in a rhythm that felt so familiar, and she understood. This wasn't going to be mutual participation. He didn't want her to give; he wanted her to take. To accept him and what he was giving her without wanting anything in return.

"This isn't a good idea," she said between nibbling kisses. She could feel him already hard beneath her, and her sex grew wet for him. How easily, how masterfully he'd trained her body to respond to him. With only his hands on her lower back now, urging her closer, and his erection against her core, she ached for him. Her legs trembled with the need to squeeze him between them. Her arms were sore from the effort to hold still.

Gabriel's eyes lightened again and grew heavy-lidded as he inhaled deeply. "I happen to think this is the best idea I've had all day."

Amelia couldn't stand it anymore. She slid her hands down over his chest, needing to bring herself closer, to press her breasts against him. He caught her exploring hands instantly and pulled them to the small of her back. Imprisoned that way, she ended up hugged to his hard chest. She moaned, frustrated that she might have gotten what she'd wanted, but now she couldn't move at all. Gabriel's mouth settled on her shoulder, brushing back and forth while his free hand smoothed down over the center of her spine, slipping between the globes of her bottom. She reacted on reflex, grinding down on him, and he groaned.

"Gabriel, please," she gasped out, already on the verge of coming. "I need you."

His hips curled up into her in a sharp thrust right against her clit, and she cried out. So close! "Do that again!" He stilled beneath her, harsh breaths rumbling in and out of his chest. She couldn't begin to fathom why he'd stopped.

"Do you trust me?" he growled against her neck.

"Yes," she said without hesitation.

"Lean back."

"What?" There was nothing *back* except the ground.

"Do it," he said, licking the column of her neck from her shoulder to just under her ear.

Her tongue darted past her lips, hungry for another taste of him. *Trust him.* With only his arm at her back for support, she did as he asked and leaned away from him. Her back arched, her sex ground more fully against him, and the fabric of the dress pulled taut over her clit, making her core spasm. Still not enough to bring her off! She was tense, helpless without the use of her hands to stop herself if his arm gave out and she toppled back.

Gabriel groaned, his eyes glowing. With his free hand, he ripped the shoulder seams of her dress. The front pooled in her lap, and he bent over her to capture her breast. At this strange angle, Amelia dangled from his arm, her knees braced on the couch no longer enough leverage for anything. When his mouth latched onto her nipple and sucked, Amelia's eyes nearly rolled back in her head. She went limp, trusting him fully, and he growled his approval, moving her against him to keep up the rhythm he'd instigated.

And all she could do was take it, accept what he gave her. When his teeth rasped over her nipple, her belly tightened, and a perfectly timed thrust shattered her. She cried his name as she came, arching more to press her breast deeper into his hungry mouth. He pulled her back up and held her tight against his chest, thrusting his hips steadily against her to keep the pleasure coming wave after delicious wave.

"I thought I'd never get to do that again," he rasped.

When he finally released her hands, she grasped his hair and kissed him. She was out of breath, still rocking from her orgasm, but her hunger for him hadn't abated at all. She channeled it all into the kiss, holding on to him so he couldn't pull away.

He didn't. With a savage snarl, he met her in kind, and within moments he was overpowering her again, his control shattering. His kisses became wild and hot, the way she loved them. He devoured her, hardly ever coming up for air, as if he couldn't stand for their lips to part even for that short tick of time. He pulled his kilt aside and snatched the remains of her dress from under her, the fabric sliding over her sex and making her shiver against him.

At first contact of his cock with her wet heat, Gabriel nearly lost it. His balls pulled up tight, and he grew harder. Amelia settled her slight weight over him, rubbing herself up and down his length, drenching him with her juices. His mouth watered to taste them, but he wouldn't last long enough to try. The scent of her orgasm was making him lightheaded, bringing the panther to the fore. His teeth ached to sink into her shoulder and hold her still while he pumped into her.

"Do it," she whispered, inflaming him even more. "Make love to me. I'm ready."

Gabriel's chest ached with the harsh thud of his heart. His arms twitched, muscles roiling; he had no control over them. His hips thrust up against her, but it wasn't enough. With an animalistic growl, unrecognizable from his own voice, he snatched her down to the couch and rose over her. She was breathing hard, just like him, eyes unfocused, hands roaming over him. When she skimmed them over his abdomen, his muscles tightened in reaction, bugling and then receding. No, changing. Into something else.

He could feel fangs sharpening in his mouth. When she locked her legs around him, pulling him down, the head of his shaft lined up perfectly with her entrance, something inside him snapped. Gabriel pushed her legs away from him, flipped her so fast she gasped. His clawed hands grasped her hips, pulling her ass up in the air, arching her back so temptingly he wanted to rub his face over the hollow of her spine. He spread her and impaled himself in her heat up to the hilt with one strong thrust.

Amelia cried out, but it wasn't a sound of pain. It egged him on, and he lowered his face to her neck, nipping lightly as he pulled out almost all the way and slammed back in, going as deep as he could. The slap of flesh against flesh was so loud in the silent cave. He did it again and again, trailing his fangs over her perfect skin. Her hands curled into the edge of the couch, digging in and holding tight. "More," she said.

It snapped the last of his control as if it had never existed. Gabriel caught her shoulder between his fangs, holding her still with his bite as he rutted over her like a frenzied beast. He felt her sex squeezing him, demanding more. And he gave her more, pounding into her as her moans became louder, faster. She screamed when she came, milking him like a fist. He shuddered at the feel, the scent, the taste of her.

It wasn't enough.

He released his bite and flipped her again, without relinquishing her orgasm for an instant. Face to face now, he snaked an arm underneath her hips and pulled them up into his thrusts. She was too far gone now to lock him in, too boneless to do anything but accept him, wild as he was. With a gasp and an arch of her back, she came again, harder this time, her fingers digging into his hips. Gabriel never let up, guiding her into another orgasm before the last one had had a chance to ebb.

He fell over her, pulling her tight against him as he moved inside her like a piston, letting the clench of her body wrench the pleasure out of him, as well. The roar that tore out of his chest shook the world around him, and he heard nothing, saw nothing, felt nothing but

Amelia coming apart in his arms.

It could have taken minutes or hours for his breathing to level out. And even then, satisfied purrs rumbled in his chest. He couldn't stop that if he wanted to. Gabriel could feel Amelia's heartbeat against him, felt her soft breath on his skin. Her arms were around his neck, one of her hands tangled in his hair, and he'd never felt so calm and content in all his life. A curious sort of peace settled over him, as if everything was right with the world.

Not ready to relinquish the feeling, he maneuvered so they lay on their sides, facing each other, still joined in the most intimate of ways. Amelia smiled the sort of sleepy, sated smile that made him feel like a god among men. She yawned delicately and cuddled closer to him, settling trustingly in his arms to sleep.

Gabriel buried his nose in her hair and closed his eyes, breathing a sigh of relief. Everything would work out. With Amelia by his side, there was no way it could not.

~

Rain pelted down on him in heavy sheets, stinging his eyes like acid. The sand beneath his feet was mud, puddles of water mixing with the blood of his opponents. It was all over him. As the rain washed the blood away, so the pooling water at his feet stained him with it once again. There was no getting rid of it.

He raised his twin swords high and roared his courage to the heavens, his voice bouncing off the arena walls. The crowds leapt to their feet, cheering madly, thousands of people screaming and waving, gesturing for whatever outcome they wanted to see most.

This time, they were all for one.

Gabriel lowered his swords to the neck of his defeated foe. The gladiator knelt before him, head bowed in submission, neck exposed for the killing blow. The blade of one sword kissed his nape, but Gabriel didn't move more. He raised his gaze to the faraway balcony where the Caesar sat underneath a makeshift umbrella. She would give the final order.

He focused on her impassive face, her cold eyes, and not the bodies littering the arena. The fallen dead were everywhere, their faces frozen death masks.

Faces he knew.

Gabriel held steady, refusing to look at them and remember. Names swirled in his mind, demanding to be acknowledged. Male and female, so many he could hardly keep track of them. Amaya, Malcom, Ruby, Seth—his training mates. Desiree, Juliana, Roland, Braiden, Thom— servants and slaves hired to see to his needs. And the ones that hurt the most: Alex, Jack, and Paige. He'd plowed through them without mercy.

And it had felt righteous. His chest puffed up with primal aplomb. He stood unmatched another day. None would dare challenge him on his turf again. He was master of his demesne.

The Caesar rose from her seat, as graceful as a swan, draped in nearly transparent white silk, her hair glittering gold—a wig. She was magnif- icent. Hatred oozed through his veins like thick sludge. It choked him, infuriated him. He'd bested his enemies. He had. All on his own. He'd proven himself champion among them all, yet his hand was still stayed, waiting for her decision. Her command. He might have won the battle but she chose whether or not he could end it.

Fury uncoiled in his gut, and he ground his fangs together, clawed hands gripping his swords until they shook. The prey was his to end, not hers! Still, he could not move. She held him prisoner with her gaze, the powerful magic of her glacial eyes searing the tattered remnants of his soul to ash. He had no more will than she chose to grant him. She chose not to. And so he could not move.

One delicate arm rose, fingers curled, thumb held out sideways. Ga- briel held his breath, waiting for her to choose. Despising every second that ticked by while she stalled.

My prey! Mine!

At last, that pale thumb turned up.

The crowd screamed approval, their voices rising to a fever pitch as Gabriel raised his sword. Without looking, he brought it down, smoothly severing his opponent's head. Only then did he deign to look upon the challenger's now useless body.

Breath left him.

At his feet, a female form lay still in death, her blue dress now black, soaked with rain and blood. She lay in a pool of it, fingers still twitching with the last of death spasms. She looked so small, so delicate, the silver bulla at her bleeding throat glinting at him, blinding him. He knew the symbol etched on it: Asclepius, the healer god.

A wretched wail tore from his throat. He fell to his knees, battle-hazed mind refusing to comprehend what he was seeing. A shaking clawed hand reached for the body lying so still, but recoiled. She was dead, her head severed from her body. It was far too late to fear hurting her. But he did.

Gabriel tossed his head back and let loose another wail that almost punched a hole through his chest. He clutched it, feeling his own heart still as he rocked back and forth. Hot tears mingled with the icy rain running down his face.

My angel…

Mine…

No longer.

A peal of laughter echoed in the suddenly empty arena. Soul-numbing wrath made his heart beat fast and strong again. He zeroed in on the Caesar, rising to his feet taller than before. His fangs shot longer as he stared at her, his claws sharper. The woman paid him no heed, lost in her amusement.

Muscles tightened, a growl rose from deep within, clawing its way up his throat until it bled. He tasted his own blood, the blood of his mate. The absence of her breath in him made his insides twist and wrench. He doubled over and fell to his hands and knees.

But the pain made him stronger, even as his back bowed from it near the breaking point.

He raised his gaze once more to his prey. A snarl split his upper lip and made his claws dig into the mud. With a powerful launch, he shot after her, leaving his human self behind to bleed and die with his mate…

~

The agonizing spasm twisted his insides until he was certain he would cast them out. Gabriel levered himself up on a shaky arm, mind still hazy with dreams, and looked down at the still body nestled against him. Shock propelled him away from her, off the couch onto the hard rock floor. He scrambled away as fast as his trembling limbs would allow, claws scraping rock like nails on a chalkboard.

His heart hammered against his ribs, too large, too strong to contain. It bruised him from the inside. Another spasm laid him flat, and the next arched him off the floor. He felt muscles twisting and tearing, bones grinding as they changed. His throat locked up, allowing neither breath nor scream to escape him.

When he toppled to his side, his back bowed the other way, stretching and distending while his limbs contracted toward his body into a fetal position.

"Gabriel?"

His head raised, gaze locking on the pale, golden-haired female draped in white rousing on the couch. *The Caesar!*

Gabriel snarled at her, showing off his huge fangs as his spine stretched and grew into a long tail. The wrenching agony made him howl.

The female gasped. "Oh, God!" He could hear her heart thundering, could scent the disgusting tang of her fear. It would taint her blood and stink up this whole place when he tore into her. He couldn't wait.

But her voice was different. "Gabriel!" she cried, and instead of running, came off the couch toward him.

He shook his head, at the last second recognizing Amelia's face. Claws dug into the rock as his limbs broke and snapped into a different shape. The panther was frenzied, its bloodlust spreading across his mind, blurring everything but the need to hunt. And to kill. On a rising growl, he managed to grate, "*Run.*"

And then the panther took over.

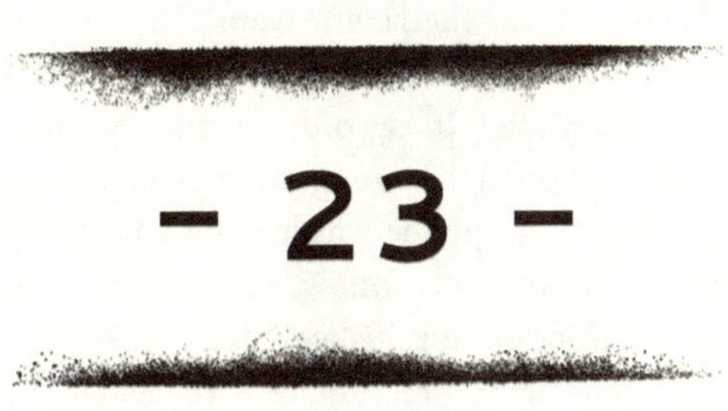

– 23 –

Amelia snatched the blanket tight around her and sprang to her feet, running out into the tunnel. She didn't stop to think; didn't even slow to grab her glasses. Squinting at the blurry world in front of her, she ran for her life. Part of her knew the worst possible thing she could do was run from a predator, but she was in no way prepared to face it head-on. Heart in her throat, she hurried through the passages, praying she wouldn't trip one of the booby traps and get herself killed.

The panther's roar echoed through the cave system. She ran faster, a shot of adrenaline propelling her whichever way she could go. He was closing in on her. She could hear him making his way toward her, stalking her. He wasn't running, as if he knew there was no way she could escape him. Amelia rounded a corner and nearly fell into a deep pool of water. The underground stream emptied here, into what looked like a thousand-foot-deep pit. The light shone down as far as it could go and then the water was… black. Not gray rock, but black abyss. There had to be an outlet down there somewhere, another crevice in the rock where the water disappeared, otherwise it would have flooded the tunnels by now.

Dead end. Amelia spun on the balls of her feet, cutting one on the sharp rock, and ran back, taking another way. The panther at her heels was growling now, a purring rumble that bounced off the walls, as if he enjoyed this cat-and-mouse game.

She turned another corner, trying a different branch of the tunnel.

This place was a labyrinth and she'd already gotten so turned around, she had no idea which way she'd come from. *I'm going to die here,* she realized. If not in these tunnels tonight, then somewhere out in Rome tomorrow. Or the day after. It was only a matter of time.

The premonition sapped the strength out of her and she stumbled, the cut in her foot stinging. She was leaving a trail of blood in her wake the panther could easily follow right to her. Amelia couldn't have made it any easier on him if she'd tried.

A crossroad. *Left or right?* Both tunnels were pitch black and deathly silent. She'd be completely blind in there and ridiculously easy prey for a creature with exceptional night vision. Amelia tossed a frantic glance behind her. *Left or right? Left or right!*

She dashed right, feeling her way along the wall. Without the benefit of her sight, she was reduced to a snail's pace, carefully sliding one foot in front of the other. The pain in her foot barely registered, nothing more than a dull ache at the moment, but when she calmed down—if she lived long enough to do that—she knew she'd be in agony.

A pebble skipped down the rock wall behind her. She stilled, turning around blindly while keeping hold of the wall. If she let go, she'd be completely lost. No sense of direction at all. She could feel her pulse hammering in her neck. Her eyes darted left and right and she struggled to keep her breathing as quiet as possible so she could hear. It was making her dizzy with lack of oxygen.

Another pebble skittered across the floor. It thumped off her big toe, and she gasped. "Gabriel?"

Silence answered her.

The hairs on the back of her neck stood on end. She could feel eyes watching her and shivered with dread and cold. The blanket wasn't nearly enough to stave off the chill of this cave. Her hands were starting to feel numb and the ache in her foot intensified. Her teeth chattered as she spoke. "Gabriel, listen to me. You have to control this. It's your mind, your body. Don't let the panther rule you. You're stronger than that." She eased her foot back a little, skimming her hand on the wall.

The growl he emitted sounded like an avalanche somewhere above ground, and she stopped. When he fell silent again, Amelia squeezed her eyes shut, accepting her fate.

His prey was wounded. The beast thrilled at this. He tracked her by her blood through the maze of tunnels, taking his time. There was no need to hurry. His prey would be easier to take down now. She would tire soon and then he'd have her.

Unease.

Why? He did not understand. The female was a menace. She made him kill for sport. He remembered the names and they hurt him inside his head. He shook it out, irritated, and hastened through the tunnel. But his step slowed with hesitation again. Something wasn't right. His senses pricked up, sorting through every little detail.

He could scent blood and fear; his prey was close by, slowing. The panther lowered closer to the ground, ears twitching. There was the soft trickle of water from back where she'd started bleeding. There was the low howl of air rushing through the maze from somewhere unknown. There was his prey's heartbeat. That made him snarl.

He took a whiff of the blood in front of him. His nose wrinkled, and his heart beat a little faster. Excitement? No. Apprehension. Concern.

He snarled again and shook himself out as though wet. No reason for that!

Still, he trotted forward, ears flat, eyes sharp for any movement. He rounded the corner where her scent became stronger, and slowed. Two paths before him, but only one carried her scent. He eased to the opening of the dark tunnel, his tail tapping the wall, accidentally loosening rock.

He saw her a little way off, his vision perfect, when she was all but blind. She didn't see him, her eyes darting left and right frantically. The unease returned. Her face was different. Blonde hair, white dress, but her eyes were wrong. She smelled wrong. Good, but wrong.

The panther lowered to the ground to watch. His tail swished along smooth rock, sending another pebble across it, right to her. Another wave of her fear hit his nose. She spoke. Human words that somehow made sense. Had he heard them before? His head tilted to the side.

The woman eased a step away from him, and he came to his paws again, growling. She was two steps away from the edge of a precipice. He could scent a lot of old air from that place. The hole went down far. When she stopped again, he felt relief.

The panther huffed in agitation. It was the *other one*. The human him was frantic, holding him back. He supposed that meant this was the wrong prey. She did look a lot like the interesting one from before. But he couldn't be sure… hadn't been *himself* then.

"Gabriel?" she spoke again.

Get her safe! The other one demanded. He would take over if the panther refused.

Huffing, grumbling, he trotted around the frightened female and nudged her away from the precipice. She squealed, which made him growl, but she did move. *Sloooowly.* When they emerged into the lighted tunnel, she sighed with relief. So did the other him.

The panther huffed and trotted off back to the cave.

"Wait!" the female called, and he growled again for her to hurry up. Bad enough that he had to argue with the other him about what to do with her, he was in no mood to be waiting around until she caught up. He had things to do while he was out here. Caves to explore. The other him knew where the traps were and he wanted to see them for himself.

At the next corner, the female caught his tail, and he stopped dead.

Inconceivable! With the other him laughing in his head, he rounded on her and roared.

She jumped, but didn't release him. "Slow. Down," she ordered. *Ordered.*

Baffled, the panther stared at her.

The other him rose to the fore, and he growled, shaking his head to get him loose. But the human was strong, and fighting him was not easy. He pawed at his head, roared inside it, did everything he could to intimidate the human, but he would not back down. The more he struggled, the less ground he had until… until…

Until there was no more panther and the other one.

Gabriel opened his eyes, feeling the panther inside him, all around him, but they weren't separate anymore.

"Hey, are you okay?" Amelia said, concern in her voice. He still had the scent of her blood in his nose. He turned to her, and she flinched. Moving slowly, cautiously, he brought his nose to her feet and sniffed.

Fresh wounds. Her foot had to be cut up pretty bad. No wonder she'd been lagging behind.

Gabriel nosed her ankle, then rasped his tongue over it, savoring the taste of her skin. All of his senses were a hundred times better in this shape; he'd have to explore them thoroughly. Later. Right now, he had to lead Amelia out of here, back to safety. How she'd managed not to trip any traps was beyond him. But he was grateful.

Now he picked his way carefully, going slow so she could keep up. Every once in a while she hissed in pain, and he cursed himself for having been the cause of it yet again. This was the second time his nightmares had hurt her.

Gabriel could keep her safe from the Romans when he was with her. He could get Soren's men off her back and keep Honoria in her place. He could even show her the nicer, gentler sides of Rome. But how in the hell was he supposed to protect her from himself?

The tunnel opened into his cave lair again, and Amelia sighed next to him. She hobbled to the couch. He felt like shit with each step she took. Bloody footprints marked her trail. As soon as she sat, she raised her foot to examine it. "Crap," she muttered. "I don't suppose you have a first aid kit in here?"

He did. But against common sense that said to shift back to his human shape and get it for her, instinct told him something else. Instinct won out. Gabriel rounded the couch, nudging her hands away with his nose.

"Gabriel?"

She was nervous. Having a carnivore sniffing around a bloody limb couldn't be the most comfortable feeling to have. But she was handling herself masterfully. She kept still, though her heart was racing again; she looked at him warily, but didn't fight him or try to get away. Meeting her gaze to reassure her, he gently licked her wounded foot. He was relieved to find that even though the taste of blood was interesting, he didn't feel any uncontrollable urge to take a bite out of her foot. Always good to know.

"Ever heard of sepsis?" Amelia asked.

He grunted in answer since he couldn't exactly voice his opinion. And even if he could, there was no way to explain why he needed to do this when he himself didn't know. It felt right. He licked the wound again, cleaning off the blood and dirt to gauge the severity of the cut. The ball of her foot had an arching groove ripped into the skin by a jagged edge.

"Yeah, okay," she said, pushing at his head. "That's enough. I could really use some antiseptic, and your whiskers tickle."

Gabriel shook off her hands and put a paw on her leg when she would have moved it away. His claws barely touched her skin, but she went still as a statue. He wasn't exactly doing a jig either. A baffled sound was all he could manage as he stared at Amelia's foot. Was it his imagination, or was it healing?

He distinctly remembered the wound being bigger and bleeding. Now the very edges looked like they were… closing? Gabriel looked up at Amelia for confirmation. She met his gaze but seemed to have trouble forming words.

Curious, he lowered his head to her skin again and swept his tongue over her foot in a long, slow lap.

The ravaged skin pulled together and mended before his very eyes.

His paw slipped back down to the floor, and he sat, at a loss. Was this some sort of side effect of the change? He already knew his body healed quickly to compensate for the damage done by shifting shape. Amelia had never mentioned this ability could be passed on to someone else.

Amelia touched her foot to the ground, testing it. "That's a new one," she said.

Gabriel's mouth pulled to the sides in an awkward snarl-smile. He didn't know why Amelia was looking so serious. This was great! He couldn't wait to test all of the applications. Would it work when he was human, too? What exactly could he fix?

There was one thing he knew he could do.

He got up, startling Amelia backwards. Using her momentum, he hooked a paw beneath her other leg and nudged it up. She got the hint and proffered her other foot. This one wasn't as bad as the other. It wasn't bleeding, just scratched up a bit, but that didn't stop him from showing it the same meticulous attention. When he was finished, he sat again, head high, feeling like a rock star. He tried to waggle his eyebrows, but it felt weird.

Probably looked it, too, given the face Amelia made.

"Uh, thanks," she said.

Gabriel rolled his eyes. He knew those wheels of hers were already turning, calculating all the facts and possibilities. Him? He was over the moon to be alive—and a *panther*! With healing saliva. Ha! He wanted to run. He wanted to jump into the pool of crystalline water and romp around. How high could he jump? Could he scale those rocks?

"It had to be the regenerative serum," Amelia said, brows drawn in concentration. "I amped up the dosage, hoping it would lessen the pain of transformation. I never imagined…"

Gabriel hopped up on the couch next to her, his tail flaring out to balance him. Cool. Face to face with her, he savored the sight of her eyes going wide, staring into his. He could distinguish every shade, every speck of color in them.

Amelia raised a timid hand, touched his face. His ear twitched when she brushed it, and she grinned. "How do you—"

He licked her face.

"—feel?"

In answer, he laid on his back and put his head in her lap.

"You're enjoying this way too much."

Gabriel barked a strange-sounding laugh. Hell yeah, he was! Now that he'd worked out the double personality issues, this was the most amazing thing he'd ever done. He was strong, he was fast, he could scent things above ground and see in the dark—and not just animalistic, catching what little light there was and interpreting it. No. He could see. In pitch black darkness. Whatever Amelia had done in the past, this had to be her greatest achievement yet. She hadn't just combined human and animal DNA; she'd joined the strengths of both to make something that surpassed them. Gabriel felt invincible.

Amelia smiled, her eyes sad. "It worked."

And that was bad news?

"You don't need me anymore."

The muscles in his core contracted. He turned over as his body began to roil again, shifting out of its animal shape. It wasn't pleasant, but neither was it the bone-breaking, gut-twisting agony he'd gone through to get to this point. When it was over, Gabriel was left gasping, sore and bruised, but whole. He cupped Amelia's cheek with a shaky hand. "I'll always need you," he grated. His jaw felt stiff; he couldn't open his mouth enough to speak normally, and his voice was a scratchy growl.

She took his hand in hers, pulled it away from her cheek. "We had a deal. It didn't include emotional attachment."

"Yeah, well it didn't include you getting kidnapped to Rome either. I guess we'll have to renegotiate."

"You got what you wanted. What's left to negotiate?"

A week ago, he wouldn't have seen it. He'd have taken her nonchalance at face value, accepted defeat, and walked out of her life. It'd have killed him, but he'd have done it. But too much had happened. He knew her too well, and the heightened senses didn't hurt either. He could see in her eyes the raw vulnerability she strove so hard to conceal. He wasn't in this by himself. Amelia was right there with him, just as deep. There was no way out of the hole they'd dug for themselves, and he thanked all the gods above for that. Even the son of a bitch Trickster who'd gotten them into this mess to begin with.

Gabriel could feel Amelia's pulse on the soft inside of her wrist. The rhythm matched his own. Their hearts beat not in unison but in harmony, complementing each other. On some level, she had to feel it, too.

Now he had to get her to admit it.

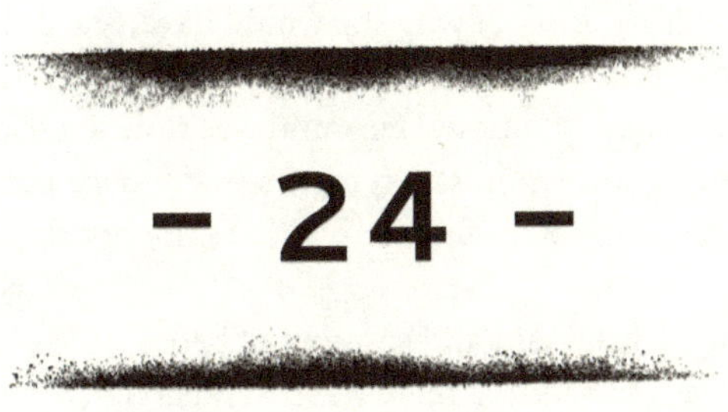

– 24 –

A low beep pulled on Amelia's consciousness, dragging her out of a warm, pleasant haze of dreamless sleep. It was dark; not a sliver of light penetrated her eyelids. As the noise faded, so did she, drifting back to sleep.

But the beep returned; an irritating gnat in her ear. Amelia didn't want to move ever again. She was cuddled against her lover, cocooned in his warmth and strength, puffs of his breath caressing her neck. He'd held her all through the night, as if he couldn't sleep unless he felt her with him. She was warm, sated, and so relaxed, nothing could bother her.

Except that damn beep.

Amelia forced one eye open, squinting in the darkness, unable to make out even the tip of her nose. She groaned in displeasure to be so rudely awakened in the middle of the night. Behind her, Gabriel rumbled an answering growl, pulled her closer, and buried his face in her shoulder.

She would have been content to snuggle in and sleep, but the beep returned yet again, and she got that annoying tingly, startled feeling in her belly, sharply shedding a layer of sleep. Irritated, she ground her teeth, waiting for it to stop. Beeps always stopped after a while.

This one didn't.

Gabriel purred—actually purred—from deep in his chest where she could feel it against her back. "Did you set another alarm?" he mumbled.

Amelia couldn't think of why she would have. She didn't have any appointments, and there was nothing pressing in her schedule that would demand her attention. Her mind was slow to kick in. She was almost asleep again when she remembered where they were. She tensed and felt Gabriel do the same. "That's not my alarm."

Beep.

"I'm on it," Gabriel said and shot out of bed.

Except it wasn't a bed, and there was barely enough room for the two of them on it. Jarred from her position, Amelia tipped forward and, with a squeal, toppled to the hard, cold ground as the lights came on.

She got up and wrapped last night's dress around herself for cover if not warmth. She found her glasses neatly perched on a pillow next to the couch. Amelia felt a bloom of warmth in her belly. Had Gabriel put them there, out of harm's way?

Gabriel swore, dispelling most of the enchantment, but not all.

"What is it?"

"A seeker signal."

"I'm guessing that's exactly what it sounds like?" She padded over to him, taking care with her still-sore feet.

"It's like a fishing net tossed over a wide area. Most systems are designed to automatically respond with a ping if they're capable of communication."

"Honoria?" Did she suspect Gabriel had a com somewhere?

"I don't think so," he said with a frown. "I'm tracing the signal back to its origin. It's coming from off-world."

Amelia read the results on-screen. The computer was still on the signal's path, and a small map in one corner displayed the trace—a mad flight across the galaxy far from Rome. "That's…" *not possible.* The direction it was heading… No, it couldn't be. But the possibility made her heart beat a little faster.

Gabriel noticed. "You know something I don't?"

Amelia didn't respond. She held her breath, watching the map zero in on a solar system, and then a planet.

"Torrey," they said in unison. Amelia grinned, almost giddy with hope. They had a plan B!

"Torrey, where your sister recorded that thing with the virus?"

Amelia shook her head. "Torrey, where Tristan lives." She couldn't quell her enthusiasm. By some miracle, Tristan was calling here! All the nastiness of last night's machinations by the Caesar disappeared for one shining moment of utter joy. She was going to get out of here. Tristan would find them and come rescue them, and she was going to go home!

Then she looked at Gabriel and her mood plummeted. "Why are you looking at me like that?"

He said nothing.

Amelia shook off the strange feeling she'd somehow disappointed him and turned her attention back to the computer while she put the dress on properly. "Did you ping back yet?"

"No," he said.

"Well, what are you waiting for?"

"A good reason."

Amelia blinked at him. "That's our ticket out of here. What more reason do you need?"

He pointed at the blinking red light on the console. "That little shield is all that stands between this place and the outside world. I have to deactivate it to send the ping, and the second I do, Honoria will know. How sure are you that your knight in shining armor will be so eager to help you?"

Amelia flushed, unable to answer him. She had no reason to think that Tristan would help her; no reason to think it was him at all. And if it was, and if he decided to intervene, there was no way he could get to them before Honoria did. If Gabriel exposed this place, the Caesar would destroy it without hesitation, and who knew what other retribution she would take? It was a huge risk to both of them.

Beep.

A lifetime of logic shut down. Her gut told her she needed to make that call, to get some sort of signal out, no matter what. It could be their only chance at getting out of here alive. "What choice do we have?" she asked, her voice barely above a whisper. "We're not getting out of here on our own."

Gabriel swore. "I could—"

"What? Fight your way past the legion of trained soldiers?"

"I can get you out of here safely," he growled. "You don't need that guy."

"And what about you? Oh wait, I forgot. You never planned on leaving once you got here."

"Amelia…"

Beep.

"We're too far. Your knight won't be much help from across the galaxy."

That set her teeth on edge. "Ping him," she said. "That's all I'm asking. Let them at least get our coordinates so someone outside this godforsaken world knows where're here."

"He'd never know who it was from."

Beep.

"Oh, believe me, he has his ways."

Gabriel's eyes narrowed. "You won't trust me, but you'll trust some-one who isn't even here?"

Beep.

"Yes," she said without hesitation. Amelia had no way of knowing if Tristan would take up their cause, but she knew without the faintest shadow of a doubt that if he did, he would succeed. He would get them out. They had to at least give it a try.

"I don't like it," Gabriel said.

He was wasting time! "It's a ping, it can't take longer than it takes to say the word."

Beep.

"Long enough to get us noticed. Honoria is cruel beyond your imagination. By the time your knight gets here, he might have only pieces of us to pick up."

"So we should let her rule our lives? I won't accept that. You are so eager and prepared for death, but now I have a chance to get out of here—we have a chance to get out of here—and you hesitate?"

Beep.

"Your kni—"

"I swear to God, if you call him my knight one more time, I will slap the hell out of you." This was getting them nowhere and every second he did nothing was more time for her to get angrier. She hated not being in control of a situation. Gabriel was keeping her deliberately off balance and helpless. Why? So she would have to rely on him? When he himself didn't expect to survive?

Gabriel's eyes glowed, his anger palpable, yet she was unafraid. Amelia was just as pissed and ready to fight him if need be. "What did he do to earn such trust from you?"

Beep.

"You're wasting time." She could feel the window of opportunity closing on them. That signal wouldn't be there forever. "Just ping him already."

"Not until you tell me."

Beep.

"What does it matter? The point is I trust him with my life, isn't that enough?"

Gabriel slammed a fist down on the console. "What did he do?"

BEEP.

"Ping him!"

"Answer me!"

"*He lived!*"

Silence.

They stared at each other, their harsh breaths the only sound in the underground chamber.

And the silence stretched on.

Amelia was so furious, she could cry. She set her teeth against angry tears, refusing to blink and force them out. "Did we lose the signal?" she grated.

Still glaring, Gabriel turned to the computer. "I'm not getting anything anymore."

Helplessness nearly crushed her again and she wanted to wail in denial. She blinked, and a tear rolled down her cheek, unchecked. "Can you still ping him back?"

He sighed heavily. "The seeker was wide range. He's probably getting a billion pings by now. Even if I did, he wouldn't be able to sort through them all to find mine."

Amelia hung her head. She'd been through a lot in her life. She'd kept her composure for years in New Alaska, had faced a shape-shifter in a blood rage. She'd seen her sister destroy her life and struggle to get it back. But none of that compared to what she felt now. Her legs held steady, but inside she was shattering.

Gabriel muttered something she didn't catch. She heard him typing, but didn't trust herself to look up and see what he was doing. "It's done," he said.

Amelia raised her gaze to the computer screen, where a confirmation message blinked. The two of them watched the screen without a word, waiting for something. A call from Torrey. Another alarm warning that they'd been discovered. Amelia's heart thumped so hard in her chest, she shook with it.

After a while, when nothing happened, Gabriel sighed. "We should go."

"Wouldn't it be safer to stay here?" she asked.

"I'm hoping the ping won't register on Honoria's system as more than a tiny blip, but if her monitors are looking for it, they'll have our position by now."

Her instinct went against leaving a perfectly good hiding place. The cave was so well camouflaged and fortified, it felt like they could be safe here forever. But it was no better than a child closing her eyes and pretending it made her invisible. Sooner or later, they'd be found. Much better to take their chances outside than to corner themselves in here.

"We go out there and you get taken to the arena," she said. She hadn't forgotten today was his big day, the champion's return to glory.

Gabriel shrugged. "Just another workday." He wasn't nearly as self-assured as he wanted to appear. Whatever Honoria had planned would be bad, made worse by his alter ego. There was no telling how the panther side of him would react to so much blood and death.

"As your doctor, I would advise against excessive stress, both mental and physical."

He rose and caught her face in his hands, brushing away her tears. "As your lover, I would say don't worry. At the end of the day, I'll always come back to you."

~

Planet Torrey

"Sweet Jesus, if you don't stop that noise, I will hurt you." Hailey wasn't really sure which she was talking about: the deafening beeps echoing in the lab, which had become dusty while she'd been on her honeymoon, or the screech of the wriggling infant in her arms. The threat didn't work on either.

Hailey bounced the child in her arms, hoping it would calm the girl enough to stop crying, but it only agitated her more. Why couldn't she have gotten the male instead? Tristan's son, Jonathan, was snuggled in his mother's arms, cooing softly and tugging on Dara's loose hair as if none of the chaos fazed him. That kid was a marvel.

Juliana, the evil spawn of Satan, screamed so loud, her entire body shook. How could something so small be so freaking loud? "Oh, my God!" Hailey yelled. She couldn't take this. Her head was splitting open and she'd about had it with the way everyone ignored her.

"Where the hell's the sound control?" Tristan growled. He had to be in as much agony with his super hearing. His skin wasn't just tattooed with stripes anymore; it was turning orange. She wasn't sympathetic at all.

"How should I know?" Jer yelled back, fumbling with the computers.

Hailey growled and marched over to the tiger man, shoving his uncooperative daughter at him. "Take that and move," she told him.

Tristan took the girl, snuggling her against his chest, and within seconds, Juliana quieted. Like he'd flipped a switch. Hailey snarled at them both and took over the controls. This was Amelia's system, a purpose for everything and everything with its purpose. The only problem was that someone—meaning the striped, orange moron—had the brilliant idea to route the program's output through the alarm system rather than straight audio.

"I can't turn it down," she said. But she could damn well turn it off. The flood of responses they were getting was turning into one long beep instead of hundreds of thousands of short ones. Never again was she letting Tristan Hunt near her stuff again. She typed a few commands, because voice was beyond the realm of possibility right now, and shut off the alarm. Blessed silence filled the lab. Though she could swear the ringing in her ears was still echoing.

All of them breathed a sigh of relief.

"Did it stop?" Dara asked. She was perched on the gurney, where not so long ago Hailey had died. A couple of times. Dara wasn't looking much better than Hailey had back then. She was pale and still weak, having to deal with two newborns and the complications she'd had giving birth to them. That little psychotic episode she'd had in the night hadn't helped, either. The woman should be on bed rest, not traipsing across town with her hulking husband and infant twins in tow.

But damn, Hailey was glad she had.

Tristan went to Dara, took Jonathan from her, and put both babies down into the makeshift crib they'd made out of an old incubator. She wanted to tell him it had been used to mix toxic chemicals. For all she knew, it had been.

But the way he looked at his wife when he sat down next to her locked her mouth shut. "You shouldn't be here," he said, rubbing Dara's back. "You're still weak."

Dara leaned against him. "Better here, than at home by myself." She shuddered.

Tristan pulled her into his lap to cradle her. He exuded peace as if he was willing Dara to relax, and Hailey found herself swaying on her feet, suddenly very tired.

Then Jeremy grasped her hand and the feeling was gone. *Did he just…?* she asked in the privacy of her mind.

—*Dara needs it,*— Jeremy answered in kind. —*Don't worry, he's not trying to calm you down on purpose.*— There was wry humor in that she wanted to kick him for, but then he put his arms around her and said, —*Amelia will be fine. We'll find her.*—

Now you're trying to calm me down on purpose, she groused. But she was grateful.

Hailey felt sorry for Dara. The woman had enough problems without adding freaky, telepathic nightmares into the mix. When the four of them had shown up at Jeremy's doorstep at four a.m., she'd looked like the hounds of hell were chasing her.

Jeremy said it was like the dreams they shared sometimes, only theirs were pleasant. Dara's weren't. The telepath couldn't seem to shake them.

Tristan speared Hailey with his glowing yellow gaze. "Has it stopped?"

Hailey shook herself inwardly and checked the computer. "It seems to be winding down. There's too many responses, though. The program is storing them instead of tracing because it can't keep up. It might take a while."

Dara shook her head, looking up at her husband. "No, we don't have a while."

If the look on Tristan's face was anything to go by, that small plea was enough to make him go berserk trying to change the universe so it made sense for his mate. Too bad this time there was nothing he could do.

"What exactly did you see?" Hailey asked. All she knew was that Dara had had some sort of nightmare involving Amelia. She wouldn't say what it was about, but offered to show Hailey—and no, thank you. She'd tried before with a non-Jeremy person. Not about to do that again.

Dara closed her eyes. "I'm in darkness, like a cave, or a tunnel. Everything is blurry; I can barely see where I'm going. I'm so cold, and my feet feel like I'm walking on glass. There's so much fear and confusion, but not only for myself. And I can feel something coming after me."

Tristan rumbled some primitive purr that soothed Dara.

"And you don't know where it's coming from?"

Dara sighed. "No, just a general direction. But I know there is a computer of some sort there."

That's what she'd said earlier. That she knew even that much was apparently a big deal. So they'd pointed the seeker and let it do its thing. None of Amelia's equipment was designed for something like this. Dara could point at the sky and they could aim the signal that way, but it wasn't laser-straight. The farther it went, the wider it spread out. Who knew how long they'd be getting flooded with responses before it stopped?

If it wasn't her sister Dara was channeling, Hailey wouldn't give a damn, but she owed Amelia her life in every sense of the word. And because she wasn't the only one, here they all were, grudgingly putting their heads together for her.

The numbers slowed from three thousand pings per second to a hundred, then rapidly down to ten. A few moments later, it was one every couple of seconds, then a long stretch of nothing, during which the computer started analyzing all of the inputs. A whole lot of entries started streaming down, virtual addresses of every single response they'd gotten. "Looks like it's over."

And it was a giant mess. Hailey wondered what sort of divining rod Dara would use to find the needle in that haystack.

"Just wait," Jeremy said.

Hailey hated waiting. She wasn't the sit-on-the-sidelines kind; she wanted something to do. She was already contemplating using an algorithm to sort through the mess, when the computer blinked one more time, a new response ping delayed enough that it hadn't registered as part of the massive group.

Hailey paused the analysis before the ping disappeared, and traced its address back to the source. *Wait...* "Is that right?"

Jeremy leaned in closer, and Tristan came over with Dara to see for himself. The two exchanged a long look that made Hailey want to growl. "Non-mind reader on board here. *Talk.*"

"It's Rome," Tristan said.

"Oh, well, that's nice. Should we call them back?"

"No," the three of them barked.

Dara was wringing her hands, and the brats were getting fussy again.

Jeremy brought up a map of that solar system. "That's Rome," he said, pointing out one of the planets. "See the big glow right there? That's a very strong signal. Means whatever is there has massive power."

"But that's not where the ping came from," she said. If it was, the computer would have already matched an entry to it, but it hadn't. The last ping to come in had come from close to there, enough that they had to zoom in to a continent to see its origin, but it was a distinct entity of its own and one much dimmer than the one Jeremy was talking about.

"Right," he said. "This one hasn't responded, which means someone is overriding it."

"Which means it's being monitored," she said.

Jeremy wasn't liking this. His agitation was making her inner Hell-cat very unhappy. "It doesn't mean that's where she is," he said, and it sounded like he was willing it to be true.

"She's there," Dara said bleakly.

Jeremy sighed and rubbed his face wearily. "The Chase women don't do anything by halves, do they? One tries to prove her mettle and what does she do? Nearly kills herself. The other gets herself into trouble and where does she end up?"

"In Rome," Tristan said with a growl.

Hailey looked at Jeremy askance, and in response, knowledge trick-led into her mind through their link: rumors, gossip, innuendo, and a few cold, hard facts so disturbing she sucked in a sharp breath and braced herself against the desk, fighting down a sudden wave of nausea.

Jonathan and Juliana started crying. Dara looked in their direction and hissed a shushing sound. The babies calmed a little.

"Are you sure?" Tristan asked out loud.

Dara met his gaze. "As sure as I am that she's not there alone. But whether it's a friend or a foe, I have no idea." She sighed. "We have to help her, Tristan."

Tristan squared his jaw in bleak determination. "Looks like we're taking a trip."

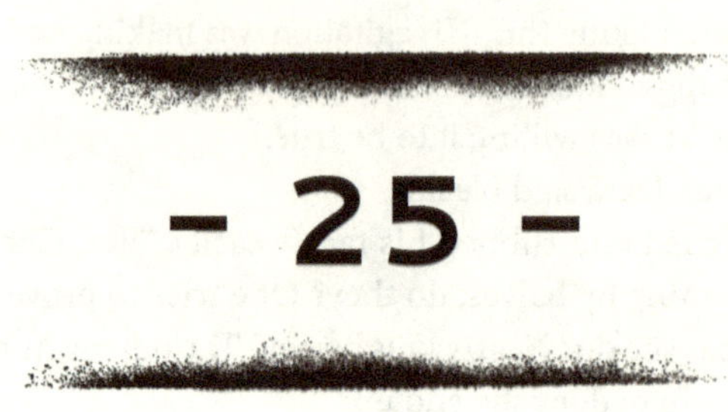

Gabriel took his time dressing. Amelia was trying to knot the ties in some sort of order to keep her gown in place and avoiding his gaze.

The way she'd looked when they'd traced the signal, as if the sun had come up in her world, was making him want to growl. She'd looked so damn happy because of some other guy, it had stabbed right through his heart.

What the hell would it take to have her look at him that way? What would it take to make her see that his heart beat stronger, surer when she was around? The Caesar didn't have to dream up any tortures for him; it killed him to know Amelia was stuck here and he might not be able to keep her safe. Worse, she was fully aware of it, ever the realist, looking at the facts. They were trapped, outnumbered, and soon it might not be "them" anymore, only her.

It killed him that she was probably right to pin her hopes on someone other than him. Gabriel had dug this hole for himself, but he'd never expected her to fall into it right along with him. He didn't want this—any of it. Amelia belonged at home, in her exotic garden, weeding her plants and being happy. He wanted to give her that.

Gabriel looked around his little sanctuary, knowing once he left, he wouldn't be coming back to it. Whether Honoria knew about it or not, whether she chose to destroy it or not, it wasn't enough anymore.

Amelia's bulla lay on the floor, half hidden beneath the couch. He bent to retrieve it, hating what it represented. Yet as he held it in his hands, it didn't feel like a leash; it felt like a symbol. Amelia had given him a gift he never could have imagined. For a few hours last night, he'd felt peace. In the Caesar's hands, the pendant was a distortion of its true purpose, but to Gabriel, this particular one would always be a reminder that for a little while he'd slept in peace, with the woman he loved tucked safely against him, her heart beating a lullaby to him alone. Her scent would never leave him as long as he lived. Her taste would never be surpassed.

Her warmth would never be forgotten.

"I guess it's time," she said.

Gabriel tucked the bulla into his belt. "Guess so." He held out his hand.

Amelia hesitated, eyes unsure when they looked into his. He'd never seen her looking so vulnerable. When he thought she would refuse, she squared her shoulders and placed her hand in his, allowing him to lead her out into the tunnel.

He'd set the system to deactivate on its own. As soon as they left the cave, the computers powered off. The lights had motion sensors, turning off behind them when they left a section of the tunnels. It was more than a little eerie to have the deathly silent darkness nipping at their heels. Amelia kept close, clutching his hand, looking behind them often. Gabriel could scent her fear, her need to go faster, but the faster they went, the sooner the lights would go out.

"It feels like we're closing a crypt," she said nervously. She shuddered and faced forward. He quickened his stride, forcing her to hurry to keep up with him.

By the time they emerged into the main tunnel and he could see the ladder at the end, she was winded. "Hey," she said. "Slow down."

"Were you in love with him?" He stopped so abruptly, she collided with his shoulder. He hadn't meant to ask; didn't know he wanted to hear the answer.

"W-what?"

"Tristan," he said. "The tiger man." Who she'd told him was dead. "Did you love him?" He turned his head sideways, but his gaze never touched on Amelia. If he looked at her now, it would mean acknowledging something he wasn't ready to face. He was having a hard enough time holding her hand.

Amelia straightened, hesitant. "At times, it felt like love," she said softly.

Gabriel closed his eyes. "Do you still love him?" He knew what awaited him up the ladder. There would be a troop of men with swords outside the house, patiently waiting for him to come out. There was nowhere for him to go, except toward them. And he knew where they'd be taking him. Honoria had a full slate planned. The games would be epic to celebrate his return, and the sands would be thick with blood by sunset.

He had the wherewithal to come out on top, Amelia had seen to that. Gabriel was the ultimate predator now, sure to champion over man and beast alike. He had all he needed.

Everything, but will.

What the hell did he have to fight for? He'd wanted revenge for so long, he'd never planned beyond each little step to getting it. He'd gone along with the program, telling himself one day he'd take out Honoria and do his friends proud. Rome had taken everyone from him. It had taken the lives of the few people he'd ever loved.

And for that… he'd joined it.

It hurt like hell to admit it, but there it was. All these years he'd been here, reaping a bloody path in the arena, and he hadn't gotten one step closer to what he'd ultimately wanted. Honoria had always been there. Right in front of him. Countless times so close, he could have poisoned her. Strangled her. Reached out and snapped her neck or stabbed her through her black heart.

But he hadn't done it.

In the end, he'd done nothing but betrayed the people he'd sworn to avenge. He'd become the very image of everything he despised. He'd held strong so long, focused on surviving, he'd never realized that with each win, with every kill, he was losing more of himself.

What was he fighting for, *living* for? Revenge? He wanted to scoff at himself. Justice? That was a pipe dream. Freedom? Where would he go, what would he do with it? Years ago, Gabriel could have made something of himself. He'd chosen to become this. He had nothing and no one left outside of Rome. And the one good thing he'd had the amazing fortune to find, the one thing that might have redeemed him, he'd dragged back into this hell with him.

"Do you?" he repeated, waiting for the answer; dreading it.

It was a yes or no question, but instead of answering, she let go of his hand. Her gaze dropped to the ground, and she said, "There's so much you don't know. So much that's happened, more than anyone should have to go through."

"How touching," he said, his voice dripping with acid.

Her chin lifted, and she met his gaze, her spine straight. Signature confident, unflappable, untouchable Dr. Chase. Except her lips were pressed into a thin line, and her eyes glittered wetly behind her glasses. "He lived," she forced out through gritted teeth, her fists clenching at her sides. She'd said it earlier and it made as little sense now as it had then. "After *years* of hurting people. All those lives—they're all on me, I know that. I have so much blood on my hands…" She shook her head, taking control of herself, cleanly shutting out the horror and pain that had shadowed her sapphire blues for a second. "But he lived."

And Gabriel understood.

This had nothing to do with tender feelings, puppy love, or every female's infernal obsession with the wrong kind of guy. Amelia didn't *love* Tristan Hunt. He was for her what she was for Gabriel: salvation. Tristan had survived. If that didn't justify all of the people who'd come before him, it at least lightened the stain of them. He'd lived, and Amelia got out. She got free. If anyone should understand, it was Gabriel.

I have so much blood on my hands. Gabriel had seen the evidence of it in the file of pictures she'd shown him. But she'd always been so aloof about it, he'd never realized how big of a burden it was for her to bear. *Idiot.* Of course it had to weigh on her. Not only that, now she had three huge responsibilities walking around.

Gabriel cleared his throat and shifted uncomfortably. "I guess I should learn to keep my mouth shut."

Amelia's lips twitched in a wry smile. "I don't know. That sudden outburst of irrational jealousy was kind of cute."

The lights overhead switched off, plunging them into total darkness. That wasn't a problem for Gabriel; he could still see. But Amelia blinked, squinted, and blinked again, trying to make out anything at all. She reached out cautiously. "Hey, are you still there?"

And he was secretly thrilled there was something she needed him for. "Always," he said, taking her hand again and drawing her closer so she could feel him with her. It was as close to a promise as he dared to get. "Come on, the ladder isn't far." It was, in fact only ten yards or so away. With Amelia literally dragging her feet, it took them a good five minutes to reach it. Gabriel didn't mind in the least. Every moment he got to spend with Amelia was a blessing he wasn't about to give up so easily.

He cast a look behind them, able to see a fair distance down the pitch black tunnel. Honoria didn't like secrets, unless she was the one keeping them. She'd destroy this place the first chance she got. Good. It was time to bury the past.

"Up you go," he said, maneuvering Amelia to the ladder. The first step opened the hatch and locked down the house above. There was enough light up there, filtering in through the shutters, that he knew it was day. Not enough to illuminate anything but the top two rungs of the ladder.

Once they were both clear of the tunnel, there was nothing more to do except face the men waiting outside. And they were there; Gabriel could scent at least two dozen and the tang of steel.

He was beginning to learn that distinctive smell. The scent of clean, sharpened metal, stained countless times with blood, and sweat, and dirt, the stench of fear and rage seeping into leather-bound handles like cheap perfume. It overwhelmed his nose, stamping out Amelia as if she wasn't there.

Gabriel met eyes with her. She was her professional, strong, and unflappable self again, ready to stand her ground and fight. He loved that about her. "So what happens now?" she asked.

"Now we face the firing squad," he told her. Part of him roused for a good fight and he couldn't say for sure it was the animal part. This was it. Whatever happened today would put everything to an end, at least as far as he was concerned. He was eager to be done with it. Gabriel's fangs itched in his gums and it made him grin. "A kiss for good luck?"

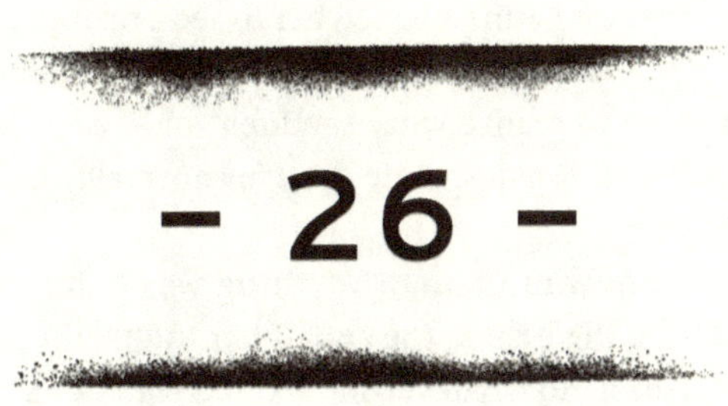

– 26 –

The first time Amelia had met Tristan Hunt, he'd walked into her lab with two guards behind him. His wrists had been bound, his ankles shackled, and he'd been harsh-faced and glaring as the guards escorting him snickered and taunted him.

Two armed guards, trained to handle a prison riot.

Tristan had broken one's nose beyond repair and twisted the other's arm out of its shoulder socket. When they'd been huddled on the floor, weeping, Tristan had taken one's keys, removed his restraints and calmly taken a seat in the exam chair, placing his arms into the manacles which promptly locked him in. "Name's Tristan Hunt," he'd said. "Nice to meet you."

In all the years she'd known him, Amelia had never seen Tristan intentionally harm someone who hadn't had it coming. There'd been times in New Alaska when she'd locked the doors of her lab to keep the guards out. She'd kept a tranq gun on hand every time an inmate had been brought in for treatment or examination.

She'd never been afraid of Tristan.

How easy it would have been to love him. Six years ago, Amelia had dreamed of the man showing the smallest hint of interest in her. She'd treated him, examined him, spoke to him, always keeping an impassive mask in place, but inside she'd been a mess, torn between having to do her job and wanting to protect him, wanting a hell of a lot more than she knew she'd ever get.

And then Dara had shown up. Quiet, unassuming, deceptively boring Dara. To say it hadn't affected her to see a relationship develop between her and Tristan would have been a lie. But observing them, Amelia had come to realize what she'd felt for Tristan was nothing more than infatuation, a desperate need for normalcy in a world that was anything but.

What she felt now more than anything was gratitude. Tristan's survival had been the light at the end of her tunnel. Because of him, she was alive, free to do whatever she wanted with her life. She could love him just for that.

In the tunnel, she'd been caught off guard by Gabriel's question, unable to find the right words to make him understand. Amelia could explain the inner structure of DNA, in detail, to a ten-year-old, but she couldn't tell the man holding her hand like it was precious how much he'd come to mean to her.

She didn't want to distract him and put him in more danger. Emotions split focus between needs and wants. Regardless of what Gabriel thought he wanted, right now, he needed to stay alive so they could get out of here.

And what then?

She didn't know.

When Gabriel closed the trap door, the house unlocked and the shutters opened automatically. He led the way to the door and Amelia didn't need to be told anymore to step exactly where he stepped. In the light of day, she could see the glint of metal through the small cracks and holes in the wall. She could tell where the floor was uneven; detected the edge of some sort of pressure trigger with her toe.

The moment she stepped foot outside, it was déjà vu all over again. Only this time, there were no adoring crowds lining the streets, no petals raining down on them, and no carpet held in place by slaves. There were only the soldiers, hard-mouthed men in armor, with helmets obscuring their features. They stood motionless like statues, but Amelia wasn't fooled. Especially with Soren at the front, mockery oozing from his cold eye.

"Did you really think we wouldn't find you?"

Next to her, Gabriel held steady. "Did you really think I'd care if you did? Have to say I'm disappointed. I thought you'd get here a lot faster. What's the matter, Soren, trouble getting *up* in the morning?"

Soren's eye twitched, the only indication he got it.

Gabriel leaned toward Amelia and stage whispered, "*I certainly* don't have that issue."

Amelia took her cue from him. She moseyed closer to Gabriel and caressed his arm. "You most certainly don't," she purred. To Soren, she said, "He's quite the morning person."

Soren's jaw tightened, and for a second, she had the satisfaction of scoring at least some small victory. There was enough animosity between Soren and Gabriel she suspected there was something very personal behind it. For now, that wasn't important. While Gabriel drew himself up and smirked, Soren turned red, and she'd bet his hand was itching to reach for his sword.

But then his eyes narrowed, and he smirked, too. "I can see that," he said, a little too pleased with himself for Amelia's comfort. Did she have something on her dress? "Looks like you got dressed in a hurry, Doctor. Are you sure you didn't forget something?"

Amelia frowned. Forget something? Was her sheet on backwards? Was it tucked the wrong way, something showing that shouldn't be? She patted herself down. It wasn't as if she'd know if she'd tied the ropes wrong.

"He means the necklace," Gabriel said.

Amelia's hands curled in the sheet. That damn necklace! *Oh, bad, bad!* She couldn't remember having taken it off. It must have stayed behind in the cave. God, how could she have forgotten?

Soren's smirk stretched into a predatory grin. With the exception of last night's party, this was the most emotion he'd shown so far.

She was in so much trouble.

"I did warn you about him, didn't I?" Soren crowed. "Sooner or later he was bound to betray you."

Amelia felt her face turn cold and pale.

Gabriel squeezed her hand a little; the smallest thing, but she felt it, and it reassured her. Gabriel had never given her reason to doubt him. With every word and action he showed her, he was there for her to lean on. He wouldn't betray her.

He wouldn't betray me.

The knowledge was there, as sure and as real as the sun above her head and the sand beneath her feet. Once she believed it, Amelia knew nothing Soren said would make her doubt Gabriel again.

Gabriel sighed dramatically and dropped his chin almost to his chest, slowly shaking his head. "It's almost not worth the effort to make you look like a dick when you keep doing such a good job of it all by yourself." And with that, he produced the shining pendant and held it up for all to see. Then he moved behind her and fastened it around her neck. He took his time about it, too, probably to get on Soren's nerves. From the looks of the man, it was working.

"Remember what I told you," he murmured at her ear. "Let *no one* take this. Someone even looks at it too long, you run, you hear?"

"Nothing wrong with my ears."

"You think this changes anything?" Soren snapped. "She wasn't wearing it when she came out. I have a full battalion as witnesses."

Before Gabriel could jump to her defense, Amelia drew herself up. "Don't you threaten me," she said, stepping forward. He was starting to piss her off, and she was done taking it lying down. "You may be a trained soldier, but sooner or later you will need to sleep. And I'm a doctor. I know how to make it hurt."

Amelia expected them to scoff, laugh at her, underestimate her, and maybe even ignore her. She definitely did not expect Soren's grin to fade at the edges and a few of the men behind him to shift an infinitesimal amount.

What was this? Fear? Was it possible they were actually afraid of her? They definitely looked uneasy. "Ah," she breathed, understanding dawning with a delightful tickle in her belly. "I see my reputation precedes me." For once, she was glad of it.

Gabriel grasped her arm lightly and pulled her back. "Don't push it," he told her.

"But I want to," she replied, feeling cocky enough to take on the world. Because she was as dangerous as any of these men. The only difference was she didn't need an arsenal strapped to her person to show it off.

"Pick your fights," Gabriel said.

When Soren drew his sword, she was forced to admit his strategy made sense. Soren pointed the blade at Gabriel and made a sweeping motion to the right. A dozen men came forward to separate them. They didn't bother restraining Gabriel, but each and every one of them had his weapon drawn and his eyes sharp for any tricks. "Take him to his cell," Soren said. "I'll escort the good doctor to the Caesar."

"Shot in the dark, here, I'm guessing we won't be taking the scenic route."

Gabriel glared at her.

Soren's eye twitched. He jerked his chin at one of the remaining soldiers, and the man pulled out a set of leather straps. Amelia backed almost all the way into the house as he came for her. They whipped people here. Those straps would probably take skin.

Gabriel lunged for the soldier, but his guards held him back.

Amelia yelped when the soldier reached for her, flinching in anticipation of the first lash. It never came. The soldier took her wrists and bound them with the leather straps, tight enough so she couldn't twist them. He tied a long lead to them and handed the other end to Soren.

"Scenic route it is," Soren said. "*Move out!*" He kicked his horse and the monster reared with a loud whinny and took off at a trot. Amelia was jerked off balance and barely managed to catch herself before she fell. She had no choice but to run after Soren or be dragged across the sand behind him.

~

Three against one usually weren't fair odds for the other three. Today the son of a bitch Soren had Gabriel tied up and hung by his wrists from the rafters. His feet touched the ground just barely so he could support himself and stay put. He couldn't get enough leverage to fight back properly, and those three were giving him all they had.

They didn't hit his face; Soren wanted his eyesight and mental faculties unaffected for the games to come. In a strangely chatty moment, the general had told him, "You've been a thorn in my side for long enough." Which Gabriel supposed meant that today was about to be his last.

He'd broken Soren's nose with his forehead in reply.

The bastard had dragged Amelia behind him all the way to Honoria's palace. Just for that, he would be dying bloody before Gabriel went down.

Easier said than done when his shoulder joints strained and his wrists throbbed with almost his full weight hanging on them. His body was one huge bruise, and he was pretty sure he'd be pissing blood soon. The three behemoths Soren had summoned were gladiators in training. Little more than muscle, they were still learning how to strategize and keep a fight going to entertain the masses.

But goddamn, they had fists like anvils.

One of them—Gabriel lost track of which—punched his side, and he felt something rupture. Almost immediately, he felt it start to knit together again. "Didn't quite catch that," he said. It hurt like a son of a bitch, but he was still standing. If he somehow got out of this, he'd have to thank Amelia. Maybe a candlelit dinner or something shiny. Women liked shiny, didn't they?

The one with the braids drove his knee into Gabriel's midsection. He felt it all the way to his spine, and for a few minutes, all of his insides locked up and he couldn't breathe. He was keeping his human shape solid with thoughts of more pleasant things. His pain threshold was usually pretty high, but this was too much to ignore.

"That was almost"—he coughed—"a good kick. Lean into it a little next time."

"Why won't you stay down!" the third yelled and swung the flat of a wooden training sword at Gabriel's back. For a second, he lost feeling below his waist, but it returned quickly, leaving his lower body tingling from waist to toe.

That blow would have broken his back or even severed his spine, if not for Amelia's treatments. If he could, Gabriel would have laughed, but his muscles were locking up and cramping in quick spasms, as if they couldn't decide whether to hold shape or shift. He was balancing on the balls of his feet and that felt more natural than letting his heels touch the sand. That couldn't be good. Yet the more of the animal he channeled, the faster he healed. His pains were little more than a dull ache. By all rights, he should be minced meat on the inside now, and he was still standing.

Gabriel reminded himself to breathe, forced air into his tired lungs and let it out. A tight grin pulled on the corner of his mouth. He could still see Amelia's scrawled message on her e-pad, underlined three times. These guys had nothing on that woman and her needles. "Come on, children, man up a little," he taunted. "You won't last ten minutes in the arena like that."

Their fury made him grin outright. They would really lay into him now, tire themselves out before the big fight. Served them right for being such brainwashed morons. Survival of the fittest—which happened to be him. Something else he'd be thanking Amelia for with a whole lot more of what they'd done last night. Just for that, he was willing to let them have their fun. The sooner they tired, the sooner they would leave. It wasn't like there was much to do here before a fight. At least time went by faster this way.

"Leave us," Soren ordered.

The three gorillas obeyed, giving him looks that promised a painful death in the arena later on. He sent them air kisses and memorized all of their faces. He'd be looking for them, too. There were others waiting just out of sight; Gabriel could scent them. Gladiators, soldiers, slaves, too. All were curious to see what was happening, but not brave enough to come look. It pissed him off how much they feared Honoria and her minions. He wanted to scream at them to wake the fuck up. He didn't expect them to rally behind him like Spartacus part deux, but was it too much to ask that they not help their jailers? If half of them had the guts to stand up to this regime, they could rule the damn place.

Soren grabbed Gabriel's chin and lifted his face so he could look in his eyes. "I know I can't make you talk," he said, "so I won't bother asking whom you called."

"You mean you don't know?"

Soren said nothing. Meaning no, they didn't. They must have registered the ping he'd sent and its source, but not the destination. *Oh, that's gotta chafe.* He almost laughed. He'd never hear the end of it if the tiger man showed up like Amelia said he would. But shit, he wouldn't care. He'd be alive to listen to it.

"You might be interested to know Honoria is choosing to keep your doctor friend close at hand for the time being."

The reminder made Gabriel's heart beat double time. It was going so fast, it hurt. He bit his tongue until he tasted blood, but that made it worse. Claws curled out of his toes, and he dug them into the sand, out of sight. He *felt* bruises fading all over his battered body.

Soren looked down on him, appraising his enemy. He'd wiped the blood off his broken nose, but it was swelling. He'd set it himself with hardly a grunt, probably causing more damage in the process. Gabriel could see the wheels turning in his head as Soren watched him healing right before his eyes. A cold fist squeezed his insides.

"Seems to me you have an unfair advantage," he said and released Gabriel.

A second later, Gabriel felt fingers digging into his side where a moment ago a rib had been broken. He groaned, but the rib was whole. Sore and bruised, but whole. He met Soren's gaze in defiance, but didn't say a word. He didn't have to. For all his faults, Soren wasn't an idiot. He knew something wasn't right. And like the good little lap dog he was, he would run right along and report it to his mistress.

Gabriel strained against his bonds, fighting for enough leverage to stop him.

Soren slid out of his reach, farther off to a rickety wooden table with a box from which he pulled a syringe.

Gabriel jerked on the binds, felt them loosen and snap taut again. That wasn't rope or leather he hung from, it was a synthetic material they used for building. It could withstand a full ton of force and not show any wear. Gabriel twisted his wrists, felt the binds cut into skin. If he could get them slippery enough, maybe he could pull his hands free. He couldn't let Soren take blood samples.

Soren set the syringe aside and picked out a vial. "Let's see if we can't even the playing field a little."

Relief was quickly replaced with a deep unease. Soren didn't want his blood; he wanted to inject him with something. Drugs? Poison? What would it do to him? There were rumors Honoria had gathered chemists and biologists from every known corner of the inhabited universe to find just the right poison to off the old Caesar. They said she'd collected toxins and compounds to achieve any and every possible outcome, from a mild stomachache, to total baldness, to death.

They said she could make death instantaneous, or drawn out over two agonizing months.

Soren filled the syringe, not bothering to measure the amount. He returned to Gabriel and instead of administering the injection with the surgical precision that made him famous in battle, he stabbed the syringe forcefully into Gabriel's liver.

The acid burned through flesh with rapid efficiency. It spread through organs, into the blood, but also his abdomen. It seared like hellfire, burning him from the inside. For a moment he couldn't move; couldn't see past the blinding pain. Gabriel gasped for breath, and when he coughed, blood filled his mouth, tasting foul. He smelled the acid, the liquefied mess his insides were turning into, and it made him want to retch. The beating had barely affected him. This was going to kill him.

Somewhere nearby, animals driven out of their heads with starvation and abuse caught the scent and threw themselves against the doors holding them in their pens. The tigers roared, the leopards screamed, and Gabriel knew on instinct there were a handful quietly pacing back and forth, feral eyes locked on the gate, waiting for someone to open them. Those were the ones he dreaded most; the ones who'd learned to bide their time.

Soren cut his ties, letting him drop to the floor. Gabriel curled in on himself instantly, a vain attempt to contain his insides. He was shaking from the searing pain, feeling his organs giving way little by little. Soren laughed low, finally satisfied to have achieved his ends. The general walked out, leaving him unattended, unguarded, dying.

And all Gabriel could do was pray Tristan would get Amelia out of here safely.

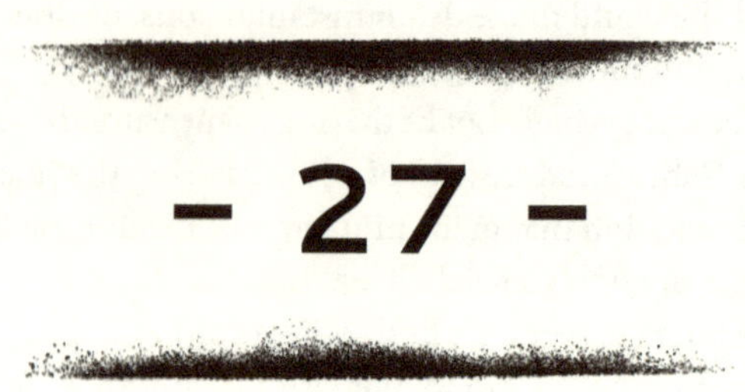

– 27 –

All pretense of civility had been abandoned. Guards followed Amelia everywhere she went. They stood at the entrance to the baths while she washed, and though they kept to their stations, they watched every move she made. She felt dirtier coming out of the bath than she had going into it.

Another atrocity of a dress was waiting for her. This one pure white with dark blue silk scarves instead of ropes to hold it in place. They tied at her lower back, with the ends left to trail down almost to the floor. She could really hate this fashion. There was nothing to go underneath this thing; Romans didn't bother with underwear. But knowing they were waiting for an excuse to put her in her place, Amelia kept her mouth shut and her pendant tight in hand. She'd removed it from around her neck and looped it around her wrist. It felt more secure that way. Even though her wrists were chafed raw from her little enforced exercise earlier, the pain reminded her the pendant was still there.

As the servants led the way to another chamber, this one with food laid out on long tables, she worried the pendant, looking around for any sign of Gabriel. There was no one she knew and no one who would tell her anything. She was afraid something bad was going on. They'd had to shackle his wrists and neck to keep him in line on the way here, and Soren had been in a temper when they'd led him away to his cell. The man was loyal to Honoria to the point of obsession. If she ordered Gabriel not to be harmed, he would obey, but he had to have his limits. If Gabriel pushed him past them…

And what if Honoria didn't give that order?

"The fair Caesar has provided breakfast," one of the servants told her with a deep bow, but his eyes were terrified. Amelia nodded her thanks, which was a signal for this man to leave. She was left on her own with a banquet fit for a legion. Well, except for her guard dogs.

"Are you two hungry?" she asked them.

They didn't even twitch.

"Not even a little? It looks delicious."

No reaction. They'd showed more awareness that she was alive while she'd bathed. She shuddered and turned away to hide her blush. It didn't help; she still felt them at her back and it was worse to not have them in sight. She hated feeling this way!

"Oh well, more for me, then." But there was no way she was eating or drinking anything else Honoria gave her. Besides, she was too unsettled to feel any hunger. Being here, humiliated and guarded every second, as if she would jump out the window and fly off, was the least of her problems. Worse was the ever-present fear that had physically manifested as slight dizziness and vertigo. She couldn't shake the suspicion that everything since the moment she and Gabriel had stepped foot in Rome had been deliberate. Every action, reaction, and set up, every time she knew she was being watched, and the times she felt safely out of sight, had been Honoria moving the players into position.

But for what?

The Caesar already held the "or else" card against her. Amelia could only hope Gabriel wouldn't be so easily controlled.

She felt her own puppet strings pull taut, and she wanted to swipe the fancy dishes off the table and hear them shatter. Uncertainty, any deviation from the known parameters, wreaked havoc in her life; she'd learned that long ago. Now, here, the only solid parameter she'd had, had been taken from her, and fear for him was as bad as the fear she felt for herself. It was a constant hum in the back of her head, distracting her when she needed to keep her focus.

Her patient was out there somewhere, having God knew what

done to him, and she could do absolutely nothing about it. What if he changed? What if they found out somehow? What if they did to him what Amelia had always feared someone would do to Tristan? Far too many people would be willing to do anything to possess the ability to change their shape. Even more to possess someone else with that ability.

And what about Tristan? He could be on his way here right now. Just what was she supposed to think about that? He could get her out of here. The chances of there being anyone on this messed up planet who could stand up to Tristan's telepathy were astronomically in their favor. If he found her, they could probably walk right out of Rome without anyone noticing until they were long gone.

But what if someone did notice? What if *he* changed and got caught?

Objectively speaking, she ought to be praying Tristan would get here soon. Yet for once, Dr. Amelia Marguerite Chase was beyond objectivity.

Emotions clouded judgment, and for once she couldn't shut hers out. She worried for herself, for Gabriel, for all of her friends, each of whom was now in danger because of her. Simply by knowing her, having associated with her in the past, they might be on Honoria's radar right now.

She could never go home. Probably not to Torrey, either. Which left her… what?

That was assuming she got out of here in the first place. Amelia was on extremely thin ice now; one wrong move and she could find herself in a very unpleasant situation.

"You are not hungry?"

Amelia started and spun around to face the speaker. The woman was a stranger, Amelia was certain of it, but she still got the feeling she should know her. "After a night with Gladius, I wake up famished."

Breakfast, with a side of poison. Amelia smoothed her dress slowly to give her hands something to do besides wrap around the woman's throat and squeeze. It never ceased to amaze her how some women had a natural gift for destroying others with a well-aimed, perfectly delivered remark.

But looking closely at the woman, Amelia noticed something that eased her jealousy. The other woman felt it, too. Last night, the harem gossiping about Gabriel had stung, true. Today, this woman simply did not pack the same punch. For one thing, she was by herself. For another, Amelia suspected whatever she'd had with Gabriel had been over for a long time. That was what really made her so bitter.

Amelia kept her back straight and her chin high, her expression carefully blank, checking her childish impulse to thumb her nose and say, *Gabriel's mine now. Yay for you, you got to have him for one night. You never will again.*

The only reason she didn't say it was Gabriel wasn't hers to claim. Amelia had seen to that with the deal they'd both agreed to. No emotional attachment. She was beginning to regret it now. Every time Gabriel said something that made her melt for him, she felt him steal a little deeper into her soul. He made her want to believe he meant it.

"I apologize," the woman said with a smile too sharp to be called bright. "Where are my manners? I am Galanta, the Caesar's lady-in-waiting, so to speak. She asked me to keep you company this morning, as she is quite busy with matters of the republic."

What good would it do to hope for more? In a week, a month, maybe a year, she might be in Galanta's shoes—bitter, lonely, alone. Only it would be her own doing. "Don't trouble yourself on my account."

Galanta's saccharine smile was all venom and bile. "Nonsense," she said. "I relish any opportunity to share gossip." She looked Amelia up and down. "Maybe compare notes."

You took your pleasure from him. I changed his life. The two weren't in any way comparable. She didn't know how much of what she'd done had changed Gabriel. That the regenerative abilities could be used externally indicated there might be more anomalies. She needed him in a controlled environment for tests to make sure his anatomy and chemistry were stable. He shouldn't be running around in an arena, playing gladiator for the amusement of the masses.

Amelia uncurled her nervous fingers from her dress, ignored the satisfaction on Galanta's face. "What could be keeping the Caesar so busy she can't attend to her guest?"

Galanta didn't press. "My dear, I don't know, and would never dare to ask. It's not our place to question what the Caesar does or does not do with her time. But I can wager a guess she's picking up where you left off. Gladius is a man of varied and vigorous tastes, after all."

The viper was fishing for a rise, but she'd cast the wrong bait. Amelia smiled. "Somehow I doubt that."

Galanta measured her again, wandered to the fruit platter and toyed with a grape. Curiously, though, she did not put it in her mouth. "We have a history, you know. Gladius and I. I was his first."

Ah, that was where she knew her from. "I'm sure he remembers that time with the same fondness." Suspicion confirmed. This wasn't an adversary worthy of anything but Amelia's sympathy, just a lonely woman carrying a torch for someone who'd forgotten her a long time ago.

She could see by the way Galanta's smile turned brittle that she still wanted him. She might have been his first, but not his only, and holding that rank over others was a vain attempt to make herself feel better about having been left behind.

"You pity me," Galanta said with disgust.

"No," she replied gently. Amelia felt sympathy for what Galanta had lost, perhaps, but she, along with every other noblewoman here, was much too cruel and unfeeling for pity.

Galanta sneered. "Yes you do. I can see it on your face. You think you're somehow special? That you will fare any better?"

"I think you're grasping. How do you know I want the same things from Gabriel you did?"

"Has he told you that you make his world brighter?" she asked, eyes narrowing with malice. "Has he looked deep into your eyes and thanked you for easing his pain? Has he called you his everything?"

"No," Amelia said. Considering what he'd been dealing with as a gladiator, Amelia could well believe any moment of intimacy would have been a solace to him, would have eased him. But Galanta had taken far too much meaning from his words. As for being his everything, coming from Galanta's mouth, the sentiment sounded so utterly insincere, she couldn't imagine Gabriel ever uttering it to her.

"What?"

Amelia shrugged. "He hasn't told me any of that."

Galanta frowned. "But he has promised you something, hasn't he?"

I won't ever let you go.

Amelia had completely forgotten about that raw declaration. And then earlier, what was it he'd said? *At the end of the day, I'll always come back to you.*

She'd never wanted any promises from him, and anything that might have been construed as one, she'd let pass. But it was getting more difficult to ignore them. The way he spoke to her now, the way he looked at her and touched her felt like a promise in and of itself.

Oh, Ams, you're dreaming. Emotions were running high on both ends. Tense situations tended to bring people closer together than they would get under normal circumstances, but sooner or later everything would return back to normal. What would happen then?

Gabriel might want to renegotiate their agreement now, but he might change his mind later on. He might die. No, whatever they had had always been temporary, and that was the way it needed to stay. It was the only way Amelia could walk away from it in one piece. She'd played the emotion game before. She'd laid all of her cards on the table and had lost every time.

It would be a thousand times worse with Gabriel. They'd shared too much already, and there would be a price to pay.

I won't ever let you go.

"In his case, I think it was more of a threat," she said to Galanta. Good thing the woman was so preoccupied with her own misery, she didn't hear the subtle difference in Amelia's tone.

Galanta scoffed. "It's true what they say about you. You're as cold as ice. Completely heartless."

Amelia flinched.

"Oh, I wouldn't say so, my dear." Honoria made her entrance with a train of attendants following in her wake. She wore a golden wig today, glittering strands braided intricately over her head. Silver adornments secured the design in place, and delicate chains hung around her face, almost like a knight's chain mail, but much more feminine and graceful. Her dress was a midnight blue with pearlescent white scarves tied over it. She'd dressed a mirror image of Amelia.

"My lady." Galanta curtsied so low, she nearly knelt before the Caesar.

Over her head, Honoria smiled at Amelia, amused by the bowing and scraping. "Our good doctor is much more complicated than that, aren't you?"

"As you say, my lady," Galanta agreed, still down in her curtsy.

"Leave us," Honoria said. "Dr. Chase and I have a ceremony to oversee."

Galanta left without a word.

"You must excuse her," Honoria said. "She really is a delightful companion, but I'm afraid the topic of my Gladius is not a favorable one to bring up in her company. I've had to reprimand her for her zeal before."

"No harm done."

Honoria looked her over. "Quite. Shall we? Our citizens are getting impatient for the show to begin." She motioned for Amelia to join her, and they left the room, side by side.

Amelia had never felt so out of place as she did in that moment, walking next to the Caesar, with people staring at her as if she'd taken something that didn't belong to her. Each and every one of their gazes slid over her, noting the absence of a pendant at her throat. As they descended down the grand staircase to street level, Amelia brought her hand up to her stomach so the pendant on her wrist would be easier to see.

"Very clever," Honoria said. "But it won't save you if somebody is overcome with passion for you."

"What a lovely way to put it." Actually, it had done exactly that last night. For all the violence Rome engendered, even when mindless with an aphrodisiac, that pendant had kept everyone to each other and away from her. Apparently, some laws here were absolute. And the Romans picked and chose which ones.

"I've become somewhat of a wordsmith in my time as Caesar. It's a necessity."

Amelia kept looking forward, taking her cue from everyone else. "And a fairly adept strategist, socially speaking. Although I fail to see what the purpose of last night was."

"Everyone played their parts," Honoria replied vaguely. There was a disturbing veil of civility they were speaking through. It made Amelia think of a snake dancer. The melody was haunting, the movement of the instrument hypnotic, but the venomous snake following both could strike with deadly precision at the slightest misstep. "I learned what I wanted to know, and my goal was achieved."

"Meaning what?"

Honoria turned to smile at her. "I wanted to see exactly how attached my Gladius has become to you. On that score alone, my dear, I should tear your heart out where you stand."

"Our arrangement is purely physical, if that's what worries you," Amelia said. She delivered the line flawlessly, but the words felt hollow.

"Even if that were true, you are enough of a distraction to him that I have no doubt your presence here will affect his performance. Although I must confess to some curiosity. I do not for one second believe you to be as heartless as poor mistreated, misguided Galanta claimed. And it would take a woman completely devoid of feeling to not be moved by Gladius' tale—which, again, you are not. So either you are hiding your feelings for him, or you've sufficient reason to not feel for him at all. Which is it?"

What was it, a pastime for Romans to psychoanalyze her? Three telepaths and her sister hadn't bothered asking so many questions about her emotional state. She was the one putting others under a microscope, not the other way around.

"Is there someone else?"

"Dozens," she lied.

"Is it his scars? I've always been quite fascinated by them. They're a testament to his determination."

Maybe not all, maybe not most, but Amelia knew many of those scars could be traced directly to Honoria and Gabriel's wanting nothing to do with her. She kept her hands flat against her thighs and bit her tongue against a scathing response. When they got out of here, Amelia would treat each and every one of those scars and make them disappear. She had the tools; it was only a matter of calibration. Gabriel would have no reminders of his stay in Rome if she had any say about it.

They entered the arena, where a path had been cleared for them up a staircase to the Caesar's private balcony. The very same one Amelia had seen in the recording Gabriel had smuggled out of here. It was such a tight fit in the staircase that emerging onto the wide-open platform was a shock. Going up to the railing and looking out over the vast arena, already vibrating with thousands of voices, made her speechless.

All of those people, chanting together, standing as one and demanding blood. Multitudes of human beings stomping their feet and raising their voices in unison to see gladiators slaughter each other. Amelia had thought she'd seen the worst of what humanity had to offer. But this...

"Or is it because he shared with you the particulars of his contract?"

Amelia blinked, tearing her gaze away from the disturbing sight, back to the Caesar.

Honoria smiled. "I see he might have failed to mention it."

"Mention what?" She almost grated the words.

Honoria made her wait two whole minutes before she said, "Gabriel Connors' time here is not being measured in days, but in victories."

"You mean kills," she said, glad she hadn't eaten anything at breakfast. She remembered Honoria's little visit to her lab, her parting words to Gabriel that day. It hadn't occurred to her to wonder if the blood debt she'd called in might have been literal.

"You make it sound so base and vulgar," Honoria said. "There is much more to gladiator battles than death. It's almost an art. You'll see."

Amelia didn't trust herself to answer, or to look at the Caesar.

"This round of games is not just a homecoming for him. It's a sort of graduation, as well. If he can manage to best three opponents, his contract will be fulfilled."

Three. He has to kill three more. How many had he killed by now?

Honoria's mouth compressed in displeasure. "Although the stunt he pulled, leaving Rome and running to you, should be considered a breach of contract. If I choose to see it that way, his quota will be expanded indefinitely."

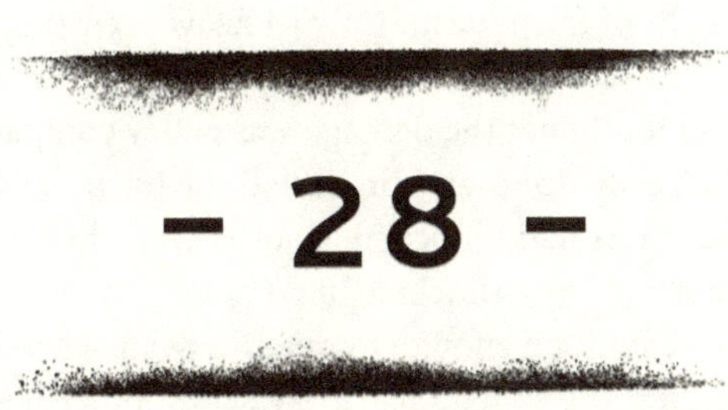

- 28 -

Minutes… hours? Couldn't be days. Could be eternity, for all he knew. Gabriel was a shivering heap of misery on the sand, deaf and blind to everything but the acid wreaking hell on his insides. He was losing himself, part by part, inch by inch. Soon, there would be nothing left of him but a shell filled with blood.

Then something changed. It was subtle; a different kind of pain that speared down his back and into his legs. His muscles contracted, curling him into a tighter ball, spine straining under the pressure. That he still had muscles was amazing. The pain concentrated, condensed, intensified in his midsection. Another contraction squeezed it even tighter. The next one would snap his neck.

Gabriel gasped a shuddering breath, wishing he could have seen Amelia one last time. Grateful she wasn't there to see him this way. He prayed for another chance, knowing he didn't deserve it. Just to tell her…

Another spasm made him whimper. A sound. He'd made a sound. Gabriel held as still as he could; held his breath and waited. The pain in his limbs had lessened. It was… receding? It felt as if the acid was being pushed back together, channeled somewhere else. As it shifted back from outside in, the pain coalesced in the very center of the mess his insides had become. He could wriggle his arms now and felt he had the use of his legs, though his abdomen was filled with a searing hot agony that kept him immobile.

Then the burning center shifted, and somehow his body felt like it was insulating itself from harm. Gabriel heaved, casting up the vile stuff, ridding himself of every last drop. It burned its way up his throat and out of his mouth, but the damage was paltry compared to what the acid had already done, and he healed the burns so well that by the time his muscles had unlocked, Gabriel was whole again. Weak as a kitten, shaking, shell-shocked, but whole.

He barely had strength enough to raise his head, when he felt footsteps approaching. The animals had grown eerily quiet; he could scent their fear and confusion. He wasn't one of them, but he was close enough to be familiar. They recognized a creature in torment. Did they pity him? Were they capable of sympathy? Or was he another prey, a meal made easier because it would limp instead of run?

Gabriel didn't have time to dwell on it. Slaves approached. They hauled him to his feet and dragged him through the catacombs beneath the arena to the armory.

They passed the gladiator cells, where each and every man stood and came forward to see him be carried past. They were silent, all of them familiar enough with the games to know now was not the time for jokes and insults. Now was when they sized each other up, committed to memory the face of every opponent, their strengths and weaknesses.

They would see him as an easy target. Good. That meant they'd fight each other first while they still had their strength. It gave him minutes more to live and recover before all hell broke loose.

The slaves dumped him on the floor of the armory. They dressed him in his own clothes, strapped on his own breastplate and leg guards. His bracers needed to be laced, which took time. But with three slaves working at them, Gabriel watched the laces slip in and out of their holes and tighten just right.

One of the helpful eunuchs settled a helmet on Gabriel's head and handed him a pair of swords. Gabriel couldn't hold them steady, let alone up. They clattered out of his hands.

The slaves exchanged a look. Someone removed his helmet, grasped his shoulders and made him look up. "What do you need?" He didn't recognize the face, but the voice was familiar.

"To get out of here," he said, voice hoarse.

The man grinned. "Try something we can actually get you."

"Water."

An earthen jug appeared in front of him. They had to hold it up to his mouth so he could gulp down half of the contents. The cool liquid soothed his ravaged throat. It revived him enough that he could sit up by himself and breathe in deep.

"How are you still alive?" one of the other two asked, baffled.

"The gods show me favor?"

The third snorted. "Yeah, right."

The one who sounded familiar wasn't amused. "When Soren finds out, he won't be happy."

"Don't plan on sticking around long enough for that," Gabriel said. He straightened in his seat. "The woman I was with. Where is she?"

"With the Caesar," the eunuch replied. "As far as anyone can tell, she has not been harmed."

The *yet* remained unspoken.

Above them, the hum of the crowds became a steady beat of thousands of people stomping in unison, demanding their money's worth.

"That's your cue, Sword of Caesar."

They helped him to his feet. He could stand on his own now, barely, but his hands still refused to cooperate. Rather than send him out unarmed, the slaves tied his swords to his hands. They pulled him aside so the others could arm and assemble. Puppets with weapons. So well trained that within moments they were lined up in two rows, all but holding hands, waiting for the doors to open and release them out to slaughter.

Sometimes the Caesar felt merciful and let a handful live. This time, Gabriel saw a dozen new faces, fodder for the beasts. They were the ones chosen specifically to die, only no one had bothered to tell them. There was nothing Gabriel could do for them. They wouldn't listen, not when he was swaying on his feet like a drunk and couldn't hold his own swords.

"Rico," he called to one of the men at the front of the formation. He and a few others were still sane enough to know they were in hell and strong enough to look for a way out. They'd helped Gabriel escape the training rink the day he'd hitched a ride out of Rome. He was counting on them now more than ever.

The gladiator turned, face grim.

"Today's the day."

Rico didn't crack a smile. "You had your day, Gladius," he said. "You failed, and we paid the price."

Several men grunted at this. Honoria would have been livid when she found out. Had they been beaten? The punishment couldn't have been that bad. Rico wasn't showing any bruises or marks consistent with torture.

"You're right," Gabriel said. "There is no way I can ever atone for my failure. I can't ask you to fight for me, but you can spare lives. Any hand that can hold a blade at the end of the day is a victory." The best way he knew to get back at the Caesar and all of her nobles was to deny them what they wanted so badly: blood.

"Honoria will punish us again!" someone snarled. "Last time she had our wives whipped. What will it be next time?"

Gabriel's stomach dropped. These men had simply created a diversion for Gabriel to slip away. Nothing more than they would have done any other day for any other guy who couldn't wait until sunset to see his girl. And for that, their women had suffered. Probably suffered still. Honoria had struck these men where they were most vulnerable. That he bore the responsibility for their pain was unforgivable. There were no words. Nothing he could say or do would ever be enough. "I would have spared them if I knew," he said.

"Worry for your own woman," said the one who'd spoken before. "Ours live. Yours won't." The warning sounded so much like a threat, Gabriel clutched his swords tighter.

Rico didn't show any reaction. He was a warrior to his core and would sooner die than show weakness. He looked Gabriel over, measuring him. "Who are you fighting for, Gabriel? Do you even know?"

The faces of his friends appeared in his mind's eye, replacing the grim expressions of the warriors lined up to slaughter each other. They were his answer.

They were a lie. And somewhere deep inside, he'd always known it.

Jack, Alex, and Paige had died for Rome's ambition. None of them would have wanted this. He'd told himself that he was avenging them. In truth, all he'd been doing was venting his rage and grief. He'd killed a hundred men in the arena, slaughtered the ones ordained to whet the others' appetite. And when he'd gone to the Caesar, knife in his bracer, thinking his contract was fulfilled, she'd told him with an indulgent smile the full terms of it.

One hundred *duels.*

"Any thug with a weapon can take a lesser life. *You*, my Gladius, are an artist. What I want from you is art."

He hadn't taken another life unless it was in a duel. And the bitch had kept him on a fucking leash, doling them out when she saw fit, sometimes out of spite, then later to give him hope. But no matter how he entertained, how well he killed, she always chose which fights counted and which didn't.

Who do you fight for?

With the growl of an animal kept too long by a cruel master, Gabriel silently admitted: *For myself.* He selfishly wanted to be free of his shackles. He wanted to stand beneath the roaring heavens as icy rain poured down on him and lightning struck all around, and breathe in the freedom of it. He wanted to look at his woman and feel at peace. Gabriel had fought his way in. It had been reckless, and he'd carry the stain of it on his soul forever, but he'd done it. If there was another way out, he would take it. But there wasn't.

Gabriel was going to fight his way back out.

The challenge was there in his eyes when he met Rico's gaze again. *Fight with me or don't. But I'm getting out one way or another.* The surety of that made him smile. No matter what, this fight would be his last.

Rico didn't smile back. One nod was all he allowed. "I won't kill unless I have to." It was more of a concession than Gabriel had expected. Rico was a fierce fighter and he respected the man for that. For whatever reason, Honoria had never pitted them against each other. Probably because she wouldn't be able to match such a spectacle ever again. Gabriel was thankful. He never wanted to fight Rico.

A pair of fresh meats right next to Gabriel looked at each other and snorted.

He leaned toward them and warned, "Don't make him have to."

The crowd cheered and the gates opened. Gladiators marched out like the proper little army, taking center stage on the sand. Gabriel limped out after them, dragging his swords.

Do or die time.

~

The warriors came out, spreading into formation, a perfect square of ten by ten. One hundred men, armed to the teeth, faced the Caesar's box, eyes straight ahead while all around the arena holographic screens flashed with the face of each one, and their names and statistics. Among them, the odds of winning, so everyone would know exactly how much they stood to gain in a wager.

When Honoria stood, they looked up as one, each thumping a fist or a weapon against his chest. Their greeting rang out flawlessly synchronized. "*Ave Caesar! Morituri te salutant!*"

Honoria smiled. "Not exactly traditional in ancient Rome, but it certainly has a nice ring to it," she purred. "They say, 'Hail Caesar. We who are about to die, salute you.'"

"You say that like it's something to be proud of."

Soren entered, taking his place by the door. He had a broken nose, but the smug look on his face made Amelia's stomach turn. What had he done?

The general met her gaze and gave a jeering smile.

Amelia wanted to beat the smugness out of him. She bit her tongue to keep quiet. Anything she might say would amuse him that much more. *He's strong,* she told herself. *He's gone through the treatment and survived, came out stronger for it. Whatever Soren can dole out, Gabriel can take.*

Then: *He'll come back to me. He promised.*

She would not cry. Gabriel needed her to be as tough as he was.

"Look at them down there," Honoria said, drawing her attention away from the general. "One hundred strong, all loyal to me and only me. All willing and eager to fight for me and die if I ask it. Who wouldn't be proud?"

"A sane person, for one." She spat out the retort before she could filter her words.

Honoria didn't seem to mind. "Sanity is so subjective. All those people out there cheering their champions are living their dreams. It's what we all strive for, even you."

"So what happens when they wake up and all they're left with is the blood and carnage to clean up?"

Honoria chuckled. "Who says the dream ever has to end?"

"They do," Amelia said, nodding at the gladiators down below. They were shifting to make way for one lone man. He limped, dragging his feet and his swords.

Amelia wanted to kill Soren.

And she wasn't the only one. Honoria turned on her general with such a scorching glare, there was no doubt Soren would pay a high price for this misstep.

The general's face turned stone cold. He drew himself up and stood his ground, but Honoria wasn't letting it go. Her silence said far more than any reprimand would have. Soren had lost the Caesar's favor. He would come to regret it bitterly.

Good. It was no less than he deserved.

Amelia transferred her gaze back down to Gabriel making his way to the front of the group. With each halting step, her hands curled more and more, until her nails dug crescents into her palms. When he reached the front, instead of touching his chest, Gabriel raised his sword high, and then swept it sideways and bowed low like a knight.

"*Ave angelus aureus*," he called. "*Indignus te salutant*."

Honoria smiled beatifically and raised her chin higher. But Gabriel wasn't finished. He straightened and added in English, "And hail Honoria. Today you die."

Honoria turned her frigid gaze on Amelia and hissed furiously as the crowds fell deathly silent. Amelia clasped her hands in front of her so no one would see them shaking. Down below, every gladiator present turned to stare at Gabriel. Some clutched their weapons, ready to make something bleed, while others appeared as stunned as the audience.

Oh, God, Gabriel, what have you done?

"Shall I gather the troops, my liege?" Soren asked, stoic.

Honoria was breathing hard, nostrils flaring. If she was anyone else, she would be screaming. But the Caesar pulled herself together again, at least enough to speak. "Get me Lucia," she said. "*You* are dismissed. I'll deal with you later."

Soren's jaw muscles twitched, but he did as his mistress commanded him. With a curt bow, he left, and moments later a woman with closely cropped red hair and a black tattoo on her face came in. She was a soldier, dressed in the same type of uniform as all of Soren's men, except her armor was altered to accommodate her breasts and she had daggers strapped to her body.

"Stay close," Honoria commanded without looking at her. She'd given the signal and the gladiators were dispersing, picking out their places in the arena. Gabriel was the only one who remained standing where he was, his gaze locked on Honoria. "What are you up to?" she said to herself.

"He was very clear in his speech," Amelia said, just to annoy her.

"You must care for him very much," the Caesar said, making a cut motion with her hand. "To hold out hope he will survive what is coming, when he can barely keep his feet under him."

The gates opened, and a flood of more people rushed in like a maddened mob. They swarmed the gladiators, outnumbering them five to one, and the battle began.

It was a slaughter. Dozens fell, then dozens more as the warriors methodically plowed through the masses. Amelia kept watching Gabriel, wincing each time he took a hit. Despite the Caesar's mockery, he was still standing, still fighting, and with each opponent who fell, Honoria's posture became a little more rigid and Amelia smiled a little wider.

The hordes were weakening, bodies littering the arena, but shockingly more of them were still moving than not. Many more. The gladiators were fighting to win, not to kill. Amelia wanted to get up and cheer them on. She had absolutely no doubt this was Gabriel's doing and couldn't hope to temper the grin that lit up her face. *Take that, you viper.*

"Touching," Honoria said. "But you're getting ahead of yourself. This is just the beginning."

The gates opened again. From one side, bowmen in horse-drawn chariots rolled into the fray, stomping those still on the ground into dust without a backwards glance. From the other side, wild animals charged anything still moving, ripping limb from limb. Those horde fighters who were still able, picked up their weapons again and joined in the fight, as if that was all they lived for. It was chaos, war. More kept coming in, more kept falling.

Amelia couldn't look at it as people dying anymore; there were too many to distinguish. Now it was an overwhelming, mad slaughter without an obvious victim. All were killing and all were dying, even the animals. She lost sight of Gabriel in the mess. So much was going on, the arena was sheer chaos. The crowds ate it all up, shouting and throwing things, which only riled the fighters more.

A sharp smile creased Honoria's face. She watched it all without blinking, her eyes feverish. She was enjoying this!

Amelia couldn't take it anymore. She stood and turned for the exit.

The short-haired Lucia blocked her way.

"You will sit and see this through," Honoria ordered.

"And if I refuse?"

"Then I will have Lucia here slit your throat and toss you down there for the beasts," the Caesar said with an easy shrug, as if she wouldn't blink an eye at giving the order, wouldn't mind either way unless she got blood on her pretty dress. "Besides." She turned her head to spare Amelia a cold look. "He fights for you. It would be rude to abandon him."

Amelia looked from Honoria to her red-haired assassin. They waited for her to make up her mind. The redhead was as still as a statue, stone-faced but sharp-eyed. If Amelia twitched toward the exit, she would be instantly subdued.

Stiff-legged, she turned and went back to her seat. Her knees nearly buckled as she lowered herself into it. She clutched the armrests, shaking with helpless fury. The puppet strings weren't merely taut now; they were tightly wrapped around her neck. The more she fought, the more she choked. She hated Honoria for it with a passion she hadn't known she was capable of until now. "This is all just a game to you," she accused. "Just a day's entertainment, isn't it?"

Honoria inclined her head. "If it pleases you to think so."

"You want me here to rattle Gabriel."

She didn't deny it. "I'll admit I've had my fun with him. But he's become a nuisance."

The confession made Amelia's heart beat faster, and that damn vertigo intensified until the entire world moved beneath her feet. "You manipulated us. You wanted Gabriel to come for me last night. You hoped it would distract him in the arena."

Honoria said nothing. Which was pretty much a confirmation.

"My God," Amelia said, unable to comprehend such ruthless calculation. "How long have you been screwing with us? Since you dragged us here? Since you found us in Miramar?"

The Caesar laughed at that. She looked at Amelia through eyes bright with amusement. "Oh, you fanciful creature. You think this is about you?"

Amelia looked down into the arena. She couldn't see Gabriel anywhere. Not a sign of him, not a gleam of his swords, not the blue plumes of his helmet. If he'd lost it somewhere, it had gotten covered with sand. Her pulse throbbed in her temples as she sought his familiar form in the throng of fighters. On the ground. In the darkened doorways that stood open wide like the waiting gates of Hell.

He was nowhere to be seen.

"No, my dear," Honoria was saying. "My purpose is, and always was, only Gladius."

Her indulgent voice made Amelia cold to her core. "Since when?" She could hardly hear herself say the words; dreaded the answer, learning the true depth of Honoria's obsession. She imagined the Caesar watching her gladiators with lust in her gaze, catching on one among many. The tall, brave fighter who stood victorious again and again. How long had she been trying to mold him into her toy?

"Since long before he ever stepped foot on Roman soil."

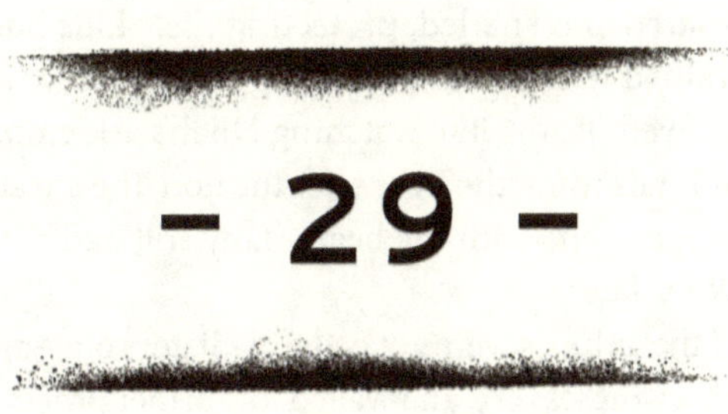

– 29 –

The fight went on until the only ones left standing were the gladiators. The horses had run, taking the chariots with them and destroying three of the gates. Ever-efficient slaves had repaired them in a flash to keep the animals contained. The beasts themselves were ripping into the dead, gorging themselves on human flesh. Some lay dead, but most were scattered about, minding their own business now that there was plenty of meat to go around.

As for the gladiators, at least twenty had fallen. From this far up, they were indistinguishable from the rest of the bodies and there was no telling who'd survived and who hadn't. At least that's what Amelia thought. The remaining warriors once again faced their Caesar, winded, wounded, wary of the carnivores mere feet away, but they stood proudly, having fought a war and come out the victors.

Honoria shoved to her feet and clutched the railing. "Where is he?" she hissed.

"My lady?" Lucia said. It was the first time she'd spoken since she'd arrived. Her voice was hoarse, as if her vocal cords had been damaged somehow. Amelia winced, hearing her. She wanted to sit the woman down and run a scan to figure out what was wrong and then fix it. But that was her MD talking.

"Find him," Honoria ordered.

Lucia bowed and gave a signal.

Down below, the gates opened again, all of them this time, and men with whips came to herd the animals back into their cages. The beasts roared and snarled, protecting their kills but they must have been trained to fear that particular type of attire because they eventually obeyed. It was like watching Noah's ark empty out. Two by two the animals went, the tiger with the lion, the cheetah with the panther, and the hyena with the bear. Many still had a limb in their jaws, a snack for later.

Once all of the animals were gone, the gladiators once again saluted, this time with a wordless cry, and waited for further orders. The Caesar was too distracted to issue them. She and Amelia both searched the arena floor, looking for Gabriel among the fallen. It was like looking for a needle in a haystack.

Lucia went to the man wearing a bright red sheet and said something into his ear. With a nod, the man turned to the audience and raised his arms high. His image appeared on every screen, and the crowds cheered, then quieted. When the man spoke, his voice resounded everywhere, but didn't echo. Amelia couldn't tell if there were hidden speakers or if he was simply that good.

"Today, the Caesar's legions have overcome their first challenge! But there are far more difficult trials yet ahead! Beasts of legend, treacherous spies, cutthroat pirates, and deadly traps are but a few things awaiting the brave men of Rome in the days to come! But for now, they go to their much deserved reward!"

Hoots and cheers accompanied the entrance of what could only be a group of prostitutes. They were topless, with only golden paint and glittering jewels to disguise their nudity, and diaphanous skirts to accentuate their sensuous gait. They glided around dead bodies, gracefully making their way to the warriors left standing as if none of the gore touched them.

A woman to each man, they kissed them on the cheek and led them by the hand from the arena. One of the men tossed his woman over his shoulder and carried her out. Another backed his against the wall and kissed her hard right there.

A third didn't move when his woman beckoned. Instead, he pulled her back to him and painstakingly brushed her hair back over her shoulder without getting blood on her. That simple act showed such unexpected gentleness after all of the carnage, Amelia's insides warmed a little. What incredible strength it had to take to do what these men did and not be warped by it. When those two left, they did it walking side by side, holding hands and looking into each other's eyes. Amelia was sorry to see them go.

Slaves took over the arena once the warriors had left. They started clearing out the bodies as the stadium seats emptied. Amelia couldn't look away. Most of the bodies were picked up and tossed on waiting wagons like so much trash to be disposed of. The slaves were meticulous, leaving nothing behind except the blood soaking into the sand. But one group of slaves, dressed all in white, had a different approach. She could only assume they tended to the valuable dead. They stopped at each of the fallen, touched them, and arranged the bodies to lie straight with the arms at their chests. They gave them their weapons back. Only then did they pick them up and place them on one of the wagons. And when they wheeled the fallen out, the slaves chanted some sort of funeral dirge. It was as much respect as those men were ever going to get.

Did they have families outside of Rome? Would any of them know what had happened to their sons and brothers? Would they care? Somehow Amelia couldn't imagine the Caesar going to the trouble of contacting them.

When the last of the bodies was cleared from the arena and the audience was gone, Honoria snarled, turned away and left, her attendants following their angry mistress. All but Lucia, who stayed behind, staring at Amelia. "I'm guessing that means I'm supposed to follow."

Stone-faced Lucia said nothing, just waited. Amelia was almost certain the woman was ten times more deadly and ruthless than Soren. She still preferred her to the general.

She followed the entourage down those narrow steps that were beginning to feel like a press closing in on her. It wasn't much better outside. The streets were full again, people going about their daily lives. There were markets filled with merchants selling everything from fine silks, to flatbread, to weapons both decorative and deadly, and holographic posters everywhere showed highlights of today's battle and touted attractions still to come.

It was an absurd dichotomy between the merchants dressed in rags, shouting their wares and shoving them into the face of every passerby in hopes of earning a coin, and those sleek, modern advertisements that belied Rome's apparent age.

There were merchants selling oil lamps and candles, but even though the main street was lined with torches, the posts were too solid in the ground to be mere wood. Amelia ambled closer to one and ran her fingers across it. Metal. Probably hollow to channel fuel up to the flame.

None of it was real. It was all an excuse for rich people to give in to their sadistic fantasies and not feel guilty. It made her sick.

The silent assassin at her back shoved into Amelia, steering her back onto the main path. She'd almost taken a wrong turn, so lost in her surroundings she couldn't see the Caesar and her entourage anymore. The distraction was a welcome one and she looked Lucia over, trying to catalog her in her internal encyclopedia of Rome. "What are you supposed to be?" she asked.

Predictably, the redhead didn't answer.

"I meant you don't look like the rest of the Romans." She navigated around a leather merchant who was determined to sell her a corset of some sort and looked back at Lucia. "The tattoo isn't a trademark feature of Rome."

No answer.

At a particular deadlock of foot traffic, Amelia looked over the holograph advertising hair adornments. She'd seen them on a few of the ladies today, sticking out of their hair at the temples. Nothing between them, but *something* had cast a shadow over their eyes. Sun screens.

Lucia shoved into her again and, annoyed, Amelia stepped through the holograph, enduring the momentary field of static that made fine hairs all over her body stand on end.

"My people hail from Gallia," the assassin said.

"I see." There was nothing else to say to that, since Amelia wasn't familiar with the term and had no idea whether the woman was serious or playing a role. "Is that near Rome?"

No answer.

Amelia shrugged. She didn't see much point in trying to carry on a conversation after that.

They were not going to Honoria's palace. Instead, Lucia steered them to some sort of meeting hall where men robed in white were running out as they were trying to get in. "She's gone mad!" one of them said to himself, looking over his shoulder.

Took you long enough to notice. The Caesar wasn't what Amelia would call a pillar of sanity. It was good her own people were beginning to notice. It meant Honoria's position had become more precarious. "She's dismissed her most trusted general," she told the man in an aside, giving him a meaningful look.

His eyes went wide.

"Tell everyone," she said.

Lucia shoved her to get her moving, and Amelia complied, knowing full well the power of a little rumor. She smiled at the redhead. Lucia looked at her as if she couldn't decide whether punishment was required, but there was a hint of admiration in her eyes. It made Amelia stand a little straighter. She'd earned a little respect from the assassin. "Pride goeth before a fall," Lucia said.

"Then let's hope my angel wings hold steady," she replied, thinking of Gabriel. She hadn't seen him go down. He hadn't been among the fallen, and she would have recognized him among the ones still left standing. Where could he be? The gates had remained open until they'd released the animals. Could he have slipped out somehow? Was it too much to hope he'd escaped before the worst of it? He could be hiding somewhere now, biding his time.

Don't press your luck. She wished she could make him hear. *They'll be looking for you. Don't make it easy for them.* But where could he hide?

The corridors gleamed with polished marble. Someone had infused the cracks with gold to seal them, and those veins running in every direction created an intricate web across the floors. Such a waste of wealth. It was a symbol of status, nothing more. Means that would have been better spent caring for the people of Rome. Every carved bust they passed had a smug, haughty look on its face. A dozen, then another, of old men who had ruled this place, but not a single woman. Not until they reached an arched doorway. There, on one side, was the statue of a woman in a helmet, with a sword in her hand, almost hidden against the flow of her gown. It was as tall as Amelia, and her eyes were so empty and detached, it was uncomfortable to look into them.

"The goddess Athena," Lucia said. "Justice."

"Justice without mercy," she countered, indicating the sword.

"As it should be," Lucia said, then nodded to the other statue. Honoria in all her glory, taller than the goddess, her robes made of some kind of blue stone, with emerald inlays for the belt and clasps at her shoulders. Her body was pure white marble, without a single crack or flaw. Her hair was painted with gold and her irises glittered with ferric diamonds.

Amelia looked closer. At least one of them did. The other had a marble in the socket instead. She bit back a smile, remembering the diamond Gabriel had given her. It was about the right shape and size. And it currently lay on her kitchen table, underneath a tea cup turned upside down. Her chin was a little higher when they entered the chamber, her eyes a little sharper, and her mouth stretched the slightest bit into a faint smile. Honoria would not win.

In a circular room with benches set up around a stage of some kind, the Caesar and her attendants were gathered. Honoria was red in the face, pacing like a rabid animal, while the others warily kept their distance. Amelia expected her to start frothing at the mouth.

"I'll ask again, and don't you dare tell me you don't know. Where. Is. Gladius?"

Three slaves in loincloths knelt before her, foreheads to the floor, arms outstretched forward. "Glorious Caesar," one of them said, "we did not find him among the de—"

"*Don't tell me that!*" she screamed and kicked the speaker viciously in the head.

Amelia started forward, but Lucia caught her arm and held her back.

With good reason, it turned out, because the Caesar rounded on her next. "You," she said, and Amelia took a small step back on instinct, only to meet with Lucia's chest. "You helped him with this. What did you do? Where is he?"

"I don't—"

Honoria rushed her, one hand latching on to her arm, the other holding the tip of a dagger to her throat. "Lie to me again and I'll have the skin pulled off your body."

The tip pierced skin and a warm drop of blood ran down her chilled flesh. Amelia dug her nails into the Caesar's wrist. It did nothing to dislodge the hold on her arm.

"My lady," Lucia said, unmoved.

"What?"

"I would not presume to question you—"

"Then don't." The tip pressed deeper, and Amelia sucked in a sharp breath, squeezing her eyes shut for a second. Defiance made her open them again. If she was about to die, she would look Honoria in the eye and hold her gaze until the last breath left her body so the Caesar knew Amelia didn't fear her.

Lucia grasped the Caesar's shoulder. "She is a bargaining chip. Wherever Gladius is, he will come back for her. But not if she's dead."

Amelia's eyes watered. The blade was about two pounds of pressure away from piercing through her trachea. If that happened, Amelia would start choking on her own blood. Honoria kept the pressure up a moment longer, then released her with a shove. Amelia fell back awkwardly against a bench, slapping a hand on the wound to stop the bleeding.

"Get rid of them," Honoria said to her assassin, who nodded grimly.

Amelia held her throat and winced in pain when she swallowed. Lucia pulled one of her knives and set her jaw as she walked over to the slaves. *No!* Amelia wanted to shout, but no sound came out. Horrified, she could do nothing but watch as, one by one, Lucia grasped the slaves' hair, lifted their heads, and sliced across their throats like cattle. The last one, now kneeling in a pool of his friends' blood, had enough time to beg for his life before he was mercilessly silenced.

As Amelia struggled to process it, another group of slaves rushed in to clear away the bodies. It was so efficient and coordinated, Amelia wanted to retch. Her eyes blurred with tears and she was glad of it, grateful she wouldn't have to watch as they mopped away the blood.

"Search the arena again," Honoria ordered, untouched by the horror. "I want no corner left unchecked. Then spread out into the market. Find him."

Lucia nodded. "And what of her?" she asked, indicating Amelia.

Amelia felt the Caesar's gaze on her but refused to acknowledge her. Shock was beginning to wear off, leaving her shivering and cold, and terrified she would be the next one to die. Not for any good reason, except that Honoria was in a temper. She made an effort to lever herself up to sit, but couldn't brace her feet because they kept slipping over her skirt.

Honoria came to crouch in front of her. She waited until Amelia looked at her before she said, "Either you helped him escape, or he got away on his own and left you behind to distract me. Either way, I'm going to show you why it's ill-advised to tangle with me." With a quick strike, she snatched the silver pendant at Amelia's wrist and tore it off.

She didn't have time to gasp before Honoria pushed to her feet and ordered, "Take her to the slave barracks."

Amelia tried to scream when she was hauled up off the floor, but her voice came out as a feeble croak. She fought against Lucia and the other soldier holding her with everything she had, furious tears streaming down her face uncontrollably. She might as well have been a fussing kitten in their grasp. Lucia was trained and very strong for her stature. The other soldier was a man, probably one of Soren's troops. He wasn't necessary to subdue her. In some corner of her mind not screaming in helpless, terrified fury, she knew he was there because he enjoyed it.

They dragged her out of the chamber and past those damn unfeeling busts again. When they emerged in the streets, the larger sun was right in her face, blinding her. "Let go of me!" Each time she bucked in their grasp, her shoulders wrenched a little, her arms bruised more. It was useless to fight them, but she couldn't stop.

"You're only hurting yourself," Lucia told her.

"Let her," the soldier said. "I like them feisty."

Lucia's grasp on her loosened as she glared at the other soldier. It wasn't much, but it was enough that when an overzealous merchant got shoved out of the way by a passerby and barreled into Lucia, she lost hold of Amelia's arm.

Amelia swung wide, heedless of the consequences. She hit the male soldier purely by chance, right in the throat. He choked, his fingers on her loosening for a second before he could compensate. Amelia pulled her arm free, shoved away from him so hard, she lost her balance and tripped over someone's foot. She slammed against a stall, and it knocked the breath out of her. Legs unsteady, Amelia righted herself and ran for it, shoving her way through the crowds, weaving left and right as fast as she could.

The two guards shouted and came after her. Their approach gave her a much needed boost of adrenaline, and she ran faster. But she looked behind her. It only took a second, a foolish instinct to check if they were gaining on her. Without seeing where she was going, she ran right into someone. The burly merchant caught her to steady her. He might as well have been the guards' accomplice. Amelia didn't scream, but she fought him until he released her. She stumbled against his table and nicked her palm on the blades he sold.

Knives! They gleamed so sharp, so powerful in the sunlight. So many, they could arm a battalion.

"What's yer hurry there, luv?" the merchant grumbled. "Fancy lady don't like me grubby hands on ya, eh?"

"*Stop her!*" the male soldier roared.

Amelia gasped, palmed a needle thin, sharp knife, shouldered her way past the merchant, and ran again.

She ran straight into Lucia and screamed.

"That would have been commendable if you'd run left instead of right," the redhead said. "Now you pissed him off."

The soldier caught up, grabbed her arm again and yanked to make her face him. Then he backhanded her so hard, Amelia's vision went dark and she went limp in his hold. Her glasses flew off, instantly trampled by the crowds flooding through the market.

Gabriel... She couldn't even call his name, vain though the effort would have been.

Amelia had no idea which way they took her after that. She had no recollection of the path they took while her head throbbed and her mind shut down. The next thing she knew, her ears had stopped ringing and it was silent all around. They were past the market, in a part of Rome that looked abandoned. The houses were damaged, some in ruins, others black after a fire.

The few people they passed close enough for Amelia to make out details were disfigured with disease and injury, staring up at them with bleak eyes and hollow expressions on their gaunt faces. The air reeked with refuse, and if Amelia didn't keep smelling blood, she would have retched.

She raised her head to look forward and could barely distinguish a big building at the end of the alley. There were no stairs leading up to a terrace, just a thick wooden door with a barred little window.

The male soldier banged his fist on the portal and it opened from the inside. Some other guard let them pass. "A new concubine? Ah, Julian, you spoil me."

When he reached for Amelia, Lucia caught his hand. The man was twice her size, yet the redhead had no fear of him. "This one isn't for you," she said.

"The Caesar said—"

Lucia cut the male soldier off. "She said to bring her here. Not to hand her out."

"You know that's why she's here," the soldier growled and his fingers dug into Amelia's arm more. She bit her lip to keep from crying out.

"You presume to know the Caesar's mind, Julian?"

The other guard scratched the back of his bald head. "I always try out the new ones," he said. "The Caesar would understand."

Lucia drew a knife. This one was long and curved. "Unless I hear otherwise, she is not to be touched," she whispered menacingly. "Is that clear? To both of you?"

The two men pulled back from her as if they feared her. How many times had she had to prove herself to earn that sort of reaction?

"Clear," the guard said.

Lucia looked to Julian, waiting for his answer. The man nodded, his Adam's apple sliding up and down in a nervous swallow.

"Stay here," Lucia said.

Julian let go of Amelia, and Lucia shouldered her entire weight, taking her the rest of the way alone.

"Thank you," Amelia said, getting her feet under her to walk on her own.

"Don't thank me," the redhead replied. "I bought you a few extra hours. If I were you, I'd be praying for a rescue before time runs out."

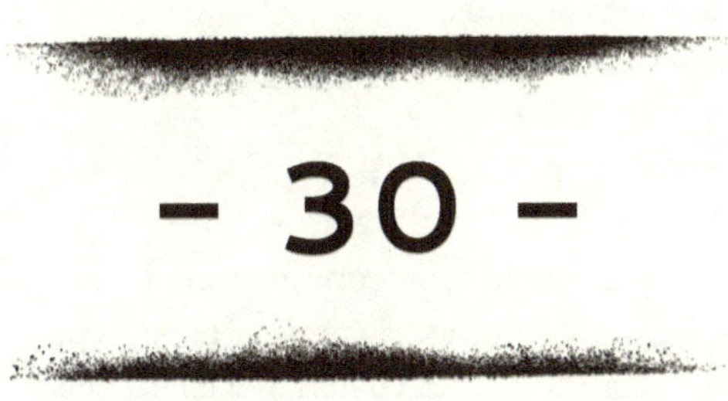

– 30 –

There were soldiers everywhere, combing through every corner and shadowy passageway of the arena and the catacombs beneath it. Their agitation translated into the very air and sand. The ground rumbled with their footsteps; the hallways echoed with their voices.

"Nothing!"

"Search again. Search a hundred times. *Find him!*"

"The Caesar dismissed Soren," someone whispered. That was curious. The news traveled through the ranks, and soon the entire complex was humming with it. Soren had lost favor with the Caesar. The Caesar had him punished. The general was gone.

In the way of rumor, the message escalated, and soon they were saying Soren was dead.

Gabriel listened patiently, waited for everything to quiet again. The gladiators who'd survived were nursing their wounds. Those sponsored by influential nobles had already been seen by healers and compensated for their services with a good meal and a warm body to take away the chill of battle.

The others had to see to themselves.

As the news spread that the Caesar's champion was missing and her general wasn't in command any longer, more whispers joined the shouted orders. The gladiators were stirring. Order as they'd known it had been disrupted. If it was true, they said, the Caesar was losing control over her underlings.

The soldiers searching the catacombs were doing as ordered, but their discontent was obvious.

"Look at that one, he's about ready to kill someone," a man said, chuckling.

"And three already gave up!"

"Gladius is gone?"

"Wasn't among the dead," someone answered.

Gabriel huffed and turned away from the noise to pace. He couldn't shut out their voices, but he could damn well ignore them. They weren't saying anything of use. He didn't give a damn about Soren and Honoria having a lover's spat; he wanted to know what happened to Amelia.

A snarl pulled on his mouth. He had to get out of here.

"He's not here."

"Spread out, search the market."

Fools. If he'd gotten out of the arena, he could have been miles away from Rome by now and they'd still be clueless. Honoria was slipping. Or perhaps this was a true show of her genius. She searched first where he was least likely to be—the best hiding place. But they would never find him here.

Gabriel flexed his claws, raking the sand in anticipation. It had been a huge risk to shift, but a calculated one. In the madness of the fight, when the beasts flooded into the arena, no one had noticed. He'd been able to stay out of the worst of it and unless he got in someone's way, no one bothered to engage him. He'd been led out right along with the other beasts with no one the wiser.

Now that their snacks were devoured, many of the animals drowsed in their individual pens. But some were still alert. They sensed something was off and they didn't like it. A tiger in the next pen over kept growling and scratching at the wall between them. On Gabriel's other side, a hyena was yipping. It threw itself against the wall every so often, and then promptly retreated to the other side, as far from him as possible.

The doors were thick transparent plastic, reinforced with iron bars. Through it, he could see into the pen across from him. The two lionesses in it stared at him, watched every move he made, seemingly calm, lounging one against the other. Still, there was tension in their bodies and their tails were twitching. Their steady gazes unnerved him. They told him his presence was tolerated only as long as he didn't cause trouble. The second he broke that unspoken rule, they would rip into him like a lame deer.

Riled from the fight, impatient to get out, and frustrated with the wait, Gabriel roared and raked at the door. They didn't twitch, not in the least bit intimidated. They would have learned nothing was getting through these doors unless humans allowed it.

Biding their time.

Eerie.

He went all the way to the back of his pen and lay down there, keeping his eye on them. The larger sun was setting. Even though no natural light penetrated here, he could feel it somehow. The soldiers were gone, leaving only gladiators and the beasts. Soon the trainers would be coming by to fill water trays for the animals as Gabriel had seen them do dozens of times in the past. The water was dosed with a tranquilizer so the animals could be safely seen to.

He would wait them out. There would be only one chance to get this right. He wasn't about to screw it up; too much rested on his ability to get out of here and find Amelia.

The suns had set. Rome plunged into darkness pierced only by the light of torches and candles in every window. Honoria stood on her balcony, translucent drapes billowing in the evening breeze over her naked skin. She looked out across her beautiful city, watching her soldiers search through each street, house, and sewer like efficient little cats seeking out a rat.

They'd left the arena, having found no trace of Gladius. The sergeant in charge had passed his message on through a slave, the coward. She'd deal with him when he showed his face next time. Honoria had no patience for weakness; didn't allow it in herself and refused to tolerate it in others. Rome was far too magnificent for that.

"You are restless, my lady."

She didn't turn. "You have not pleased me well enough," she said.

How could he have, when all she could think was that her most prized weapon had slipped her grasp? Her champion, her sword, was free, sharp as ever, deadly as always, and out for *her* blood. She'd grown complacent with him, let her guard down far too much. She'd hoped he was broken, finally hers to command.

It should have been him in her bower this night, not the useless pile of muscle currently chained to her bedposts.

The chains rattled. "Allow me to make amends," he said.

His tone made it clear he wasn't talking about finding Gladius and taking his head, as she needed. Honoria caressed the railing, deep in thought. She was the most beautiful, intelligent, cunning and powerful female in Rome. She was the Caesar, for all the gods' sake. She should be mating with her equal. Why couldn't he have accepted her? Everything would have worked out perfectly if he'd swallowed his pride and accepted her. With Gladius as her consort, guarding her blind side, she would have been unsurpassable. With him inside her every night, pleasuring her as she knew he could, she would have been a happy Caesar indeed.

Years of strategizing, tactical missteps that would have undermined her rule if anyone had suspected the cause, sacrifices—true, none of them her own, but they still counted for something—all of it had led them together. The Caesar and her Champion.

She'd stolen him from right under Shadow noses, with none the wiser. Gabriel wasn't just her Champion. He was her trophy, a testament to her strength and ruthlessness.

He could have been epic.

Instead he'd spat blood in her face, taken harsh punishments rather than the pleasures she'd offered him. Insult on top of injury, and he'd continued to refuse her. Was it any wonder she'd reacted harshly?

Her council had advised to be rid of him. Every time Gladius spurned her and she allowed him to live undermined her authority. They'd warned it would all come to a bad end. She had not listened.

Anger filled her to the brim. That she had sunk so low as to be rejected by a *slave*!

Honoria turned her back on the night and faced her bower. The sight disgusted her. Another man tied to her bed, his cheeks and chest red where she'd beaten him, his wrists and ankles chafed raw where he'd strained to touch her. She hadn't allowed it; hadn't wanted his filthy, incompetent hands on her. She'd ridden him hard, losing herself in climax, struck him whenever he'd spoken and marred her fantasy. She wanted it to be Gladius. This one was a paltry replacement.

A temporary one.

He gave her a lecherous smile, hips curling up off the bed, his cock already hard and thick, weeping a drop of pre-semen for her. It maddened Honoria, the way her body tingled, hungry for the feel of it inside her. But she had more self-control than that.

"Come to me," he commanded. He dared! His own lust made him reckless. He'd craved this for so long, he didn't care how he achieved his ends, only that he did. For hours he'd endured her screaming rage, taking her blows without a sound, meeting her each time she slammed down over him, taking him so deep it hurt. He'd watched her the entire time, his eyes burning as they had for months at her side. Every touch, gentle or harsh, had only aroused him more. She'd allowed him to come three times, never inside her, and he still hadn't had enough.

Her faithful, useless, idiotic Soren.

"When I am good and ready," she replied. "Remember your place, peasant."

"Oh, I know exactly where I am," Soren said, strong fingers curling tight around his chains. His arms strained again, but he could not budge them. He didn't want to. He merely showed off for her pleasure.

It wasn't enough. He'd harmed her Gladius against her express orders. By rights, she should have him castrated and tossed in with the slaves. She still might, if she was of a mind come morning.

"If I had known this was how you would punish me, I would have killed him sooner." He scowled. "He should be dead."

Honoria rushed him with a hiss and cracked the back of her hand against his face. The ring she wore left a scratch in its wake. She caught his jaw, nails digging into his skin, and forced him to look at her. "Watch your tongue," she said. "Or I'll have it ripped out and fed to the dogs."

Soren strained more, breathing hard, hips bucking toward her. "You would do that? When it's so much more pleasing to you in my mouth?"

Honoria released him and straightened with disgust.

His gaze swept every inch of her and her nipples beaded beneath it, her woman's core growing wet. She let him look his fill, tormented him with the sight of what he could never possess. What she allowed tonight was all he would ever have of her. And he would yet come to regret everything he'd done.

"Bold words for someone completely at my mercy."

He licked his lips.

"You have failed me miserably, general." He would not hear the gravity of her words past his own unslakable lust for her. Honoria placed one pale knee on the bed by his head, pinning his arm down with her ankle. Soren started panting. Shifting her weight, she placed the other on the far side of him. When he flexed his biceps, it nearly swayed her off balance. "Show me why I should let you live."

He groaned deep when she lowered herself over his mouth.

She would let herself have this pleasure tonight, to nurse the dream of Gladius a few hours more. When the suns rose big and bright over Rome in the morning, it would die.

Along with pathetic, insolent Soren.

– 31 –

Lucia shoved her into the room so hard, Amelia fell forward, landing on her hands and knees. Her hand hit something hard and the impact sent a numbing tingle up her arm to her shoulder. She blinked in confusion at the thin, sharp knife gleaming on the ground.

The door closed and locked behind her, leaving her to the mercy of whoever else was there with her. She could hear people moving around her, but didn't dare look up. Not while the knife still lay unseen in her grasp. How had she not lost it?

Amelia sat back on her heels, sliding the blade beneath her skirt and out of sight. Only then did she look up. The room was vast, with a set of four columns spread out evenly to hold up the floor above. There was no furniture, only piles of worn pillows, a water fountain built into one wall, and a trough of a stream at the base of the other. The woman crouching over it by the window confirmed her suspicion this was the equivalent of a toilet here.

She shuddered. The window was more of a lack of wall. It was barred in a crisscrossing pattern with the holes barely large enough to fit her head through. There would be no escaping that way. It was dark now that both suns had set. The only light came from two small oil lamps, and everyone was huddled around them.

Amelia counted twenty-five blurry shapes in all. The ones closest to her were wearing haunted expressions like she'd seen on rape victims in the past. They ranged in age from late teens to late forties, and they hardly noticed her. One more addition to an already terrible situation.

While she was still fairly invisible in the darkness by the door, Amelia took one trailing end of the ribbon around her waist and ripped off a long strip, then one more. She hiked up her skirt and tied the knife to her thigh. Without a proper scabbard, it was a risk. She could either cut herself on the blade or lose it somewhere if the ties weren't tight enough. It was still better than not having a weapon at all.

When the ties were as tight as she dared to make them, Amelia pushed to her unsteady feet. This was a harem. Not at all like she'd imagined one should look. There was no opulence here, no lush satin sheets tenting around the room, or colorful pillows where finely dressed women lounged, waiting for their master to choose them. This place looked more like an abandoned brothel. The light, though dim, cast harsh shadows. The walls were bleak like some ancient prison, and the floors were rough, uneven, and slanted. She was walking up a slight incline to get to the window and picking her way carefully around the other residents.

Amelia hadn't been in this much pain in, well, ever. Once, as a child, she'd broken her arm in a bad fall down the stairs, but after so many years, she didn't remember how much it had hurt. Whatever pain she'd felt then had been quickly dulled by medication, and all she recalled was ice cream and a bright pink cast she'd been proud to show everyone.

What she felt now was beyond her mind's ability to comprehend. Her body hurt, bruised and abused. Her throat hurt more, the wound still fresh enough to throb with sharp stings. But it was more than physical discomfort. Amelia's fear and vertigo had turned inward somewhere along the way. She no longer tripped over her feet, but her thoughts.

She was exhausted and wired at the same time. Heart beating too fast to sleep, mind too sluggish to stay awake. Memories mixed with imaginings that rattled her more than anything Honoria could have done. Blind to everything else, Amelia made her way to the window and sat.

Somewhere out there, Gabriel bided his time, waiting for the tide to ebb so he could come for her. Somewhere out there, he might be biding his time to escape without her. Maybe he was already gone.

Or maybe he was already caught, imprisoned, dead, and she would live out the rest of her days in this hell.

None of that got a rise out of her. They were the musings of a tired, traumatized psyche trying to make sense of what was happening. She had precious few facts to support any theory and no desire to look for more.

No one had found Gabriel yet, of that she was certain, otherwise they would have come for her already. That meant there was still hope he might find her and get them both out of here. And then there was Tristan. Strong, steady, unpredictable Tristan. He could be on his way here right now. She looked up at the starry sky, searching for a subtle flare of shuttle engines. Gabriel didn't believe the tiger man would make it here in time.

In time for what?

Time was incomprehensible here. It moved, and it stood still; she never knew how quickly it was passing when one moment raced away and another lasted forever. At some point, she might decide one of those was worse than the other, but right now all she had was measurements of night and day. It was day when the suns were up, and night when it was dark.

It was dark now.

Amelia blinked. She didn't know how long she'd sat there, staring out the window at the darkness beyond the bars. It was long enough that full night had fallen and passed, and now the faintest light of day was beginning to cut the darkness. Where had the night gone?

The others were already wide awake. Their whispers jarred her out of the pleasant void her mind had become.

"Fancy lady fell from the Caesar's grace."

"Look at her clothes..."

"Haven't seen cloth so clean in ages."

"Little princess," someone spat. "Her spine will droop soon enough."

"She smells like flowers," a woman said wistfully. But her tone turned sharp when she raised her voice. "What's the matter, princess? Too good for the likes of us?"

Amelia sighed, hugged her knees to her chest. She kept her gaze outside because it was the safer direction. Out there, she could see her freedom and pretend it was within reach. In here, the despair and bitterness was overwhelming.

"Hey! I'm talking to you!"

Amelia should be able to maintain her detached objectivity, rise up and rally these women, give them hope, however fragile and fake, that things would get better if they were strong enough to will it that way. *People hurt us because we allow it,* she would say. *If you give them that power, they will destroy you with it.*

"Leave her be, Reena."

It would have been a lie.

The most insidious thing about Rome wasn't that it was deadly; it was that it made you doubt yourself. It made a strong man feel weak and insignificant, a proud woman feel like a cheap whore.

Amelia had no defense against this. For every strategy she came up with, a dozen reasons why it wouldn't work followed. Even at the worst of times, in New Alaska, when she'd believed herself in Hell, Amelia had never felt this helpless. She'd always had her secret weapons, little exit strategies, and always the knowledge that she had science on her side. The one thing that always worked in her favor and against all others.

And now here she was, in a place where science as she knew it literally did not exist as far as she could see. They might as well have cut off her hands.

Grunts and curses alerted Amelia to a woman coming at her. The threat was audible in every move she made, and Amelia felt for the handle of her knife, keeping her face casually averted. Anger made her spine straighten more and her limbs tense for a fight. Hurt, fear, uncertainty, grief—it all blended together inside her; so much emotion, she couldn't possibly shut it out, only mold it into something else.

That something was rage.

"Leave her alone," someone said, and Reena's progress stopped for a moment as the speaker caught her.

"You'll get us all in trouble," another whispered in harsh reprimand.

Amelia swiveled her head to look at the woman who would confront her. In the meager light, her eyes glittered with anger fueled by her own helplessness. She needed to lash out, if only to prove she still could.

She would get more than she bargained for if someone didn't stop her.

"Quiet!" an older woman ordered.

Someone gasped. "I hear the guard."

Reena snarled, fisting her hands. She shook off the one who held her back and advanced again. "You think you're better than us?" she demanded.

Holding her gaze, Amelia shook her head slowly from side to side.

That simple thing infuriated the woman. "Don't you look at me!" she screamed and lunged forward.

~

Here they come. Like clockwork. Punctual little ants going about their business. Gabriel lay tense in the shadows, listening to the trainers' advancing footsteps. He could hear their heartbeats, scent the blood rushing through their veins and part of him thirsted for it. He hadn't eaten all day, was starved for a hunk of juicy meat. So what if it still had a heartbeat?

The lionesses still watched him. They hadn't moved an inch, except for their tails. They waited to see what he would do next. *You'll get your show.* At one point, while waiting, he'd debated letting all of the beasts out, giving them the freedom they craved. He ultimately decided against it. Even if they weren't crazed from constant confinement, they were still carnivores. He didn't need more obstacles in his path.

The lights came on, and the beasts came to their feet. All but the lionesses. Whips cracked in the air, signaling the trainers' entrance, and the beasts riled into a frothing frenzy. Their aggression polluted the very air until Gabriel was afraid to breathe and be infected by it. He needed a level head to do what had to be done. Going into a blood rage was not part of the plan.

Time moved in freeze frames. Empty hallway. Lionesses staring.

Trainers with whips. Water troughs in every pen. Waiting. Waiting. Waiting.

Gabriel closed his eyes, pretending to sleep. He had his paws under him, ready to spring forward the second the door opened, but he made himself lie still, while he felt those damn lioness eyes on him.

They hadn't drunk.

The trainers waited for-*fucking*-ever to do their job. Gabriel counted a good ten minutes after the last animal went down with a groan and a thud. First pen open. The scent of blood intensified, mixed with something chemical. That one had gotten hurt. Second pen open. Nothing in there but shit and rotting flesh. Gabriel wrinkled his snout, almost showing a fang. Third and fourth pens open, first two closed.

Two by two the trainers went until they got to Gabriel's door. He heard them on the other side. Three heartbeats. He waited.

"These ones are awake," one of them said.

"Leave them," another replied.

Key in the lock. *Click. Clang. Whoosh.*

Gabriel lunged before he'd opened his eyes. The trainer went down with a startled yell, breath knocked out of him, eyes wide with terror. Gabriel didn't want to kill the guy, or any of them, but they had weapons and tranqs with them for protection. The other two were already reaching.

He roared at them so loud, it brought the lionesses to their paws, and they roared with him, raking the door, maddened, demanding release. They would kill anything that moved. He tackled the second trainer, bit into his shoulder enough to draw blood. It poured so sweet into his mouth, he salivated for more. Just a bite.

Third guard shot off a round.

Gabriel shook off the sting of the tranq, released his prey, and bounded off before another could hit him. His paws tingled as he ran down the corridor and out of the holding dock. Idiots had left the door wide open.

He tripped and fell on his face, rolled over from the momentum in the gladiator barracks. Breath huffed in and out of him; the world tilted and swam. The tranq was a strong one. He shook his head hard, got up again, and slipped into shadows against the wall, moving forward as silent as death. Gladiators in their cells. Most were lost in thought or someone's orifice. A few noticed movement. Shot to their feet to see what was happening.

One or two reached for a shard of clay or glass, the only weapon at their disposal. They stared at him with wary eyes as he slunk past them. His paws dragged. He had to get the hell out of here before they caught up to him.

The tunnels led out into the arena. He could already scent the night air mixing with dry blood out there. Many had been there, their scents lingering. He could make it. Just a little farther. Almost there.

Gabriel's head swam. Footsteps approached and voices shouted directions. More now than before. Had the trainers released gladiators to help them search? Then he would be dead on the spot when they found him. *If* they found him.

Now or never.

He'd need hands to open the gate outside.

Gabriel stopped by the supply room. There were clothes in there, weapons and armor all waiting for gladiators to pick them up. He was leaning against the wall, barely keeping his paws under him. The dart was still embedded in his shoulder and he couldn't reach it with his teeth to pull it out.

Now or never.

Fucking change!

It wasn't easy, short, or painless. But it *was* working. Even in this state, he still had control over it. Paws became hands and feet, his tail receded into his spine. Limbs elongated and face collapsed into a different shape. A human one. He was left gasping, weak. It felt impossible to raise his arm, but he did, and he yanked the tranq dart out.

"Sweet gods above," someone whispered.

Gabriel turned his head to seek out the threat. Rico and two other men stood not ten feet from him, weapons in hand, mouths agape.

They'd seen.

He should kill them.

Rico's jaw worked, his face contorted in disgust. "This is what you did with your freedom?"

It took too much effort to keep looking at him. "You wann'kill me," he drawled. His tongue felt strange in his mouth. "Then do it. Or you c'n lethe others out 'n go home." Gabriel reached for the first set of clothing he saw. Missed it by an inch. Hand-eye coordination shot to shit. He reached again; his hand barely made it halfway there.

"Do you see it?" someone called. Gabriel froze. He turned again, enough to see Rico from the corner of his eye.

"This is insane," one of his men muttered.

"Can't be real…" the other said.

"*Where is it?*" the trainer shouted.

Rico held Gabriel's gaze. "It was in the south corridor," he shouted back. "I think it's wounded."

Gabriel breathed out in relief. Hung his head. Too much effort to hold it up.

Strong hands caught his arms, dragged his sorry ass up.

"The hell are you doing, Rico?"

"Getting the fuck out of here. You coming or what?"

The two swore and split up. One in each direction, they opened every cell and let the men out. Neither said a word about Gabriel—he would have heard. His head was beginning to clear by slow degrees, but the world still spun. He had no choice but to let Rico help him put some clothes on. Pathetic.

"I hope to hell you have a plan."

"Get out, find Amelia, kill the Caesar, disappear."

"Just like that."

Gabriel looked at him. "What else you wanna do? Go sightseeing?"

"How are you going to get off-world?"

Gabriel grinned, feeling drunk. "Got fifty men at m' back. 'N I hear Soren's dead." Or would be soon.

Rico stared at him, then a savage little smile stretched across his face, too. "Do or die time."

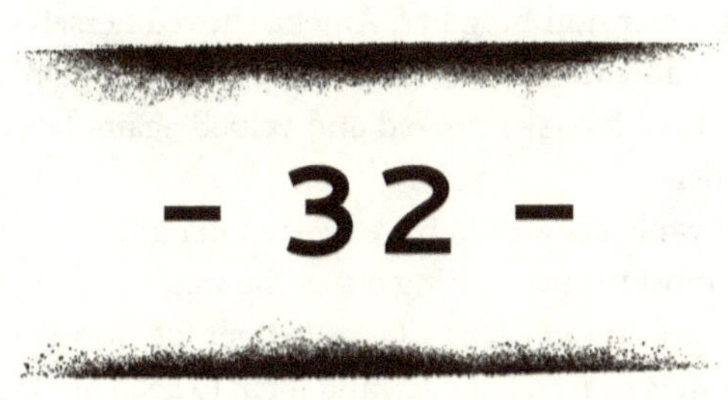

- 32 -

Someone tripped her. Reena went flying but managed to put her arms up to break her fall against the window bars. It infuriated her even more, and Amelia scrambled to get away from under the cage of her.

A dozen women got to their feet, shouting encouragement or warning. Amelia didn't know which won out; she was too busy weaving around Reena's unpracticed attacks. Someone caught her arms from behind, and Amelia cried out. Reena was smiling. "Got you," she mouthed.

Amelia couldn't get her arms free. Couldn't get away from the beating Reena was about to deliver—for what? She did the only thing she could. Used her captor's strong hold to lift her legs and kick out. She caught Reena in her solar plexus. Her face turned red as she fought for breath, fought the nausea that made her torso spasm. There were tears of pain in the woman's eyes, which only focused the hatred in them the way a magnifying glass focused sunlight into a single point.

When Reena came at her again, it was without mercy. A fist drove into her midsection so hard, she felt it in her spine. As she doubled over, the person holding her let go, and she fell to her hands and knees. Reena kicked out at her side. Again. And one more time. She was already tiring, but the damage she'd done was enough to make Amelia want to pass out.

Clutching the knife hard so she wouldn't lose it, Amelia rolled away, kept rolling, though it was agony, trying to keep one small step ahead of those stomping feet. She ended up in the water trough, face-first, the freezing water numbing her. Amelia shoved herself upstream as Reena's foot came down. The woman slipped and yelped. Snarling in Amelia's direction, she moved and yelped again, her foot caught in the channel.

With that yank, she would have twisted her ankle.

Amelia almost tripped getting out of the water, the stupid skirt wet and tangled around her legs. She didn't get far. Some of the others blocked her way, shoved her back and forth to keep her in place while Reena hobbled toward her.

"*What the fuck is going on in here!*" The roar was followed by screams as the guard forced his way inside, shoving and punching women out of the way.

Reena made an awkward run for it, seeming determined to get her beating in before the guard could stop her. She didn't make it. The guard backhanded someone so hard, there was a sickening snap, and the woman *flew* into Reena, mowing her down.

"It was her!" the other one who'd blocked Amelia yelled, pointing. "She started it!"

The guard slapped her down with the full force of his tree-sized arm. Broke her jaw and left her moaning on the floor.

Amelia backed away from him, tripped over the dead girl and went down.

The guard grabbed her by the hair and pulled her to her feet, his fetid breath stinging her face. "All this trouble for some whore," he muttered, his free hand curling into a massive fist. If he aimed it at her, she was dead.

Amelia moved lightning quick. Hand cramped around the knife, she stabbed it into the guard's neck, closing her eyes at the last second. She hit her mark—at least she thought she did—and twisted the knife for good measure.

The hand in her hair curled tighter for an instant, then loosened and yanked so hard it nearly twisted Amelia's neck. Not on purpose. He was trying to get free. When he did, Amelia dropped as he reached up to the knife with a baffled look on his face. Gurgling, he pulled the blade out, the worst possible thing he could do. With nothing to plug the hole, blood sprayed out of his jugular to the rhythm of his beating heart.

By the time he dropped to the ground, dead but still twitching, the room had gone quiet. No one moved, no one breathed, except Amelia. She pushed up unsteadily, finding her feet, but her legs felt weak and her body was one massive pain. Breathing hurt. She gasped in small breaths, tears stinging her eyes.

When she turned for the door, shuffling her feet through the puddle of blood everyone else was backing away from, no one stopped her. She reclaimed her knife, not ready to give up the only protection she had, and wiped it on her now filthy dress. The feel of soaking fabric clinging to her skin disgusted her. She was covered in human waste and blood, and noted with the last speck of wry humor she possessed that this was as low as she could have possibly fallen from her sterile scientific pedestal.

The door had been left open. The others should have been stampeding out of here. Amelia braced her hand against the doorframe to keep her balance as she looked back at the others. Every last one of them stared at her with wide eyes filled with something she didn't dare put a label on. Fear? Shock, definitely. Confusion, most likely. Or was that hope?

Amelia was no one's hero. She didn't have time to make speeches, rally troops, or comfort anyone. Who knew how many guards were in this place? Had to be more than one. She had to get out of here before the others came to investigate the commotion.

Walking as fast as her current state allowed, which meant a slow, careful shift of her weight left and right so she could slide the opposite foot forward, she reversed the path she'd taken here in her mind and followed it to the main gate.

Noises behind her. Soft hiss of whispers and gentle thumps of many footsteps. Amelia didn't look behind her to see who was following. Keeping her blurry gaze straight ahead, she shuffled on, gritting her teeth against the pain.

Her heart sank when she got to the gate and found it barred by a thick wooden beam. The massive guard would have had no trouble lifting it out of its braces. Amelia didn't stand a chance.

Defeat making her dizzy, she leaned against the wall to catch her breath.

More whispers.

Then four bedraggled, emaciated women, went past her to the gate. They nodded at each other, and on some silent count, put their entire meager weights into it and lifted the beam. Four more came to help them set it down quietly.

Amelia made herself look over her shoulder. There were others. At least a dozen, if not more. She couldn't be sure, but it looked like they were keeping watch. Working together to get out of here.

Gabriel had been right. One person really could affect many others.

Without its brace, the gate groaned open a few inches. The women who took down the beam looked at it, and then looked at her uncertainly.

"We're going south, out of the city," Reena said, coming up from behind her. "You can come with us," she added grudgingly.

Amelia shook her head and pushed away from the wall. "Someone I love is still in the city. I have to find him first." She didn't realize what she'd said until she pushed the gate wide open, and then her step faltered. How easily the words had slipped out. How obvious it was. She loved him.

She. Loved. Him.

Amelia picked up her step a little. She had to tell him before it was too late.

"Good luck to you," one of the women whispered. They were heading south, a path branching off to her right. Amelia's road lay straight ahead. Back the way she'd come, to the heart of Rome and the viper at its center. A always led to B. If Gabriel had been caught, he'd be close to the Caesar. If he was free, he'd either look for Amelia or go after the Caesar. Right now, Amelia had a bone of her own to pick with the bitch.

C and D eliminated. B, here I come.

Only the street she was on ended a few feet ahead in a T. And she had no recollection of which path Lucia and the other soldier had taken to get to this point.

Amelia squinted first left then right, trying to make out something, anything that might be familiar. Without her glasses, everything was a blur of the same. Yellow sand, paler yellow houses. Strings hung from one house across to the other, with something hung from them, billowing in the breeze. Clothes. Amelia reached up, wincing at the pain, and snagged the very fringe of something. When it fell, she held it up, relieved to see it was a long shirt. Long enough to cover her from shoulder to below the knee. She stripped out of the sodden dress, uncaring of who might see, and pulled the shirt on. It was rough, but it was dry and clean. She felt a hundred times better already.

Decently covered, Amelia squared her shoulders and turned down the left path.

Wait, left?

Yes, definitely left.

But wait. She frowned in the other direction. Why not that way?

Left. Go left.

Still frowning, Amelia continued down the left street. A few more steps and she stopped again, glancing behind her. Maybe she ought to try that way instead.

Go left!

Amelia flinched at how loud the thought was. She might have called it instinct, except she wasn't one of those people who had it. Amelia didn't *feel* her way out of trouble, she *thought* her way out. And there was no logical reason for choosing this path over the other when they both looked the same.

Shaking her head, she went back to the intersection to consider this properly.

Woman, are you physically incapable of following directions?

Somewhere in the middle of that thought, the voice of it morphed from hers to one decidedly male and extremely agitated. Amelia stopped as if she'd hit a glass wall.

Heart pumping double time, she searched the sky, hardly daring to hope.

—*Go. Left,*— Tristan growled in her mind—and it was definitely Tristan.

Where are you? She had no idea how this telepathy thing was supposed to work. Would he hear her?

—On approach. Can't risk breaking atmo in the shuttle. We'll use the life pod to get down and back up, and you have to be there when we touch down.—

He was here! They were getting out!

But wait…

How many will the pod hold?

A pause. *—Why, you suddenly got the urge to liberate a planet?—*

There was pressure in her head that bordered on pain. Her feet turned involuntarily down the left street and carried her step by step where Tristan wanted her to go. But he wasn't the only one in her head anymore. Before she could start freaking out, Agent Calen's voice rang out. *—Amelia, your sister says she's going to kick your ass when we get back.—*

I know how that feels. She thought it before she could censor herself, and winced.

Her sister's husband, though, was amused by it. *—You girls can sort that out later. Right now, I need you to let Tristan lead you to us.—*

Amelia stopped at the very edge of the narrow alley. It was already full day and people were beginning to stir. The streets would fill up soon, with everything from peasants, to nobles, to soldiers.

I'm not leaving without Gabriel, she thought, trying to somehow aim it at Calen.

—Unless you come across him along the way, you damn well are,— Tristan growled back.

She was shaking her head.

As if he could see her, his agitation rose. *—Amelia,—* he said in warning.

No. No way. *I'm not leaving without him,* she decided loudly. *So figure something out.* She would find her way back to the arena somehow, even if Tristan refused to help her.

—How the hell are we supposed to find one man in fucking Rome?—

Well that was the easiest thing on this world. *Just look for a panther walking on two legs.*

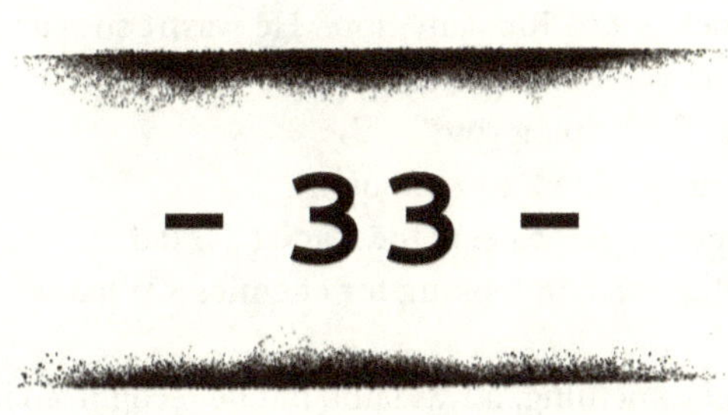

– 33 –

It was day. With Rico's help, Gabriel had managed to get out of the arena, sword strapped to his side. The others had gone a different way. They would scatter for now, retrieve their women while they could, and then disappear. None of them had any ties to each other and no reason to risk their necks unless there was some tactical advantage to it. With Gabriel as the main target, they were better off being far away from him.

This wasn't a revolt against the Caesar, it was a free for all, and everyone who could was taking the opening and getting the hell out of town.

Why Rico stayed, Gabriel had no idea.

He was still shaking off the damn tranq and regretted not having bitten the trainer's throat out. But he was walking on his own now.

"What does it feel like?" Rico asked.

"What? Sticking it to the Caesar?" He winced at his poor choice of words.

"Funny guy."

Gabriel almost smiled.

"Well?"

Persistent bastard. "You've broken a bone before, right? Got your skull bashed in?"

"Many times."

"Well, imagine that, but everywhere."

Rico grunted in a noncommittal reply. Gabriel had to admire that. Nothing much got to Rico anymore. He wasn't sure anything ever had. "Why are you helping me?"

"Who says I'm helping you?"

Now Gabriel grunted. Fair enough.

They stopped in the center of the market. Or rather, Gabriel stopped and Rico followed suit, looking for enemies. "What is it? You hear something?"

He *smelled* something. It was faint, but he recognized it; he would never forget that scent. If there was a hint of it in his nostrils, he would follow it through Hell or high water to get to her. Amelia had come this way. He inhaled deeply, swayed on his feet in relief. She was alive. He felt his face ripple in a slight change, nose flattened, fangs sharp, eyes glowing like candlelight. All because of her. He'd find her. He was sure of it.

Rico was staring at him. "That is messed up."

Gabriel grinned, felt his lip split wider and made himself purse his mouth to fuse it together again.

Rico stifled a shudder. He looked away, scanning their surroundings. "Which way?"

Right to Honoria's bedchamber. She would be asleep after an eventful day like yesterday. Easy to sneak in and slit her throat. Or rip out her black heart.

Straight to Amelia. Somewhere out there. He could follow her scent right to her and get them both out of here. There was a shuttleport outside of Rome, one of only two, including Mt. Olympus, which they'd never make. He could get her to the other one easily.

But he couldn't do that *and* kill the Caesar.

Straight or right?

Rico cursed and pulled him behind the shelter of a street cart as a contingent of soldiers rode by on horseback. "Make up your fucking mind. I'm not dying here for you."

If he killed Honoria, it would be over. He might make it out of Rome, he might not. He would definitely lose Amelia. If he went right, she would be forever out of his life one way or another.

If he let the Caesar live, she would never stop hunting him. On another world, another time, he might have an advantage, or he might grow complacent and be caught off guard. He hated the idea of sleeping with one eye open for the rest of his life.

He hated the idea of losing Amelia more.

So. Straight or right?

Instinct made him look up. A sound not heard but felt drew his eye to the sky. There! A tiny wink of light, so far he'd have missed it had he not been looking for it. Something on approach. Something small. Hardly a speck in the sky, no telltale burn of entry, meaning low velocity short range pod, in all likelihood. But the pod had come from somewhere.

Gabriel sighed. He'd never hear the end of this.

But he might stay alive long enough to listen to it.

For now, no one was looking that way. It wouldn't take long before it was noticed, though. He had to find Amelia before that.

Gabriel charged across the market, heading for the alley straight ahead. Rico swore and followed. A glint of movement to his right caught his eye, and before he ducked into the safety of shadow, Gabriel looked for its source. Honoria's bower. His eyes adjusted to see farther, clearer. There she was, the bitch hell had spat out for trying to oust the Devil himself. Honoria in all her morning glory, standing at the top of her stairs with only a bed sheet wrapped around her. Were those bloodstains?

She looked up at the approaching pod, the only person who noticed it—but of course she would have been alerted to it already—and pointed an imperious finger, shouting orders at everyone around. Then, as if she felt Gabriel watching her, she looked right at him. No way she could see him from so far away. She couldn't possibly know he was there.

It still made him uneasy. If he ran, Honoria *would* find him. She'd stop at nothing to get him back, to get even.

A breeze brought him another hint of Amelia. The scent was fading. It would dissipate soon.

Make a choice.

Gabriel's spine stiffened. He looked at Rico, but the gladiator wasn't looking at him. His eyes scanned the crowds for threats the way he'd been trained. He had not spoken.

Make a choice. The words were plain enough. It was the growling anger behind them he didn't get. As if somewhere in those two words and a letter there was a hidden threat: *it'd better be the right one.*

Holographic panels flickered on next to him and made him twitch. He'd never realized before how cloying the static charge was against his skin. Gabriel edged an inch farther from it.

Choooooooose.

"Knock it off," he growled, startling himself.

"The hell's the matter with you?" Rico said.

He had no clue. The longer they weren't moving, the more on edge he felt. Time was running out. He *knew* that. Had been preparing for this for so damn long, there was no reason to feel restless. It was about to be over. He should be calm, steady. Ready to get this over with and move on.

This inner turmoil was foreign to him. His head kept turning right, even after Honoria had retreated inside, presumably to get dressed for the occasion.

His feet were shifting to follow Amelia's scent. It was subconscious, only it wasn't. His mind and body were at war, and it was so unnatural, he fought it on instinct.

A snarl split his lip again. He took off, following Amelia's scent. A second later, Rico was on his heels. A minute later and the scent was gone. Utterly and completely, as if he'd somehow gotten off the path it had created, taken a wrong turn somewhere. But his feet were still moving, running headlong for something.

And he couldn't stop. He couldn't fucking make his feet stop.

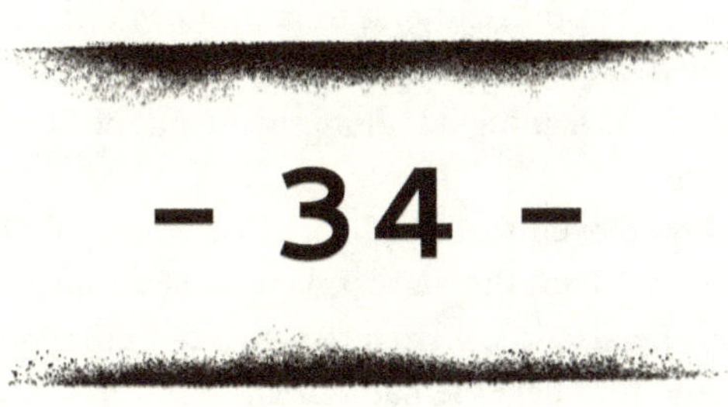

– 34 –

—*We found his mind,*— Calen said at the same time as she shouted, *I see you!*

She would have shouted it out loud, but caution stopped her. The hooded cloak she'd found on another clothesline fit as if it had been made for her, but the hood kept slipping over her eyes. She shoved it back up again. Amelia was breathing hard from her tromp through the city. Tristan was a merciless navigator. When she would have turned right, walked straight into a contingent of guards, he'd projected a high-pitched squealing noise into her head to stop her. It had worked like a charm; she'd stopped so fast, she'd fallen back on her ass.

She'd give her last penny for one shot of pain killers straight to the spine.

The problem was Tristan didn't exactly know *where* she was, but he knew what, or rather who, was around her.

When she asked Calen why they didn't simply tell her where to go, rather than navigating her turn by turn, he explained that telepathy didn't work that way. Tristan didn't have a convenient glowing dot on a map to mark her location. He was steering her on a safe route, but he had to drop all of his shields and let in everything to do it. It was taking a tremendous effort on his part to sort through all of that to maintain contact with her. He didn't have the mental capacity to do more than navigate the maze. No one alive did.

Amelia slowed down a lot after that, paid better attention to where she was going.

Now she saw the pod readying to land outside the city. She was still far, but down one of the streets she'd passed, Amelia had seen the market. Tristan was leading her alongside it, out of sight and toward the landing site.

Her step slowed even further. Gabriel was that way. To her right, somewhere in the chaos the marketplace had become. Amelia knew he'd be there. She also knew she'd never find him in that mess. But what if he could find her? He had his super senses—although right now she smelled like a lot of things, just not herself.

And what if he's not interested in finding you?

The thought brought hurt with it. And it pissed her off—it wasn't her own. *Don't you dare use your tricks on me, Tristan. I expect better from you.*

The hurt receded immediately. —*You want to know what he's thinking right now? He's got this Honoria woman in his sights.*—

Hope flared bright hot. He was alive! She headed for the next corner, fully prepared to make the turn and go after him.

—*Think, woman!*— Tristan's words were a growl in her mind, and on their trail, she caught a glimpse of what he thought of her just then. He was surprised, had never expected her to react this way when the right, *safe* course of action should have been clear. She was supposed to be rational, always thinking ahead and coming up with solutions to problems others hadn't thought might occur. Now she was a stranger, a lovesick female running headlong toward her own demise for someone who…

That was it. He cut himself off before she could catch the end of the thought.

Someone who what? she demanded.

The pod was landing, and unless Honoria was dead or her soldiers completely inept, it was already surrounded by troops. Already she felt the crowds two streets over shifting, pouring in that direction, propelled by curiosity. By the time she made it there, the pod would be surrounded, and Amelia would never get through the crowd now unless someone cleared a path for her.

—*We can do it, but you have to hurry,*— Calen said.

Not without Gabriel, she replied with iron resolve.

The response from Tristan was wordless, furious, and probably very unflattering. But he didn't stop her when she turned toward the marketplace. It was her own caution that kept her from rushing headlong into the crowds. Amelia flattened herself against the wall of a house, behind a holographic panel, squinting through it. With her vision already blurry without her glasses, she couldn't see a damn thing through the flickering screen. If she stuck her head around it, she'd be seen.

—*You don't trust me,*— Tristan said with something like hurt surprise in his mind-voice.

Amelia's cheeks heated. He and Calen had flown in from Torrey to rescue her. Of course she trusted them. Amelia knew she was safe now that they were here. *She* was. But Gabriel was something else. She couldn't trust his well-being to them because they simply did not care. Their priority was Amelia, and whether or not she had others was incidental.

It felt like spitting in their faces for their efforts, but Amelia couldn't walk away from this. It was too important.

I can't leave him here, Tristan, any more than I could have left you and Dara in New Alaska.

—*You can't stay here for him, either.*— That was Calen.

She knew that. Intellectually.

But her intellect wasn't calling the shots right now. There was a choice to be made.

—*He has a choice to make.*—

She could leave him behind, get to safety—

—*He can go after Honoria, get his revenge*——

—and figure out a way to get him out later, risk something happening to him in the meantime…

——*or he can go to you. He has your scent, Amelia.*—

Or she could go after him. He was close, she could feel it. They could take their chances together. Live or die, but not alone.

She hesitated.

—*He hesitates.*— That accusing voice was Tristan's. His way of saying, *I would already be stalking Dara.* It was a mark of inferiority to Tristan that Amelia wasn't Gabriel's first and immediate priority.

Amelia knew better. She'd seen enough of Honoria's madness to know they might never stop looking over their shoulders if they ran now. Honoria would never let Gabriel go willingly. And he had to know that. He'd make the same decision he'd made all along, since the beginning. He'd choose to secure her safety before anything else. He'd go after the Caesar to make sure Amelia was safe.

You can't let him, she thought frantically. *Tristan, you can't let him do it—he'll die!*

There was a long enough silence from both men that Amelia thought they'd abandoned her. She waited, worrying her lower lip, nails digging into the wall.

—Everyone is heading toward us,— Tristan finally said, his mind-voice gruff. *—Honoria will, too. Go back one street and keep coming toward me.—*

The reasoning was implied, but she felt him nudge her thought process to understand what he did: Gabriel would follow either Honoria or her. Either way, all of them would end up in the same place. He wasn't issuing an order but directions.

—Oh, and Amelia? They know you escaped. They're hunting for you already. Run.—

Amelia ran.

~

"Slow the fuck down!"

He couldn't. His legs pumped faster, propelled him onwards. Two streets over, the market crowds were moving the same way he was— toward the landed pod. That wasn't where he wanted to go. Amelia had to be in the other direction somewhere. He'd lost her scent a while back.

What the hell was happening to him? This couldn't be part of the panther asserting itself, could it? Gabriel didn't sense the animal part of him behind it.

Up ahead, a red curtain billowed out of a window, and he ran straight through it. Three steps beyond it, he was in the middle of a crossroads, and his feet stopped dead, as if he'd hit a wall. His breaths were growls, his nails were claws. Gabriel was furious, unable to move an inch. His muscles rippled, shifted, but the act of changing shape was denied to him. All he could do was stand there and breathe.

Rico caught up, panting and glaring. "Are you out of your mind?"

Possibly. He couldn't move his mouth to speak. The growl became constant. Breath or not, it rumbled in his chest so hard, he felt the vibrations down to his fingertips.

"We should be heading the other way," Rico said.

This was insane. A person didn't lose control of motor function out of the blue. Whatever was causing this had to end, and soon. Amelia was on borrowed time alone in Rome. She was the most capable woman he'd ever known; beautiful, and smart, and so damn strong it humbled him. If there was a remote chance of her getting out of here on her own, he had absolutely no doubt she would somehow make it work.

But he didn't want it to change her in the process, as it had him. He never wanted to look into her eyes and see a stranger staring back at him. Gabriel needed to get her out of here, before he did anything else. He could wait out Honoria, or come back here and finish it on his own.

Rico snapped his fingers. "Hey! Wake up!"

Gabriel dragged in a deep breath, and his eyes widened. He hadn't noticed before, too distracted to pay attention. He breathed in deeply again and sagged with relief. The scent was back.

And he could move again.

Rico swore when he took off, but Gabriel could only laugh. He followed his nose one street over and spotted a hooded figure far ahead, almost at the edge of the city. It jogged, slowed, jogged a few more steps, and then stopped for breath.

He slowed so he wouldn't frighten her. She had to be exhausted. How far had she come? How did she know to go this way? The cloak wasn't hers. None of what she was wearing was. He still scented her beneath it all, almost went to his knees in gratitude to whatever messed up side effect had made him turn onto this path to find her.

He could almost hear an irritated voice growl, *You're welcome.* Gabriel didn't care. Whatever it was, Amelia would have the answer.

They were getting out of here, both of them, and alive. He could live with hallucinations for the time being.

Next to him, Rico drew his sword, but took his cue from Gabriel. Stayed close enough to cover his back, but left plenty of room for Gabriel to move fast if he had to.

A tingle of apprehension made him slow. Something was off. He scanned the street front and behind, looked into the windows he passed, down every alley and around every corner. A hint of movement drew his eye up.

Archer on the roof. Arrow to string.

Gabriel sucked in a sharp breath.

Aiming for Amelia.

"*Rico!*" he shouted, putting on a burst of speed. Amelia stopped, turned around. The hood fell over her face. Ah, God, she wouldn't see it coming! He ran faster, willing his feet to movemove*MOVE!*

The string loosed with a snap.

Gabriel launched forward as she drew her hood back and smiled beatifically. Sunshine illuminating Heaven deep in Hell. He would die for that smile.

They collided, and Gabriel hauled her close, hunching over her to shield her. The arrow slammed home into his back, jagged edges tearing a hole through his flesh.

He would die for that smile.

Amelia's scream deafened him to the world at large.

He would die.

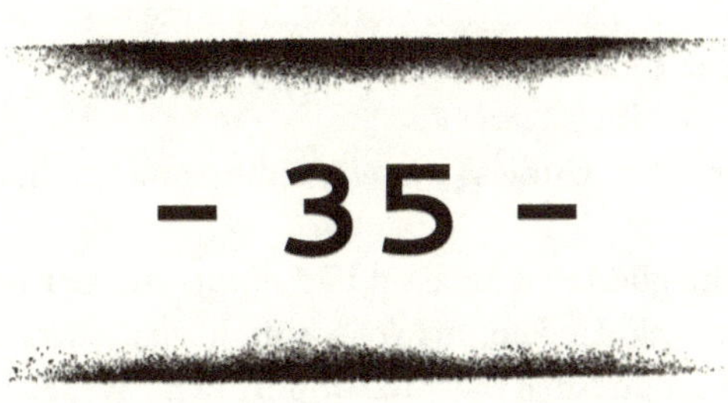

- 35 -

The arrow pierced through him. Gabriel groaned. The pain wasn't severe; it hardly swayed him. It was Amelia's cry that nearly killed him. He pulled away from her, wincing as the arrow's shaft slid through his flesh before the sharp metal head came free of Amelia. She clamped a hand over the wound immediately to stop the bleeding, and Gabriel staggered back.

Up on the rooftop, the assassin died beneath Rico's blade. A quick death to silence the man before he could raise an alarm, but the damage had been done. Gabriel broke off the arrowhead, and when Rico jumped down to the street, he pulled the shaft out of Gabriel's back. The wound started closing almost immediately, like every other injury he'd had since Amelia had changed him. He waited for the pain to stop, too. It didn't.

"Ow," Amelia said. Understatement. The arrow had pierced her shoulder just beneath her collarbone. It was a flesh wound but deep enough that she had to keep pressure on it to stop the bleeding. She was hurt. The scent of her blood baffled him for a moment. The message from his nose got stuck in his heart en route to his brain and refused to move along.

A flesh wound, he told himself, she would be all right.

So why couldn't he make himself believe it?

Because nothing was ever that simple anymore.

Gabriel stared down at the arrowhead still in his hand. The piece of shaft still attached to it was stained red, not with blood, but paint. He brought it to his nose and sniffed. *That* message came through loud and clear. Closing his fist tight around it, he turned his back on Amelia and met Rico's gaze.

Rico nodded in wordless understanding and ran ahead to clear the path.

Poison. The goddamn assassin had dipped the arrow in poison. "Come on, angel." He kept his voice soft, his gaze averted when he put his arm around her waist to support her. "We're almost there. Your knight came through after all."

"I can walk," she said peevishly.

Not for long. The poison was hemlock.

Amelia stopped and looked up at him. "Conium is a neurotoxin," she said. Her heart beat faster, spread the poison quicker. He had to get her onto that shuttle.

"What?"

"Hemlock," she said. "Latin name, Conium. It's a neurotoxin."

"Huh." What, was she a mind reader now? "That's interesting." He moved forward again, but she stopped him.

"It means it acts on neural impulses, messages between cells, rather than cell structure." After a moment's pause, she added, "Means you won't be able to heal from this on your own."

Shit. "All the more reason to get moving." Gabriel propelled her forward, kept her in front of him so she wouldn't see his feet starting to drag.

There was a vast field out beyond the city. It stretched for miles like a sea of golden wheat swaying in the breeze. At least that was what it used to look like before the pod had flattened a good portion of the crop. Romans had gathered en masse and soldiers had their hands full holding them back. There were mostly peasants and slaves, those desperate enough to escape that they would fight soldiers and each other for a spot on that pod. And they could plainly see not many would make it. There were already fights breaking out. Enforcements were coming in from all sides to keep the mob contained.

A small group of nobles had come out as well, keeping their distance from the dirty crowds; they were flocked around Honoria and her personal guard, watching the pod's passengers disembark.

"There has to be a med kit on the shuttle," Amelia said. "Maybe I can improvise something."

That's my girl. Always thinking two steps ahead.

"I might be able to slow the progress of it until we get to my lab."

He said nothing.

"Crappy way to die," she muttered. "Stops muscle function 'til you can't move, or breathe. You asphyxiate slowly but your brain keeps working until the end."

Comprehending every terrifying second of it.

Honoria had equipped her men with different varieties of the same thing. The one soldiers dipped their arrows and blades into was a concentrated version. Introduced straight into the bloodstream, it killed fast, but not too fast.

They were on the very edge of the crowd, with nearly a clear path to the pod. Nothing stood in their way except a couple of serfs and three soldiers with sharp eyes currently trained on something else. Gabriel raised his knee high, testing mobility. Already it took more effort than he'd like to put one foot in front of the other. He couldn't feel his toes, and Amelia was limping, leaning on him for support. She tried not to, knowing he was suffering from the same, but every time she pulled away, he dragged her back.

Ahead, two men emerged from the pod. The taller one might as well have been a gladiator. He had the posture and physique, the same vicious killer look in his eyes. He didn't walk, he slunk, as if his feet never made a sound on the metal ramp. The other was leaner, more refined. Not a man who toiled with his hands, more someone who used his brain. There was something about him that put Gabriel on guard. The buttoned up composure held an air of authority, but it was a mask for something far more unpredictable underneath. He would not be underestimating that one.

"Almost there."

The soldiers weren't looking at them. They were keeping an eye on the crowds, moving in closer to herd them back, leaving the path completely clear and unguarded. What was this, another trick? Honoria's last little amusement before she shut him down? *See how far you can get, little rat, before I catch you by the tail and rip your head off.* He wouldn't put it past her.

But what choice did they have?

"Now or never," Amelia said quietly. Her face was set; she wasn't about to give up now, no matter what. She was squinting at the pod. Where were her glasses? When he slowed, she nudged him to go faster.

At the front, Honoria detached from her entourage and met the strangers halfway. Gabriel couldn't see her mouth moving but some sort of communication must have passed between them because the Caesar nodded, turned to the crowd, and raised her arms to silence them.

No one did. No one cared about the Caesar now that her reins had slipped. Gladiators were running free. Rico was not far away, egging the crowd on, busting soldiers' heads together. The others were rallying behind him, following his lead. Rome's downtrodden had found their hero. *Good luck, my friend.*

The moment Honoria turned away from them, the two strangers turned in unison to stare right at him—or rather through him—with an identical expression of impatience, annoyance, and something only an animal would recognize. Gabriel bared his teeth at them, driven by instinct to warn them off.

The men exchanged a long, speaking glance. Who the hell were these guys?

He was so focused on them that Honoria's words didn't register in his mind until they'd almost cleared the guards. Despite no one except those members of her court closest to her listening, ignoring the danger she was in, the Caesar was talking, her tone casual, composed, and regal, as every other time she'd addressed a crowd. Her words were anything but.

Had she really just confessed to the old Caesar's murder?

Not that everyone didn't know already. A woman didn't simply take over in Rome the way Honoria had by accident. But to hear the words aloud, spoken like some sick introduction to an awards acceptance speech, had to be a bad joke. "When I slit Caesar Marius' throat…"

The court hens gasped, all equally baffled, and Honoria just kept on talking. They hissed with whispers behind politely raised hands, their eyes wide, frightened, some calculating.

A few tried to stop her, to get her to shut up, but the Caesar ignored them as if they didn't exist.

The crowds were getting more and more violent. The soldiers had concentrated closer to the pod and Honoria, but many of them were recognizing a lost cause and tucking tail.

Honoria brushed off warning hands, sighed, and turned to Gabriel with an indulgent smile. His hackles went up instantly, and he drew Amelia tighter against him, shifting to shield her from view. "And Gabriel. My Champion. The unequaled among titans. You were my great hope for the future."

Gabriel snarled.

"Gabriel, let's go," Amelia said.

He couldn't move a step, felt the gazes of both the strangers on him the entire time, and for some reason it pissed him off. This was a test of some sort.

"You all probably know him as Gladius," Honoria was saying. "A warrior never bested in the arena. If I'd allowed him to join the ranks of my soldiers, he would have risen to surpass them, as well."

A rock flew out of the crowd. It struck Honoria on her pale shoulder, turning her sideways. As if she hadn't noticed she now had a gash on her skin the size of a plum, bleeding freely down her arm, Honoria righted herself again, with that same smile on her face and continued. "Gabriel has never met an opponent he could not defeat, never met a woman he could not charm. Not even me."

The ground shook. But it wasn't the ground, it was him. Amelia laid a hand over his rumbling chest. "Please," she said. "We have to move."

He could not look away from the bitch Caesar.

Only a handful of soldiers remained, but it didn't seem to matter that the crowd was free. Most of them were too busy fighting, brutally bashing and pounding each other instead of turning on their rich patrons. There was smoke in the air, the kind that usually preceded a firestorm.

Half of Honoria's court had run. The other half stood there, crying, shaking with fear, but they would not move.

"No one would have expected a man like that to end up here, killing for our pleasure. A few years ago, the world had been open to him, and if the scales of fate had tipped another way, he would have been king in his own right." Honoria's smile dimmed, her eyes became sad. "How could I let that happen?"

The rumbling stopped. The crowds disappeared, and the world plunged into silence broken up by the beat of his heart.

Amelia said nothing.

The strangers stared.

Chooooooose…

Choose what?

Honoria turned back to the crowds, her movements no longer as smooth as before. The muscles in her neck and jaw twitched, as if she was fighting a compulsion to speak. They were minute signs, hardly visible except to those who knew to look for them. Her voice never changed when she continued her little speech. "I first saw him in a back alley brawl put on by lowlife scavengers, facing two opponents, cornered and unarmed. He defeated them with such elegance. Even then, I was smitten by this man."

"Gabriel, we need to move." The alarm in Amelia's voice hardly registered. He felt her tugging him to keep going, but he couldn't move more than a single step. And it wasn't toward the pod.

Choose.

The more Honoria spoke, the more her eyes changed. From dreamy, to shocked, to terrified. Her posture became rigid, her muscles tense. Fear rolled off her in sickening waves, and still she kept talking and smiling, while fires erupted left and right before her. From the corner of his eye, he could see the bright orange flames flicker higher. No one was fighting them. Several had torches in their hands, weaving through the crowd like fireflies.

It meant nothing to him. Gabriel was wholly intent on the Caesar and her speech as it dawned on him she couldn't stop herself. Like him, she was being forced to do this, to say things never meant to be heard, and she had enough sense to know it.

Gabriel listened to her talk about her affection for him, how she couldn't rest until she had acquired him for the glory of Rome, and for herself. Shock had formed a shell over his body, locking him in place, but inside, a furious storm was growing.

With a proud raise of her chin, the Caesar exulted her own genius, the way she'd planned every step, manipulated her way into the lives of four friends while they had no idea who was behind it all. Gabriel screamed denial in his head.

It had been an amusement to her to see her architect build up a city as an homage to the girl he was so enamored with.

Cute little Paige, hopping from foot to foot in front of him, tiny, ineffectual fists raised in front of her nose. She'd made him laugh. She'd had the brains and the courage, just lacked the physical strength. He'd been teaching her. *Arms high, doll, guard up.* Gabriel would have gladly called her sister.

Dead.

A tactical maneuver to remove her from the picture.

Brilliant Alex, with his pencil always on a notepad, or a napkin, anything he could reach, drawing magnificent designs unlike any-thing ever seen before. Paige was in every single schematic, secretly hidden away in the code of measurements. He would have changed the face of the world.

Dead.

And Jack with his concoctions, always finding something new, something better. Never the same dish twice, never an unsatisfied stomach leaving his kitchen. Never a harsh word to say about anyone, always quick to laugh.

Dead.

And Gabriel wanted to howl with anguish.

"Don't listen. Don't let her hurt you more."

The girl, her architect, and finally the cook.

Family to Gabriel.

Obstacles to *her*. That's what she'd called them. They hadn't been human to her, just roadblocks between her and what she'd wanted to achieve. The panther stayed quiet as the human raged on the inside. This wasn't its fight. Gabriel's hand fisted so tightly around the sword's handle, he could feel it crack.

As the last of her court finally broke apart and ran, Honoria bragged about the way she had moved meddlesome pawns off her playing board one by one to make way for her king… "And he came, as I always knew he would. He came to me, and Rome was going to be ours."

The mob had all but overpowered the soldiers. The fire was spreading, devouring house after house, toxic fumes poisoning the air he breathed. He somehow knew all of this, though his gaze never left the Caesar's face.

Choose.

Honoria doubled over as if in pain. When she straightened again, she smiled and kept on talking.

Amelia's forehead touched his shoulder. She was getting weaker by the second, holding on to him instead of keeping her wound covered. The scent of her blood was so thick around him, it overpowered the smell of Rome burning itself to the ground, and it maddened him.

Honoria spoke about how hurt she was every time he refused her, how much she'd wanted to take care of him each time he'd been injured, but could not bring herself to overcome her repulsion of blood. She turned to him again and, as if in a brief moment of clarity, broke through the compulsion to speak her true mind. "I killed my general for you."

His eyes widened. Gabriel cast around for Soren, fully expecting him to jump out of the crowd. He tightened his hold on Amelia, nearly knocking himself off balance, but he would fight the fucker from the ground if he had to.

"I gave you *everything*!"

Except Soren never appeared. Gabriel frowned.

—*See!*— The word hissed straight into his ear, so close, Gabriel's head whipped around, sword raised to meet the threat. But there was no one. The strangers hadn't moved an inch, still watching him with those damn unnerving eyes. Then the civilized one nodded his chin by slow degrees, and Gabriel swayed on his feet.

For just a moment, his vision split between the present and some other place, just as the small sun rose. He saw Soren sprawled on the marble floor, naked and bruised. He looked the picture of serene repose, except for his eyes. The terror in them made Gabriel shudder. Soren didn't move because he couldn't. But his chest rose and fell in quick, shallow pants, and his voice carried in short, quiet whimpers.

The vision moved, as if Gabriel was really there, standing over the general while those petrified eyes of his followed him step by step. He could almost feel an echo of someone else's emotions—betrayal, anger, disgust, and revulsion, yet at the same time, excitement and arousal. The eyes he was looking through swept over the general, lingering on the frantic pulse beating in his chest, then on his flaccid member.

A pale, feminine foot reached out to caress it, and Gabriel almost retched.

Then Soren coughed weakly, the paralysis allowing for only the smallest of movements while blood sprayed out of his mouth. He was choking on it, helplessly drowning while his murderer stood there and watched, amusing herself. When Soren started to gurgle and Gabriel saw a feminine hand reach down, the vision mercifully ended.

Gabriel squeezed his eyes shut and shook his head. What the hell was that?

He felt the strangers watching him regain his bearings and an impossible thought crossed his mind, as impossible as a man who could turn into a panther. Could one of them have shown him this? Could it be true?

As if he'd heard him, the taller one rolled his eyes and shifted his weight. The other didn't have a single tell; he simply met Gabriel's gaze and waited for him to form his own opinion.

The thing was, Gabriel could believe it.

Huh… Soren really was dead. And the woman he'd been so devoted to had killed him.

Time unfroze, and Honoria's voice pierced through the din, aiming straight for his heart. "I would have given you everything, and you left me for that insipid bitch," she hissed.

Everything inside him quieted in a moment of true clarity. Gabriel's gaze turned inward, back through time, seeing his life as he never had, not since the recruiter showed up at his dorm room. It hadn't really been his life at all. It had been Honoria's.

She'd manipulated him, played him to her advantage, and every move he'd made had had her invisible hand behind it. Because as long as he played, she had his attention—had *him*. Everything she'd worked for, killed for, was the notion that Gabriel would eventually choose her.

All this time he'd been blinded, oblivious to the games she'd played. But now he knew. And it was his move again. His choice.

Chooooooose...

He did.

His jaw was cramped shut, fangs sharp and poking into the soft tissue of his mouth. Gabriel hooked an arm under Amelia's knees and picked her up. The woman who kept his heart beating sighed, her breath warm on his chin, and it calmed him. Her arms looped around his neck and he was home. He chose this.

Honoria could go fuck herself. He was done playing her games.

When Gabriel turned to the pod, the Caesar turned back to the crowd with a pained moan and kept on talking, spilling all of the dirty little secrets that would have torn this place apart from the inside if it wasn't already happening. The words were ripped from her, and even a rock striking her temple didn't stop her. Gabriel hoped this crowd tore her to pieces.

The riot would last for days. He was glad he wouldn't be around to see it.

The strangers met him on the ramp like a hostile welcome party. If they made him set Amelia on her feet again to fight them back, he would be taking body parts and proffering them to her as presents. Just as he was about to tell them exactly that, a white-haired female came running out of the pod, dressed in black leather pants and a silver top that molded to her every curve.

"You're Amelia's sister," he said by way of greeting. He recognized her from the video.

Amelia raised her head a little and smiled. "Hey, sis," she said.

Hailey nodded. "Are we done here?"

Gabriel glanced over his shoulder at Honoria. She was visibly in pain now, struggling to stop herself, but the words kept coming. He allowed himself one second of resentment, of hoping that her torment lasted a good long while and that after it was over, she burned forever in the deepest pits of Hell.

And then he let it all go. "Yeah," he said. "I think we are."

The taller male raised an eyebrow at him. "You sure? You don't want to go tear apart the woman who single-handedly killed everyone you loved and destroyed your life? You're going to walk away?"

So much death. Gabriel couldn't unmake any of it. But he could do the one thing that Honoria would never understand and never forgive. It was the perfect revenge. He'd only needed someone to make him see it. The worst thing he could ever do to the Caesar of Rome was to deprive her of the satisfaction she so craved. Just walk away and forget her. "Got everything I need right here," he said. "You want to tear someone apart, though? Be my guest. I won't stop you."

The man regarded him through a steady golden gaze. Seeming to make a decision, he nodded. "Get Amelia on board. I'll take care of this."

Gabriel frowned at him.

"She'll keep coming," the other man explained. "Trust me, it's safer for all of us if she's… no longer capable."

Hailey came forward and brushed Amelia's hair back. Gabriel almost snarled at her. "Whatever you're going to do, do it fast," she told them. "We need to get her home ASAP."

Ankles numb. He'd fall over soon if he didn't sit down.

Amelia waved her sister away. "I'll be fine."

Gabriel met eyes with the other female's glowing silver ones. They started up the ramp in unison. The two men didn't follow until he was at the very top, one foot in the pod. As the ramp rose, he glanced over his shoulder at the carnage on the ground.

His last sight of Rome was its glorious Caesar standing at the front of a stampeding mob. Shoulders slumped, eyes vacant, she stood silent and motionless, lost in the face of her impending death, blood and drool dripping down her chin as the masses bore down on her.

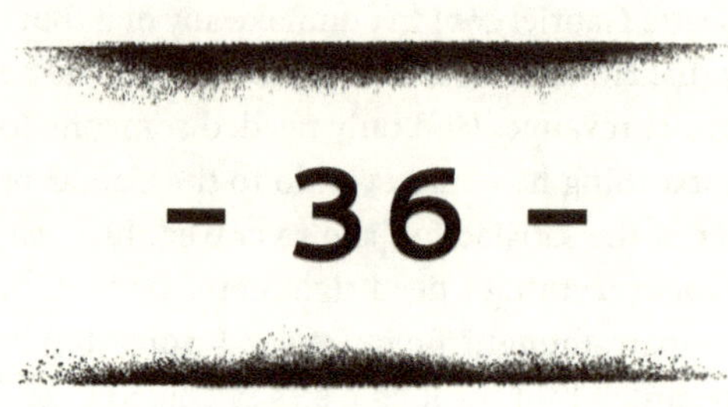

– 36 –

Amelia's world plunged into darkness, and then the din of Rome imploding was gone. She heard Hailey snapping out directions, and miraculously, the men were obeying. Calen was at the helm, raising the pod off the ground before they'd had a chance to sit, and her world lurched and tilted as Gabriel lost his balance and careened into the wall. But he never lost his hold on her, not once, even though she could feel his arms beginning to twitch with strain.

She couldn't move her own anymore; one hung lifelessly over Gabriel's shoulder, the other in her lap. Warm blood tickled her side as it seeped out of her shoulder wound.

"Sit down, you idiot," Hailey ordered, "before you both drop and I have to kill you."

"Hailey!" Calen snapped.

Gabriel growled but stumbled into a seat, clutching Amelia to his chest.

Tristan was nearby. She couldn't see him, but she felt him. Somehow, without any telepathic skills whatsoever, she felt his mind like a low-level hum in her head. Whatever he was doing, it had to be taking tremendous energy.

She felt the shift in gravity as they left the planet's atmosphere. It was a fast ascent, enough that her ears popped when they shouldn't have. Amelia swallowed compulsively to clear them.

Gabriel nuzzled at her temple and murmured, "You don't get to die on me, angel, so just put it out of your head right now."

She smiled against him as she felt the paralysis inch up her legs. The poison was acting too fast. Maybe it was the way it'd been introduced into her system, maybe just some enhanced form of it, maybe her rapid heartbeat and stress were accelerating the process; maybe if she had her microscope and a sample, she could study it and calculate exactly how long it would take to kill her. What Amelia could tell from the feel of it was that she didn't have long. Certainly not long enough to reach a lab and administer an antidote.

Her wound was still bleeding sluggishly. It should have slowed, at least.

"Hold on to something," Calen said. "It won't be a smooth dock."

The pod scraped the shuttle's hull with a teeth-clenching screech before the mechanism locked into place. A hiss of air signaled a pressure seal engaging, and then the door opened.

"Hurry," a familiar voice said. It couldn't be who it sounded like.

—But you already know it is.—

You brought Dara? she thought incredulously.

—I'm not letting her or my kids out of my sight again,— Tristan said.

Amelia said nothing. Gabriel lurched to his feet and nearly went down again. She had no idea how he was still able to stand. Strange hands reached for her to pry her away from him, and the snarl he emitted was so violently vicious, she shuddered. Or would have, if she still could.

"Jesus," Hailey said with breathless astonishment. Had he shown his fangs? Had his face changed? They already knew he was a shifter like them.

Light. Too bright, too fast. Amelia squeezed her eyes shut against it, wondering if she would ever be able to open them again. Around her, her friends were talking; loud, agitated voices snapping at each other. Scared. She recognized their fear, could hear it as easily as Gabriel could probably smell it. They were terrified, and none of them had the training to keep their heads under this kind of pressure.

"It'll be okay," she said softly. Not sure if anyone heard her. Her lips were beginning to tingle. "You'll be fine."

—You mean you *will,—* Tristan corrected.

"Shit! She's still bleeding."

"There must have been an anticoagulant on the arrowhead. We have to stop it. She can't afford the blood loss."

"Put her down here."

I mean what I said. For the first time, after everything, keeping secrets, creating them, creating creatures that were more human than most of the people she'd met in her life, surrounded by them now, Amelia realized how utterly insignificant she really was. All this time she'd thought she had to protect them. They didn't need her. She'd guided them through the gauntlet and now, safely on the other side, they were so much stronger. She was the one who needed them.

"Put. Her. Down!"

Gabriel growled. And kept growling.

—*Ironic,*— Tristan said. —*How the tables have turned. I remember being in his place not too long ago.*—

"We may need to sedate her," Hailey said, but Amelia heard her own voice, saying the exact same thing to Tristan, holding a traumatized Dara in his arms.

Unlike Tristan back then, Gabriel didn't move a muscle. If anything, he hitched her a little higher in his arms, adjusting his hold more securely around her.

—*Too little, too late,*— Tristan growled.

"Will you listen to me?" Hailey snapped. "She needs to be treated; she's in pain."

"I can take care of her. Get out." Gabriel's voice was inhuman.

"What are you gonna do, lick her wounds?"

That was exactly what he would do.

Amidst the argument from all sides around her, Amelia was baffled by how she could understand every word that was said, as well as carry on a conversation in her head.

You're judging him? You? When you brought your post-birth telepath mate and, unless I miss my guess, your shape-shifter babies to Rome?

—*He walked away,*— Tristan said. —*When face to face with his mortal enemy, the greatest threat to him and you, he just walked away. They stoned her to death, in case you were wondering. You're safe.*—

He chose me over his revenge, she countered, ignoring the comment about Honoria. *That's really what bothers you. He did what you couldn't.* She knew the story of Dara's abduction and Tristan's heroic rescue. *You took the time to make Dara's kidnapper suffer. You tortured him while Dara hung bleeding, dying, not twenty feet from you. I wonder if she would have suffered the coma, the weeks of hospitalization and unconsciousness, if you had just reached out to her sooner, found her before she got lost.* She said it without mercy. Maybe he deserved it, maybe he didn't, but right now, Amelia didn't care.

She felt his baffled silence at her unexpected attack, felt the smallest twinge of regret, but not enough to back down. *Don't you dare cast judgment, Tristan Hunt. You have no moral high ground here.*

There was a quiet, contemplative pause in which outside voices registered again. Hailey was yelling, Gabriel snarling, and somewhere nearby, she heard the faint sound of babies fussing. He really had brought them all here. It was unfathomable to her.

"Hailey, back off," Tristan said aloud. Amelia's world jerked again as Tristan shoved Gabriel onto a makeshift gurney. Gabriel collapsed onto it but twisted immediately to shield her with his body. Breathing hard, he still clutched Amelia as if nothing else in the world mattered, not even his own life.

There was a commotion, and from the corner of her eye, Amelia saw Hailey lunge for Gabriel.

Calen caught her around the waist. "Whoa, hey, we're not doing that again." He turned to place himself between the two shifters. "Go help Dara put the IV together."

An entire list of ingredients automatically scrolled through Amelia's mind. A cocktail that would keep her heart pumping, her lungs working until they got the antidote. She didn't have the oral motor skills to voice them anymore.

She didn't have to.

—*We don't have all of that,*— Dara's gentle voice said in her head. —*Hailey is putting together what we do have. She's thinking it won't be comfortable, but it'll keep you alive. What's he doing?*—

Gabriel was bending over her, an awkward enough angle, especially given how precarious his balance had become. He was trying to reach her shoulder. Amelia flexed what few muscles she still had control over and twisted to bring her shoulder closer to his mouth.

His tongue lapped at the wound once, twice, three times. Then, as if he couldn't hold his head up anymore, he dropped his forehead to her neck and just breathed. "You don't get to die," he said again. "Not you. Not now."

You're just as bad off as I am, she wanted to say. They'd probably die together. Strange, she wasn't afraid.

"Lie down," Dara told him softly.

He complied, keeping Amelia against his side. "Help her," he said.

"I'll try," Dara replied. "This will make you both sleep. Try not to fight it. It'll be easier that way."

A needle pricked Amelia's arm as the IV was attached. There would be one for Gabriel, too. She wanted to tell them it wouldn't work, but what the hell did she know? It had taken ten times the normal dose to put Tristan out. Gabriel's chemistry was even more altered.

"Look at him," Hailey said. She sounded shocked. Amelia couldn't lift her head to see for herself. Her eyelids drooped, and with the rumble of Gabriel's growl beneath her cheek, she gave in to artificial sleep.

Some time later, she floated in a hazy state between sleep and waking, boneless, fuzzy, but still aware of what was happening. The shuttle was dark and quiet, with only a few lights blinking sporadically. It was hard to breathe, but she was still breathing, somehow dragging air into her lungs and expelling it. Amelia shifted a little, her sleepy mind sending a command small enough for her body to obey, and her hip nudged back against something.

Gabriel rumbled a sleepy purr behind her, nudged his hip right back at her and she became aware that he was plastered against her back, as close as skin would allow. Heaving a labored sigh of contentment, she settled into welcoming darkness.

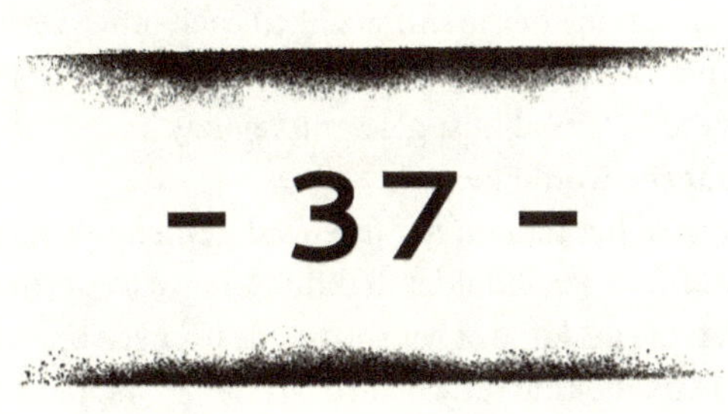

– 37 –

October 4, 3032 – Torrey

Amelia woke to birdsong. She breathed in deeply of dew-scented air and stretched her legs down to her toes, relishing the feel of it. The bed was soft, the linens clean, the air fresh and cold and the sun dim on her closed eyes, but sharp at the same time. Everything was wonderful, because it wasn't Rome.

"Good morning."

Amelia opened her eyes and squinted at her smiling brother-in-law sitting in a chair next to her bed. "Hi," she said. She felt a hundred years old when she lifted herself up and arranged the pillows behind her to lean against. Jeremy handed her a pair of glasses and she put them on, relieved when the world sprang into sharp focus. "Am I under supervision?"

There were no monitors, equipment, or medication around her. She just had a patch on the inside of her wrist, which someone was probably monitoring from elsewhere.

Jeremy grinned. "No. This was Hailey's idea. She says it's 'Wake after a near-death experience to someone you don't want to see' day. Hunt saw you, Hailey saw Hunt, Gabriel is seeing Hailey, and you get to see me. Aren't you lucky?"

Amelia stared at him for a few seconds. "I have absolutely no trouble believing that." She briefly worried about how Gabriel would react to

Hailey. Then she shrugged it off. They would probably try to rip each other apart since none of the shifters liked each other very much. But unlike her, they'd heal within a day.

He chuckled. "We're all just glad you're okay."

Not yet, but she would be.

Amelia pushed her hair off her forehead, remembering too late the puncture wound to her shoulder. It didn't sting, except from memory, and she pulled the neckline of her shirt aside to check on it. A faint scar marked her skin, looking fully healed as if it had happened years ago.

"That's some trick," Calen said. "We tried to give you Hailey's regenerative serum but—"

"It didn't take."

It wouldn't. She had zero chem-resistance. Her DNA was locked down tight.

"Yeah. Lucky your newest project has some additional perks."

Amelia groaned. She still had to figure out exactly how that had happened. "How is he?"

"Restless. We kept him under, but he's shaking it off pretty quick. Now you want to tell me what the hell happened?"

"Shouldn't you already know?"

Calen shrugged. "I don't like to pry. And Tristan took Dara and the kids into town for a while. Not that I blame him."

Amelia cast an uncertain glance at the door. She didn't like being on this side of the doctor-patient playground. Experience told her she would heal faster if she took the time to rest, but how could she?

"Amelia," Calen said in warning.

"Did I say anything? No. So back off." She blinked in surprise. Had she really just said that?

Calen shook his head. "Doctors should never be patients. It's too cruel to the rest of us." His easy smile was contagious, but as she felt her own mouth curve, Calen sucked in a sharp breath and his expression turned thunderous.

"What is it?"

"'Scuse me." He shoved to his feet and raced out the door.

Amelia threw off her covers and stood off the four-poster bed. The floors were wood but freezing cold to her bare feet. Weak and a little dizzy from so much bed rest, she hurried after her brother-in-law, following the sound of mayhem.

Only vaguely did she note that the hallways had stone walls covered with tapestries every few feet, and large double windows, half of which were open to let in fresh air. She was shivering with cold by the time she passed the grand staircase to the other side and turned the corner to see something fly out of an open doorway and shatter against the wall.

Amelia winced.

"Arrogant, pain in the ass, pig-headed *moron!*" Hailey was yelling. "Let go of me!"

Amelia picked up her step to intervene.

"*Get her out of my sight!*" Gabriel roared, and the sound of his voice was so sweet to her ears, she slowed.

He was okay.

They were both alive and on the mend, and far away from Rome.

It was over.

Then sounds of a struggle broke her out of her little reverie. "I'm trying—*ack!*"

Amelia all but flew in the doorway. Calen was holding Hailey up off the ground while she kicked and flailed to get at Gabriel. "Lemme at 'em! Lemme at 'em! I'll scratch your face off, pussycat, just you wait!"

They were so busy in their little battle that neither of them noticed Gabriel freeze at her entrance.

"She doesn't mean that," Calen said. "She just needs to cool off a little. I'll go dump her in the lake."

Gabriel's pale, feral gaze zeroed in on her and did not blink.

"You just try it, freak boy," Hailey snarled, "see what happens tonight. *Nothing*, that's what! *Let me down!*"

For a long moment, neither of them moved as Calen and Hailey made their noisy exit. The voices faded down the hall, and Amelia was suddenly alone with Gabriel, completely at a loss for words.

"H-how do you feel?" she finally asked lamely.

In two ground-eating strides, Gabriel was in front of her, his predator's gaze never straying from her face. He came toe to toe with her and stared her down. Sniffed at her and growled.

Bending his knees, he braced an arm beneath her ass and stood up with her. "How do I feel?" he said, walking her back to the large bed that looked like something had exploded out of it. That would be Gabriel. "I got shot, poisoned, knocked out, and I woke up alone. How do you think I feel?"

Amelia shrugged as he rearranged the covers into some semblance of order over her. "Hungry?"

"Ravenous," he growled, his mouth a fraction of an inch from hers. "But that can wait." He nudged her to lie down and slid under the covers with her.

Amelia didn't want to wait. She turned to him instantly, starving for the feel of him, cold without his body heat to warm her. Gabriel must have sensed how desperate she was because he met her halfway, and with his arms around her, rolled so she was tucked safely beneath him, sheltered and held immobile by his steady weight. He nuzzled at her and rumbled soft purrs that somehow felt like praise and love words.

It completely undid her.

Amelia was mortified to feel tears spilling from her eyes. She tried to hide, but there was nowhere to turn; Gabriel wouldn't let her. Letting more of his weight rest on her, he kissed every one of them away. "What is it, angel? What's wrong?"

Amelia sucked in a breath and held it to try and stop herself, but it just made everything worse. Her breaths turned into choppy, hyper-ventilating hiccups, and she couldn't trust her voice to come out in words rather than sobs. It frustrated and scared her how completely she was falling apart.

Gabriel swore and shifted so they lay on their sides facing each other. He squeezed her to him so hard, her bruised torso protested, but the pressure eased her a little, held her together so she could shatter to pieces. "It's… o-ver," she managed to wheeze between hiccups. "It's… r-really… over. W-we're… s-s…"—*gasp*—"…safe."

"Shh, easy. Just breathe. Slooow breaths." He rubbed soothing circles over her back and rocked her a little. Patiently held her while she cried until she just couldn't cry anymore.

"It's just shock," he murmured when her crazed heartbeat had stopped pounding in her ears. She could finally breathe, if a little shakily, and there were no more tears to shed. "You held up through all of it, Amelia. You were so damn brave. Now it's over, and it's all just catching up."

She knew that. Of course she did, but that didn't mean it made any kind of sense to her. "This sucks," she said, grateful that the words came out in one piece.

Gabriel chuckled and pressed his lips to her temple. "It'll pass."

"You're not freaking out."

"Of course I am."

She sniffled. "Why?"

Gabriel shifted her so he could meet her gaze and answered with his signature lack of reservation. "Because I didn't think it was possible to care for someone so much. There is no way a human body is capable of carrying it all. I thought the panther would make it easier, you know? Extra room to breathe. And then you went and made me love you even more."

Amelia melted at his words.

A lifetime of cold silence, of looking over her shoulder and carefully monitoring every move she made and every word she spoke, flashed across her mind. Her past. She couldn't escape it. It was always with her, putting her on guard.

It sucked, but it didn't have to be her future.

Take the chance offered. There's only loneliness to leave behind.

And to have *this* to wake up to every morning, Gabriel's strength to lean on, his heart, so wide open to shelter hers, wasn't that worth the risk?

She took a deep breath for courage. "Gabriel?"

"Yes?"

"I think I'm ready to renegotiate our agreement now."

His chest rose on an inhale that lifted her by several inches. "No," he said. "No more agreements, contracts, or conditions." He rolled them over, trapped her beneath him and stared her down, nose to nose. "You wanted me to make up my mind, well I have. This is it, angel. I want you. All of you—mind, body, and soul, including that efficient muscle that pumps blood through your body. No holds barred, no turning back, one hundred percent stunning, brilliant Dr. Amelia

Chase. I told you I would never stop once I started. So you better learn to deal with it, because I'm—not—leaving."

That efficient muscle pumping blood throughout her body swelled to impossible proportions inside her chest. She let that joy fill her to near bursting and couldn't hope to keep from smiling. "Good," she said, for once taking a chance and saying exactly what she wanted, exactly the way she wanted to. "Because I don't think I could ever let you leave."

An answering smile broke over his face, and it was like watching the sun be born in the morning sky. "That's my girl," he growled.

ALIANNE DONNELLY is an avid lover of stories of all kinds. Raised on a healthy diet of fairy tales in a place where they almost seemed real, she grew into a writer who seeks magic in the modern age and enjoys sharing a little bit of it with the world through every story she writes. Her books span the spectrum from fantasy to science fiction with varying degrees of romance sprinkled throughout. Alianne now lives in California, where she spends her free time reading, writing, and daydreaming. For more books, news, and updates, visit aliannedonnelly.com.